HOLIDAY WIZARDRY!

"Tree lights, free lights," I said, and suddenly there was a swarm of little green lights above me. I closed my hands right away to stop the power flow. These lights didn't disappear. They started out in a globular cluster, then peeled off, darting everywhere. Some flew into the living room, some headed for the dining room, three flew into Gyp's bowl of cookie dough, and one landed on her forehead.

"Hey!" she yelped. . . .

—From "LaZelle Family Christmas"

**Plus many more
amazing tales of
Christmas magic!**

Tor anthologies edited by David G. Hartwell

The Ascent of Wonder (with Kathryn Cramer)
The Dark Descent
Foundations of Fear
Christmas Magic
Christmas Stars
Christmas Forever
Northern Stars (with Glenn Grant)

Christmas MAGIC

EDITED BY
DAVID G. HARTWELL

A TOM DOHERTY ASSOCIATES BOOK
NEW YORK

CHRISTMAS MAGIC

Copyright © 1994 by David G. Hartwell

Cover art by Nicholas Jainschigg

A Tor Book
Published by Tom Doherty Associates, Inc.
175 Fifth Avenue
New York, N.Y. 10010

Tor® is a registered trademark of Tom Doherty Associates, Inc.

ISBN: 0-812-53447-6

First edition: November 1994

Printed in the United States of America

0 9 8 7 6 5 4 3 2 1

COPYRIGHT ACKNOWLEDGMENTS

I would like to acknowledge the expert assistance of my editor, Greg Cox, whose patience and wit eased my way to completing this book. Great title, too, Greg. Special thanks, also, to Nick Jainschigg, the right artist at the right time. Special thanks are also due to Janet Kagan, Roger Zelazny, and Virginia Kidd, for special help.

CONTENTS

Let the search for
Christmas Magic begin here.

SCRAMBLEPIPE TRIES
TO UNDERSTAND

The Gnomes Who Set Out For Christmas and
Found That The World Is Round

Anonymous

IT WAS THE twenty-fourth of June. The twenty-fourth of June is Midsummer Day. Screwworm said to Scramblepipe: "Christmas is coming."

Every gnome had a vast respect for Screwworm. When Screwworm spoke, everybody listened. When Screwworm asked a question, everybody thought, reflected, took a turn round the garden, or sat with their heads in cold water, before making an answer. Screwworm, in short, was immensely wise.

Now, the only gnome who was not in his heart convinced of Screwworm's wisdom was Burrowjack. Burrowjack was a gay little fellow. Once a week he had a punning day. It was the same day as Mrs. Burrowjack's washing day. She filled the house with steam; he filled the air with puns.

When Screwworm said to Scramblepipe on Midsummer Day, "Christmas is coming," Scramblepipe immediately leaned his brow upon his hand and plunged into profoundest thought. He knew that there was something deep in the idea. Screwworm had uttered it.

Burrowjack, who was sitting on a toadstool outside the cave, blowing bubbles with soap water from his wife's washtub, pricked up his ears and listened.

"I can't get it," said Scramblepipe, after a long meditation. "I'm sorry, Screwworm; it's stupid of me, but I can't get it. *Christmas is coming.* No; I don't follow you. Perhaps if I went out, took a Turkish bath, and lay down for an hour or two, it might come to me and I might understand."

"There isn't time," said Screwworm. "Scramblepipe, make yourself easy. This is not a usual thought. It surprises *me*. It's TREMENDOUS!"

"Then I give it up," said Scramblepipe, with a grateful sigh.

"It is, if I may say so," said Screwworm, "one of those ideas which come to the brain of only the wisest, and that only once in a million years. Be quite easy, Scramblepipe, but reverent; I will explain. Christmas is coming *because summer is going.* If summer is going, Christmas must be coming. Now, in a certain sense, it may be argued that, while summer is here, Christmas cannot be here, too. But that is not my point. Summer undoubtedly is here, as much here as any one thing can ever be said to be here at all. But, what is Here? Have you ever seen Here? Have you ever taken it in your hands, examined it, punched its head, heard it squeak, or counted its waistcoat buttons? *Has it got waistcoat buttons?* We are in profound ignorance. Scramblepipe, I will let you into a secret. I don't believe there is any such thing as Here."

"It's coming to me," said Scramblepipe thoughtfully.

"Now, if Christmas is coming," continued Screwworm, "it is something that is alive and real. Far from going, it is coming. The two movements are as different as life and death. If summer is going, it is something mortal; if Christmas is coming, it is something immortal. If we stay here waiting, while something is going, we shall be left."

"Oh, I feel as if I am being tickled all over!" exclaimed Scramblepipe, interrupting. "I've nearly got it, nearly, almost, practically got it; but not quite. It eludes me, just as I think I'm certain of it."

"A thing that is going is ceasing to be; a thing that is coming must exist, to be coming," said Screwworm.

Scramblepipe leaped to his feet.

"Got it! Got it!" he cried excitedly. He began to dance—singing, grinning, laughing, cackling, and whistling. Suddenly, he stopped dead, his face livid. "Screwworm," he said, "it has gone!"

"My point," said old Screwworm, "is this: a thing that is coming must have a place from which to come. If, instead of waiting for that thing to come, we go to the place from which it is coming, shall we not be in the possession of something that is never going at all? In other words, if—"

Scramblepipe buried his head in his hands.

"Come with me," said Screwworm kindly; "I will show you what I mean." They rose up and went out together.

"Can you tell me," said Burrowjack, "who bade the field farewell? I am speaking of the bird. Say it over slowly to yourselves, thus: Who—bade—the field—fare—well."

"His mother," said Screwworm, "for no one else would take the trouble to do so."

"No," replied Burrowjack. "Beautifully no. The answer is Adieu drop."

"Burrowjack," said Screwworm, "leave this silly jesting, and hear my words. We go to discover Christmas."

For many days and nights these intrepid explorers journeyed across the earth to find Christmas. Weeks and months passed. Their clothes were in rags, their shoes were worn to shreds, their legs were so stiff that they could scarcely lift their feet. But still they journeyed on.

"Courage!" said Screwworm, "courage! All we need is courage."

"It's certainly a splendid idea of yours," said Scramblepipe. "It takes time to come to it; but it's a magnificent idea!"

One day they arrived at a place where snow was falling. Their eyes shone with enthusiasm as they saw it.

"I feel," said Screwworm, "like a king approaching his coronation. Columbus discovering America is not nearly big enough for my feelings."

"I never saw such a splendid country in my life!" exclaimed Scramblepipe.

"You can feel the very air is Christmas, can you not?"

"I can smell it!" cried Scramblepipe, with enthusiasm.

They traveled on. Night fell. The whole earth was buried under snow. Above this white earth the sky was glittering with stars. An immense moon shone through the trees.

"The moon looks very different," said Screwworm.

"There's no man in it, for one thing," said Scramblepipe; "it smells different."

They traveled on and on until suddenly they heard a horn blow in the distance.

Screwworm fell on his knees. His face was dazzled with ecstasy. He waved his arms above his head.

"My idea!" he exclaimed. "My idea! I thought of it! Alone I got it! Oh, what it is to be a thinker!"

Scramblepipe cried:

"It is the horn of Christmas!"

Screwworm rose.

"This night the dream of my existence is realized. We have penetrated into the unknown. We have conquered Time. We are in the very land of Christmas!"

The horn blew again.

"Santa Claus is calling us!" said Scramblepipe.

They went on with joy.

"Think, Scramblepipe, think of that foolish Burrowjack, sitting on a toadstool, and waiting, *waiting* for Christmas to come to him!"

They rubbed their hands and laughed.

At last, they came to the place from which the horn had sounded. They started and turned a little pale.

"I seem to know this spot," said Scramblepipe suspiciously.

Screwworm admitted:

"It certainly has a miserably familiar look about it."

"Why," cried Scramblepipe, "it's old Cuddledick blowing the horn!"

"It certainly looks like it," said Screwworm, whose face was green.

"My dear old boy," exclaimed Scramblepipe suddenly, "do you know where we are?"

"I do."

"We are at home!"

"Too true!"

"Home—in our own land, in our own country, in our own territory, in our own neighborhood!"

They entered the cave, and sat down.

"Hallo!" said Burrowjack. "Where have you been? Oh, I forgot! You've been to Christmas. How did you find the old gentleman?"

"Gentlemen," said Screwworm, "I and Brother Scramblepipe have been upon a scientific exploration. We have made an amazing discovery. I will tell it you."

"Not at Christmas! Not at Christmas!" pleaded all the gnomes, holding their heads. But Screwworm heeded not their pleading.

"Gentlemen," he said, solemnly and mercilessly, "the World is Round!"

A classic Christmas fantasy—black
magic and dark psychology herein.

NACKLES
Donald Westlake

DID GOD CREATE men, or does Man create gods? I don't know,
and if it hadn't been for my rotten brother-in-law the question
would never have come up. My *late* brother-in-law? Nackles
knows.

It all depends, you see, like the chicken and the egg, on
which came first. Did God exist before Man first thought of
Him, or didn't He? If not, if Man creates his gods, then it fol-
lows that Man must create the devils, too.

Nearly every god, you know, has his corresponding devil.
Good *and* Evil. The polytheistic ancients, prolific in the creation (?) of gods and goddesses, always worked up nearly
enough Evil ones to cancel out the Good, but not quite. The
Greeks, those incredible supermen, combined Good and Evil
in *each* of their gods. In Zoroaster, Ahura Mazda, being
Good, is ranged forever against the Evil one, Ahriman. And
we ourselves know God and Satan.

But of course it's entirely possible I have nothing to worry
about. It all depends on whether Santa Claus is or is not a god.
He certainly *seems* like a god. Consider: He is omniscient; he

knows every action of every child, for good or evil. At least on Christmas Eve he is omnipresent, everywhere at once. He administers justice tempered with mercy. He is superhuman, or at least nonhuman, though conceived of as having a human shape. He is aided by a corps of assistants who do *not* have completely human shapes. He rewards Good and punishes Evil. And, most important, he is believed in utterly by several million people, most of them under the age of ten. Is there any qualification for godhood that Santa Claus does not possess?

And even the nonbelievers give him lip service. He has surely taken over Christmas; his effigy is everywhere, but where are the manger and the Christ child? Retired rather forlornly to the nave. (Santa's power is growing, too. Slowly but surely he is usurping Hanukkah as well.)

Santa Claus *is* a god. He's no less a god than Ahura Mazda, or Odin, or Zeus. Think of the white beard, the chariot pulled through the air by a breed of animal which doesn't ordinarily fly, the prayers (requests for gifts) which are annually mailed to him and which so baffle the Post Office, the specially garbed priests in all the department stores. And don't gods reflect their creators' (?) society? The Greeks had a huntress goddess, and gods of agriculture and war and love. What else would we have but a god of giving, of merchandising, and of consumption? Secondary gods of earlier times have been stout, but surely Santa Claus is the first fat primary god.

And wherever there is a god, mustn't there sooner or later be a devil?

Which brings me back to my brother-in-law, who's to blame for whatever happens now. My brother-in-law Frank is—or was—a very mean and nasty man. Why I ever let him marry my sister I'll never know. Why Susie *wanted* to marry him is an even greater mystery. I could just shrug and say Love Is Blind, I suppose, but that wouldn't explain how she fell in love with him in the first place.

Frank is—Frank was—I just don't know what tense to use. The present, hopefully. Frank is a very handsome man in his way, big and brawny, full of vitality. A football player; hero in college and defensive linebacker for three years in pro ball, till he did some sort of irreparable damage to his left knee, which gave him a limp and forced him to find some other way to make a living.

Ex-football players tend to become insurance salesmen; I don't know why. Frank followed the form, and became an insurance salesman. Because Susie was then a secretary for the same company, they soon became acquainted.

Was Susie dazzled by the ex-hero, so big and handsome? She's never been the type to dazzle easily, but we can never fully know what goes on inside the mind of another human being. For whatever reason, she decided she was in love with him.

So they were married, and five weeks later he gave her her first black eye. And the last, though it mightn't have been, since Susie tried to keep me from finding out. I was to go over for dinner that night, but at eleven in the morning she called the auto showroom where I work, to tell me she had a headache and we'd have to postpone the dinner. But she sounded so upset that I knew immediately something was wrong, so I took a demonstration car and drove over, and when she opened the front door there was the shiner.

I got the story out of her slowly, in fits and starts. Frank, it seemed, had a terrible temper. She wanted to excuse him because he was forced to be an insurance salesman when he really wanted to be out there on the gridiron again, but I want to be President and I'm an automobile salesman, and *I* don't go around giving women black eyes. So I decided it was up to me to let Frank know he wasn't to vent his pique on my sister anymore.

Unfortunately, I am five feet seven inches tall and weigh one hundred thirty-four pounds, with the Sunday *Times* under my arm. Were I just to give Frank a piece of my mind, he'd surely give me a black eye to go with my sister's. Therefore, that afternoon I bought a regulation baseball bat, and carried it with me when I went to see Frank that night.

He opened the door himself and snarled, "What do *you* want?"

In answer, I poked him with the end of the bat, just above the belt, to knock the wind out of him. Then, having unethically gained the upper hand, I clouted him five or six times more, and then stood over him to say, "The next time you hit my sister I won't let you off so easy." After which I took Susie home to *my* place for dinner.

And after which I was Frank's best friend.

People like that are so impossible to understand. Until the baseball-bat episode, Frank had nothing for me but undisguised contempt. But once I'd knocked the stuffing out of him, he was my comrade for life. And I'm sure it was sincere; he would have given me the shirt off his back, had I wanted it, which I didn't.

(Also, by the way, he never hit Susie again. He still had the bad temper, but he took it out in throwing furniture out windows or punching dents in walls or going downtown to start a brawl in some bar. I offered to train him out of maltreating the house and furniture as I had trained him out of maltreating his wife, but Susie said no, that Frank had to let off steam and it would be worse if he was forced to bottle it all up inside him, so the baseball bat remained in retirement.)

Then came the children, three of them in as many years. Frank Junior came first, and then Linda Joyce, and finally Stewart. Susie had held the forlorn hope that fatherhood would settle Frank to some extent, but quite the reverse was true. Shrieking babies, smelly diapers, disrupted sleep, and distracted wives are trials and tribulations to any man, but to Frank they were—like everything else in his life—the last straw.

He became, in a word, worse. Susie restrained him I don't know how often from doing some severe damage to a squalling infant, and as the children grew toward the age of reason Frank's expressed attitude toward them was that their best move would be to find a way to become invisible. The children, of course, didn't like him very much, but then who did?

Last Christmas was when *it* started. Junior was six then, and Linda Joyce five, and Stewart four, so all were old enough to have heard of Santa Claus and still young enough to believe in him. Along around October, when the Christmas season was beginning, Frank began to use Santa Claus's displeasure as a weapon to keep the children "in line"—his phrase for keeping them mute and immobile and terrified. Many parents, of course, try to enforce obedience the same way: "If you're bad, Santa Claus won't bring you any presents." Which, all things considered, is a negative and passive sort of punishment, wishy-washy in comparison with fire and brimstone and such. In the old days, Santa Claus would treat bad children a bit more scornfully, leaving a lump of coal in their stockings in lieu of presents, but I suppose the Depression helped to change that. There are times and situations when a lump of coal is nothing to sneer at.

In any case, an absence of presents was too weak a punishment for Frank's purposes, so last Christmastime he invented Nackles.

Who is Nackles? Nackles is to Santa Claus what Satan is to God, what Ahriman is to Ahura Mazda, what the North Wind is to the South Wind. Nackles is the new Evil.

I think Frank really *enjoyed* creating Nackles; he gave so much thought to the details of him. According to Frank, and as I remember it, this is Nackles: very very tall and very very thin. Dressed all in black, with a gaunt gray face and deep black eyes. He travels through an intricate series of tunnels under the earth, in a black chariot on rails, pulled by an octet of dead-white goats.

And what does Nackles do? Nackles lives on the flesh of little boys and girls. (This is what Frank was telling his children; can you believe it?) Nackles roams back and forth under the earth, in his dark tunnels darker than subway tunnels, pulled by the eight dead-white goats, and he searches for little boys and girls to stuff into his big black sack and carry away and eat. But Santa Claus won't let him have *good* boys and girls. Santa Claus is stronger than Nackles and keeps a protective shield around little children, so Nackles can't get at them.

But when little children are bad, it hurts Santa Claus, and weakens the shield Santa Claus has placed around them, and if they keep on being bad pretty soon there's no shield left at all, and on Christmas Eve instead of Santa Claus coming down out of the sky with his bag of presents Nackles comes up out of the ground with his bag of emptiness, and stuffs the bad children in, and whisks them away to his dark tunnels and the eight dead-white goats.

Frank was proud of his invention, actually proud of it. He not only used Nackles to threaten his children every time they had the temerity to come within range of his vision, he also spread the story around to others. He told me, and his neighbors, and people in bars, and people he went to see in his job as insurance salesman. I don't know how many people he told about Nackles, though I would guess it was well over a hundred. And there's more than one Frank in this world; he told me from time to time of a client or neighbor or bar crony who had heard the story of Nackles and then said, "By God, that's great. That's what *I've* been needing, to keep *my* brats in line."

Thus Nackles was created, and thus Nackles was promulgated. And would any of the unfortunate children thus introduced to Nackles believe in this Evil Being any less than they believed in Santa Claus? Of course not.

This all happened, as I say, last Christmastime. Frank invented Nackles, used him to further intimidate his already intimidated children, and spread the story of him to everyone he met. On Christmas Day last year I'm sure there was more than one child in this town who was relieved and somewhat surprised to awaken the same as usual, in his own trundle bed, and to find the presents downstairs beneath the tree, proving that Nackles had been kept away yet another year.

Nackles lay dormant, so far as Frank was concerned, from December 25 of last year until this October. Then, with the sights and sounds of Christmas again in the land, back came Nackles, as fresh and vicious as ever. "Don't expect *me* to stop him!" Frank would shout. "When he comes up out of the ground the night before Christmas to carry you away in his bag, don't expect any help from *me*!"

It was worse this year than last. Frank wasn't doing as well financially as he'd expected, and then early in November Susie discovered she was pregnant again, and what with one thing and another Frank was headed for a real peak of ill-temper. He screamed at the children constantly, and the name of Nackles was never far from his tongue.

Susie did what she could to counteract Frank's bad influence, but he wouldn't let her do much. All through November and December he was home more and more of the time, because the Christmas season is the wrong time to sell insurance anyway and also because he was hating the job more every day and thus giving it less of his time. The more he hated the job, the worse his temper became, and the more he drank, and the worse his limp got, and the louder were his shouts, and the more violent his references to Nackles. It just built and built and built, and reached its crescendo on Christmas Eve, when some small or imagined infraction of one of the children—Stewart, I think—resulted in Frank's pulling all the Christmas presents from all the closets and stowing them all in the car to be taken back to the stores, because this Christmas for sure it wouldn't be Santa Claus who would be visiting this house, it would be Nackles.

By the time Susie got the children to bed, everyone in the house was a nervous wreck. The children were too frightened to sleep, and Susie was too unnerved herself to be of much help in soothing them. Frank, who had taken to drinking at home lately, had locked himself in the bedroom with a bottle.

It was nearly eleven o'clock before Susie got the children all quieted down, and then she went out to the car and brought all the presents back in and ranged them under the tree. Then, not wanting to see or hear her husband any more that night—he was like a big spoiled child throwing a tantrum—she herself went to sleep on the living-room sofa.

Frank Junior awoke her in the morning, crying, "Look, Mama! Nackles *didn't* come, he *didn't* come!" And pointed to the presents she'd placed under the tree.

The other two children came down shortly after, and Susie and the youngsters sat on the floor and opened the presents, enjoying themselves as much as possible, but still with restraint. There were none of the usual squeals of childish pleasure; no one wanted Daddy to come storming downstairs in one of his rages. So the children contented themselves with ear-to-ear smiles and whispered exclamations, and after a while Susie made breakfast, and the day carried along as pleasantly as could be expected under the circumstances.

It was a little after twelve that Susie began to worry about Frank's nonappearance. She braved herself to go up and knock on the locked door and call his name, but she got no answer, not even the expected snarl, so just around one o'clock she called me and I hurried on over. I rapped smartly on the bedroom door, got no answer, and finally I threatened to break the door in if Frank didn't open up. When I still got no answer, break the door in I did.

And Frank, of course, was gone.

The police say he ran away, deserted his family, primarily because of Susie's fourth pregnancy. They say he went out the window and dropped to the backyard, so Susie wouldn't see him and try to stop him. And they say he didn't take the car because he was afraid Susie would hear him start the engine.

That all sounds reasonable, doesn't it? Yet I just can't believe Frank would walk out on Susie without a lot of shouting about it first. Nor that he would leave his car, which he was fonder of than his wife and children.

But what's the alternative? There's only one I can think of: Nackles.

I would rather not believe that. I would rather not believe that Frank, in inventing Nackles and spreading word of him, made him real. I would rather not believe that Nackles actually did visit my sister's house on Christmas Eve.

But did he? If so, he couldn't have carried off any of the children, for a more subdued and better-behaved trio of youngsters you won't find anywhere. But Nackles, being brand-new and never having had a meal before, would need *somebody*. Somebody to whom he was real, somebody not protected by the shield of Santa Claus. And, as I say, Frank was drinking that night. Alcohol makes the brain believe in the existence of all sorts of things. Also, Frank was a spoiled child if there ever was one.

There's no question but that Frank Junior and Linda Joyce and Stewart believe in Nackles. And Frank spread the gospel of Nackles to others, some of whom spread it to their own children. And some of whom will spread the new Evil to other parents. And ours is a mobile society, with families constantly being transferred by Daddy's company from one end of the country to another, so how long can it be before Nackles is a power not only in this one city, but all across the nation?

I don't know if Nackles exists, or will exist. All I know for sure is that there's suddenly a new level of meaning in the lyric of that popular Christmas song. You know the one I mean:

You'd better watch out.

The poor are always with us at Christmas.

Another Dime,
Another Place
A.J. Austin

"Postcard, mister?"

The wind seemed colder now, damper, as he tried to pretend he couldn't hear the tiny old woman at his side. His briefcase in his left hand, he pulled his overcoat more tightly around his throat with his right against the chill of what seemed a harsher-than-usual December.

"Postcard? Nice views, mister. Only ten cents."

Jesus, why doesn't she leave me alone? he thought. Can't she see I'm ignoring her? Damn, why can't you ever get a cab when it's raining?

"Only ten cents, mister." She reached out tentatively, touching the sleeve of his expensive overcoat. He quickly jerked his arm away.

"Don't you dare touch . . ." he started to say, seeing the old woman, really looking at her for the first time. Although she was as deplorable as he had expected, there was still a dignity there that made him stop and reconsider how he spoke to her.

"Postcard?" she asked again, holding out a bundle of cards perhaps an inch thick. Despite the newspaper wrapped around them, it was obvious they had seen little protection from the weather.

"Uh, yeah," he said finally, thinking that if he bought one of the stupid cards maybe she'd go away and bother someone else. Tucking his briefcase under an arm, he took the bundle gingerly, careful not to touch her, careful not to actually make contact with one of *those* people. He flipped through them hurriedly, barely seeing them, and picked one from the middle of the stack.

"I'll take this one." He slipped the card inside the overcoat and fumbled in his pockets for change, wet hands making the task more difficult and time-consuming than he would have liked. He finally found a coin, a quarter, and gave it to her.

"Taxi!" He ran for the curb, aware that his shouting was more to further distance himself from the old woman than to actually hail the cab now rounding the corner. Whether the driver heard or saw him was irrelevant; what mattered was that the salt-encrusted car pulled to an abrupt halt at the curb nearest him.

"Union Square," he barked, throwing himself into the backseat. Reaching for the handle, he was both startled and dismayed to see the old woman standing there, preventing him from closing the door.

"They're only a dime, mister," she was saying, the tiny voice nearly lost in the traffic noise. "Let me give you your change."

"It's OK; you keep it. Please, I'm in a hurry."

"But, mister, I—"

"It's all right, really." He gave her his best smile and watched as grimy fingers closed tightly over the coins in her outstretched hand. The old woman moved away from the curb, a smile appearing on her own face.

"Thank you, sir. God bless you." She was still standing at the curb as he closed the door and told the driver to go on. He looked back once through the water-streaked rear window of the taxi; he couldn't be sure because of the distorted image, but he thought he saw her wave.

Pathetic, he thought, and meant it not as a curse, but as a literal statement of fact.

* * *

"Greetings from Niagara Falls" was written in bright-red letters across the picture. As such, it was typical of most postcards bought at any tourist-attraction gift shop. Turning the card over to the message and address side, he read the description: "View from Goat Island. From the unique vantage point of the island can be found the best location to view the magnificent splendor of both the American and Canadian falls."

As bad as Manhattan was right now, it would be totally miserable at the falls this time of year. Not yet frigid enough for the beautiful ice cascades to form but too cold to be out in the constant spray. He didn't envy anyone there right now.

I can't imagine how Doug has stood it there all these years, he thought. I wonder how he's making out. He glanced at his watch and picked up the phone. Why not? He had time before the nine-thirty meeting.

"Cara, make a call for me please?"

"Yes, Mr. McKee." A slight pause. "OK, go ahead."

"Look in my Rolodex and see if you still have a card on Douglas Harper. If it's not under 'H,' then try Curry and Glassman in Buffalo."

"Yes, sir. It'll be just a moment."

He replaced the receiver and swiveled the plush chair around. The sleet had changed to a strong, driving rain and the headlights on the cars jammed along Park Avenue forty floors below his office window sparkled like a string of Christmas lights.

The phone chirped softly behind him and he turned back to the desk. "Mr. McKee? Mr. Harper on line five."

"Thanks, Cara." He quickly punched up the blinking button. "Doug? Hi. It's Ed McKee in New York."

"Eddie? Jeez, it's been, what, five years at least. How the hell are you?"

"Freezing my onions off right now; outside of that, I guess I can't complain. How about you?"

"Oh, hey, things are going great. In case your secretary didn't mention it, they answer the phone 'Curry, Glassman, and Harper' around here now. We've expanded the firm again, added a half-dozen associates this year alone. How's Bonnie and the kids?"

"Fine, they're all fine. Jimmy's taller than I am, and on the varsity basketball team. Donna's in junior high, now—straight-A student, too."

"Congratulations. Sounds like they've really turned out great. I can hear the pride in your voice."

The phone chirped. "Damn, can you hold a second?"

"Sure, no problem."

He pressed the receiver cradle momentarily to answer the page. "Yes?"

"I'm sorry, Mr. McKee, but Mr. Knox says he needs to see you upstairs before your nine-thirty."

"All right, thanks, Cara." He touched the phone once more. "Doug? Listen, I'm sorry to have to run like this, but—"

"Same old Fast Eddie," Harper joked. "Always in a hurry. No wonder Jimmy's gone out for sports. Before you sneak away, let me just ask: You still a big shot at the insurance company?"

"Yeah. Why?"

"Well, as I said, we're growing pretty fast up here and our old coverage is getting expensive as hell. We're making changes and I'm in a position now to make some of the decisions. Be interested in taking us on?"

"Of course."

"This is perfect. I can't believe your timing, calling out of the blue like this. Put me through to your secretary and I'll have her schedule us a time when we can talk a bit longer than two minutes."

"You're on, Doug. I'll talk to you later."

"Good talking to you. I'm glad you called, Eddie."

McKee looked absently at the postcard on the desk blotter. "Greetings from Niagara Falls . . ."

"Yeah, me too."

"Postcard, mister?"

It was almost as if she was waiting for him when he stepped off the elevator. Ed McKee looked around the lobby for a security guard, but couldn't spot one. At well past six the normal crowd of people leaving the building had long since thinned to a trickle.

She held the bundle out as she had that morning, and McKee noticed that the stack was thicker and unwrapped; now, out of the weather, there was no need to wrap them.

"Nice views, only ten ..." She stopped in midsentence, only now recognizing him. "Oh, sir, it's you. I was hoping I'd see you again. I have more cards, now. Most of them were in my coat to keep them dry, but see? I have them all here now, many more views to choose from. Wait, wait. I think I got some more in here...." She began digging through an enormous plastic shopping bag, chattering even more excitedly than before about her vast selection of cards and about how kind he had been to her earlier.

McKee wasn't sure if it was the prospect of another sale or the fact that she was indoors in a warm, dry place that accounted for her good spirits, but he couldn't help grinning as she searched through the seemingly bottomless bag. He still felt a certain revulsion for her, for all street people, but there was something about her that touched him.

"Yes, I think I might want another postcard."

Her eyes grew wide with delight and she stood quickly, dropping the bag to the marble floor. Handing him the bundle, she waited silently while he examined them.

"How about this one?" he asked finally, choosing one from the stack and showing it to her.

She looked carefully at it, shaking her head.

"No, not that one. It's badly damaged from the water. Let me find you a better one." She took the bundle away from him, shuffled through them till she found the one she wanted. "Here you are," she said, extending one of the cards to him. "Much nicer one."

The card was a Christmas scene. A perfect tree, brilliantly lighted, with dozens of wrapped gifts under it. In the center with a large red bow around its neck was a stuffed teddy bear, leaning against the front wheel of a tricycle. The stitched-on eyes made the bear look sound asleep. Beneath the picture in Old English lettering was the legend "Not a Creature Was Stirring ..."

"You're right, it's very nice," he said as he looked for change. Remembering he'd used the last of it in the soda machine, he reached for his wallet. "Listen, do me a favor. I don't know how you managed to get past the security people, but it's really not a good idea to hang around here, understand? They sometimes get a little rough when any of you . . . Well, they sometimes get a little rough, that's all."

She nodded, her eyes never leaving the wallet for a second.

"Here." He handed her a crisp, new five-dollar bill and watched as her face widened into a huge grin.

"Thank you. Oh, sir, I'm so glad I picked you that one. It'll be an extra special one for you. Miss Lacey thanks you. Merry Christmas, sir." Swiftly gathering up the stack, she snapped the rubber band back around the bundle and dropped it into the bag. She hustled toward the front entrance, and McKee nearly laughed out loud when she ducked behind a huge pillar just as the security guard rounded the corner.

"Good evening, Mr. McKee. Working late again?" The guard, a tall, muscular man in his late twenties, tipped his hat as he approached. The strength in the man's shoulders and upper arms was obvious even in the security company's one-size-fits-all blue shirt.

"Afraid so, Brad. Landed a big contract today, added it to the list of things to take care of before the holidays."

"Yeah, I know what you mean. Well, you have a good night, sir. Watch your step, getting kind of slick."

"Sure thing. Thanks." He made a show of buttoning his overcoat and listened for the guard's footsteps to disappear around the other side of the elevators before calling out. "Pssst! It's all clear."

Without a word the tiny woman darted for the front entrance. She struggled for a second with the heavy door and then quickly slipped out. Once outside, she turned back for a moment and waved, then lost herself in the crowd.

The guard had been right, he realized as soon as he left the building. The temperature had dropped rapidly and the steady rain had turned to snow, but despite the cold, the crowded sidewalks were more slushy than icy. Besides, the falling snow made even the Manhattan streets look good tonight.

And it was quiet; the traffic still made the same sound, the shoppers and other passersby still talked as loudly as ever, but the soft, heavy flakes had a dampening effect on the entire scene. In the middle of the city, it was almost peaceful.

It might be nice, he thought, taking a quick peek at his watch. I've got some time. Enjoying the snowfall. McKee strolled past his usual taxi stand.

It was nearly seven when he finally stopped at a stand. No cab was waiting, of course, and with the rush of holiday shoppers all around him, he resigned himself to a long wait. Standing beneath a wide awning that ran the entire length of the front of a huge department store, he passed the time by watching the shoppers and looking at the various window displays.

After several minutes, the arrangement of one of the displays, a lovely Christmas morning, caught his attention. It took a moment before it suddenly occurred to him where he'd seen it. Setting the briefcase down, he reached into his coat for the postcard. The scenes were the same, or nearly so. Some of the details were different—the tree a bit smaller, the colors of the wrapping paper varied here and there—but the teddy bear, the tricycle, even the small sign declaring "Not a Creature Was Stirring" were all identical.

He marveled at the similarity and headed for the entrance to get a better look from the inside. A large knot of people was shoving and jostling to enter the store, and he took his place in the line waiting for the revolving doors. Just as he stepped in, the blast of car horns caught the crowd's attention. Too late to get out of the spinning doors, he tried to make out what was going on from inside the revolving chamber.

At the end of the block, several cars, apparently the same ones honking, were swerving in all directions. Through the wet, heavy glass, McKee couldn't quite make out what was happening, but the danger was apparent as soon as the doors came fully around. A driver had lost control of his car and was literally plowing through the traffic; cars, buses, and delivery trucks alike were making their best efforts to get out of the way.

A woman at his side screamed and dropped her shopping bag to the pavement, dragging her two kids quickly to one side as she did. Others were yelling all around him, all of them moving, running, pushing at the same time as the car approached. McKee felt frozen where he stood, the scene unfolding in slow motion as he stared.

The car hit the curb hard with the right front wheel, bouncing sideways into the air. In an imitation of a fairgrounds stunt driver, it continued on two wheels as it came onto the sidewalk, the angle of tilt almost, but not quite, giving it enough clearance to miss the streetlight. The bumper just caught the pole about four or five feet up, snapping it; right next to it a newspaper machine bolted to the sidewalk went flying in the opposite direction, hitting the street and scattering dozens of *USA Today*s into the confusion. As the pole hit the sidewalk not thirty feet from the crowd of shoppers at the door, the glass globe shattered and sparks flew from the electric wiring pulling free from the stump of the pole. Still on two wheels, the car slammed into the polished granite storefront, dead center between two display windows. In a moment frozen in time, it hung there at that impossible angle, then fell to a level position.

It was over in seconds, and a stunned quiet came over the crowd. Most of the traffic had come to a stop and the only sound was the hissing from the car's smashed radiator and the intermittent popping of sparks from the demolished streetlight.

An approaching siren broke the reverie of the crowd and everyone began talking, moving, shouting, crying, pointing at the same time. Two teenagers, taking advantage of the sudden confusion, scooped up several handfuls of change from the smashed vending machine before disappearing down the street. The sight of the blatant theft made McKee realize he didn't have his briefcase. He looked around, but his attention was drawn away when the door flew open on the wrecked car and the driver stumbled out; he had a cut on his forehead, but appeared otherwise all right.

Besides the driver there were, amazingly, very few people hurt as a result of the accident. Some of the bystanders had been cut by flying glass from the streetlamp, and one of the shoppers had suffered a broken wrist when she fell on the slippery pavement during the excitement; but other than that, police were calling it a miracle that somebody wasn't killed.

McKee had never believed in miracles, but when a tow truck pulled the twisted wreck from the sidewalk, the sight made him give the subject serious thought.

Jammed into the grille of the battered vehicle was his brief-case.

He got lucky at the eighth newsstand he tried.

"Yeah, I know Lacey," said the vendor, looking suspiciously at McKee. "I always give her the outdated stuff. Any cards that get torn or wet, I give them to her for nothin'. What's it to ya?"

"I need to find her."

"What for?"

"I . . . I have something for her," McKee said.

The vendor looked him over again. "You got a grudge against her for something, hangin' around your fancy office maybe? How do I know you ain't gonna try and push her around?"

He was getting nowhere, so he tried a different approach, leaning in to the man and lowering his voice. From time to time he'd look to his side to make sure no one was listening, as if what he was about to say was important enough that it shouldn't be overheard.

"Listen, you give her your old cards, right? So do dozens of other newsstands around the city. Well, she stopped me on the street the other day and I bought one of the damned things just to get her off my back. But get this . . ." McKee leaned closer, taking the man into his confidence as he lied. "Some of those 'outdated' cards, as you call them, are collector's items. The one I bought from her was worth over a hundred bucks."

The man let out a low whistle.

"Now, all I want to do is buy some more of her outdated cards. Get it?"

McKee could almost hear the wheels turning in the man's greedy little brain as he thought. He took a candy bar from one of the display boxes and unwrapped it slowly as he said, his voice a low whisper, "Yeah, I get it. So, uh, what's in it for me if I tell you where she lives?"

McKee reached into his coat for his wallet and pulled out two bills, giving one to the vendor. "Here. Let's call this a finder's fee. And this," he said, as he gave him the other, "is an advance on any other 'collectibles' I come up with. What do you say, uh—"

"Mike."

"—Mike? Have we got a deal?"

Mike thought it over for all of three seconds. "You ain't gonna hurt her, are you?"

"Of course not, I sell insurance. Do I look like an arm-breaker to you?"

"No, I guess not. OK, it's a deal." He extended his arm and the two men shook to seal the bargain. McKee noticed that Mike's hand was sticky from the candy bar and idly wondered how long it would stay that way before he washed it.

The alley was only a few minutes' walk from the newsstand, and McKee found it easily enough. He wasn't sure just what he had expected, but the sight of it stopped him in his tracks. He'd seen these places dozens of times before; the TV news programs had shown them locally, and *Time* and *Newsweek* regularly did features on the conditions of the homeless, but the reality of it stunned him.

Thank God for the snow, he thought. It hides a lot of the filth. Several inches had fallen and a blanket of white covered every trash can and fire escape. Here and there were small cardboard and plywood lean-tos; he saw no one in them, although whether they were permanently abandoned or just temporarily empty, he had no way of knowing. Again, the weather was a blessing; he couldn't imagine what this place would have looked like—or smelled like—in the heat of summer.

He made his way down the dark passage, nearly falling several times on objects hidden in the snow. The noise of the busy street faded the farther away he got, and the quiet made him more nervous than before.

There was an intersection of sorts, and seeing what appeared to be a small fire down the alleyway to the right, he turned in that direction. His heart pounding, he approached a small group sitting around the tiny blaze. Although their clothing was tattered and filthy, the four of them looked surprisingly warm wrapped in blankets around the fire.

"Excuse me," he said, his voice shaking. "Is there a Lacey or a Miss Lacey here?"

They ignored him as he looked from face to face in the group. Had they even heard him?

"I'm looking for a woman who calls herself Lacey," he repeated, a bit louder this time. "Have any of you seen her or know where I can find her?" They turned to him this time, but remained silent.

Finally, one of them, McKee guessed him to be in his fifties, lifted a thin hand from beneath his blanket and pointed down an alleyway.

"Thank you." McKee headed in the indicated direction. The alley made several turns and he tried to remember each as he went. Looking back the way he'd come, he was relieved to see his footprints, easily visible in the snow. The alley was dark, but the glow of the city reflected well in the mantle of white at his feet. He should have no trouble finding his way back. Somewhat more at ease, he turned and was about to continue on his way, but stopped dead when a cigarette fell into the snow a few paces in front of him. He stared dumbly at it for several seconds, watching as it melted the snow and extinguished with a soft *sssst.*

McKee heard a clattering sound from behind, and above, him. He turned to run back the way he came, but another sound—also from above, but in front of him this time—made him freeze.

"Don't do it, man," shouted a voice from yet another direction. The young punk stepped quickly from the shadows of a doorway set invisibly into the wall on his right and was on him in a flash, a knife just inches from his face. The boy grinned wickedly at him, turning the knife over and over in his hand. He started circling McKee. "Well, now, what do we have here? Danny! Jackson! Get down here." The clattering resumed from front and back as two more youths scrambled down from the fire escape on his left.

McKee heard one of the boys approach from behind; he wanted to swing around now with the briefcase and run, run as fast as he could, but he knew he wouldn't get ten feet. "Nice coat, mister," said the one from behind as he felt the fabric of the collar. "You get that around here?" All three of them burst into laughter at the remark.

"Danny, ain't no stores around here carry these coats," said Jackson, the one who'd jumped from the ladder ahead of him. The one from the doorway stepped back and put the knife away, lighting another cigarette as he leaned against the building.

He must be the leader, McKee thought, hanging back to study me while his two buddies go to work on me.

"What d'ya think, Blade?" the one identified as Danny asked his companion in the doorway. "You think we can find us a couple coats like this? I think we'd look pretty damn fine if we all wore 'em."

"And how 'bout this, Blade?" said Jackson, jerking the briefcase from McKee's hand. He looked at it closely in the dark alleyway, fingered the dented-in side. "Hey, this looks like genuine alligator, Blade. That what this is, man, alligator? You should take better care of it."

McKee tried to say something, anything, but was frozen with fear. Sweat flowed down his face, melting the occasional snowflake that landed on his skin.

"Hey, Danny. You know what this is? This is flyin' alligator." With that, Jackson flung the case against the nearest building with a crash. It caromed off the wall and landed in the snow several feet away as the two burst into laughter again. They continued prodding and taunting him for several minutes until Blade, the one in the doorway, finished his cigarette and flipped it with a finger into the snow.

"That's enough," he said, stepping up to stare evenly into McKee's face.

"I have money . . ."

Blade hit McKee suddenly with the back of his hand. The other two grabbed his arms, pinning them painfully behind him. "No shit, man! You think we're out here screwin' with you 'cause we like the weather?"

McKee tasted blood, felt a small cut on the inside of his lip with his tongue. "Please, take my money. I won't give you any trouble."

Blade laughed, pulled the knife from his pocket. "Yeah, I heard that. Let him go." Danny and Jackson released his arms and took a few steps back. Still holding the knife in his right hand, Blade extended his left. "OK, Mr. Uptown, let's have it."

McKee's hands, numb from both cold and fear, shook uncontrollably as he reached into his coat, which seemed to be a source of great amusement to his tormentors.

"What the hell you doin' here, man?" Blade demanded. "You lost?"

"I was looking for someone." McKee handed the wallet over.

Clicking the knife closed, Blade opened the wallet, took a look inside, and beamed; he gave a quick thumbs-up to the others.

"All *right*," said one, McKee couldn't tell which.

"Well, whoever you was lookin' for did me a favor," Blade said, waving the wallet in the air as the three turned to leave him. "You ever find him, you tell him I said thanks."

"Please, wait. You've got my money. Tell me, do you know someone named Lacey?"

Blade froze in his steps and turned to him, all traces of humor gone from his face. Danny and Jackson continued down the alley. "What you want with her?" he demanded, approaching him menacingly.

"Blade! You comin', man?"

"I'll be there in a second; you guys go on." The two stopped, stared at him a moment. "I said go on! I'll meet you back at Carlos's place. Now!" He waited till they resumed walking, finally disappearing in the falling snow.

Blade turned abruptly and grabbed him by the collar of his coat. "I asked you why you was lookin' for Miss Lacey."

"I . . . I need to see her."

"You want her cards, don't you, Mr. Uptown?" Chuckling, he let McKee go and reached for a cigarette. He lit it and, as an afterthought, held out the pack.

McKee took the offered cigarette and cupped his hands around the flame of Blade's lighter as he lit it. He was still shaking, but no longer afraid for his life. Inhaling the warm smoke deeply for several moments, he forced himself to relax.

"I got some bad news for you, man," Blade said finally. "You're wastin' your time. If you're after Miss Lacey's cards, then you must know what they do. And if you know that, then you're just wastin' time."

Despite the fearful respect he felt for the young man, Mc-Kee began to feel a certain sense of fascination for him. "You know about the cards, what she can do with them?" he asked.

"Yeah, yeah, I know."

"Then why the hell are you hanging out in alleys, waiting for strangers to rob? Why don't—"

"You ain't payin' attention, are you?" Blade snapped, throwing his cigarette to the ground. "Listen, man, if you know about it, it don't work."

"What do mean, 'if you know about it'?" McKee could barely believe what he was hearing.

"Look, there's somethin' special 'bout Miss Lacey. Sometimes when she sells one of her cards, she . . . I don't know, she gets a feeling 'bout the person buyin' it from her, see? And that card has some kind of special thing for the person. They see somethin' in it and they act on it, and whatever it is they do turns into somethin' good for them. Understand?"

He glimpsed the battered briefcase, lying in the snow several feet down the alley. "Yeah, I think I do."

"But if you know about it, then you start lookin' for stuff that ain't there, and it just don't work no more."

The snow was falling more heavily now, and the two moved beneath the fire escape to get out of the worst of it as they talked.

"Who is she, Blade?"

"I don't know, man—just some crazy old woman. All of them livin' around here ain't right in the head. These ain't the kind that like livin' out here, ya know? These are the ones the homes throw out 'cause their budgets keep bein' cut. She don't even know what her cards do for people. Some of us tried to tell her once, but she don't listen." Blade rubbed his hands together to warm them, then slipped them into the pockets of his jacket. "So we look after her and the others, make sure they get some food, blankets when they need them. Who do you think it was built that fire?"

"You followed me all the way from there?"

Blade laughed, dug out the cigarette pack, and lit one up, blowing a plume of smoke up toward the fire escape. "Shit, man. We saw your ass comin' when you stepped off the sidewalk." He put the pack away, then reached suddenly into a hip pocket, causing McKee to jump slightly. "Take it easy, Uptown," Blade said with a smirk. He opened the stolen wallet, rifled through the several bills inside, and removed a single twenty. Pocketing the bill, he handed the wallet back to McKee.

"Thanks."

Blade turned to him, a look of deadly seriousness on his face. "Leave her alone, you got that?" McKee nodded. Blade started down the alley, stopping at the briefcase now almost buried in the snow. He picked it up, shook some of the snow from it, and tossed it back to McKee, still standing against the wall beneath the fire escape. Without another word, the young man turned and disappeared into the darkness.

McKee wasn't surprised, the following night, to find that the city of New York didn't plow the alleys—at least not the ones this far below Fourteenth. Nearly eight inches had accumulated during the snowstorm, but foot traffic and delivery trucks during the day had packed it down enough that walking was fairly easy. More snow was predicted, but for now the skies were merely cloudy and the light from several high, barred windows was unhampered by falling snow.

He found his way easily enough, following the familiar landmarks he'd seen last night. Several of the lean-tos showed evidence of having been occupied during the night. He hesitated at the intersection of the two alleys and looked around but saw no one. Too early, he thought. He passed the spot where the fire had burned last night, the embers still smoldering, and he guessed that by midnight there would be a small group huddling around it once more.

Reaching the place where he'd confronted the gang, he

found, an old man sitting in the doorway, a dirty red blanket draped over his shoulders, eating the last of a McDonald's hamburger. Several wrappers littered the snow at his feet. The old man stood up as he approached.

"Leave me alone. Go away."

"It's all right; it's OK. I won't hurt you."

The old man stopped whimpering, but stayed in the protection of the doorway.

"Do you know Miss Lacey? Do you know where I can find her?"

"Please. Leave me alone." The old man was terrified and leaned shaking against the door, dropping the remains of the hamburger to the snow. Suddenly, a look of relief spread across the man's face as he looked to a spot over McKee's shoulder.

"You heard what he said, man!" In one smooth, calm motion McKee reached into his pocket and pulled out a small handgun, pivoted around, and brought it to bear on the center of Blade's forehead. The young man was no fool; he froze, extended his hands at his side.

"From this distance, I won't miss, Blade."

"Be cool, man."

"Let's see it." Blade reached slowly into a pocket and took out the knife. "Don't even look like you're going to open it. Toss it into the snow, over there by the wall. Good. Now, take me to her."

"Why, man? I told you, she ain't got nothin' for you anymore."

McKee gestured menacingly with the gun. "Maybe not. But I've got something here for you if you don't take me to her. Now move."

"Shit, man. And I thought *these* people were crazy," he muttered, indicating the old man now on the ground brushing snow off the cold hamburger. Blade moved down the alley and McKee followed a few feet behind, the gun never wavering.

"And if you see any of your friends hiding around the corner, Blade, tell them to back off. You'll have a hole in your neck before any of them could get near me." McKee tried to sound like he meant it, but didn't stop wondering if he could really do it. Best to hope we don't pass Danny and Jackson on the way, he thought.

They had gone only a short distance and McKee was already feeling lost in the maze of alleyways when he saw the glow of a fire up ahead. Someone sat warming himself at it, and he could make out Danny and Jackson, too, standing over to one side talking animatedly to another young tough he didn't recognize. They either heard or saw them approaching, and waved in greeting.

"Hey, Blade! Where you been . . ." The boy stopped short when he saw McKee. All three reached for pockets.

"I swear to God, Blade," he said as calmly as he could, "call them off or you take one in the head."

"Danny! Carlos, Jackson! This crazy mother has a gun. Don't do it."

"You heard him. Get them out and toss them. Down the alley—now!"

They obeyed. Each had a knife; Jackson also carried a Saturday-night special. All the weapons were tossed into the snow as the person at the fire watched, never moving, never speaking.

Feeling safer now, McKee prodded the young man closer to the light. It was her sitting by the fire, he realized as he neared. Her back was to him, but he recognized the scarf and the plastic shopping bag at her side. "Over with your friends, Blade. That's it. Now, you four stay at least thirty feet away from the fire, you got that? I see so much as a flinch in my direction and I shoot."

They cursed and chattered softly to each other, but moved away steadily, if slowly, and stood leaning against a wall.

"Miss Lacey?" McKee knelt at her side and she turned to face him for the first time since he'd gotten there. The snow had begun gently falling once more and tiny flakes stood out against the bright colors of her scarf. My God, she's old, he thought. She really can't care for herself. He saw now just how much a help Blade and his friends had been to her and the others.

"Yes? Who is it?"

"My name's McKee, Miss Lacey. You sold me some post-cards yesterday."

She looked puzzled for a moment; then her eyes brightened suddenly in recognition. "Yes. Yes, I remember you. The man at the office building. You helped me when the security man came. I remember you were so nice to me and I made sure you had a special one."

"That's right. The one you gave me yesterday evening was a very special one. Do you know that it saved my life?"

Her eyes twinkled in disbelief as a tiny smile appeared on her weathered face. "No. It was just a pretty postcard."

"I told you, man," Blade called from the far wall. "She don't even know."

McKee looked to the young men and, satisfied for the moment that they were keeping their distance, set the gun down next to him on the packed snow. He reached into his coat and pulled out a small bundle.

"I brought you something, Miss Lacey. Here, look at these." He quickly rolled a rubber band off a stack of cards and showed them to her one by one. "Look at this one, Miss Lacey," he said, holding a picture of a beautiful sunset on a tropical island. "Isn't it pretty? And how about this one?" A peaceful little village overlooking a quiet lake. "And this one? Look at the details; imagine what it would be like to live there." He continued through them, and each time she'd look at one of the scenes her mouth would go wide in a soft *ooooh* and she'd take the card and turn it over and over in the growing pile of postcards in her lap.

"They're all so beautiful," she gasped. "I can't decide."

"No, you don't understand. They're yours; I want you to have them all."

She couldn't grasp it. Tears welled up in her eyes and she began sobbing. "But I don't have enough money for them. It isn't right."

Blade and his friends stirred uneasily when they heard her crying, and McKee reached quickly for the gun. "Don't try it, boys," he said as forcefully as he could. They backed off, and he set the gun down again.

"No, it's not right," she repeated. "I don't have enough

money." She started gathering them up, trying to push them back at him.

"All right," he said, realizing he couldn't make her understand they were intended as a gift. He knelt closer, extending what was left of the stack. "You pick one, then. Pick the best one, and I'll let you buy it. Do you have enough for one?"

Her eyes gleamed. She nodded excitedly and reached for the rest of the cards, unbalancing him as she did.

It was the break Blade had been waiting for. Before McKee could recover his footing, the four were on top of him, wrestling him away from the fire, away from Miss Lacey. Blade grabbed the gun and stuck it hard under McKee's chin.

"Freeze, Mr. Uptown! Danny, you and Carlos go get your stuff. Hold him, Jackson." He remained motionless, panting heavily as the strong youth held him tightly. Lost in the cards, Miss Lacey was oblivious to the violence going on around her.

"Shit, man, we ain't gonna find that stuff till springtime," Danny said when the two returned.

"I told you not to come back here," Blade said. Still jamming the gun under McKee's chin, he punched him full in the stomach and watched as he fell gasping to his knees. "Get up."

"You heard the man!" Jackson grabbed him by the collar and swung him up once more to stand wobbling before them.

"Let's go for a little walk." Blade kept the gun on him while his companions chanted and took turns jabbing and pushing him down the alleyway.

McKee hurt all over and wondered if they planned to beat him to death, or just shoot him and leave him in a dumpster somewhere in one of the alleys.

"Mister! Wait!"

The youths froze at the sound of the old woman, running to catch up to them as best she could in the snow. As she approached, Blade hid the gun in his jacket; the others pocketed their hands and stood back silently. McKee fell to the ground on his hands and knees, panting, already exhausted from the beating he'd taken. He looked up when she neared, saw her dimly through clouds of his own breath. His nose was bleeding and he wiped his face on his coat sleeve. As with the ac-

tual occurrence of violence before, she didn't notice the
effects of it now. She knelt on the packed snow before him.

"I like this one," she said simply, holding the stack of cards
out and tapping the top one with a grimy fingernail. She
waited, smiling, while McKee looked at it. "Greetings from
the Suncoast!" it said across the top. It was a beach scene, but
unlike so many postcards of its type with half-naked young
girls frolicking with beach balls, this one showed an older
couple. They strolled along the sand, just at the edge of the
lapping water. The couple wore matching, comfortable-
looking shirts and hats of handwoven palm fronds. The legend on the reverse side said, simply, "Christmas in Florida.
Wish you were here!"

"It's lovely," he said, giving the top card to her.

She took it, held it up so Blade and the others could see.
They nodded nervously and muttered a few words of agreement about how nice it was. She stood up, a look of pride on
her face as she reached into the pocket of her oversized wool
coat.

"Here. Ten cents, right?"

McKee held out his hand and nodded. She placed the dime
gently into his palm, then curled his fingers over the coin as
if afraid he might lose it.

She walked slowly back to the fire. Now, he thought, while
their attention is on her. If I break now, I might be able to get
away. They know the alleys, but I'm in better shape; I just
might make it. But when she turned to wave, as she had the
other times he'd seen her, they also turned their attention back
to him. They were nervous about this, he could tell. Blade—
and to a lesser degree, Danny, Jackson, and Carlos—looked
anxiously back and forth from the old woman to the bruised
man at their feet.

No, he admitted to himself, I have to see this through. He
tried to stand up, fell to one knee, and tried again, succeeding
this time. One of the youths grabbed his arm, the strong fingers digging through the fabric of the sleeve.

"Look at the picture, Miss Lacey. Look at it. . . ." Jackson
shoved him again and he fell, scattering the cards on the
snow. They pulled him upright, and one of the cards stuck

momentarily to his cheek before falling, blood-smeared, to
join the others on the ground.

"What do you see in the picture?" he gasped, unable to tell
if she was even listening as she walked away from them.
"Look at it! Imagine what—"

Blade slammed him against the nearest building. "I have
had it with you, man!" He released the lapels of McKee's
coat, sending him flailing sideways against a trash can. The
contents spilled noisily across the alley. "Carlos! Danny!"

The two jerked him again to his feet and he leaned, his
head swimming, against the solidity offered by the brick wall
at his back. The breath burned in his lungs as he blinked, trying to focus his eyes on his captors. He saw Blade reach into
his jacket.

"Miss . . . Miss Lacey. Look at it. Look how warm, how
nice it must be!" Blade aimed the gun at his head.

"Jesus! Blade," screamed Jackson, staring back behind
them. He was tugging now at Blade's jacket, pointing fear-
fully at the old woman. Blade looked, and the gun drifted
down and hung limply at his side.

She had stopped about halfway to the fire, and where she
stood the snow was glowing in a circle of brilliant orange
light. The circle glowed brighter and expanded till it touched
the buildings on either side of the alley. She stood motionless
in the center, head tilted back, her eyes closed. The gently
falling snow swirled within the circle, looking like nothing so
much as tiny gemstones sparkling from some inner glow.

The snow spun faster and faster about her in an eerie silence so complete they could hear the sounds of Manhattan's
ever-present traffic. The orange glow became yellow, then a
white brighter than the snow itself. Finally, it grew so bright
they were forced to shield their eyes from the sheer radiance
of it, and all the while, it remained as soundless as the night.

They could barely see Miss Lacey in the center of the
glowing swirl. No, not in the center of the glow—part of it,
the brightest part of the light itself. She lowered her head and
turned to them, and smiled.

"Merry Christmas," she said softly, "and have a nice New
Year." Her image faded from the center of the tiny whirlwind,

and was gone. The glow faded gradually as the snowy vortex slowed, from hot-white to white, then yellow, then orange; finally, a dull red, then nothing. The snow fell softly on the spot once more, and throughout the alley it was as if nothing had happened.

Blade crossed the few yards to the spot. McKee pushed himself away from the wall to follow and one of the others made a move for him. "Leave him be," Blade snapped, and the youth backed off. "Sweet Jesus," he whispered as McKee approached his side. Blade bent down and picked up the card, looked at it a moment before passing it to him. "Sweet Jesus," he repeated.

The snow was falling harder now and McKee wiped the card on his coat. He looked at it once and nodded, then handed it back. "Here, you keep it."

Blade stared at the now-forgotten gun in his hand, and with a grunt heaved it as far down the alleyway as he could. "Thanks, man." He looked at the card, chuckling softly to himself as he read the back. " 'Christmas in Florida. Wish you were here!' "

"You were right, Blade," McKee said quietly. "The magic only works if you don't know about it."

The two regarded each other in silence for several long seconds. Blade turned to his friends and jerked his head in the direction of the far alley; they nodded and wordlessly left the two alone. McKee took his handkerchief and scooped up a bit of snow, dabbing at his face. His nose had stopped bleeding and the icy handkerchief felt good on the cuts.

"Hey, man, I'm sorry. I really—"

"It's all right, Blade. Forget it." McKee finished with the handkerchief, wadded it into a ball, and threw it into the rest of the trash lining the alleyway. "Save us both some embarrassment."

They looked at each other for a moment longer, then, almost simultaneously, turned and went their separate ways through the silently falling snow.

A story set in a stable one Christmas Eve.

Bedlam Inn
Madeleine Robins

It was not yet midnight when Ivo reached the inn. He could just make out a sign, twisting in the icy wind and lit by a waning moon: a palmer walking, one hand outstretched, the words BETHLEHEM INN beneath. Ivo was cold through, his face whipped raw by the wind, his fingers numb; he was in no mood to be amused by the irony of finding such a place on Christmas Eve. The inn was a sprawling place and old, by its look: half-timbering, some rosy brickwork; despite the hour smoke still plumed from its chimneys and there was a candle lit in an upstairs window. He reined in his horse and swung down off him. No ostler appeared to take the reins and lead the animal off to the stable, and after a moment Ivo lapped the rein casually around a post and went to the door.

It was locked. Cursing all rural innkeepers, Ivo pounded on the door until at last he heard the bolt being lifted and a man's voice imploring him to lower his voice and give over the racket. The door opened a crack and the landlord peered out and muttered, "No rooms, sir."

This time Ivo saw the joke in it, although perhaps the innkeeper had meant none. He would have laughed, but a shudder of cold overtook him in the same moment. *"No room at the inn?"* he asked. The landlord regarded him as if he were an escaped lunatic. "Come on, man, let me in. It's freezing out here. I'll take whatever you have. I'll share, if I must."

The landlord shook his head. "We'm full up, sir. There's even two gennelmen sleeping on the tables in my coffee-room. Squire's daughter's to be wed on Boxing Day. Whole inn's bespoke for the week, sir." The man's west-country vowels marked him as a local; and vowels or none, he was about to close the door.

"In God's name, at least let me come in and warm myself," Ivo barked. His voice, which had oft enough cowed a ragtag company of peninsular foot soldiers into order, drove the landlord back a pace. Ivo pushed the rest of the way in and found himself in a dark, square hallway, facing an elderly man in nightshift and cap, with a gray shawl across his shoulders. "Now," Ivo began again, more civilly. "I am not proud. Turn one of your ostlers in with the other and I'll sleep in his quarters. Let me join your gentlemen on the coffee-room tables. A place to sleep and a brandy-and-water are all that I require."

The innkeeper shook his head helplessly. "I can't sir. There's no room, 'tis God's own truth. My missus'd skin me alive do I take another soul into this house. Have mercy, sir, it's Christmas Eve." He began to edge closer to the door, as if to herd Ivo out before him into the snow.

The warmth in the hallway was tantalizing; for the first time in hours Ivo could feel the tip of his nose and his fingers. It was all he could do to keep from shaking the landlord as a terrier shakes a rat. He drew a breath. "Is there another inn nearby?"

"Only the Dartcaster Arms, over Radstock way. But Squire's bespoke them, too." It struck Ivo that the innkeeper was beginning to enjoy the litany of bad news.

"A private house which might take me in?"

The landlord shook his head.

Ivo cast a look over his shoulder. His horse had gathered a powdering of snow in the last few minutes; poor damned creature wanted only a dry stable and a few handsful of oats, which he seemed unlikely to get. Even a stable would be warmer, and drier, than riding through the night. The humor of the idea suddenly welled up in Ivo, as warm as drink. Why not? "Did the Squire bespeak your stables, too?"

The landlord shook his head, apparently deaf to Ivo's meaning.

"Can my horse and I find a place there, do you think? I will pay."

"Sleep in my stable, sir?" The man seemed dumbfounded. He cast a look back over his shoulder and up the stair. Doubtless wondering how his missus would take the proposal. Then he shrugged. "If you like, sir."

Negotiations were brief, and when they were concluded Ivo shouldered through the wind with a bottle of brandy tucked into his pocket and a borrowed lantern in one hand. He gathered up Orion's reins and made for the stable. When he threw the door open the lantern light bit through the blackness inside and made little sparking reflections in the animals' eyes. Hanging the lantern high, Ivo saw horses, cows, a goat, several sheep, some chickens, all of them watching him balefully.

"Good evening," he said to the night air. One of the cows tilted its head slightly, then returned its attention to the silage in the manger. The other animals appeared to take this as a signal and went about their business: the goat sighed, the chickens clucked and settled together in a brooding, feathery mass, the horses went back to sleep. Ivo, finding that the floor of the stable was cobbled, swept a patch clear, found a little kindling near the doorway, and lit a fire, small enough so that the horses would not wake and shy at the smell of it. Then he took the bottle from his pocket, allowed himself a long draught, took off his greatcoat and scarf, and began to groom his horse, working up a sweat as he did. In the army there had been a man to see to his horses; since he'd sold his commission, Ivo did all himself. He wondered if he would find the old head groom still at Ash House—since he'd had word of his father's death, the thoughts of home he'd had were all of that sort: who he would find there, after four years abroad. He'd felt little grief for his father, but he told himself that war

made it hard to grieve for one man when so many others were
dying around you daily. His father had forced him to learn
groom's work as a boy, if he wanted to ride at all. Now Ivo
was grateful.

Warmed by exertion and brandy, he finally folded himself
up on the floor near the fire, drew his greatcoat up over him,
and fell asleep to the cascading peal of midnight bells welcoming Christmas Day.

He woke in darkness, his fire a graying glow before him,
the lantern flickered out. What had waked him? It was not yet
light. Then he heard a whisper. "Now there's two of 'em," the
voice said testily.

"Aye, so?" came another voice. "They's sleeping. Why pay
'em any mind?"

"Because it's C-c-c-c-christmas morn," a third voice stuttered. "The one night of the year. I say we b-b-b-b-be rid of
'em."

"What would you, Cally? Do our visitors in? Fine spirit of
Christmas that'd be." A fourth speaker, with a low, musical
voice.

"Keep your voices down!" Another voice, old and trembling. "If the man wake and light his fire it's all up with us."

The talk subsided to whispers Ivo could not unravel. He lay
wondering what to do: Feign sleep and listen? Sleep in truth,
as the safest course? They spoke of two visitors: who was the
other? If I've fallen in with the local smugglers, Ivo thought,
true sleep is probably my best defense. He shrugged his greatcoat higher up on his shoulder and was about to try for sleep
again when a voice rose above a whisper. The stutterer
screeched angrily, "I don't care who they is or where they
been! It's C-c-c-c-christmas morn!"

"All the more reason, then," the low-voiced speaker said.
Which seemed, for now, to settle the matter. There was quiet,
and Ivo, warm enough under his coat, let his eyelids drop
down and tried to imagine himself in a bed with dry sheets
and velvet curtains, a fire crackling in the grate. He was just
drifting on the cusp of a dream when there was an explosion

of noise, of voices screeching in argument, that brought him
bolt upright.

"Who's that!" A woman's voice cut through all the other
voices. She was frightened nearly to death, by the sound of it.
"For the love of God, who's there?" It was an educated voice,
the words crisp and clear, vibrant with fear.

"Accch, that's torn it," someone said. There was a scuffle
of sound, a sharp, fearful intake of breath from the woman.
Near the door: Ivo thought she must have stolen in after he
fell asleep. Caution vied with chivalry: he could not very well
sit still and let a lady be terrorized, despite the unwisdom of
tangling with smugglers. Ivo felt about for a few twists of
straw and touched one to the fire. The sharp, sudden flare
of light caused gasps across the room—Ivo did not see the
others, his eyes were too full of the dazzle—as he lit the lantern. Then he raised the lantern up to survey the stable.
Horses, cows, a goat, sheep, some chickens; a large black and
white cat washing herself unconcernedly. And near the door,
a woman in a tumble of blue and gray garments, drawn back
as close to the wall as she could go.

"Good evening," Ivo said. There was the woman; he saw
no one but her, and she was eyeing him as if he might be the
Devil himself. Her bonnet, or what there was left of it, was
clutched in one hand, the only weapon she possessed. He
could make out that she wore a gray pelisse and a blue dress,
both plainly but well made, with two venerable Norwich
shawls over all. Her curling light brown hair was short-
cropped, speckled with bits of straw. And her face, which he
thought must in the ordinary way have been full-lipped and
merry, was drawn and sheet-white. Old clothes but good, Ivo
thought, and no commonplace voice. Scared half to death, on
top of it. "What in God's name is a lady of quality doing
sleeping in a stable on Christmas morning?" he asked blandly.

"I've taken nothing," the woman said quickly.

"My dear ma'am, I don't believe I said that you had done.
I merely asked—"

"Oh, let her alone, do," another voice piped up. "Anyone
can see she's scart to death of ye."

Ivo almost dropped the lantern. "I beg your pardon?" he said after a moment, watching the speaker.

"I said, let her alone," the black and white cat said impatiently. "She's scart to death of ye. Probably had some bad handling by some man, haven't you, love?" The cat eyed its paw thoughtfully, then went back to washing.

"Blackie, you never could hold your tongue," one of the cows said irritably.

The cat stuck its long pink tongue out at the cow, elegantly disdainful. "They was both awake, listening. If we're to have our fete, I reckon we'd have to let 'em in on it. Less, like Cally says, we're simply going to be rid of 'em entire, which I *don't* think."

Feeling distinctly light-headed, Ivo hung the lantern on a peg and sat down again. I've lost my mind, he thought. Or this is the damnedest dream I ever heard of. I'm still in Spain, I took a bullet, I'm in a fever dream . . . Cats don't talk, nor yet cows. There *must* be someone else here, someone I haven't seen yet. *Cats don't talk.*

"You w-w-w-watch your mouth, Blackie," one of the chickens clucked.

The stutterer, Ivo realized dizzily. "Say something else," he said at last.

"Such as?" the cat drawled.

Ivo looked around the stable once more, seeking another human speaker, but saw none but the woman. She was still pressed back against the stable door; as he watched she raised her hands to her parted lips and pressed them there, as if to keep any words inside. Her eyes were wide and dazzled. I can understand that, Ivo thought. I'm feeling mightily dazzled myself.

"Such as?" the cat prompted again. "Were you wishful to ask directions, maybe?"

The cat was talking. The sound came from him, no doubt of it, and the voice itself sounded . . . cattish. *The cat was talking.* Ivo shook his head, unable to think what to do, until at last his childhood training, the company manners drilled into him in the nursery, came back to him.

"Excuse me," he said at last, to the room generally. The

woman—without the gloss of terror, she was younger than he had at first thought—dropped her hands from her mouth and turned to look at him. As did a cow, the cat, the goat, and one of the sheep. "It seems we have intruded on a festivity of some sort," he began. "I hope you will forgive us."

"N-n-n-n-not likely," the ill-tempered chicken stuttered, but the cow spoke again, more graciously this time.

"You and the lady are welcome, sir." Her voice was sweet and musical. "I am Rebecca. This is Sarah, this is Bess." As she spoke, the two cows beside her paused briefly in their feeding to nod their heads.

Ivo bowed. "Ivo Connell," he said. "Returning from His Majesty's peninsular force." He turned, hoping the woman would introduce herself, and saw that she was shivering deeply. "My dear ma'am, please draw near the fire; it will warm you as well as me, you know."

The woman shook her head. Her curls shone in the lantern light. "I do well enough where I am, sir." Her tone should have frozen Ivo colder than the wind outside, but the effect was ruined by the chattering of her teeth.

"I should hate to call a lady a liar," Ivo said smoothly. "But if you force me to, I shall gather you up bodily and bring you to the fire rather than see you freeze solid before m—"

He had meant it to sound teasing, but the woman paled again and drew back against the door. Ivo cursed himself for a blundering fool: a young woman without a protector, in such profoundly irregular circumstances, would see any man as a predator. *Have I been away from polite society so long that even my common sense has disappeared?*

He began again. "My dear ma'am, I did not mean to frighten you. If I spoke too jocularly, it is the fault of my wretched funning tongue. Only come to the fire. You have my word I'll not come near you."

"Your word?" To hear her, you'd think I'd spoken obscenities, Ivo thought grimly.

"If it matters," another voice broke in, "I've never known Master Ivo to break his word—and certainly not to a lady."

Ivo turned, slack-jawed, to see his own horse regarding him blandly. "Thank you, Orion," he said finally.

" 'Tis no more than the truth," the horse said. He spoke, Ivo realized, like the head groom at Ash House. "Now, I could tell you tales about young Forsyth, or Sir Redmond Archer—"

"Pray don't," Ivo said hurriedly. He was so long past wonder he could hardly find the words to ask what was happening. "Orion, how does it happen that you can talk?" he managed at last.

"Christmas morn," the horse said simply, and went back to his oats.

There was a laugh from the woman. Ivo turned back to her, relieved to see that she had drawn nearer to the fire and was warming her hands there. Orion's word seemed to have been good enough for her. His own certainly had not been. Was it as the cat *(the cat? good God)* had said, and she had been ill-used by some man past trusting any other? Some sort of ill-use it must be, he reflected, to send her into the night, into a barn, dressed in little more than she might have worn for a walk in her garden.

"My nurse used to say that the cats would gossip about us all on Christmas morn," the woman said quietly. "Do you?" she turned to the cat, who was busily cleaning her left hind leg.

"Oh, aye," she said, raising her head for a moment. "When we can be bothered to. Mostly there's little enow to gossip over, dearie."

Ivo laughed. "Surely people must give you enough to shake your heads over during the year?"

The cat shrugged. "Don't expect much of man-folk at the best of times. Find I'd rather smack my lips over a mouse than some man's business. Don't know about the rest of you; horses gossip some, that I do know." Orion snorted; one of the other horses switched its tail at the cat, who dodged neatly and went back to washing.

"I think I must be asleep in a ditch somewhere," the woman mused. "Freezing to death and dreaming this all."

"I'd had something of the same idea," Ivo said. "Dreaming or turned a lunatic. When I think of what I've seen in the last few years, life's a madhouse enough. And this seems a pretty enough delusion for a winter's night."

"You're right cheery at the notion," the goat bleated.

"I suppose I am. I've fetched up in Bedlam, after all, so I might as well be companionable."

"What do you mean?" the woman asked.

"The name of this place. It's the Bethlehem Inn." He gave it the country pronunciation, which turned the word to *Bedlam*. "Appropriate, isn't it? For the night, and for lunacy as well." Ivo shared it as a joke, but his human companion had returned to staring into the fire, to appearances miles distant. The tight, drawn expression returned to her face. Ivo, remembering her face lit with a smile, had a sudden powerful urge to help her, to bring that smile back.

"Ma'am, my name is Ivo Connell, and if I can be of any service to you—"

She did not raise her eyes from the fire. "I can imagine the sort of service you're offering, sir."

"Girl, he's given you no cause to take him up like that," the goat bleated. " 'E was being civil, like. Tell 'im your name, at least. That's manners. And it's Christmas morn, we'm supposed to be peaceable, like."

The woman's back stiffened, but she turned to Ivo and introduced herself. "Emma Tarliff, sir. I beg pardon if I sounded ungracious, but I've had occasion—"

"So I apprehended, Miss Tarliff. But is there no way I can help you find your friends—"

"I have none, sir," she said sharply. "I beg you will believe there is nothing you can do to help me. I have considered the matter rather closely, as you may imagine." She gave a hard, hollow little laugh.

"My, what a mystery, I don't think." It was the goat again. "You're a—poor relation, a lady's companion, something like?"

"I *was* a governess," Miss Tarliff said.

"Master chase you round the nursery?" the goat suggested. "Missus send you packing without a reference?"

"Addie, hold your tongue," the cat spat. "Have a little kindness, for Christmas' sake if no other."

The goat had hit a nerve, Ivo thought. Emma Tarliff had gone ashy white, her mouth set in a straight line of dismay. "The master did nothing of the sort," she said slowly, with a kind of exact truthfulness. "But his damnable brother did, and when I said I would not have him, he stole one of Mrs. Cheveley's brooches and put it in my workbox, to make it seem as if I'd taken it. And Mrs. Cheveley said she was sorry but of course she had to dismiss me, without a reference. And there—" Her voice shook with the enormity of it. "—almost at the gate of the house, was Arthur Cheveley, waiting for me to go docilely along with him. Since, as he so kindly put it, I will never find a new position without a reference, he thought I might like to reconsider my refusal as an alternative to starving to death. Well, I would rather *die*. I suppose, when I have run through my little savings, I *will* die."

Blackie, the cat, had been biting the base of her tail; she twisted her head up and asked, "What did you do, then?"

"I left the house and I walked to the village. But I'd missed the stagecoach, and the next wasn't for two days, and I could not—*could not*—go back to the Cheveleys. I told the man at the posting house that I'd send for my luggage, and I started to walk. That was two days ago," she added in a small voice. "I haven't eaten since breakfast that day, and my boots—I'd no idea how far it was to Wells. I thought I'd freeze to death tonight, until I saw this place and came in."

"My dear, you have been hard-used," the cow, Rebecca, said in her slow, mellifluous voice. "But have you no family—"

"I would rather die," Miss Tarliff said again, "than be a charge on my sister's family, dwindle into an unpaid servant, be reproached for each bite of food, each cast-off dress. I would rather *die*."

The word rang in Ivo's ears, cold and hard, conjuring up the battlefield at Ciudad Rodrigo. Memories he hoped he had lost came back to him: Will Stuart with his lungs torn open, his life bubbling away; Ned Hargrove, crying for his mother and for the leg that had been blown off by cannon fire. "Rather die?" he repeated. "How do you imagine it, Miss Tarliff?" His voice was rough as he asked again. "How do you imagine it? A neat, pretty, poetical death, freezing easily in a field somewhere? Wasting away in a decline like Clarissa Harlow, martyred on the altar of virtue?" He saw her draw back, heard the brutality in his own voice, damned himself for a fool but could not stop. It was as if she had torn open a wound he could not stanch.

"I've spent the last two years watching friends die, so you'll pardon me if I've a little less glamorous notion of death than you. *Rather* die? When you've seen a friend with his guts hanging out of him, joking because there is no other way to deal with the pain, or seen the man to the left of you, and then the one to the right, dropped by rifle fire, and waited for the bullet which would take you—"

"And smelled the blood," Orion added, whickering at the memory. His eyes rolled wildly; the hide at his neck twitched. "And the cannons and the smoke. And heard the scream of horses, and seen the flashes of light from the guns. And still they expect you to go on, they put blinders on you, thinking you'll not see the worst there is to see, but it's everywhere. Horses dying, men dying under them and on top of them. Some of them think nothing of using a sword to whip a horse, others will just whip you raw, until you're foaming and bleeding—"

Ivo rose and went to his horse, running a hand along the animal's neck, murmuring to him. After a moment or so Orion's head bent again. "Sorry," he whinnied softly. There was a rustling of words from the other animals, comfort and reassurance.

"If we spoke too strongly, Miss Tarliff, I apologize," Ivo said at last. "But for the love of God, let's have no more mooning talk of death. Death is no deliverer; I've seen too damned much of it."

For the first time Emma Tarliff met Ivo's glance straight on. She had fine eyes, Ivo thought idly. Direct, blue, quite honest. "It's I who owe the apology, Mr. Connell," she said at last. "I've been wrapped up in pity for myself, thinking of the alternatives before me. Although I must say that all I can see is death, soon or late. Now, as you say, from freezing. Soon, if I cannot find employment, from starvation. Later, if I take Mr. Cheveley's solution; I doubt I've the temperament for a courtesan." Her tone now was wry, less bitter. She had courage, Ivo thought, to be able to face the future she envisioned and not take the easiest path. "But what I am facing pales before your experience." She bowed her head. "And yours," she added, nodding to Orion.

"He never did," Orion said, his thoughts evidently still on the battlefield. "Even when we was cornered and I thought sure to die, he didn't even use his crop. Dug his knees in so hard I thought they'd have to pry 'em out with a knife, but never whipped me at all—"

"I never fancied the whip," Ivo said mildly. He was oddly moved by his horse's testimonial.

"Mr. Connell, I should think this would be a compliment any man would kill for," Miss Tarliff said gently. "Saving only your valet, who knows you better than your horse?"

Ivo smiled broadly. "Did I say life was a madhouse? It's Christmas morning and I hear the animals talking. Orion has paid me compliments. If that don't qualify me for Bedlam, I should like to know what does. As for you—" He turned back to his horse again. "How is it you can talk and have never said a word to me in all our years together?" He rubbed his hand affectionately along Orion's nose.

"Don't you know?" Miss Tarliff asked. She had come back to the fire again and knelt there, holding her hands out to the warmth, looking at Ivo. Her smile was broad and full of light. "My nurse told me that on Christmas morning all the beasts in the world can speak. Until dawn."

"Ay, and we'm wasting t-t-t-t-too much time on you and he," Cally the chicken stuttered. "We've had no games, no song, B-b-b-b-becca hasn't even told the story yet. You ha-ha-ha-had to come the one night of the year—"

"Oh, Cally, give over, do," Rebecca lowed. "There's more important things than a song."

"We did not mean to intrude on your fete," Miss Tarliff said, and Ivo found himself insisting that the party continue "as if we weren't here."

"Easy enow for y-y-y-y-you to say," the chicken muttered resentfully.

"Then tell the story, Rebecca," the goat bleated. "Dawn's not so far off."

Without being quite aware of it, Ivo drew near the fire and settled an arm's length from Miss Tarliff, who looked at him warily but said nothing. The chickens strutted forward to sit almost at the feet of the cow, who turned, looking from side to side as if to gather all in the stable in to her story, and began. Ivo recognized the tone of a practiced storyteller starting a tale her audience knew well. The pauses were measured and exact, the breaths precise, her voice musical.

"Long time now, before even my old Grannie's time, or her Grannie's or hers again, Man and his Wife was traveling to a great city. Were wintertime, as 'tis now, and Woman was near to time with a baby, and they come along in company with a donkey. So when they reached the town the man began to look out for a room for the night, only there were none to be had at all . . ."

Ivo listened, delighted and awed, to the animal's version of the story he had heard told every Christmas Eve since childhood. Emma Tarliff listened with a slight smile on her lips, her expression a mirror of what Ivo imagined his own to be. As Rebecca spoke he could see the Wise Men as three crotchety elders riding patient camels through the night; saw shepherds leading resentful, uncomprehending flocks to Bethlehem for a purpose they did not understand themselves. Saw the animals in the stable itself one by one give gifts to the Baby.

" 'Twas a cow gave the Babe a place in the manger," Rebecca reminded them.

" 'Twas a bird sang the B-b-b-b-babe to sleep," Cally clucked proudly.

"A nightingale, maybe," Blackie said dauntingly. "*Not* a chicken."

"Tell about the Baby," one of the sheep said sleepily.

" 'E didn't cry like man-children do. He watched 'em all, cows and kings alike, and took they's measure. My Grannie used to say that the Babe understood the speech of animals as well as men, right from the beginning. And when they wrapped Him up and Man and his Wife started on to leave the

stables, with the kings and shepherds and whatnot following
after, the Baby turned and gave us our gift, the gift of speech
one night a year, from the last midnight bell to the sun's first
light."

There was a respectful silence when Rebecca was done,
only the crackling of the fire and the whisper and clatter of
the wind through the trees outside. Then Addie, the goat,
called for a song. "Something proper and merry!"

The cat started with "God Rest You Merry, Gentlemen;"
she had a surprisingly sweet and carrying voice. Then they
had "Green Grow the Rushes," and a country song Ivo remembered from the nursery—Orion sang along on that one—
and church songs and carols. Ivo found himself dancing
country dances, cutting the figures in a square dance with his
fingers outstretched to the wingtip of one of the chickens,
skipping up the line of a reel with the cat, sliding down the
line with Miss Tarliff, who now was blushing with exertion
and laughter. And later they played the same games Ivo had
played at holiday parties all his life: lotteries, blindman's buff,
and charades. When the fire burned low, a dog Ivo had not
even realized was in the stable helped him to fetch more firewood, and the singing continued.

When they came back to report that the eastern sky was
lightening a bit, he found Miss Tarliff in counsel with Rebecca, Blackie, and Addie.

"—surely your old mistress would understand," Rebecca
was saying.

Miss Tarliff shook her head. "Mrs. Creveley is a good
enough woman in her way, but she'll never take the word of
her governess over the evidence of her own eyes: she found
the brooch in my workbox herself. And if I tell her Mr.
Creveley stole the brooch himself, and to what purpose, she'll
only think it's a tale I'm telling because he spurned my
advances—"

The cow looked shocked. "Your advances? But—"

"Give over, Becca," Blackie said brusquely. "Use your
brains, not your udders. Yon Creveley will say our Emma
made the advances, whether she done or no. And the lady will

believe him because he's her man's kinfolk. Villainous piece of work, that man."

Rebecca persisted. "If you cannot talk to her—have you no friends?"

"None who will take me in after something like this. How can they? You cannot imagine how a blackened character compromises me; any friend who harbors me will be tarred by the association. I cannot permit it—"

"You make me ashamed of my sex," Ivo said grimly. "And of my neighbors."

"You needn't be," Miss Tarliff said straitly. "It's the way of the world, Mr. Connell."

Ivo cleared his throat. "If I might be permitted?" Rebecca nodded. "Miss Tarliff, if you wish—only if you wish it—I am going to my family home in the morning; it should be only another five or six hours' ride. Orion and I would be grateful for the company, and my mother will certainly give you aid."

It was the wrong thing to say, he knew at once. Miss Tarliff stiffened again; the smile that had strayed into her eyes and played across her face disappeared abruptly.

"Thank you, Mr. Connell," she said crisply. "I will manage."

"You'd rather die," Rebecca said crossly.

"No, of course not, but—"

"Then why not take the man's offer? 'Tisn't as though he's offering marriage, just help. And his mother to help you, too."

"If he *has* a mother," Miss Tarliff muttered.

"He has one," Orion said, plainly amused. "A tartar she is, too. He'll need all the distraction he can come up with just to keep her from trying to run the estate, and him too—"

"Orion!" Ivo began, and stopped, overcome again with the ridiculousness of his situation. Why upbraid his horse for telling God's own truth about his mother?

"—and he'll have a hard enough time discovering what straits his father left the estate in without struggling with his dam on top of all. Would be a kindness for you to come along of us, Miss."

"That's *enough*, Orion. Although, Miss Tarliff, if you cannot take my word for it, you might listen to my horse. He is,

as you can hear, compulsively honest." Ivo grinned. "Come
dawn, I mean to turn Orion here toward Ash House; if the
roads are not too bad we might arrive there in time for nun-
cheon. If you will trust me that far, I promise my mother will
see you safe."

"Surely she won't want a woman who—"

"Who was badly treated by a neighbor and victimized by
the perfidy of a man? My dear lady, my mother lives to show
her neighbors their mistakes, and believes all men guilty until
proven innocent."

Miss Tarliff smiled. "Rather as I had been doing, I think."

"Then that's settled," Blackie purred. "Only about time.
Deely," she called to a chicken who was roosting near the
window. "Give us a song?"

The chicken shook its head. "T-t-t-t-too late. Sun's almost
up."

"Then we must say good night," Miss Tarliff said regretfully.

"And thank you for your hospitality," Ivo added. "I wish
we had a gift to give you in return."

"You gave us a proper romance," Rebecca said comfortably. She was aware, as Ivo was, that Emma Tarliff stiffened
at the word *romance* and glanced at Ivo as if daring him to
believe it. "Acch, d'you think all romances end with a kiss?
Don't bridle so, dearie. The best of romances is made up of
folk giving each other second chances. Think about that."

"A second chance is not the meanest gift one could receive
on Christmas Day," Ivo ventured mildly.

Miss Tarliff sighed. "You make me feel the veriest ingrate."

"Not at all, dear—" Rebecca began. What she might have
said next was lost in a mournful lowing: the sun had risen
enough to send a few rosy shafts of light to pattern the walls
of the stable.

Emma Tarliff patted the cow's ears and neck gently.
"Thank you," she said. Blackie hopped onto the manger and
rubbed her jaw along Miss Tarliff's shoulder. "Thank you
all."

Ivo bent to extinguish his fire. "You will come, then?" he
asked Miss Tarliff.

She looked at the cow and the cat, who returned the look steadily. "It would be churlish not to, I think," she said at last.

Blackie nodded and jumped off the manger as if satisfied.

"Good-bye, then," Miss Tarliff said, and Ivo echoed the words. He took up Orion's reins and led the horse out into the dawn light. Miss Tarliff pulled the Norwich shawls up tight about her collar and followed.

"It's a beautiful morning," she said, as Ivo lifted her up onto Orion's back.

"It's Christmas morn," Ivo answered, echoing Blackie's tones.

Orion turned to look at them, shook his head as if in exasperation, and, as Ivo mounted behind Miss Tarliff, turned his head toward the road, plainly feeling that the last word should have been his.

The myths and traditions of Christmas
transformed in the far future.

THE LAST CASTLE
OF CHRISTMAS
Alexander Jablokov

"WHAT'S THAT MADMAN doing out there?" Dalka asked, rousing herself from her half doze.

Tessa tugged the reins, slowing the wagon, and looked off through the last traces of morning ice mist. For a moment, nothing: the black-on-white of pipe plants, tulap trunks, insulated bundles of sprouting plants waiting for spring, the canyon wall rising beyond them. Then: a single erect, flapping shape, sliding frantically across the ice of a pond.

"Ice skating, it looks like," Tessa said.

Dalka snorted. "His way of celebrating Christmas?"

"Maybe it is." Now that Tessa thought about it, it *was* disquieting. Old Man Lewis usually did not appear in the lower parts of the canyon so openly, even in winter. She'd known him all her life, so she knew when something disturbed him.

It was early morning and they were the first wagon down the road. A damp current had slid down from the high Shield during the night, and the twin ice rails were hidden by an unbroken blanket of flat ice crystals standing on end like scales evolving into feathers. The low-slung mule Legume crunched

phlegmatically through them with its wide feet, tugging its
burden easily along behind it. The insulating hide covering its
back and vertebral spines, painstakingly applied by Tessa's
brother Benjamin, gleamed in the early-morning sunlight.

"Tessa!" Lewis's voice drifted across the wagon. "Tessa
Wolholme." He windmilled his arms and fell flat on his back
on the ice. Ice skates gleamed as he kicked his legs in the air.

"He wants you to celebrate with him." Dalka was contemptuous.

A gentle rein tug and the mule, splayed legs ungainly,
bounced the wagon's runners out of the ice-filled ruts onto the
sloping embankments. Huffing, somehow realizing that it had
been granted an unexpected rest, Legume wiggled its bulging
belly into the frost, stuck its head under a front leg, and was
promptly asleep.

"Then I will," Tessa said. "Want to come along?"

She jumped out of the wagon. The older woman lowered
her bulk after, grunting and complaining. Dalka and Tessa had
spent the night in a high cleft, extracting physiologically active fractions from rare fungi. The fractionating procedure
could have been carried out more easily in someone's kitchen,
but Dalka held to a romantic tradition, and made it a part of
Tessa's training.

Lewis lay sprawled on an irregularly shaped pond. It
opened up for swimming in the summer, but densely packed
leaves now closed in its surface, preserving carefully cali-
brated concentrations of salts and sugars. The pond was actually the bell of a subterranean flower, water storage for the
dry period at the end of winter.

But pure water had seeped through the insulating leaves,
and the pond was surfaced with ice. It always did, no matter
how carefully the farmers grew the leaves and arranged their
interlocking edges, leading Tessa to conclude that the leakage
was deliberate on the part of the original plant breeders.
Maybe it provided an extra seal. And maybe it was just for
fun.

By the time Tessa got to Lewis, he was laughing.

"Ah, Miss Theresa Wolholme! You are too late to save me
from falling. Years too late!" Lewis grinned at her, his eyes

wide and blue. His white hair flopped around his head. With Tessa's help, he climbed to his feet, slipping on his skates. "That ice is cold good on the skin, ah? Keeps it tight aware against the bone." Lewis wore little under his black cloak, and Tessa could feel his sagging, stringy flesh. "Once you've seen a planet burned to death, cold makes more sense. Die with a chip of ice under your tongue, die relaxed and comfortable."

"You should get inside, Lewis," Dalka said, pleased by the unusual opportunity to play the part of conventional reason. "You look cold. The sky's clearing. The temperature will drop."

Lewis goggled at her. His hair was as white as hers, but in contrast to her carefully managed spray, his flew around like snow blown off the peak of Kardom.

"You should get *out*," he said. "Koola does not stay inside. Inside is somewhere else. Earth, maybe." His cloak flopped loosely, but he indeed didn't seem cold. Legend had it that he curled up inside of snowdrifts and ice caves for days-long naps. Even knowing him as she did, Tessa could not say that the rumors weren't true.

"I've *been* out," Dalka said irritably. "We were just coming back—" She stopped herself. Boasting to Lewis about anything to do with the defiles and cliffs surrounding Calrick Bend was as pointless as showing a bird how high you can jump. She turned her attention to the winter-hooded herbs at the pond's edge, searching for something rare and unusual to make her visit worthwhile.

"Are you all right, Lewis?" Tessa looked into his eyes, but they were the same guileless blue as always.

"I'm all right," he said. "I'm always all right. But the others—how is your father now?"

Tessa felt a moment of sadness at the question. Had it really been so long since Lewis and her father, Perin, had spoken? After all the years and the bonds between them?

"He's been well . . . but not the same. Not since my mother died."

"Ah, Sora. She was once his anchor. Now, you."

"You should come see him." In her younger days, Tessa

would have been wary of offering such advice. Lewis was her father's wild friend, not subject to ordinary laws. When she was ten, Lewis told her and her brothers to climb the rocks naked, to feel the strength of their planet, Koola, right through their skin. She and Dom, her older brother, had stripped down and done it, to be hauled off by their furious mother and sent to their rooms. Lewis's only response was to suggest trying it a bit farther from the house.

"Perin doesn't need me," Lewis said. "He has his own way."

"You should see him." Tessa had waited for Lewis to appear at the house in the days after her mother's death. He never did, as if his old comrade's marriage and family were something insignificant, a mere bad habit. Lewis was not interested in anything that gave life comfort. But Tessa now lived with the look in her father's eyes, and if Old Man Lewis could be tamed enough to do something, she would try it.

He didn't answer her. He looked at something behind her, hard enough that she finally turned to look herself. A tiny girl had appeared in the frostbitten field. Her head was bundled in a thick scarf, but the ends were flopping loose, not tucked into the collar of her coat.

"Hello, Malena," Dalka said, straightening up from her herbs. "What are you doing out?"

"I'm running an errand," the girl said in a high, firm voice. "Mama wants some reeds for the fire. For the cake, the castle. We're cooking it tonight."

"A small one, this year?"

"Very small." Malena Merewin was serene about the possibility. "But big enough for the Kings to stay for Christmas night. They're not proud, my father says. They'll stop if they need to."

"That's good, Malena."

Malena moved around the pond pulling up bundled reeds. She might have been going a little beyond the strict definition of permitted gleaning, but no one was about to protest. It was before Christmas, the trespasser a little girl, and the Merewins were poor. Tessa knew that she would be visiting their house tomorrow, on Christmas morning, towed there by

Alta Dalhousie and the other charitable women of Cooperset Canyon.

Lewis continued to watch the little girl. She didn't acknowledge his presence openly, but stood close by him, and touched his cloak. Lewis knew Malena's father, Gorr Merewin, the same way as he knew Tessa's father, Perin: they had all fought in the wars together, were all veterans of that desperate fight in the Simurad Tunnels on a planet far from Koola. And each bore his own individual scars from that fight.

But why was the girl's scarf so loose? Her mother was starting to lose her grip. When children weren't taken care of, things were almost over.

"Come here," Tessa said. The little girl obediently marched up to her and stared up into her face. Her eyes had a stern wisdom that no five-year-old's should have had, but her favorite doll still stuck its limp-necked head out of a pocket of her jacket. Her thick dark hair had come unbraided. It was cold, and Tessa did not have time to redo the braids, though she was tempted to take Malena home and do a decent job of it. She compromised by taking a couple of clips out of her own hair to provide some control. She tucked the head scarf into Malena's coat and buttoned it back up.

The little girl had continued staring solemnly at Tessa all through the operation. Her eyes suddenly filled with tears. "Don't blame my momma," she said. "Don't blame my momma."

Tessa, who did blame Malena's momma, put her arms around her. "It's all right, Malena. Wish your mother a good Christmas from Tessa Wolholme, and tell her I'll see her tomorrow."

The little girl caught her breath. "We're all right!" she shouted. "Don't come, we don't need you! Please." She backed away, still staring at Tessa. "Momma and Poppa and I . . . we all live together. We always will. Don't try it!" And then she was running, with the frantic inefficient energy of a child, up the hill.

"She's halfway there," Lewis announced. "She's halfway to Koola."

"Please, Lewis," Tessa said, feeling a flash of fear, which she masked with anger. "She's a little girl."

"None of us is old enough to make the decisions we need to." Lewis squatted and removed his skates. He stepped out onto the ice with bare feet and stared challengingly at Tessa.

"Look at this," Dalka said. "Houndsfoot." She stood up with a tiny curled plant. "It contains a useful anthelmintic. You know how mules pick up worms from winter forage. You need a lot more than this to get a useful dose, but it might be interesting for you to examine. . . ."

Tessa allowed herself to be led away by the voluble Dalka, while Lewis slid thoughtfully on the ice in his bare feet, looking up at the snow-outlined canyon cliffs above.

Tessa slid the wagon into its slot and undid the mule. Legume, despite its unexpected nap earlier, crawled carefully into its subterranean burrow, flicked its forked tongue out to taste the air, and promptly fell asleep again. Tessa could hear a low hum as it twisted around, seeking a comfortable position amid the sweet-smelling hummocks of lungfungus. The mule shared its quarters with the farm's bees during the winter, each providing the other with heat and, Tessa supposed, company. Tessa made sure there was enough dried herbage for it to eat when it woke again. The lungfungus, supplemented by beeswax, was supposed to be its sole diet, but for some reason Legume demanded fermented sweet herbs from the kitchen garden as a condiment. Her old brother Dom told Tessa that it was because she had spoiled the thing when she was a girl. At any rate, if the finicky Legume didn't get its borage and sweetsage with its fungus, it would climb out of its burrow and bellow its displeasure to the chef.

The Wolholme house itself climbed the canyon wall. Like many houses in Calrick Bend, it grew larger the higher up it went, supported by a tangle of trusses and brackets. It was made of wood and sheet plaster and was brightly painted red and blue and green. A dark pile of moss against the canyon wall nearby puffed smoke into the cold air. Tessa could see her father, Perin, bustling around, making sure the oven was supplied with the right air mixture to cook the cake walls without drying them out.

A large open area had been cleared near the toolsheds for the castle. Tessa's youngest brother Kevin knelt on the ground, playing with a toy wagon. His coat was unbuttoned, but he didn't seem to mind the cold. With avid concentration, he picked up any stray twigs or pieces of dry grass he found on the cleared area, loaded them into the tiny wagon, and hauled them over to a dump he was managing at the edge. The toy mule was apparently based on Legume, because it often refused to behave, necessitating whispered lectures to the tiny resin figurine. He hunched over his task, his back narrow, small boy butt stuck into the air.

Tessa couldn't stand it. She swooped down and picked him up, holding him easily over her head. He was heavier than he had been when she came back from Perala after the death of her mother, but she was stronger, too. She would see how long she could maintain the advantage.

"Hey!" He squirmed. "Put me down. I'm working!"

She laughed. "What are you doing?"

"It's important. We're going to build a castle! So I have to *work*."

Tessa hugged him, kissed him, and set him back down to his task. Once free, he grabbed her legs. "It's going to be the biggest castle in Calrick Bend! I'm going to help Poppa build it." Kevin was slyly confiding. "He needs my help."

"He needs all our help," Tessa replied. She looked over at the massive, hunch-shouldered figure of her father as he used a shovel to open up the moss-covered oven. His movements had grown more deliberate since his wife Sora's death, as if he were moving against a great resistance. "Where are Dom and Benjamin?"

"Hunting!" Kevin sat down and ran the mule and wagon back and forth on the ground until he had dug a groove. He looked up at Tessa. "I couldn't go."

"You have work to do."

"I do!"

He once again bent over his wagon, the rest of the world forgotten. Tessa started toward her father, though she knew he regarded the baking of the castle as entirely his own task, without any need of outside assistance. She just wanted to see him up close, to make sure he was all right.

There was the crunch of heavy footsteps behind her, as her brothers Dom and Benjamin strode into the yard. Their pants were frosted below the knee. Dom carried a dead telena across his shoulders. Blood from its mouth had dripped down his chest. Benjamin, not yet full grown, had had to be content with carrying both of their sling darts and the rest of their equipment. They both had the weary and joyful glaze-eyed look of men who had hunted successfully. Dom knelt, slung the telena off his back with a relieved grunt, and lowered the creature to the ground.

"So, Tessa," he said. "Been out chopping herbs with Dalka again?"

His tone was idly teasing, but recently his teasing had taken on an arrogant edge. A month before, he had gone on a trading expedition to Perala with some of the other men, to negotiate purchase contracts for the next year's crops. As far as she knew, Dom had played no great role, but you couldn't tell that from his attitude.

"I finished all my work before I left." Tessa had meant to sound merely matter-of-fact, but the tone of resentment was distinct.

"I didn't say you hadn't." Dom fussed with the dead animal, as if its limbs needed to be arranged in some aesthetic way before being carried in to be cut up and hung to age in the shed.

"He didn't see it!" Benjamin was overjoyed. "It stood right above him and he didn't see it."

"I was too busy making sure you didn't fall into the ravine, like you did last summer."

Dom was annoyed with himself. Tessa could see that. Ben was growing up, getting faster, smarter. Dom had had a long time to have things to himself.

"Here, Tessa." Dom slapped the telena's flank. "Can you help me with this thing?" He smiled up at her.

It was a typical Dom gesture. She could carry something heavy and get blood on her clothes to prove to Dom that they were still friends. The dead animal had curved yellow tusks at its muzzle and slender, triple-toed legs. It was a native of Koola, unlike many of the other creatures of the cliffs. Its eyes were open and staring, its blue tongue was hanging out, and it didn't look peacefully dead, not at all.

The fermenthouse was above Legume's burrow. They tied the telena's legs together and wrestled it up onto a hook. It would hang there until internal enzymes had dissolved most of the carcass's connective tissues, at which time the animal would be cut up and properly stored.

"Dom," Tessa said. She had adroitly avoided all the blood while still doing her full share of the work and felt more pleased with herself than that simple achievement justified. "Can you think of any reason why Lewis would come down out of the high canyons?"

"This time of year?" Dom sniffed. The air in the shed was thick with calculated decay, ferment, and aging. Wheels of cheese were stacked in the corner, just below tightly wrapped haunches from earlier in the year. "No."

One of Dom's more frustrating virtues was his ability to state an opinion without needing to qualify it.

"I saw him, skating on a pond. Up the station road."

"Skating? Where did he get skates?"

That was a mystery that Tessa hadn't even thought of. Lewis was not a man with many possessions.

"Maybe he's down to see Poppa," Dom said hopefully. He had been as hurt by Lewis's neglect since their mother's death as anyone. "It's Christmas, after all. Maybe he just wants to see the castle."

"I don't think so, Dom. I think it's something else."

Dom shrugged. "Then we'll have to wait until he makes it clear. If he ever does."

"Let's go," Tessa said with a sigh. "I have some cooking to do."

"All right. Pull it over, pull it over. That's it . . . no, to the right a little. Good!" Perin, normally tentative, was in his true element: building. He had secretly planned the castle for months, arranging and rearranging its features. Easygoing the rest of the time, during construction he became tyrannical in traditional paternal style. "No, no! You want to snap those ramparts in half? Be gentle."

"Sorry," Benjamin puffed, as he slid a decorated, buttressed wall into its proper place. Sugar paste cemented it. He stood and contemplated his work, licking his fingers.

"Come on. We're not half-done yet."

The castle-cake smelled vividly of spice. Still warm from the ovens, it steamed slightly in the fading light of afternoon. Its upper towers were higher than Tessa was tall. When she paused in her work, she could hear the faint popping of carwa seeds within the walls. They were always baked into the cake. The heat of the oven and the acid of the stabilizers in the dough cracked the tough shells of the offworld seeds so that, next spring, they would sprout all over the fields, where the animals had carried them.

"That's enough, Kevin," Tessa said. "You'll dissolve it completely."

Kevin guiltily snatched the sugar-crystal window from his mouth and stuck it in the appropriate opening. Tessa picked one up herself and tentatively touched her tongue to it, feeling a guilty pleasure: cloying sweetness, just cut by the tartness of the binder. Despite herself, she found herself licking it. It was an unacknowledged privilege of the labor, the bits and pieces of the construction snuck into eager mouths. She remembered working with Dom and Benjamin, when Ben had been just a child Kevin's size, and the way they would frost every single castle window with their tongues. Their mother, Sora, had been there to supervise them then, indulging and disciplining with fine distinctions. She was there no longer. Tessa sometimes found herself doing some small thing wrong, so that she could turn and hear her mother's calm reprimand. No words, scolding or caring, ever came.

Tessa sighed. Kevin was munching on a piece of the crenellations that would top the castle wall. She decided to leave him alone. Things were hard enough.

"Poppa," Tessa said, coming up behind her father as he finished the elaborate sugar-and-spice decorations on one side of the castle. "What should I know about you and Old Man Lewis?"

Her father grunted. "He's not so old, Tessa. Not much older than me."

"I saw him this morning. He was ice skating on a pond. Malena Merewin was gathering rushes."

Perin paused for a long moment, considering. Tessa held her breath. There were times when he talked, and times when he didn't, and he became shy if pressed too hard. So she let him fuss with his decorations, making sure they were ready and arranged before he tackled the next wall.

"Lewis loves the cold. Not so much for what it is, but for what it isn't. Cold is not fire. Lewis has had too much fire in his life." He started spraying substrate over the hard-cake wall that surrounded the castle's triumphal entry gate. "When I met Lewis he was lying on the ground. A rock had fallen on him. A subterranean explosion, shock waves . . . there was rubble all over. We were in a tunnel, under Simurad, on the planet Trasach. Dark, underground. I was bleeding myself, a rock had hit the side of my head." He rubbed his hair. "I can still feel the lump. Here."

Tessa put her hand up to it. His hair was rough and thick. Tessa, to her dismay, had inherited it, rather than her mother's finer tresses. The lump swelled out along the left side of his head. She'd felt it every time she climbed on his shoulders when she was a little girl, and had heard the story.

"I pulled the rock up. Fire was all around. Someone helped me rescue Lewis: Gorr Merewin. And so we met, three farmers from the Eastern Shield, somewhere we should never have been."

Perin wore the cylinder of the sprayer strapped to his right wrist. He moved his lower arm delicately, manipulating the nozzle controls with his fingers. Precise ornaments appeared, garlands, swags, the skulls of unknown horned animals.

"We were a mixed company, from all over Koola. That in itself was educational. I never understood the arrangement, really. It was all done far over our heads. All any of us were really concerned with was getting back to our homes."

"All three of you made it."

"Parts of us did." He stepped to the right and created a line of grotesque faces, their cheeks bulging out comically as they tried to blow the viewer off the face of the planet.

"Poppa. Lewis and Gore—"

"We all helped each other, here in Cooperset Canyon as well as there at war. Lewis . . . well, you know Lewis." Perin smiled to himself. Lewis had tried to help raise the children, to Sora's dismay, advising them on how to slide down into ice caves and put frogs into their mouths so they knew how it felt to be a swamp. The children had taken or rejected his mad advice, but had somehow never had trouble seeing the concern that lay behind it.

"And you know Gorr as well. At least you did." Gorr Merewin was different. The flames of Simurad had scorched some part of his soul, leaving him bleakly silent, always angry. "He and I have not spoken for five years."

Perin had always gone out to Gorr, not the other way around, and Tessa, who had been frightened of that dark man, had not troubled to find out what they did or talked about together, or why they had finally stopped.

"Why not?"

"His anger grew too great. It sprouted there, in Simurad, but somehow never stopped growing. And poor Malena. She is the creation of that anger. So Lewis had come down out of his mountains to watch over her. Dear Lewis." With his left hand, he trailed glowing stars and spheres into the setting sugar. The cake castle, already elaborate, took on another layer of fantasy. "Poor, dear Lewis. He's doing his duty, as always. I shall have to do my part too."

Tessa, as always, had no doubt that it was the finest castle in all of upper Cooperset Canyon. Perin hunched over it, as he always did over a task, and hummed to himself, his daughter forgotten.

"Poppa—"

When he looked at her, his eyes were distant. "Something's happened. I don't know what. Only Lewis does. Whatever it is, we'll take care of Malena." It was a simple statement of fact, his duty to Gorr.

"Yes, Poppa." She paused. "Will you be in soon?"

"Just a moment. There's just a few more things I have to do. Then it will be ready."

"I don't trust him," Dalka said, sitting down by the stove. "He doesn't fit."

Tessa wasn't interested in discussing Dalka's suspicions of Old Man lewis. Dalka had made them clear enough in the past.

"Gorr Merewin served with Poppa and Lewis in the war. About five years ago he got married to Fila. . . ." About the time Gorr and Perin had ceased communication.

"Ah, Gorr and Fila! They went and misbehaved, and that girl Malena is the unfortunate result." Dalka clucked her tongue.

After slicing the roast in a crisscross pattern with a sharp knife, Tessa misted the skin so that it would crisp up, and closed the oven. Dalka made Perin uncomfortable, but he still felt obliged to invite her to Christmas dinner, in homage to his dead wife, whose friend she had been.

"Yes, a sad story—you know, Tessa, if you had put dried quince under the skin, it would have made the meat more tender, and given it a tang."

"Yes, Dalka." Tessa pulled the top of the soup pot and checked the spices. The stew was mellowing down nicely, each sturdy winter vegetable giving its insistent piquancy to the whole.

"You might add some more winter basil," Dalka said, sniffing the air. "The turnips tend to absorb its flavor, so there's not enough in the stock when you're done. You've probably been tasting it too much to tell that."

Tessa controlled a surge of irritation and tore some leaves off the plants that grew over the sink. "Gorr and Fila . . ."

"They married for love," Dalka said. "He kidnapped her—so her family called it—from her father's house. And who knows? She might not have been entirely willing, at that. She was already pregnant with Malena at the time. She'd refused to take my advice—and paid the price for that." Dalka managed the fertility of the women of Calrick Bend, and took the responsibility seriously. Tessa had already had several lectures from her. Fila's refusal to take sensible advice obviously put her beyond the pale. "Some time later Gorr and Fila's brother Swern Toroma fought. Swern lost the use of his hand. I worked on it, but something blocked nerve regrowth, I got a lot of axonal degeneration. He went to a surgeon, got it stiffened up so he can use it to support things."

Swern Toroma wore a glove on the stiffly splayed fingers of his hand, covered with tool hooks and attachments. He acted as if he was proud of the thing, but then, what else could he do?

"And Gorr got that scar across his face," Tessa said. Rumor was, Fila had put it there defending her brother. Gorr concealed it with high collars and hoods, but even Tessa had caught a glimpse of it across his jaw, swelling purple. "It's not a normal scar. . . ."

Dalka's face went cold. "Oh, isn't it?"

"Dalka!" Tessa felt a chill at her anger. Her mother, she felt with sudden loss, was gone. Without Dalka, who would she have to talk to? Even if she was at times unpredictable. "It's important to me. Something's wrong, with the Merewins, with Malena . . . I have to know."

"Oh, do you?" Dalka was not mollified. She undid the top of a ceramic container and dipped herself a mug of spicy kitchen beer, a prerogative of cooks and their helpers, moving slowly, building tension. "Why?"

"The Merewins work the land under Pakor Spur," Tessa said. She hadn't been ready to speak her thoughts, and she fumbled at the words. "It was Carlyn land, before. It comes through Fila's family, the Toromas. Her father settled it on Fila before she ran off with Gorr. Or was kidnapped, whatever."

In the past six months, she had intensely studied the patterns of land use throughout upper Cooperset and adjoining drainages. The interrelationships were complex, and not entirely comprehensible, but she felt that she was starting to get some sort of grip on it. No one could work entirely independently, unconcerned with the behavior of his neighbors.

At the root of the Cooperset farming ecology was the network of pipe plants through which flowed, from field to field, what had once been the Cooperset River. All worked together for the common good, not because of some high-minded realization of emotional interdependence but because the system would fall apart if they didn't. Everyone, from the highest Dalhousie to the lowest Trepak in the huts down by Brant Spur, knew this and donated their labor. Refusal to participate was the one unforgivable sin.

"If something has happened to Gorr and Fila . . ."

"Why do you think something has?" Dalka was sharp. "They keep to themselves. And their daughter always wanders around the canyon. We've all seen her, we all know to watch out for her." Dalka shook her head. "Too much love between a man and a woman can squeeze their child out. It's a crime, an indecency."

"Lewis . . . don't make that face, Dalka, I grew up with him, he took care of me, of all of us, in his own way. And that's why he's down here, standing out in the open where you can see him from the road: he's down to watch after Malena, as he would be to look after us if something happened to Poppa. And if something has happened to the Merewins, well, then Malena becomes our responsibility, that of the Wolholmes."

"Along with her land?" Dalka seemed almost amused. "What about Swern Toroma?"

"He can't manage that land. That's clear to everyone. And so he can't take care of Malena." Tessa didn't need to temporize or conceal with Dalka. "Managing that land would help the Wolholmes survive. You know how hard my mother worked."

"I do, dear. And I think she would be proud to see you now."

"Oh, Dalka." Tessa blinked and felt the tears wet her eyelashes. "It's so hard, and I'm so afraid. What will happen to us? What will we do?"

"Hush, dear. Here, help with this, we should be getting it ready." Tessa leaned near Dalka's comforting bulk, and together they filled a platter with cooked vegetables, arranging their different colors in an intricate pattern. "What do you know about Gorr's scar?"

Tessa held her breath until she thought she could speak without her voice quavering. "Not much. But I overheard one of the Merewins' neighbors, Lessa Tergoran, describe Gorr's scar. She laughed at herself, said she was getting old, but she really thought it moved around, that it was never in the same place she had seen it before."

"Lessa Tergoran's an old gossip," Dalka said. "Don't encourage her, whatever you do. Your life will never be your own again. No one receives gossip without paying a price for it."

"Dalka. Fila cut Gorr, didn't she? To defend her brother, whatever. And she tipped the blade with—"

"Shh!" Dalka's eyes darted to the door. The men would soon be in to eat. "Be careful, Tessa."

"Tell me!"

"She should never have done it. It's an old piece of knowledge, almost forgotten, intended for marking animals, for making a brand without wrestling with the beast." A few still herded, Tessa knew, up on the step plateaus leading to the Boss, but no longer in the canyons. It was a precarious, severe existence. "It's a self-sustaining fungus infection of the basal layer of the dermis."

"She coated the knife with it!" She was half horrified, half delighted.

"Be quiet, please!"

"But why, Dalka? What did she say she wanted it for when she asked for it?"

Dalka looked disgusted. "Small doses of it tone up the skin, get rid of unwanted hair. Fila said she needed it, for her husband's sake. To be more beautiful for him."

"For her husband's sake. Did she plan it, do you suppose? Or did she just have it around and decide to use it on the spur of the moment?"

"I have no idea, Theresa," Dalka said. "I just know that she did, finally, use it. It's there, under his skin. It should stay in the epidermis, above the blood and lymphatic vessels, but her blade infected the vascularized dermis. The infection shifts sometimes, colonizing new areas. I'm surprised it hasn't spread and killed him. It will do that in human beings. It wasn't designed for them. I guess he's been lucky. He'll always have it. Something to remember her by."

The Merewin house was isolated, hanging in a shattered side crack of Cooperset Canyon. Tessa imagined them living there, the two of them, with their tiny daughter. She realized that, much as she thought she knew, she didn't really understand what went on with people. That savage coupling, a woman mutilating her husband's face but staying with him, and he agreeing to it. She wondered if she ever would understand it.

Tessa pulled the roast out of the oven. The golden skin had crisped and pulled away from the rose-colored flesh, her slashes forming the vivid network pattern of a proper Christmas feast. She undid the twine holding the legs to the body and pulled them out to their full length. It looked ready to jump.

"Come with me, tomorrow, for the Christmas visits. I'm going out with Alta Dalhousie."

Dalka made a face. "Alta? She makes me tired. I don't even know how she persuaded me to help make her the center of attention Christmas morning. You know the way she comes to the door with a question and ends up in the kitchen eating your bread? Eventually you find yourself baking it at her house, filling Dalhousia with the smells that belong in your own kitchen. You be careful with her."

"I need you, Dalka. We're going to be visiting the Merewins."

"Oho, it's like that, is it?" Dalka chortled. "Check them out while being philanthropic. But why take Alta along? She has her own interests, you know."

"I know. So I might as well have her with me from the beginning. Without her help, and the help of the Dalhousies, I don't know if I could win a fight with Swern Toroma."

"What did you tell her?"

Tessa shrugged. "That I wanted to go up Pakor Spur, to make it easier for me to collect the baskets, since we're so near."

"Such a polite girl, that Tessa Wolholme is." Dalka was delighted. "Willing to help Alta Dalhousie look her best. Ah,

dear, I will go. You underestimate her, but you're doing well.
I'll go."

Tessa arranged the massive top frog on the platter, surrounding it with greenery. She thought back to the previous
spring, when this frog and all its brethren were still tiny peep-
ing creatures, starting their season-long climb up the tulap
trees to the vines on top. This one had probably hopped
across her foot with beady-eyed intentness shortly after her
mother's death.

"Let's go out and light the candles," Tessa said. "Then we
can come back inside and eat."

The castle glowed in the night, a candle in each of its many
windows. Everyone else had gone to bed, but Tessa couldn't
sleep. Or rather, she hadn't even tried, but sat up instead going over a part of her mother's fossil collection.

Families had strolled through Calrick Bend to look at the
castles in the night, as was traditional. The castles were osten-
sibly built as a stopping place, a caravanserai, for the Traveling Kings, as they searched the endless stars for their
Messiah, born but not yet found. Each family had one, some
small and simple, some ridiculously elaborate, so that the
Kings could freely choose. Perin's was a fine demonstration
of his architectural skill, and was one of the most popular every year. A steady procession had come through the yard to
examine the high ramparts, the soaring towers, the elaborately
decorated screening walls. Children ran up and peered
through the sugar windows at the interior passages, then ran
back to their parents, who offered Perin their congratulations.

Tessa had paid more than ordinary attention to the parents
and children gathering in the yard, but had seen no sign of
Malena and the Merewins. She might have missed them, she
thought to herself. The yard was crowded and she'd been
busy. She might well have missed them.

Now Tessa stared into the darkness, her breath steaming,
indecisively balanced at the door. She'd have to close it soon,
they were losing too much heat, but she somehow didn't feel
ready to find her coat and put it on.

Her mother Sora had always kept vigil out there by the castle. It was an old habit of hers, a tribute to her husband. Heavy shawl across her shoulders, she would walk slowly around the castle, no matter how cold it was, and admire it, for even as it was finished, it began to vanish. Animals came from beneath the fields to devour the highly edible thing: the long, elaborately spike-scaled-legged snakes that dug through the soil and lived in the tulap tree roots, the field mice, the lumbering, hard-shelled land crabs, all of them in some way necessary to the functioning of the farm ecology. The castles provided them with food during the coldest and harshest months of winter, food without which they could not have survived in adequate numbers to do their work during the growing season. The castle would slowly slump down into the ground until, by the warm days of spring, when it was completely gone, the shoots of the carwa plants came up through the earth in all the fields, marking the start of planting.

Tessa gasped. A dark figure was walking slowly around the castle. But that was ridiculous. It was obviously not her mother. Taller and about twice as wide, to start with. It was her brother, Dom. And he wasn't looking at the castle, but out into the surrounding darkness, as if waiting for someone's approach.

He would be annoyed to find that she had been watching without letting him know he was being observed.

"Dom!" she said.

He gestured: come out. She grabbed her coat, feeling the cold lick at her chest and neck as she ran out into the yard still tugging it on.

"When I was little," Dom said, "Kevin's age, I would sit up and watch for the Traveling Kings. Not just because they would leave me presents, though I liked that, but because I was convinced they would come by Poppa's castle, pause . . . and go in to take a rest, since they were so tired from their years of searching. They'd be gone by morning of course, wouldn't stay for breakfast, but I wanted to see them." He looked at her. "And I was always annoyed with Momma for walking around out here. They'd see her, I knew, and go somewhere else for the night."

Tessa looked up past him. High up on the left was Kevin's window, lit by the dim glow of his night light. Was that his little head, peering down at them, worried that their unnecessary presence would frighten the Kings off, cause them to go elsewhere? There wasn't enough light to tell.

"If you'd told her, she would have stayed inside," Tessa said. "She wouldn't have wanted to scare them away."

Dom hunched gloomily in his coat. "That's true. I was always so mad at her for not realizing."

"I always wondered what you were looking at. You wouldn't tell me, and even got mad that I was asking."

"Well," Dom said. "It wasn't any of your business, little sister."

They took a turn around the castle together, just as Sora would have. Its battlements gleamed in the darkness. Dark shapes ran at the edges of their vision. To Dom and Tessa, the sight was comforting, for the appearance of these usually subterranean creatures was the first sign of the approach of the distant spring.

"I didn't want to talk about it at the table," Dom said, "but there's something I want to tell you."

Tessa knew better than to prod. Dom was giving her information to help her make a decision, and he didn't like it, feeling it should be the other way around.

"In Perala . . . you remember it, from when you were at school."

"Yes, I do." Tessa had studied at Hammerswick Academy in Perala for a year before Sora's death had brought her back to Calrick Bend, perhaps forever. She usually thought about it only late at night.

"Well, we Cooperset men were all there, and the men from the lowlands. We got good prices . . . some of the valleys west of here have had bad storms and crop damage . . . Gorr Merewin was there. So was Swern Toroma."

"How is Swern's hand?"

Dom grimaced. "Not any better after the trip. Swern and Gorr came to a fight. They always do, other people told me. It's like a regular part of the trip, that one picks a quarrel. But this one . . . Swern mentioned Lewis. That's what started it."

"They fought because of Lewis? What did Swern say?"

Dom shrugged uncomfortably. "I wasn't really paying much attention. Too much else going on . . ." He paused for a long moment. "To tell you the truth, I was drunk."

Tessa laughed, delighted by his embarrassment. "It's part of your job, Dom. Negotiations always give you a hangover. Remember when Poppa would come back, his face all green, and Momma would put him to bed for a day?"

"Yes." The memory didn't seem to comfort him.

"But it's important, what Swern said."

"I told you, I wasn't paying much attention. But it was something about Lewis and Fila. And some infection. Gorr's sick, Fila treats him, Lewis helps . . . hell, I didn't understand it, but Gorr sure did. Took a swipe at him, right at dinner. Food flying all over. Took the rest of us to hold them both down, and the lowlanders were right there, watching the canyon people beat each other up. Part of the fun for them."

"Ah," Tessa said. "That's interesting, though I don't know what it means."

Dom looked at her, his gaze sharp. "You have some plan, right? I can see it. You're smart, Tessa. We all know that. But smart isn't everything. In Calrick Bend, I'm not even sure it's much important. You went off to school, so maybe you've forgotten that."

He was trying to be helpful, but his tone grated on her nerves. The family needed protecting, and he resented her trying to do it. She could see that.

"Dom—"

He raised a hand. "You're going to be mad at me. I can tell from your eyebrows. I'm sorry. I just wanted you to know. . . ." He took her arm as they walked. "I just wanted you to know that you can count on us. All of us. If you need to. Me, Benjamin . . . Kevin too. Him most of all. He'd do anything for you. I was just trying to say that. But I don't talk good. I never have, have I?"

"Oh, I don't know. You're talking pretty good now."

Dom was embarrassed. "Okay. Just promise me one thing.

Whenever you make a decision, try to imagine that you're only half as smart as you really are."

She smiled. "I'll give it a try."

Tessa slept little that night, and was up with the sun in the morning. Kevin was already circling the wrapped presents. His takings would be small enough this year, but he would make the most of it.

"Where are you going?" he said.

She gathered up her things and put on her coat. "I'll be back soon."

"But where are you *going*?"

"To Alta Dalhousie's. We're going to visit the poor families with food."

He sat on the floor and pouted. "You won't be here to open your presents. Wait until you see what I got you." He dug through the pile.

"I'll be back soon, Kevin. It's my job, now that Momma's gone. I have to go."

He pulled out something that looked like a forked tree limb wrapped in layers and layers of silver foil. Taking it from him, Tessa realized that that was exactly what it was.

"Open it!"

"Kèvin, let's wait until—"

"Open it!"

She knew an irresistible command when she heard one. She pulled at the frenziedly taped foil, tight and thick as if the package were to be buried as a message to future generations, and finally managed to get it open.

The crotched limb had delicate, peeling-back bark, somewhat compressed by Kevin's packaging, and was bright with red, blue, and orange patches of lichen. Tessa wondered if any of them were of medicinal or enzymatic value. She'd have to ask Dalka.

"It's beautiful, Kevin," she said. Indeed it was. Of all the fallen branches in Cooperset Canyon, this was no doubt the best. He had probably taken a great deal of time over it. She thought it would look perfectly fine on a shelf in the room containing Sora's fossils.

"It's full of borer beetles!" he said gleefully. "I'm sure they'll come out when it gets warm. I like the way they wiggle their heads.

She looked more closely at it. The bark was pierced by countless tiny holes. If she set it on a shelf in the warm house, they would awaken early and come swarming out, to devour the furniture.

"Oh, Kevin . . ."

Fortunately, at that moment Benjamin appeared, blinking in his pajamas, hair a mess, looking desperately young.

"Morning, Tessa," he said, "Where is everybody?"

"I'm in here making breakfast," Dom called from the kitchen. "Poppa's up, Kevin's making trouble, and Tessa's going to be late for her appointment if she doesn't hurry."

"I'm not making trouble!"

Benjamin sat in a chair and Kevin climbed into his lap. Benjamin patted his brother's head. "Trouble's what you're best at."

Tessa winked and ran out the door. The landscape was frosted and silent. The mountains loomed overhead, the white dusting on their shoulders giving them extra dignity. Castles stood by their houses, proud battlements, towers, flags, and arches gaily proclaiming the holiday. Tessa followed a path she had known since childhood, a twisting way around storage barns, over fences, under hedges. Burrs stuck to her coat, and a few dried leaves got into her hair. She dirtied her stockings jumping over a narrow ravine. In their younger days Dom had always beaten her at it despite her most strenuous efforts. Now it was easy. She enjoyed it so much she jumped back and did it again.

The Dalhousie house was high and proud. Most of it had been designed by her father, Perin, in his most exuberant style, a style he could not possibly afford for his own dwelling.

Tessa passed through the front hall, which stretched up three stories to the balcony of the upper bedrooms, and into the back dining room, crowded with women readying themselves for their charitable exercises. They made room for her at a table, poured her tea, asked about her family, praised Perin's castle.

"Margen's hiding upstairs," Zabeth Trasker told her, "peeking over the balcony. I think he's waiting for *you*."

Several of the other women tittered. Tessa was of marriageable age, and had, as yet, not made any indication of her preferences. Margen Dalhousie was a possible mate for her, as she had known since they were both children.

"More likely he's waiting for Mark," Tessa said. This caused more amusement. Zabeth's son, one of the few other eligible males in Calrick Bend, was notorious for his dreamy lateness.

Tessa kept a good face on it, but it took effort. The Wolholmes were in a difficult situation, and, in a sense, it was her *duty* to marry, and soon, so as to assist their survival. These friendly, cheerful women sitting around her, ready to do their Christmas duty to the poor of the canyon, would slowly move themselves around her until it was all inevitable. The earlier she moved on her own, the more choice she would retain.

"Tessa has other things to worry about than my son, or even Zabeth's." Alta Dalhousie appeared, a signal for chairs to be pulled back and coats put on.

Alta smiled and took Tessa's arm. Despite her formidable reputation, Alta Dalhousie herself did not look particularly imposing. She was shorter than Tessa, and slight, with a mass of curling gray hair and bright blue eyes.

"Dalka's coming with us?" Alta was serene, willing to put up with irregular requests as long as they didn't interfere with any of her plans.

"Yes." Striving to imitate Dom, Tessa bit down on any following phrase like "I hope that's all right," or "she really wanted to." It left her feeling anxious, as if there was a hole in the conversation. How did Dom do it so easily? Dalka joined them at the front door.

For a moment, the women stood and laughed in the cold air of the courtyard, adjusting their hoods, tugging on their embroidered gloves, exuberantly swooping their long sleeves. This was a dignified assemblage, gathered for the purposes of charity to the weak and poor, but it was a glorious day nonetheless, the sun bright, the world sensible. Their children were gathered in their front rooms eyeing the presents left by the Traveling Kings in gratitude for assistance on their journey, their husbands were sleepily contemplating a day free of labor, and they themselves were happy to be doing good in such high style.

Tessa, Alta, and Dalka crossed a teetery plank over an ice-filled ravine, carrying heavy packs. Their mission was to the isolated houses that hid themselves in the cliff-base jambles and the high cracks at Pakor and Brant Spurs, far above the easy cart roads. Alta went first, to scatter sand, which she kept in a blue-enamel bucket on the livethorn fence. She used a small silver shovel with a delicate tracing of leaves up its handle and fork tines at its edge, so that the sand spread evenly. Then they climbed up the trail, over the root bulges of the hairy-barked oaks that grew in a line along the ridge, now almost thick enough to be cut down and turned into furniture, an old Dalhousie skill. It was steep and icy enough that Tessa considered stopping and pulling her crampons out of her pack. Instead, she reached out and took Dalka's gloved hand in hers. Together, the three women formed a snake long enough that at least two of them were always standing on firm ground. They writhed their way up the icy slope.

"We don't go up there," Swern Toroma said, snipping off a length of binding cord with an attachment on his hand. He had not stopped working the entire time he spoke, as if to show by the frenzy of his activity how little he really needed their help.

"But have you seen them?" Tessa asked.

He shook his head. He was slender and pale, and looked much like his sister Fila. "I don't see them. No reason to."

Tessa, Alta, and Dalka stood close together, fastidious in the midst of the messy kitchen. Swern's wife, a woman from up canyon, was not around, but it was clear that, whatever her duties were, they didn't extend to cleaning.

"You talk to your sister." Tessa was insistent. Somehow, she thought, Fila had told her brother about the nature of Gorr's wound, perhaps in a moment of unwise confidence.

Swern had used that information against Gorr at the last trading expedition.

Swern glanced at her suspiciously, then returned to his task.
"And why shouldn't I? With a husband like that ... but I
haven't talked to her in the last few days. And you know
what? I hope that bastard ran off, killed himself, whatever.
Then maybe she could bring the land back to the family." He
gestured with his rigidly splayed fingers at their basket.
"They don't deserve your help up there."

"That is not for you to decide," Alta said. "Will you be all
right?"

"I'll be all right when I get my land back."

A baby started crying in a back room. Attempts to shush it
just made the crying louder.

"Good day, then," Alta said crisply. "Thank you for your
hospitality." The three women left, and resumed their climb
up the slope.

"It's a sad situation," Alta said, as they climbed through the
piled rocks of the jambles. "The Toromas were once a proud
family."

"Richer than now, maybe," Dalka said. "But never rich. It's
hard, high near the wall like this."

"Harder when the better part of your land leaves." Alta was
making some sort of point, Tessa wasn't yet sure what. "It
went with Fila, on her marriage to Gorr. Fine, it was settled
on her, she was the most responsible. Still—"

"Do you think it should have been handled some other
way?" Tessa asked.

"The inheritance?" Alta thought about it. "It is natural that
the land should pass through the daughter, of course, but
still ... Swern and his family barely survive. Meanwhile,
Gorr and Fila make little of their land, so that they're poor
also. When it finally passes to Malena, its value will be much
lower than it would have been. Swern, with help, could work
it, but there's too much anger. So he spends his energies in
manipulating the negotiations—keep this quiet, I'm not supposed to know—so that others don't get full value for their
produce."

Tessa was pleased by the confidence, though she doubted

she was the only one Alta had told, and suspected there was a reason she was being told.

The three women walked up to the silent, shuttered Merewin house, and knocked on the door. The sound echoed hollowly in the narrow cleft where the house hung, but there was no answer. They knocked again.

Frost had grown over the cracks of the door and the sides of the shutters. There was no mark of footsteps in the frost on the front stair. And no one had built a castle.

Alta was grim. "I was afraid of this." She looked up at the sheer walls of the cleft.

"They went for a walk!" a small voice called.

"Is that you, Malena?" Tessa said. "Where are you?"

"They went for a walk. You can leave that."

The women descended the slope from the house to the beginning of the terraced gardens. Two large trees flanked the entrance to the cleft, twining around the rock outcroppings. Tessa peered up into them and finally spotted the tiny Malena, who sat placidly on a high branch.

"Hi, Malena," Tessa said.

"Hi." Malena was as solemn as ever. Her legs dangled down.

"How long ago did your parents leave?" Alta asked.

"Not long. But they said don't wait. Just leave it, they said."

The wind blew through the top of the cleft with a high, lonely whistle. It was cold, but Malena seemed quite comfortable on her perch. Tessa wasn't even sure how she had climbed up there.

"Malena," Alta said. "Could you please come down?"

"No!" Startled by the request, Malena scrambled up another branch, small enough that it sagged even under her tiny weight. "I have to wait for Momma and Poppa."

Dalka knelt and put the tray on the front stair. "Do you promise to eat this if I leave it?"

"We'll eat it!" Malena's voice was ragged, a little frenzied. "They'll be back soon. Then we'll eat it."

The reeds she had gathered from the pond the previous

morning were stacked neatly against the side of the house. The land around them was silent.

"All right, Malena," Alta said. "Say hello to your parents when they return."

"Okay."

The women climbed back down the path until Malena was invisible behind them.

"Something's happened," Alta said. "I don't know what. Fila's run off, Gorr's done something. They may not be coming back."

"Gorr's done for Fila," Dalka said with grim relish. "Finally."

"Maybe." Alta thought. "Tessa, do you think Perin knows anything?"

"They haven't spoken in years."

"Yes, I know. I had hoped that, perhaps, recently . . . well, that leaves Old Man Lewis. He must know something." Alta stared up at the cliffs. "Finding him is something else again, of course. Do you know where he is, Tessa?" Her voice grew sharper.

"I saw him, yesterday." Tessa felt as if she was betraying a confidence, though Lewis had been out on the pond for all the world to see.

"But not since."

"No," Tessa said. "I can try to find him. Meanwhile, Malena's terrified. What shall we do?"

"I'd knock her out of that tree with a broom," Dalka said. "She's not coming down otherwise."

"Dalka!" Tessa said, startled. "You don't mean that."

"No, I don't." Dalka was reluctant. "She'll get hungry and come down on her own. Then we can get her."

"Excellent," Alta said vigorously. "Then we'll bundle her up—the poor thing must be freezing—and take her over to Dalhousia. We have a spare room, Tramt is over in Perala this term and I'm sure he won't mind." She eyed Tessa. Alta was testing her, Tessa realized, waiting for her reaction to this seizure of Malena.

Dalka stuck out her heavy lower lip. "No need for you to take care of her."

"Who else will? The Toromas?"

There was little answer to that, though they were probably her closest relatives.

Dalka glanced at Tessa and shrugged. "Well, if you want to take the trouble . . ."

Dalka was putting up the effort for her sake, Tessa realized. For the Wolholmes. If Malena ended up at Dalhousia, eventually the management of her land would also, at least until she reached her majority. Dalka was not interested in land herself, but she knew that Tessa needed. At the moment, Tessa didn't care. She remembered the tiny girl clinging to the upper branches of a tree in winter, her parents most likely lying dead somewhere unknown, with no one to help her, and no comfort but a cooling tray of food brought by distantly dutiful neighbor ladies.

"She can climb down and go into the house if she wishes," Alta said. "I checked, and the key was hanging under the stairs. If we just leave her alone—"

"I'm not leaving her up there alone. She's a little girl!"

"Good idea," Dalka said. "We're through, aren't we, Alta? Tessa can stay up there with her."

"As you say." Alta was brisk. "We'll be back soon, Tessa. Keep the poor thing company, keep her out of trouble."

When they were out of sight, Tessa headed back up to the Merewin house. Despite herself, she sympathized with Dalka's urge to swat Malena out of her tree with a broom. There was something exasperating about the little girl's stubborn refusal to be helped. As she crested the hill, she searched the branches for Malena's tiny dark shape. The branches swung free in the breeze. The food had brought her down, then.

Tessa crouched and moved more quietly, as if stalking some wild animal. The air moved gently over her. The high cliffs rose above, their cracks outlined by snow and frost, a few desperate plants clinging to them. As she went, she examined the farm with a practiced eye. There was some evidence of decay—cracked pipe plants ready for infection, inadequately insulted roots—but nothing too dangerous yet. A little extra work in the spring could take care of it.

She squinted into the shadows of the cleft. The tray was gone from the front stairs. Tessa walked slowly to the house, looking carefully around her. The girl was tiny, and clever. If she wanted to hide, here on her own ground, it would be difficult for Tessa to find her. But Tessa herself had been a champion at hide-and-seek as a girl.

Tessa reached under the stairs, found the key, and opened the door. "Malena?" she called. The girl was gone.

Tessa searched slowly through the house, looking carefully. There was a family picture on the wall of the living room: slender Fila looking attentively at Gorr, his hand on her shoulder as he stared at the camera, and tiny Malena, ignored, sitting at their feet and looking off at something out of view. The girl's space in the house was tiny, just a bed that folded into a corner so as to be out of the way during the day.

A shelf above held a few toys, neatly laid out in a row. Tessa picked up a bulge-eyed duck with wheels. Its head bobbled back and forth as she held it. Spots of paint had flaked off. She set it back. There were no empty gaps on the shelf. Even Malena's favorite loose-headed doll sat floppily in its place.

The house was in frantic disarray. Drawers were pulled out in the bedroom, clothing strewn on the floor. Personal objects had been yanked out of cabinets. It didn't look like a simple matter of slovenly housekeeping. Everything was clean. The floor under the piles of sweaters and pants was buffed to a dull shine, not a spot on it. Sora herself could not have found fault. Someone had been searching for something in a frantic hurry. Had it been found? Tessa continued, hoping to find the place where the search had ended.

Cutlery and spices were tossed about the kitchen. A dented teakettle lay in the corner. And in the sink, some sort of dark liquid. Scattered along the sink's edge were the sort of seed-pod ampoules that Dalka used for dispensing medications. All were crushed, and the liquid oozed out of them. Tessa ran a finger down the thick whitewood sink and sniffed: a bitter smell that she could not identify. Half the kitchen was a mess. In the other half the cook pots and wood bowls stood in perfect arrangement, ready to be of service.

Tessa gathered several of the empty seedpods, and as much of the liquid as she could in one of Fila's food containers, and put it in her pack. Perhaps Dalka would be able to recognize what it was.

The back door of the kitchen opened into the pantry and the back storage area. Tessa poked around back there, though she felt that she had already found what was significant, even if she did not understand it. All the food was in order in the pantry, all the equipment in the storage area, ready for spring.

Sunlight glinted in through the window. It was late in the morning, the only time direct light made it into the cleft. She was about to turn away, to head home, when a gleam of metal caught her eye. She stepped forward. Hanging from a nail by the door, returned by the one who had borrowed them, was a pair of ice skates.

Alta Dalhousie stood in her courtyard and poured steaming tea from a towering urn. Search parties found their leaders, warmed themselves up, and headed out through the gates. Most of Calrick Bend was here, and despite the seriousness of the cause, they carried with them some of the conviviality of Christmas, strengthened by their common energy.

"Ah, Tessa." Alta poured for her as well. "You must be cold."

"Any sign?" Tessa drank slowly, trying not to burn her tongue. Warmth pulsed outward from her throat.

"None. But how far could a little girl go in such a short time? After all, you only had your eyes off her for a few minutes."

Tessa felt herself flush, and was glad that Alta had turned away as she said this, to add more hot water to the urn. Tessa—childishly—wanted to point out that Alta and Dalka had been chattering away too, while Malena escaped. That might annoy Alta, but it wouldn't alter anything. And Tessa needed Alta in as friendly a mood as possible.

"She did seem to vanish most thoroughly. Here, could you help me with this?" At her direction, Tessa carried wrapped bread, still warm from the oven, out to tables in the courtyard. "Most unusual. She's only five, and even the most energetic five-year-old has no stamina for distance. I remember when Margen tried to run away, we were in a panic, then found him on a vine trellis in the next field, eating his sandwiches as if he hadn't had food in days . . . but that was nothing compared to this."

Tessa was not going to tell Alta that Lewis had taken the girl. Lewis was tolerated in the canyon, but not truly trusted. Those search parties could easily turn to a grimmer purpose.

"Will you be going home now?" Alta was easy. "You must be tired."

"No, I . . ." Tessa thought about what to say. "Gorr and my father were friends. They were in the war together."

"They stopped speaking around the time Malena was born, didn't they?" Alta headed off Tessa's argument before she had even gotten to it. "Perin hated Gorr's anger. And good for Perin."

"But Malena—"

"Perin also disapproved of the way Gorr cut the Toromas off from their land," Alta continued serenely. "Gorr had the right, having married Fila, but still . . . it wasn't a good idea, do you think? Hatred is a poor basis for cooperation."

"So you think Swern and his wife could farm that land on their own?" Tessa thought she was starting to get an inkling of where Alta's argument was heading.

Alta laughed. "Oh, no, dear. Not at all. Any more than they could raise Malena. But still, they should be able to work more of the land than they do. . . ."

"I'm sure that whoever adopts Malena will allow that." Tessa was making a political agreement on behalf of her family. She'd have to explain it to them later. "It only makes sense. As long as the result does not alienate the land from the proper owner."

Alta eyed her. "Have some sweet bread. You look hungry."

"No thank you. I should—"

"Really, Tessa. I made it myself. I think it came out rather well."

Alta Dalhousie, Tessa estimated, had been making sweet bread for at least twice as long as Tessa had been alive. She *better* have figured out how to make it come out well. She took a slice, smearing sugar frosting on her hands. If the tension hadn't been making her feel sick to her stomach, Tessa conceded to herself, it *would* have been good. Her mother, Sora, had had a tendency to fear underbaking it, and as a result it had always been dry. At least she hadn't slathered it with so much sugar.

"Tell me," Alta said. "Do *you* know where Malena is?"

"No," Tessa said. "But I think I can find her." The last words came in a rush.

"When all these search parties can't?" Voices sounded on the path outside: searchers coming in for a break, some tea, some of Alta Dalhousie's famous sweet bread. They stacked packs at the gate. Someone made a joke, and a couple of them chuckled.

"Yes."

Alta smiled. "Well, if you find her, you may as well keep her, right? Since Perin and Gorr agreed. And the Toromas can no doubt be persuaded."

Tessa stared at her in wonder. "I—"

Alta waved a hand dismissively. "We can discuss it later. We both have things to do." She turned to the search party, and began to pour them tea.

It was late, and the mountains cast their long shadows across the farms of Cooperset Canyon. The air grew colder, and Tessa longed to move. Her blood felt as if it had pooled and crystallized. She shifted on her rock outcrop, and once again examined the Pong's Defile trail, just visible through the jambles below.

It was time to get home before the trail disappeared beneath her feet. Lit house windows already glowed in Calrick Bend, far below her. A moving line of lights descended the opposite canyon wall on a switchbacked trail. Searchers, returning empty-handed from their pursuit of a vanished little girl. Tessa had to find her and Lewis before the townspeople turned to searching for *him*.

Perhaps he wasn't going to come tonight ... but still she sat, watching her breath puff into the steadily darkening air. Pong's Defile, up to Born Canyon, was Lewis's favorite trail.

The Wolholme children had always known it. Lewis had
taken Tessa some way up it when she was a child, a well-
remembered first trip away from the settled logic of the canyon floor. And a trail at the edge of Cooperset Canyon,
clinging high above any habitation, led straight to the cleft
where the Merewin house stood.

Nothing of Malena's had been taken from the house, not
her clothing, not her favorite doll, not any of the food she
liked to eat. She was no doubt suffering in silence, wherever
Lewis had taken her, but he would know what she needed. No
one was at the Merewin house but the neighbor Lessa
Tergoran, and she would most likely be asleep by now.

Tessa pulled on the chain of logic, and it held. She only
hoped it was actually attached to something.

Had Alta Dalhousie actually offered to allow Malena to be
adopted by the Wolholmes if the Toromas were given access
to the land? It felt that way to Tessa, though she sliding implications of Alta's offer had left Tessa dizzy. But it all made
a kind of sense. If the Dalhousies themselves tried to adopt
Malena, the Toromas would fight, but the rights of Perin
Wolholme in the matter were well known. The solution did
not actually benefit the Dalhousies, but it didn't harm them
either, and settled several problems in the bargain. And it left
Tessa in Alta's debt. Alta Dalhousie had always taken the
long view.

That is, if Tessa managed to find Malena, and Malena herself agreed to the solution. Were things really so complicated
in Calrick Bend? Tessa had never realized.

She heard a purposeful chuffing of breath on the trail below
her. She swung out precariously on her rock, supported by her
fingertips, and looked down the trail. The dark figure, head
down, shoulders hunched, could only have been Lewis. She
looked into the darkness below her feet. She'd scooped it out
before, decided that a jump would be easy, but now the earth
seemed to have been swallowed up, leaving her with nothing
to land on.

She drew a breath. Lewis paused and raised his head. Tessa
jumped. For an instant it seemed that she had indeed been
right, that the ground had vanished; then it slapped her feet.

She almost lost her balance, then regained it, and darted forward.

Lewis stood calmly and waited for her.

"Good evening, Theresa Wolholme," he said.

"Hello, Lewis."

"You want to ask me a question."

"What have you done with Malena Merewin?"

He turned, gestured, and she found herself walking with him, slightly behind, down the trail. She thought about putting on her headlamp, but he seemed to have no trouble finding his footing. She followed his lead.

"I haven't done anything with her. Koola has done with her. I just live here."

"Lewis!" She grabbed his shoulder and tried to swing him around. Despite the light boniness of his frame, he was immovable, as if his feet interpenetrated with the rock beneath them. "She's a little girl. She's lost her parents."

"They're not lost," Lewis said craftily. "No. We've got some absolute coordinates."

"Are they dead then?"

"Their journey is over."

Tessa felt despair at his Koolan obstinacy. "Lewis. You can't keep her."

"I'm not keeping her!" He didn't shout, but his voice grew less precise. He waved his arms. "The suns burn with their own fires. Their messages take forever to reach us, but reach us they do."

Darkness had come completely, and the clear sky was bright with stars. Tessa stared up, wondering if he could see the star around which circled the flaming Simurad Tunnels. The wind blowing down the canyon grew even colder.

"All good places are hard." Lewis had calmed down. "They slide into the flesh. Unite us."

"Lewis!"

He sidled away. "The human world has rejected her. Koola accepts her. Accepts her with gracious hardness."

"We aren't rejecting her," Tessa said in despair. She thought of the tug-of-war that Malena would return to, the tensions that pulled the net of social relations in Calrick Bend tight. And she thought of the solemn little girl in the tree, waiting for her parents to come home and knowing they never would. "We need her."

"Koola needs her more! She'll learn the ways, as I have. She'll climb to the heights."

For an instant, he almost convinced her. Malena could go with her war-uncle, learn to sleep on bare rock, to eat the edible lichens of the cliffs, to walk unafraid through the blizzards. Lewis would bring her to it, with love. It was a life as sensible as any other, more sensible than some.

"Lewis," Tessa said. "Malena did not live through Simurad. Does she need to live through this?"

For the first time, she felt she had reached him. He peered at her.

"Perin has his own service to perform for Gorr's daughter," Tessa said. "So do I. I need to talk to her. Please."

"Climb, then. Show who you are."

"Will you talk to us?"

"Us?" Lewis seemed puzzled. "Who us?"

"The Wolholmes. All of us. You know who we are."

"I'm cold," Lewis said. "It blesses my flesh. Bring Perin, if he will come. We will talk."

And with that, he was gone. He jumped up, slid over a rock, and disappeared into a silent void. Fingers shaking, Tessa pulled out her headlamp and clipped it onto her forehead. The beam showed dark-shadowed rocks and sternly undecorative plants, but Lewis was nowhere to be seen. She held her breath, but heard nothing but the wind.

Tessa began to slowly pick her way down the rough path toward home.

Dom bent over and adjusted his sister's snowshoe. Tessa had thought it was set fine on her foot, but he had another opinion. She looked ahead, at the trail that led up into the high end of Born Canyon.

"We'll be sidestepping up that slope," Dom said. "It'll be easier if it doesn't slide so much at the heel."

"You'd know that if you did much winter hunting," Benjamin said in a superior tone. "We can loosen it again at the top of the slope."

Perin said nothing. He was clearly already tired, unused to the exertions of climbing the higher canyons in midwinter, but had voiced no complaint. He wiped his red, sweaty forehead with a handkerchief, then looked up into the heights. Tessa heard the ragged pull of his breath with sorrow. Her father was growing old. Hadn't she noticed that before?

Dalka, though of an age with him, seemed unaffected by the climb. She had insisted on coming with them. She and Tessa had not had a chance to talk in private, and Tessa didn't know when they would.

"Let's *go*," Benjamin said. "We've got to move." He moved upslope with little steps, jerking his head like an animal straining against a leash. "You know where we're going, Tessa?"

"Just up Born," she said. "They're up there, somewhere." But how high? They would see.

When the going got difficult, as it did here, they roped themselves together and moved slowly. The sun was deceptively bright, glaring on the snowfields. The snowfields weren't deep: there was never much water in this part of Koola, even in winter, but they were deep enough to impede travel.

"We don't usually hunt this high at this time of year," Dom said, with the air of confiding a male secret. "The game comes lower, which actually makes it easier for us than in the summer."

"Ben didn't make it sound that way."

Dom snorted. "Well, he comes up here to prove something, not to hunt. That's dangerous, but he's been doing it since that wapiti got away from him in the summer. Hunting's not for proving, it's for food, and for fun. Or maybe I'm just saying that because I'm getting old." He turned and pointed. "But hunting helps in everything. There, those dark spots? A couple of Lewis's footprints, I think. Even he can't cross a snowfield without leaving a mark, though some people think he flies. We're still going right."

As they climbed, the countless slopes and cliffs opened out

around them, their edges sharp and blue in the moody winter light. Tessa wondered what it would be like to live and farm up here, far from the density of the lower canyons. She'd heard old stories that it was possible, that at some time not long after the initial settlement of Koola, people had lived at these heights, not yet having descended to the flood-prone depths of the canyons and subdued them.

They reached the top of the steep slope and unroped. Tessa readjusted her snowshoes before Dom could come over and do it for her. He nodded his approval when he saw, thus retaining some control over the situation. The land curved gently up from this point, up to the base of a vast vertical cliff about a mile away. The top of the cliff, thousands of feet up, was cleft into three, with the middle bastion the highest, hence its name: Telena's Foot. Tessa had caught glimpses of it in the warmer months, but she had tended to climb well down-canyon. This was good territory for hunting: men's country. Women tended to stay away from it so that they would not be interrupted and annoyed during their strolls by the wails of dying animals.

"Dalka." Dalka had fallen back, and now she and Tessa were far enough away from the others to talk. "What was in those seeds?"

"Lessa Tergoran, left on watch at the Merewins', says she was attacked by ghosts last night. The house was filled with them. Actually, she fell asleep. I know her. Lewis could have lifted the entire house and taken her with it. She would never have stopped snoring."

"Dalka—"

Dalka was silent for a moment, her face stony. "Damn it, Tessa, you do give me the most difficult things, did you know that?"

"I'm sorry."

Dalka shook her head: "The High Plainsmen. They must be behind it. I see no other way."

Tessa was surprised. She looked up the canyon, toward the heights behind which the High Plainsmen lived. "Why do you say that?"

"That liquid must have been the way Fila controlled Gorr's

fungal infection. It's a fairly simple enzyme blocker, keeps the fungus from spreading but doesn't kill it. Topical application, fairly straightforward. I don't think it will be too hard for me to duplicate."

"Then what—"

"I didn't make it for her! And I don't know who did, or who she got it from."

"But you think it was Lewis."

Dalka nodded. "But Lewis didn't make it. That's not his way. He got it from someone else. Someone high up-canyon. And he gave it to Fila, to control Gorr, as if he were some herd animal himself."

Tessa remembered the argument Dom had recounted for her, during the trading trip. "Swern Toroma told Gorr about it, just before all this happened, about the infection, about Lewis."

"Ah." Dalka thought about it. "It was the balance between them, that infected wound of his. Her stake."

"If he strayed from her, he would die."

"Exactly. And that, in the end, was how he punished her."

It took a moment for Tessa to realize that she'd lost track of the logic. "I don't understand."

Dalka smiled. "You don't think Fila dumped the treatment in the sink, do you? She knew exactly where it was, she didn't need to search the house for it. No, it was Gorr. Gorr, when he found out how he had been controlled, came home and destroyed his treatment. Without it, he would die, slowly and by degrees. I might have been able to help him, I don't know. He didn't give me a chance."

"He never thought about Malena," Tessa said.

"Indeed he didn't. And he never would have, his whole life. The only person who was important to him was Fila. She was the beginning and the end. As long as *he* was in control, not she. To find that, for all those years, she had held his life in her hands ... he punished her. Punished her by taking away her control."

"And dying." Tessa looked up the slope. A jambles lay at the cliff's base, with high square blocks sticking up out of the snow. "That was how he punished her."

"She always did love him, whatever else there may have been."

"He came up here to confront Lewis," Tessa said. "He must have decided where the treatment came from."

"And Fila followed. What else could she do?"

"And what happened then?"

"That," Dalka said, "is something only Lewis can tell us."

The jambles under the cliff turned out to be the foundations of an ancient manor house, most of its structure long vanished. Tessa looked at the chisel marks on the hard rock and wondered who had built here, so long ago, and why. She climbed up on the highest part. The view down the canyon was tremendous. She could see Fulda's and Angel's Buttes in the distance, on the other side of Cooperset. The successive ranges of mountains that made up the Boss were crisp in the cloudless sky to her right.

Benjamin bounced around the rocks like an enthusiastic dog, but Tessa noticed the care with which he kept his feet on rock, off snow or soil that might hold some track or other evidence of their quarry.

Ignoring his son's outraged protest, Perin walked right into the middle of what had once been the cellar.

"Lewis!" he called. Silence. "Lewis! It's me, Perin Wolholme. I want to talk." He turned to the rest of them, who stared silently at him. "Could the rest of you please go a ways back down the slope so that we can talk, Lewis and I?"

"He hasn't even answered you," Dom said, irritated. "He's probably not even here. Why should we—"

"Please, Dom. He won't answer to a crowd, which is what we are. You know that. It won't take long, one way or another." He pointed off to a rock outcropping about a quarter-mile away. "There. You can all have your lunch. It's a nice sunny spot." Perin was as decisive as Tessa had ever heard him. His tone did not accept argument or contradiction.

Dom shrugged. "All right. But look here: there's been digging at the base of these rocks." Indeed, the snow had been disturbed and there were traces of dirt in it.

"I'll discuss that with Lewis when he appears," Perin said. "Tessa—could you stay? I may need you."

"All right, Poppa." Everyone else headed out into the snow, not saying anything, Dalka most reluctantly. Tessa watched them go.

Perin stood in the middle of the foundation, black against white, not moving, staring up at the looming Telena's Foot. After a long few minutes, he bent and slung the pack from his back.

"Here, Tessa," he said. "I'm going to ask you to do some work."

He pulled out a shovel, handed it to her, and pointed to the disturbed snow and earth that Dom had noticed. Tessa accepted it. At least it would give her something to do. She started digging carefully.

Tessa warmed up as she worked, but suddenly she felt lonely. Usually she liked being alone, but not now, not with her father standing nearby, staring off at the cliffs, ignoring her. She cocked her head. Her brothers and Dalka were enjoying a companionable lunch on the outcropping, chatting over something. Probably something completely irrelevant, she thought jealously. Something that had nothing to do with life and death and adoption and land. Perhaps Dalka was retelling the story of Lessa Tergoran, mimicking her vigorous snores. Ben picked up a double handful of snow and let it glitter away in the breeze.

Something had appeared under the snow. A hand, frozen half-clenched. Tessa stared down at it, then began to dig carefully around, revealing the arm, the shoulder, and finally the head of Gorr Merewin. The details of his body were mercifully obscured by the snow. Fila lay next to him, with a wide cut in her chest.

"Perin. You shouldn't have come."

Tessa looked up from her grim labors. Old Man Lewis stood facing her father.

"I had to come, Lewis. You know I did."

"Why?" Lewis's voice was a wail of pain.

"She's not yours to take. I'm not dead. If I were, then my

children too. would have the choice of going with you. But
I'm still here."

"This is her place. There is no other for her. Gorr—"

"Lewis!" Tessa was surprised at the strength in her father's
voice as he faced his old comrade in arms. "This is intolerable. Where is she?"

"Safe." Tessa had never seen Lewis this sullen. Usually the
words of people were as the wind for him, but Perin's words
clearly had an impact. Lewis would have liked to disregard
them, but he couldn't.

"Let me be the judge of that. Bring her out."

"But—"

"Bring her out, I said. You have breathed the air, drunk the
water, eaten the earth, and slept on the rock of Koola, but you
are not free of us all. Lewis!" Perin reached out his hands.

Lewis did not move away, but he did not respond either.
Slowly his white-haired head rose. "You want to haul her
back, hide her in a house, tear her away from her place. Is
that better than the life I lead here?" Lewis spoke gently, almost humorously. "Don't speak, I know your answer. We
have a duty to Gorr's blood. Both of us."

"You're right." The reluctance in Perin's voice was clear.

"Both of us. We swore, there in that flaming place. Didn't
we?"

"We did." Perin spoke to Tessa over his shoulder. "Keep
digging, Tessa. We still need them." He turned back to Lewis.
"But if you keep her the people of the canyons will hunt you.
They won't catch you, not you, Lewis, but they will hunt
you because they will hate you."

Tessa resumed her excavation of the two frozen bodies.
Gorr's face was peaceful. Had he died of the fungal infection?
Aside from the wound on her chest, Fila's body was un-
marked.

She brushed snow away from Gorr's face. The disfiguring
mark of the fungus was gone. He had died, and it had no further use for him. It hid, somewhere in the bloody snow, and
awaited another host. Her hands were gloved. She should be
safe from infection, since it needed to penetrate the dermis to
have its effect. Still, she moved away.

A shadow fell across her digging. Tessa looked up. Malena stood above her, staring down dispassionately at the bodies of her parents. Tessa almost jumped up, to grab her and screen her gaze, but stopped herself.

Malena looked at her. "They're dead, aren't they?"

Something caught in Tessa's throat, and she could only nod.

"Lewis told me . . . but I didn't see them. He dug them under himself. They loved each other very much."

"They loved you too, Malena."

"Not as much."

Malena jumped down and suffered Tessa to put her arms around her and hold her. She was wearing a hodgepodge of clothing, none of it adjusted properly, but, like Lewis, still seemed warm.

"Lewis wants me to live with him," Malena said.

"And what do you want to do?"

Malena looked up at her. Her dark eyes were wide. "I want to be with my parents."

Tessa did not glance down at the frozen bodies. "No, Malena."

Malena sighed. "They didn't want me anyway. They wanted to be by theirselves." Malena reached down and cast a handful of snow across her father's dead face. "They didn't even build a castle for the Kings. They were too busy and so the Kings passed us by."

"The Kings looked in on you, Malena. They always do, to make sure all the children are asleep. They don't need a castle to stop by."

Malena was not to be consoled. "We didn't even have a little one."

Lewis and Perin appeared above them.

"Malena." Lewis could not hide the despair in his voice. "You must choose. I was wrong."

The little girl sat down and crossed her arms, ignoring all of them. She was the same age as Kevin, now safely at a neighbor's house, being spoiled. She held her body tightly, as if the intolerable pressures on her were indeed physical, and she was being compressed into a space too small to live in.

Tessa squatted down in front of her and looked her in the eyes. "I'm sorry, Malena. You shouldn't have to make decisions like this. No one should."

"I'm all right." Malena's tone was resentful. Arms still crossed, she looked away from all of them, off across the valley to the mountains beyond. "Tessa?"

"Yes, Malena?"

Malena switched her gaze to the ground. "Tell me what to do."

"I—" Tessa didn't know what to say. She looked up at the two men who loomed over her and the little girl. Perin was carefully expressionless, Lewis sad and weary. Tessa was half tempted to let Malena stay with him, so that she could learn the ways of the Shield's heights and stay completely pure, like snow and rock.

"We will adopt you. The Wolholmes. Poppa and I, and Dom and Benjamin and Kevin. Will you allow that?"

"Yes." The girl's voice was the barest whisper.

"Good." Tessa kept her voice brisk and efficient. She was getting some understanding of why Alta Dalhousie enjoyed being who she was. There was a joy in making such significant decisions, much like the feeling of jumping from a high rock down to the distant ground.

"And Lewis." She looked up at him, wondering what consequences her next decision would have. "You'll have her too, as you deserve. The canyons will not claim her entire. Malena will come to you, up here. Is that something you want to do, Malena?"

Malena looked up at Lewis, the only person who had evidenced any interest in her own personal fate, and nodded silently.

"I'm afraid you'll have to be satisfied with that, Lewis," Tessa said.

His head moving in time to Malena's, Lewis nodded also.

"But can we do that?" Crisis over, Perin was once again tentative. He looked down at Malena as if he had never seen her before. "What about—"

"Alta Dalhousie will agree," Tessa said briskly. "As long as we grant the Toromas some use of their old lands."

"Oh." Perin was still puzzled, but willing to accept his daughter's decision. "Well, that's all right then. The others will want to know." He put his fingers in his mouth and whistled shrilly.

Benjamin didn't realize that there was any mystery at all. He hugged Malena, who tolerated it, then jumped up on the rocks. They'd wanted to find her, and they'd found her, and it was a noble success.

Dom was more suspicious. Decisions had been made in his absence, significant family decisions. He accepted them, but now Tessa regretted having acted in such haste. She should have talked to him . . . but there hadn't been time, everything had moved so fast. She'd have to make it up to him later, if she could.

Dalka knelt down by Gorr and Fila. "How did they die?"

"He came up to see me, to find out why I had been giving her the medicines," Lewis said. "And to forbid me to do it anymore. She came after him, much faster. They fought. He was weak, dying, but they fought, and she let him cut her, as she had cut him. The fungus went right into her, deep, even deeper than the skin. She died quickly, even more quickly than he. And after, when I found them, he had decided that his journey was over. I asked about Malena." Lewis sighed. "He barely knew who I meant. Perin and I were to decide. I decided for Perin." He looked at his old friend. "I was wrong."

"Now we bury them," Perin said. "We can't take them to the burial ground at Topfield until spring. So shall we build them their winter house?"

His family looked around at the high, inhospitable cliffs. They had all been looking forward to getting somewhere lower in altitude before night fell.

"They are family," Perin said. "It is our duty."

And it stakes our claim to Malena, Tessa thought, but did not say. It felt entirely too cold-blooded.

Perin knelt, gathered a small clump of snow, and began to roll it. "Time to get to work."

Despite the gravity of the situation, Tessa laughed and

clapped her mittened hands. "Let's go, Dom! Bet you I can roll a big one faster than you can."

Dom shook his head. "God. What a family I was born into." Then he bent over and began to roll his own snowball.

"Tessa!" Perin whispered piercingly. "Tessa. Get up, it's almost dawn."

"I'm awake, Poppa." Tessa rolled out of her sleeping bag. Malena, who had been sharing it, got out without a sound. Tessa had listened to her steady breathing during the night, wondering if she slept.

It had been a cold night, and Perin had slept none of it. After he had sent his children to bed he had stayed up. In brief waking moments, Tessa had heard him wandering around the snow structure, adding things to it, spraying it with catalyst-warmed water to freeze in the cold night air. He'd obviously planned for this. Dom had already left his own bag without waking her. She crawled out of the tent.

A dark shape bulked in the predawn darkness: the snow structure that Perin had built for the bodies of Fila and Gorr. They were below it now, encased in ice.

"Dom!" Tessa called. "Help me get this tent down." The air was sandpaper-cold. She felt it abrading her exposed skin.

Dom bounded up, thrust a cup of steaming tea into her hand, and took down the tent before she could say anything more.

Morning light filtered around the peaks. They all stood as still as they could in the cold.

"Oh, Poppa," Tessa said. "It's beautiful!"

"That's not the point, is it?" Perin said, pleased in spite of himself. "Not the point at all. But they might as well have what I can give them, right? What I can give them."

Two days after building his magnificent structure of cake for the animals to eat, Perin had built one of ice and snow to be melted by the spring sun. It thrust up from its base in the old foundation stones. Delicate, ice-encased spires gleamed above heavy, crenellated walls. The front of the castle had huge, claw-tipped paws, as if the entire building was some gigantic, frozen animal.

Tessa sipped her tea, feeling it go quickly cold.

"Well, that's it then, isn't it?" Perin said briskly. He picked up his pack. "We'd best be down quickly. Everyone has to be told."

"But, Poppa," Tessa protested. "We can't just leave—"

"We can. We can and we will, Tessa. It's just something to keep the scavengers away from them. That's all it's for." He turned away from it without another look, tightened his snowshoes, and started down the hill.

Dom, Benjamin, Dalka, Malena, and Tessa followed, Tessa in the rear. After taking a few steps, she stopped and turned. The castle was in full light now, gleaming as if dropped from some other world. The dark shape of Lewis moved across the tumbled rocks above it, as he walked slowly into the dark and icy mountains beyond others' knowing.

Tessa turned back and hurried to catch up with her family.

A very old Christmas tradition, modernized.

An Old-Fashioned Bird Christmas
Margaret St. Clair

THE REVEREND CLEM Adelburg had come out to cut some mistletoe. He tucked the hatchet tightly in the band of his trousers and shinned up the knobby trunk of the apple tree. When he got high enough, he saw that two ravens were seated on the apple tree branches, eating the mistletoe berries. There were always ravens around the cabin nowadays; he chased them away indignantly, with many loud whooshes. Then he felt a twinge of remorse.

"O Lord," he prayed among the branches, his face upturned toward the dramatic cloudscape of an Arizona winter, "O Lord, bless this little experiment of thy servant. O Lord, grant that I wasn't wrong to chase away those darned ravens. Yes, Lord."

He sighted up at the berries. He chopped with the hatchet. Three branches of mistletoe fell down on the sheets of newspaper he had previously placed at the foot of the tree. He climbed down.

It was beginning to get dark. Mazda would have supper ready. There was a premonitory rumble and then the sound of "Silent Night," played on an electric xylophone, filled the sky.

The Reverend Adelburg frowned. The noise must be coming from Parker; the municipal Christmas tree there would be thirty-five feet tall this year, and already he could see the red glow of Parker's municipal Christmas street-decoration project in the southern sky. Well, if the Lord continued to bless him, and if his next few sermons had the effect he hoped they'd have, he might be able to change the character of Parker's Christmas celebration. The Forthright Temple, in Los Angeles, was a long way from Parker, but these FM broadcasts were receivable here, too.

He went in the kitchen. Mazda was cooking something on the oil stove, an oil lamp burning dimly on the table beside her. The kitchen smelled good.

"Hello, Clem," she said, turning to face him. She smiled at him. "Did you get the berries for the tea?"

"Yes, dear." He handed her the three branches of mistletoe. "Make it good and strong this time, dear. I just want to see if there's anything in my little idea."

"About mistletoe being the common element in all religions? Sure."

He watched her as she went to fill the teakettle at the sink. She was a tall woman, with masses of puffy ginger hair and a very fair skin. Her figure was excellent, though rangy, and he always enjoyed watching her.

Most of the time Mazda's being in the cabin seemed so ordinary, so fitting (she was remarkably domestic, when you got to know her), that he simply didn't think about it. But there were moments, like the present, when her physical immediacy seemed to catch him in the solar plexus. Then he could only stand and look at her and draw deep, surprised breaths.

It wasn't so much his living with her, in the technical sense, that troubled him. He hadn't even tried to feel guilty about that. It seemed at once so extraordinary, and so perfectly natural, that it wasn't something his conscience could get a grip on. No, it was Mazda's being in the cabin at all that was the surprising thing.

Where had she come from, anyhow? He'd gone outside one morning early in September, meaning to walk up and down in the sand while he put the finishing touches on his sermon for next week, and there she had been, sitting quietly under a Joshua tree.

She couldn't have been there for more than ten minutes: her skin, as he had come to know later, was extraordinarily sensitive to sunlight, and she was wearing the skimpiest bikini imaginable. She'd have been sunburned all over if she'd been there for any length of time. And how had she got there? There'd been no sign of a car in any direction, and he hadn't even heard the noise of a plane or a copter in the sky. Had she walked over from Parker? In a bikini? Five miles?

He knew so little about her—no more now, really, than he had known on that first day when she had said, "Hi," and gone in the house. It wasn't that she was closemouthed or sullen— she just didn't talk about herself. Once only, when he had been elaborating his idea that the use of mistletoe might be the common element behind all religion, had she come out with anything that might be a personal remark. He'd spoken of the use of mistletoe in classical paganism, in druidism, in Christian festival, in the old Norse religion, in Zoroastrianism—

Her lower lip had begun to protrude defiantly. "There's no mistletoe in Zoroastrianism," she had cut in sharply. "I know."

Well? It wasn't much for the fruit of more than three months.

He couldn't help wondering about Mazda sometimes, though he didn't want to fail in Christian charity. But he knew he had his enemies. Could she possibly be a Retail Merchants Association spy?

The teakettle was beginning to hum. Mazda gave the pot of string beans on the stove a stir with a wooden spoon. "How did you come out with your sermon, Clem?" she asked.

"Eh? Oh, splendidly. The ending, I really think, will have an effect. There are some striking passages. The ravens were quite impressed." He smiled at his little joke.

"Ravens?" She turned to face him. "Were there ravens outside when you were rehearsing your speech?"

"Yes, indeed. We have ravens all the time here now. There were even ravens in the apple tree when I was cutting the mistletoe."

Her eyes widened. "Oh . . ." she said thoughtfully.

"I fear I chased them away a little too vehemently," he

said, becoming serious. "Ravens, after all, are the Lord's creatures too."

"Not *those* ravens," Mazda said.

There was a very brief pause. Mazda fingered the bracelet on her left wrist. Then she said, "Listen, Clem, I know you've talked about it, but I guess I'm just dumb. Why are you so down on modern Christmases, anyway?"

"My dear, if you'd ever attend the Temple service . . ." the Reverend Adelburg said in gentle reproof. "But I'll try to make my point of view, which I humbly trust is also the Lord's point of view, clear to you." He began to talk.

He was an excellent talker. Phrases like "star in the darkness," "the silent night of Bethlehem," "pagan glitter," "corruption," "perversion," "truer values," "an old-time America," "myrrh, frankincense," and "1776," seemed to shimmer in the air between them. Mazda listened, nodding from time to time or prodding the potatoes in the saucepan with a two-tined kitchen fork.

At last he appeared to have finished. Mazda nodded for the last time. "Um-hum," she said. "But you know what I think, Clem? I think you just don't like lights. When it's dark, you want it to *be* dark. It's reasonable enough—you're a different guy once the sun goes down."

"I don't like the false lights of modernity," the Reverend said with a touch of stiffness. "As I intend to make abundantly clear in my sermon tomorrow."

"Um-hum. You're a wonderful talker . . . I never thought I'd get fond of somebody who didn't like light."

"I like some kinds of light," said the Reverend Adelburg. "I like fires."

Mazda drew a deep breath. "You'd better wash up before supper, Clem," she said. "You've got rosin on you from the apple tree."

"All right, dear." He kissed her on the cheek and then—she had seductive shoulders, despite her ranginess—on the upper arm.

"Mmmmmmmm," Mazda said.

When he had gone into the pantry to wash, she looked after him slantingly. Her caramel-colored eyebrows drew together in a frown. She had already scalded out the teapot. Now she reached into the drawer of the kitchen table and drew out a handful of what looked like small mushrooms. They were, as a matter of fact, mescal buttons, and she had gathered them last week from the top of a plant of *Lophophora Williamsii* herself.

She cut them up neatly with a paring knife and dropped them into the teapot. She put the mistletoe berries in on top of the mescal buttons. Then she filled the teapot with boiling water. When the Reverend got back from his washing, the teapot was steaming domestically on the table beside the string beans.

He said grace and poured himself a cup of the tea.

"Goodness, but it's bitter," he observed, sipping. "Not at all like it was the first time. What a difference putting in more mistletoe has made!"

Mazda looked down. She passed him the sugar bowl. He sweetened the tea lavishly. "You haven't set a cup for yourself, dear," he said, suddenly solicitous.

". . . There isn't much tea. You said to make it strong."

"Yes, honey, but if there's any good in the tea, I want you to share it. Get another cup."

He looked across the table at her, brightly and affectionately. There was a faint flush in Mazda's cheeks as she obeyed.

Supper was over and Mazda was washing the dishes when the Reverend Clem said suddenly, "How fast you're moving, Mazda! I never saw anything like the way you're getting through those dishes. I can hardly see your hands, they're moving so fast."

"Fast?" Mazda echoed. She sounded bewildered. She held up a spoon and polished its bowl languidly in the light of the oil lamp. "Why, I'm not moving fast. I've been standing here by the sink for hours and hours, washing one dish. I don't know what's the matter with me. I wish I *could* move fast."

There was a silence. Mazda had finished the dishes. She took off her apron and sat down on the floor, her feet out straight in front of her. Almost immediately the Reverend Adelburg slid off the chair where he had been sitting, and flopped down on the floor parallel to her. Both their legs were stretched out.

"What lovely hands you have, Mazda," he said. He picked up one of those members from her lap, where it was languidly lying, and turned it about admiringly. "Your fingers remind me of the verse in the Canticles—'Fair are my love's palms as an eel that feedeth among lilies. And the coals thereof hath a most vehement flame.' They're even colored like eels, purple and gold and silver. Your nails are little dark rainbows.

"The Lord bless you, Mazda. I love you very much." He put his arm around her. She let her head decline on his shoulder, and they both leaned back against the wall. "Are you happy, dear?" he asked her anxiously. "As happy as I am? Do you have a dim sweet sense of blessings hovering over you?"

"Um-hum," Mazda answered. It was obviously difficult for her to talk. "Never felt better." A grin zigzagged across her face. "Mus' be the mistletoe."

The effects of peyote—mescal-button—intoxication are predictable. They run a definite course. None the less, the response to a drug is always somewhat idiosyncratic. Thus it was that the Reverend Clem Adelburg, who had drunk enough peyote infusion to keep a cart horse seeing beatific visions for twenty-four hours, reached, about six o'clock in the morning, the state of intense wakefulness that succeeds to the drug trance. By the time the copter came from Los Angeles to take him to the Temple, a little after eight, he had bathed, shaved, and dressed, and was reading over his sermon notes.

He went into the bedroom where Mazda was lying to bid her good-bye. Sometime during the night they had managed to get to bed. He bent over and kissed her tenderly on her loosened mouth. "Good-bye, dear. Our little experiment certainly had results, didn't it? But I feel no ill aftereffect, and I trust that you will not, either. I'll be back about eleven tonight."

Once more he kissed her. Mazda made a desperate effort to rouse herself from the rose and opal-hued heaven she was currently floating in. She licked her lips. "Clem . . ." she said.

"Yes, dear?"

"Be careful."

"Certainly, dear. I always am. Yes."

He patted her on the shoulder. He went out. Even in her paradise, which was at the moment blue and silver, she could hear the noise of the copter as it bore him away.

Mazda's drug dreams came to an end with a bump about twelve o'clock. She sprang out of bed and ran to the window. The Reverend Adelburg was gone, of course. And there wasn't a raven in sight.

Over in Los Angeles, the Reverend's sermon was going swimmingly. From his first words, which had been the arresting sentence, "The lights are going out again all over the world," he had riveted the attention of his listeners as if with stainless-steel rivets. Even the two troops of Archer Eagle Scouts in the front rows, who, with their scoutmaster Joe Buell, were today's Honor Guests, had been so fascinated that they had stopped twanging their bowstrings. The Reverend had swung thunderously from climax to climax; by now at least half his audience had resolved to disconnect its radio when it got home, and throw away the electric lights on its Christmas tree. Now the Reverend was approaching the climax of climaxes.

"In the sweet night of the spirit—bless us, O Lord! Yes, Lord, it's good to be dark—in the sweet silence of the stable let the little flame of—bless us, Lord!—let the little flame—My *Gosh*! Good Lord!"

Forthright Temple is ventilated, and partly lighted, by a clerestory in the middle part of the building. Through this clerestory eight large black birds flew rapidly.

Two of them headed straight for the Reverend Adelburg's eyes. Four of them attacked the Temple's not very bright electric lights. The other two made dive after dive on the helpless congregation's head.

Women were screaming. Handkerchiefs waved. Hymnbooks rocked and fluttered through the air. The organist burst into a Bach chorale. The bewildered choir began singing two different songs.

When the ravens had first swooped down upon him, the Reverend Adelburg had dived under the lectern. From thence—he was a man who was used to authority—he began shouting orders to the troops of Archer Eagle Scouts in a clarion, stentorian voice.

"Young men! Listen! Shoot at the birds! Shoot . . . at . . . the . . . birds!"

There was a very slight hiatus. Then bowstrings began to twang and arrows to thud.

Eight pagan ravens are no match at all for the legitimate weapons of two troops of Archer Eagle Scouts. The ravens dived valiantly, they cawed and shrieked. In vain. Inside five minutes after the shooting started, there remained no trace of the birds' incursus except a black tail feather floating in an updraft, eight or ten hymnbooks with ruffled pages, and some arrows on the floor.

For a few moments the scouts scurried about collecting arrows. Then the Reverend Adelburg summoned them up to the lectern, where he was standing. He finished his sermon with a troop of Archer Scouts drawn up on either side of him, like a bodyguard.

"That was a wonderful sermon, wasn't it," said the lady from Iowa as she and her husband walked toward their parked car. "I never heard anything like it before. He really spoke better after the birds came in than he did earlier . . . I think tomorrow I'll go downtown and see if I can get some little oil lamps to burn in the patio."

"Wonder what sort of birds those were," her husband said idly. "They were mighty big for crows."

"Crows! Why, they were ravens; haven't you ever seen pictures of ravens? I wonder what made them go in the Temple. Ravens always seem such *old-fashioned* birds."

"I betrayed my company for you," Mazda said. She hiccoughed with emotion. "I'm a rat. As far as that goes, you're a rat too. We're *both* rats."

"What company is that?" the Reverend asked with innocent curiosity. He yawned. They had been sitting in the tiny living room, arguing for hours, ever since he got back from the Temple, and by now it was nearly two o'clock in the morning.

"The PE&G. Why? Did you ever suspect?"

"I thought perhaps the Retail Merchants Association sent

you. I never understood how you happened to be sitting under that Joshua tree."

Mazda laughed scornfully. "The Retail Merchants? Those boffs? Why, I don't suppose they have more than three secret agents in the whole Los Angeles metropolitan area. They couldn't stop a baby from crossing a street on a kiddy car. Their idea of hot tactics is to hire a big newspaper ad.

"No, I'm a PE&G girl. I've been one of their top people for years. That's why I know what you're up against."

She took an earnest step toward him. "Clem, I don't think you have any idea of how serious this is," she said. "But they'll stop at nothing. They can't possibly let you get away with it. Why, last December after your old-fashioned Christmas sermons, power consumption was off twenty-seven percent all along the whole Pacific slope, and it didn't get back to normal until late February. People just didn't use much electricity. The company didn't pay any dividends at all on its common stock, and if the same thing happens this year, they'll have to skip payments on the preferred. That's why I was sent to stop you at all costs."

"How were you supposed to stop me?" the Reverend inquired. He put the tips of his outstretched fingers together thoughtfully.

"I was supposed to seduce you, and then call the broadcasters in. You know, moral turpitude. But I convinced them that it wouldn't work. Congregations aren't so touchy about things like that nowadays. It wouldn't have worked."

"Mazda, how *could* you?"

"I don't know how I could," Mazda replied with spirit. "I could have had a nice clean-cut electronics engineer . . . or one of those cute linemen up on a pole . . . and then I had to fall for a Reverend with his collar on backwards. Somebody ought to examine my head."

The Reverend Adelburg let this pass without comment. "What was the alternate plan?" he asked.

"I promised them I'd keep you from delivering any more old-fashioned Christmas sermons. That's what the peyote was for."

"Peyote? When?"

She told him.

"Oh. Then it wasn't the mistletoe," he said when she had finished. He sounded rather annoyed.

"No, it wasn't the mistletoe. But I guess I didn't give you enough peyote. You delivered the sermon anyway.

"Clem, you think that because the ravens made that silly attack on you in the Temple that that's the sort of thing the company has up its sleeve. It's not. The ravens were acting on their own responsibility, and they're not awfully bright birds. The company can do lots better than that."

"What do you think they'll try next?" the Reverend inquired. His jaw had begun to jut out.

"Well, they might try to get you for moral turpitude after all, or stick an income tax evasion charge on you or accuse you of dope smuggling. I don't think they will. They don't want to give you any more publicity. I think they'll just quietly try to wipe you out."

For a moment, Mazda's self-command deserted her. She wrung her hands. "What'm I to *do*?" she whimpered. "I've got to save you, and you're as stubborn as a mule. I don't know any magic—or at least not nearly enough magic. The whole company will be against me as soon as the ravens are sure I ratted on them. And there's just no place in the world today for anybody who's in conflict with the PE&G.

"I wish I hadn't been such a dope as to fall in love with you."

The Reverend Clem Adelburg got up from the chair where he had been sitting and put his arm around her. "Cheer up, my dear," he told her solemnly. "We will defeat the company. Right is on our side."

Mazda gave a heroic smile. She smiled at him mistily. "It's not just the PE&G, of course," she said. "Sometimes I think *they* have agents everywhere."

"The PE&G?" the Reverend cried. He let his arm fall from around her. He had a sudden nightmare vision of a whole world united against him—a world in which the clouds semaphored secrets about him to the dolphins in the Pacific waves. "What is it, then?"

"Why, it's *Nous*."

"I never heard of it."

"Very few people have. But *Nous, Infinite* is the company from which the PE&G gets its power.

"*Nous* is a very strange outfit. It operates on the far side of three thousand A.D., and selling power is only one of the things it does. When you're a top agent for the company like I was, you hear all sorts of stories about it—for instance, that it's responsible for maintaining the difference in potential between the Earth and the ionosphere, or that the weather on Venus is a minor *Nous* project—stuff like that. I've even heard agents say that *Nous* is G—but I don't believe *that*. I know about Mithras, myself."

"I thought the PE&G made its own power," said the Reverend. He was still struggling with the first part of Mazda's remarks.

Mazda laughed. "I don't mean any disrespect to the company, but what makes you think that? The company's a bad opponent, but outside of that, witchcraft, or sorcery, or ravens, is all they're capable of.

"All the really hot developments in power, the electronic stuff, comes from after 3,000 A.D. Nobody in the present has brains enough to work out a germanium transister, for example. *Nous* helps them. People nowadays are dopes. They can't work buttons on pants, or open a package of chewing gum unless there's a paper ribbon to help them.

"That's beside the point, really. The thing I'm trying to make clear, Clem, is that *Nous* is a bad outfit to come up against.

"I was supposed to go outside at one-thirty this morning and have the ravens pick me up under the Joshua tree. They were going to take me back to headquarters by air raft. If it—"

"Is that how you got here in the first place?" the Reverend inquired. "By air raft?"

"Yes. As I was saying, if I'd done that, the company would have accepted that my failure with the peyote was just a mistake. But I didn't do it. I couldn't bear to leave a chump like you all alone to face the company, and by now they must be beginning to realize that I've ratted on them. It won't be very long before the real trouble begins.

"Now, listen. There are two things you can do. The best one would be for you to go outside and talk to the ravens. If you promise them on your word of honor as a Christian gentleman that you won't deliver any more anti-light sermons—I can't see why you don't like light, anyhow; light's wonderful—if you promise them that, they'll let you go." She paused hopefully.

The Reverend gave her a look.

"Then we'll have to make a break for it.

"While you were in the washroom, I called the Temple copter." She indicated the shortwave radio on the other side of the little stone fireplace. "It'll be here any minute. I think—well, we'll try to get through."

The Reverend looked at her in silence for a moment. Fatigue had made shadows under her eyes, but they only made her look glamorous and desirable. She had never been more beautiful. She had betrayed her company for him; he loved her more than ever. He gave her a hug.

"Nix, my dear," he said. "Nix."

"N-n-n-n—"

"Nix. Never." His voice rang out, booming and resonant. "Run away from those devils and their ravens? Flee from those pagan night-lighters? Never! I *will* not." He advanced toward the radio.

"What are you going to do?" Mazda squeaked.

"I'm going to contact the TVA," he said without turning. "You have to fight fire with fire."

"Public power?" Mazda breathed. Her face was white.

"Public power! Their line will be open all night."

He turned his face toward the rafters. "O Lord," he boomed reverently, "bless this radio message. Please, Lord, grant that in contacting a radical outfit like the TVA I'm doing right."

The noise of prayer died away in the ceiling. He pressed a key and turned a switch. For a moment the room was utterly quiet. Then there was a soft flurry and plop at the window. The ravens, after all, were not deaf. They too had heard the Reverend's prayers.

Mazda spun round toward the sound. Before she could decide what to do, there was a series of tinkles from the chimney. It ended in a glassy crash. Something had broken on the stone hearth.

Mazda screamed.

"Keep back!" she yelled at the Reverend, who had turned from the radio and was leaning forward interestedly. "Keep back! Don't breathe! Damn those birds!" She was fumbling wildly with the wooden bracelet on her left wrist.

"What is it?" he asked. He advanced a step toward the shards of glass on the hearth.

"Get *back*. It's a germ culture bomb. Parrot fever. I'm going to purify it. Stand back!"

The Reverend Adelburg discounted most of this warning as due to feminine hysteria. He drew back a fraction of an inch, but still remained leaning forward, his eyes fixed on the glass.

Mazda gave a moan of desperation. "I've got to do it!" she yelled. She slid her bracelet toward her elbow and gave it a violent twist.

A strictly vertical flash of lightning appeared between the ceiling and the hearth. It was very bright and accompanied by a sizzling noise. A second later a sharp chlorine-like smell filled the air.

Mazda's artificial lightning died away. The room returned to its normal dim illumination. A faint curl of smoke floated above the pieces of broken glass on the hearth of the fireplace. There was no doubt that Mazda had purified the germ culture effectively. But the Reverend Clem Adelburg was stretched out on the floor flat on his back.

Mazda ran to him. She tore open his white shirtfront and laid her head on his chest. His heart was still beating, and his hands and feet were warm. But he was completely out—out more than any of the neon lights he had been trying to put out.

Mazda got up, rubbing her hands. She couldn't move him, and she didn't know what she ought to do for him. She hoped he'd be all right. She knew he had a strong constitution. She went into the kitchen and got a towel.

She came back with it and tied it to the poker. Carrying this homemade flag of truce in front of her, she opened the door and went out into the night.

It was a dark night. From under the Joshua tree a darker shadow detached itself. " 'Lo, Mazda," a harsh voice said.

"Hello," she replied. There was a glitter of beady eyes in the darkness around her. "Listen here, you birds," Mazda said slowly, "we've always been on good terms, haven't we? We've always got on together well. Are you really trying to do me and my boyfriend in?"

A bird cleared its throat. There was a noise of talons being shifted uneasily. "Well ... no, Mazda. We like you too," somebody said.

"Oh, yes? Is that why you dropped the parrot fever bomb? Were you going to drop a dead parrot down the chimney and make it look as if we'd died a natural death? I wouldn't call that bomb exactly a friendly thing."

"The bomb was just a warning," said the harsh voice that had spoken first. "We knew you'd purify it. We have confidence in you. We don't want to do you any harm personally. You can always get another boyfriend."

"I want this one."

"You've had better ones."

"Yes, I know. But this is the one I want."

There was a silence. Then a bird said, "We're sorry, Mazda. We only do what we're sent out to do."

Mazda drew a sharp breath. "Hell's canyon," she said deliberately. "Rural electrification cooperatives. *Public power.*"

There was a sound as of somebody's tail feathers being plucked distractedly. "Mazda, I do wish you wouldn't," said the chief raven in a wincing voice.

"I will, though. I'll get in touch with the public-power people. I don't care about the ethics of it. I'm in love."

"Haw!" the raven jeered harshly. It seemed to have regained its aplomb. "That lightning flash of yours burned out every tube in the radio. You couldn't send a message to Parker to ask for a stick of chewing gum. You're through.

"We'll give you half an hour. During any of that time you can come out unhurt. But after that you're in for it too. This time we're serious."

"What are you going to do?" Mazda cried.

"You'll find out."

Mazda went back to the house.

The clock on the mantelpiece read twenty minutes to three. The ravens would probably give her a few minutes' grace, so she had until ten or twelve minutes after the hour. Mazda knelt down by her consort and began to chafe his hands. When that didn't help, she ran to the kitchen, got a handful of red feathers from the chicken they had had for lunch yesterday, and began burning them under the Reverend's nose.

At seven minutes to three the Reverend's eyelids fluttered and the noise of a copter was heard in the sky. Mazda listened with strained attention, her eyes fixed on her consort. She longed to run to the window, but she was afraid of alerting the ravens. She could only wait.

The copter appeared to be having difficulties. The whoosh of its helix changed pitch, the motor stuttered and coughed. Once the noise seemed to recede; Mazda was afraid the plane was going away entirely. She fingered her wooden blast bracelet nervously. But the copter returned. It landed with a thump that was almost a crash.

The copter door opened and somebody jumped out. There was a sound of squawks, caws, and rapid fluttering. A vigorous male voice said, "Ouch! *Ouch!* What the bloody hell!" More fluttering, then sandaled feet thudded rapidly along the path. Somebody pounded at the door.

Mazda ran to open it. The man who stumbled across the threshold was a dark, stocky Indian who wore white duck pants and red glasses, and carried a three-foot bow slung across his back. He was bleeding freely from half a dozen peck marks on his shoulders and breast. "Lord Mithras," Mazda said prayerfully, "it's Joe Buell! Joe!"

"Mazda! Why didn't you show a light? What are you doing here? What *is* all this?"

Mazda told him. Joe listened intently, frowning more and more. "My word, what a mess," he said when she had finished. He pushed his red glasses up on his nose. "Has the Reverend come to yet?"

They turned around. Clem's eyes were open, but he was still lying on the floor. As they watched, he slowly closed his eyes again. "I guess he's not ready yet," Mazda said.

She looked at the clock. It showed two minutes to three. "Let's get him up and walk him," she said harriedly. "It might help him to get back to normal. Oh, Mithras, how late it is!"

The Reverend Adelburg was limp and slippery, but they managed to get him to his feet. As they guided his rubbery footsteps about the room, Mazda said, "I haven't seen you since you were in Canada, Joe. Those nights in Saskatchewan! I didn't know you were one of the Reverend's men."

"Since 1955," Joe answered briefly.

"How come? I thought you danced Shalako at the pueblo one year."

"I did. But you should see Halonawa now. There's a red and purple neon sign twenty feet high over the plaza. It reads, 'Welcome to Halonawa, Home of the Shalako.' After that I joined up with the Rev. A nice dark Christmas seems a wizard idea."

He plainly didn't want to pursue the subject further. Mazda said, "If the Reverend revives in time, what'll we do?"

"Can you pilot a copter?"

"I can drive a car."

"A copter's really easier." He gave her directions. "The motor's missing a little, but I don't think you'll have any trouble. Orient yourself by Parker and the dam. The dam's just north of us.

"If the Rev comes to in time, make a break for it with him in the plane. I'll create a diversion by climbing out the window and shooting at those bloody birds. I owe them some arrows, at that."

"I wish I knew what they had in mind," Mazda said.

At five minutes after three the Reverend's withy body stiffened. His eyes opened. He raised his head and looked about him. "What a lovely day," he said in a pleasant, conversational voice.

Mazda's face puckered. For a moment she seemed about to burst into wild tears. Then she blinked her eyes and shook her head defiantly. "He hurt his head when he fell, that's all. He'll be all right later. He's got to be all right. And he may really be easier to handle this way than if he wasn't goofed. He's a stubborn man."

Joe had gone over to the table and was putting out the lamp. He handed his red glasses to Mazda. "Makes piloting easier," he said. Then he opened the window on the left and swung himself out of it. He gave a high, passionate battle cry. There was a rush of feathers and some frenzied squawking. Joe's bow began to twang.

Mazda grabbed the Reverend by the hand. "Nice Christmas," she hissed. "Come along." Bent forward, one arm raised to shield her eyes, she pulled him after her at a run toward the door.

The night had grown darker. The sky was heavily overcast. Nonetheless, she could make out the improbable shape of the copter. "Hurry!" she said to Clem Adelburg. "Run!"

Wings buffeted around her. Claws struck at her face, her cheeks, her hair. The Reverend Adelburg gave a cry of pain; Mazda had to use her free arm to wipe her own blood from her eyes. Then they were in the copter and the door was slammed.

She turned the switch. The motor gave a cough and started. Mazda was trembling with excitement, but she followed Joe's instructions. Slowly the copter rose.

She had put on the red glasses before they left the house. As her eyes grew used to the darkness, she made out the glimmer of the river in front of her and the flat surface of Parker Dam. She wanted to go west, toward Los Angeles. The copter climbed a little. She tried to turn.

Wings whizzed by her. Mazda grinned. She twisted the blast bracelet on her wrist. The tiny receptor within it vibrated. There was a flash of light, and the bird plummeted to the ground.

When it hit the sand there was a faint concussion. The floor of the copter shuddered. After a second the smell of almond extract tinged the air.

The bird had been carrying a cyanide bomb. Mazda sent the copter a little higher. Her mind was a kaleidoscope of tumbling fears. The possibility of more bombs, of explosive bombs, of a kamikazi attack on the copter's propeller, played leapfrog in her brain. And what about Joe? Dear Joe, he'd been wonderful in Saskatchewan. Had they got him yet?

She looked back anxiously at the cabin. Joe had vaulted up

on the roof and was standing with one foot planted on either side of the ridgepole, like a Zuñi Heracles. The thick clouds behind him had begun to be tinged with light from the rising moon; she could see that though his bow was ready and he had an arrow drawn nearly back to his ear, he wasn't shooting. His eyes were fixed intently on the sky.

She followed the direction of his gaze. Very high up, so high that they looked no bigger than crows, seven of the big black birds were flapping rapidly northward in single file.

For the next five minutes or so nothing at all happened. The copter plodded steadily westward toward Los Angeles, down low, along the line of the aqueduct. This apparent quiescence on the part of her opponents unnerved Mazda more than a direct attack would have done. She couldn't believe that the PE&G would let her and Clem escape so easily.

Suddenly along the sky in front of her there passed a vast flash of light. For an instant the desert was as bright and white as day. Then the darkness closed down again and thunder crashed.

Mazda's hands shook on the controls. The storm that was coming up might, of course, be merely a storm. Or it might have been sent by the Company. But if *Nous* . . . but if *Nous*, that enormous and somehow enigmatic power that operated from the far side of 3,000 A.D. . . . if *Nous* had decided to stretch out its arm against her and Clem, there wasn't a chance in the world that she and the Reverend would continue to live.

There was another prodigious lightning flash. The desert, the aqueduct, a line of power poles, a small square building, burned themselves on Mazda's eyes. When darkness came back the Reverend, who had been sitting quite calmly and quietly beside Mazda all this time, stirred. "Wonderful fireworks," he said approvingly.

Mazda's eyes rolled. "Clem, baby," she said despairingly. "What'll I *do*?" She looked around as if hunting an answer. Then the bottom of the heavens dropped out.

The heaviest precipitation recorded to date in a cloudburst is two and a half inches in three minutes. What fell on the copter now was heavier. Inside of two seconds after the avalanche of water had begun to pour from the sky the copter was down flat on the ground, as if it had been pushed into the sand by a giant hand.

The noise inside the cabin was deafening. It was like being a dried pea shaken within a drum. It beat along the body like hammers. Mazda, looking up openmouthed, saw that the copter ceiling was beginning to bulge.

The downpour—the cataract—stopped as suddenly as it had begun. There was a minute of dazed silence in the cabin. Then Mazda, pushing hard against the door in the warped copter body, got it open and scrambled out.

The copter was deep in the sand. One blade of the propeller had been broken off entirely. The other hung limply parallel to the shaft.

Mazda stood shivering. She took off her red glasses absently and dropped them on the sand. The sky had cleared. The moon was almost up. She reached inside the cabin and caught Clem Adelburg by the wrist. "C'mon," she said. She had seen a building just before the cloudburst. They might be able to take cover in that.

She struggled over the sand with the Reverend following docilely at her heels. The building, once reached, turned out to be a company substation, and Mazda felt a touch of hope. She could get in, despite the DANGER and NO ADMITTANCE signs, and the ravens might be deterred, even if only slightly, by their respect for company property.

The substation door would open to a verbal signal. Mazda twisted her blast bracelet twice on her arm, inhaled, and swallowed. "Alameda, Alpine, Amador, Butte," she said carefully.

Nothing happened. She cleared her throat and began again, a couple of notes lower. "Alameda, Alpine, Amador, Butte." There was a faint click. "Calaveras, Colusa, Contra Costa, Del Norte, Fresno—"

The door swung wide. Mazda's enumeration of the counties of California had worked. She took the Reverend by the hand and led him through the opening. "Stanislaus, Sutter, Tulare, Tuolmne, Ventura, Yuba, Yolo," she said. The door closed.

It was much darker inside the substation than it had been outside on the white desert, and the air was filled with a high

humming that sounded, and actually was, exceedingly dangerous. Mazda put her arm around Clem's shoulders. "Don't
move, baby," she said pleadingly. "Don't touch anything. Stay
close to Mazda and be quiet."

The Reverend coughed. "Certainly, my dear," he said in
quite a normal voice, "but would you mind telling me where
we are? And what has been happening?"

Mazda went as limp as if she had been skoshed on the
head. She clung to him and babbled with relief, while the
Reverend stroked her soothingly on the hair and tried to make
sense out of her babbling.

"Yes, my dear," he said when she had finally finished, "but
are you sure you aren't exaggerating a little? After all, we
aren't much worse off than we were in the cabin."

Mazda drew away from him slightly. "Oh, sure, everything's fine," she said with a touch of bitterness. "We're in a
place where if we move fast we'll be electrocuted, the copter
is down in the desert with a busted propeller, we haven't
anything to eat or drink, and Joe and I have killed so many
ravens that when the company *does* catch me they'll do something special to make me pay for it. Outside of a few little
bitty details like that, everything is real real george."

The Reverend had not listened with much attention. Now
he said, "Do you hear a noise outside?"

"What sort of a noise?"

"A sort of whoosh."

Mazda drew in her breath. "Shin up to the window and
look out," she ordered. "Look out especially for birds."

He was at the high, narrow window only an instant before
he let himself down. "There was only one raven," he reported, "but there were a number of birds like hawks, with
short wings. There seemed to be humps on their backs."

Even in the poor light of the substation Mazda visibly
turned green. "Goshawks!" she gasped. She staggered against
the wall. Then she began taking off her clothes.

Dress, slip, panties went on the floor. She stood on one foot
and removed her sandals alternately. She began going through
her hair and pulling out bobby pins. She took off her blast
bracelet and added it to the heap.

"What are you doing that for?" the Reverend inquired. It seemed to him a singularly ill-chosen time for sex.

"I'm trying to set up a countercharm, and I have to be naked to do it." Her voice was wobbling badly. "Those birds—those birds are goshawks. I've never known the company to send them out but once before. Those lumps on their backs are portable *Nous* projectors. They're trying to teleport us."

"Teleport us? Where to?"

"To ... to the company's cellars. Where ... they attend to people who believe in public power. They ... oh ... I can't talk about it, Clem."

She crouched down at his feet and picked up a bobby pin. "Don't move," she said without looking up. "Try not to think about anything."

She began to scratch a diagram around him on the floor with a pin. He coughed. "Don't cough," she cautioned him. "It might be better to hold your breath."

The Reverend's lungs were aching before she got the diagram done. She eyed it a moment and then spat carefully at four points within the hexagram. A faint bluish glow sprang up along the line she had traced on the floor.

Mazda rose to her feet. "It'll hold them for a few minutes," she said. "After that ..."

The Reverend raised his eyes to the rafters. "I'm going to pray," he announced. He filled his lungs.

"O Lord," he boomed powerfully, "we beg thy blessing to preserve me and Mazda from the power of the ravens. We beg thy blessing to help us stay here and not be transported to the P&G's cellars. Bless us, O Lord. Preserve us. And help us to make thine old-fashioned Christmas a living reality. Amen, O Lord. Amen!"

Mazda, too, was praying. Hands clasped over her diaphragm, head bowed, lips moving silently, she besought her bright divinity. "Mithras, lord of the morning, slayer of the bull of darkness, preserve my love and me. Mithras, lord of the morning, slayer of the bull of darkness, preserve my love and me. Mithras, the countercharm on the floor is fading. Preserve us! Mithras ... Mithras, Savior, Lord!"

Prayer is a force. So is magic. So is the energy from *Nous* projectors. These varying forces met and collided in the air.

The collision made a sort of vortex, a small but uncomfortable knot in the vast, conscious field potential that is the Infinite part of *Nous*. There was momentarily an intense, horrible sense of pressure and tension in the very air. The substation hummed ominously. Then, with a burst of energy that blew out every generator from Tacoma to San Diego, the roof came off. All along the Pacific slope, and as far inland as Provo, Utah, it was as dark a Christmas as even the Reverend would have wished.

There was a pause. The noise of breaking timbers died away. The Reverend Adelburg and Mazda were looking upward frozenly, mouths open, necks outstretched. Then a gigantic hand reached in through the hole in the roof. A gigantic voice, even bigger than the hand, said in enormous and somehow Oxonian accents, "Very well. *Take* your old-fashioned Christmas, then."

It was just before sunrise on December 21. The Christians, who would be strangled at dawn the next day and then burned in honor of the solstice, were gibbering away in their wicker cages. There were three cages full of them. Great progress was being made in stamping out the new heresy. The Christians would make a fine bright blaze.

The druid looked up at the cages, which were hanging from the boughs of three enormous oak trees, and nodded with satisfaction. His consort, Mahurzda, would find it a hard job strangling so many people. He'd have to help her. It would be a pleasant task.

Once more he nodded. He tested the edge of the sickle he was carrying. Then the druid who had been—would be— would have been—the Reverend Clem Adelburg hoisted up his long white robe and clambered up into the nearest of the oak trees to cut the sacred mistletoe.

The annual Christmas tree shopping
expedition nightmare.

THE WILD WOOD
Mildred Clingerman

IT SEEMED TO Margaret Abbott that her children, as they grew
older, clung more and more jealously to the family Christmas
traditions. Her casual suggestion that, just this once, they try
something new in the way of a Christmas tree met with such
teenage scorn and genuine alarm that Margaret hastily abandoned the idea. She found it wryly amusing that the body of
ritual she herself had built painstakingly through the years
should now have achieved sacrosanctity. Once again, then,
she would have to endure the secret malaise of shopping for
the tree at Cravolini's Christmas Tree Headquarters. She tried
to comfort herself with the thought that one wretchedly disquieting hour every year was not too much to pay for her
children's happiness. After all, the episode always came far
enough in advance of Christmas so that it never *quite* spoiled
the great day for her.

Buying the tree at Cravolini's began the year Bonnie was
four. Bruce had been only a toddler, fat and wriggling, and so
difficult for Margaret to carry that Don had finally loaded
Margaret with the packages and perched his son on his shoul-

der. Margaret remembered that night clearly. All day the Abbotts had promised Bonnie that when evening came, when all the shop lights blazed inside the fairy-tale windows, the four of them would stroll the crowded streets, stopping or moving on at Bonnie's command. At some point along the way, the parents privately assured each other, Bonnie would grow tired and fretful but unwilling to relinquish the dazzling street and her moment of power. That would be the time to allow her to choose the all-important tree, which must then, of course, be carried to their car in triumph with Bonnie as valiant, proud helper. Once she had been lured to the car it would be simple to hurry her homeward and to bed. The fragrant green mystery of the tree, sharing their long ride home, would insure her sleepiness and contentment.

As it turned out (why hadn't they foreseen it?), the child showed no sign of fatigue that evening other than her captious rejection of every Christmas tree pointed out to her. Margaret, whose feet and back ached with Bruce's weight, swallowed her impatience and shook out yet another small tree and twirled its dark bushiness before Bonnie's cool, measuring gaze.

"No," Bonnie said. "It's too little. Daddy, let's go that way." She pointed down one of the darker streets, leading to the area of pawnshops and narrow little cubbyholes that displayed cheap jewelry. These, in turn, verged on the ugly blocks that held credit clothiers, shoe repair shops, and empty, boarded-up buildings where refuse gathered ankle-deep in the entrance ways.

"I won't," Margaret said. "This is silly. What's the matter with this tree, Bonnie? It isn't so small. We certainly aren't going to wander off down there. I assure you, they don't *have* Christmas trees on that street, do they, Don?"

Don Abbott shook his head, but he was smiling down at his daughter, allowing her to drag him to the street crossing.

Like a damn, lumbering St. Bernard dog, Margaret thought, towed along by a simpering chee-ild. She stared after her husband and child as if they were strangers. They were waiting for her at the corner, Don with the uneasy, sheepish look of a man who knows his wife is angry but unlikely to make a scene. Bonnie was still tugging at his hand, flashing sweet, smug little smiles at her mother. Margaret dropped the un-

furled tree with a furious, open-fingered gesture, shifted
Bruce so that he rode on one hip, and joined them.

The traffic light changed and they all crossed together. Don
slowed and turned a propitiating face to his wife. "You all
right, hon? Here, you carry the packages and I'll take Bruce.
If you want to, you could go sit in the car. Bonnie and I, we'll
just check down this street a little way to make sure. . . . She
says they've got some big trees someplace down here." He
looked doubtfully down at his daughter then. "Are you sure,
Bonnie? How do you know?"

"I saw them. Come on, Daddy."

"Probably she *did* see some," Don said. "Maybe last week
when we drove through town. You know, kids see things we
don't notice. Lord, with traffic the way it is, who's got time
to see anything? And besides, Margaret, you said she could
pick the tree. You said it was time to start building traditions,
so the kids would have . . . uh . . . security and all that. Seems
to me the tree won't mean much to her if we make her take
the one we choose. Anyway, that's the way I figure it."

Margaret moved close to him and took his arm, squeezing it
to show both her forgiveness and apology. Don smiled down at
her and Margaret's whole body warmed. For a long moment
she allowed her eyes to challenge his with the increased mois-
ture and blood-heat that he called "smoky," and which denoted
for both of them her frank desire. He stared back at her with
alerted male tension, and then consciously relaxed.

"Well, not right here and now," he said. "See me later."

Margaret, reassured, skipped a few steps. This delighted the
children. The four of them were laughing, then, when they
found themselves in front of the derelict store that housed
Cravolini's Christmas Tree Headquarters.

Perhaps it was their gaiety, that first year, that made
Cravolini's such a pleasant memory for Don and the children.
For the first few minutes Margaret, too, had found the dim,
barny place charming. It held a bewildering forest of upright
trees, aisles and aisles of them, and the odor of fir and spruce
and pine was a tingling pleasure to the senses. The floor was
covered with damp sawdust, the stained old walls hung with
holly wreaths and Della Robbia creations that showed real art-

istry. Bonnie had gone whooping off in the direction of the taller trees, disappearing from sight so quickly that Don had hurried after her, leaving Margaret standing just inside the door.

She found herself suddenly struggling with that queer and elusive conviction that "this had happened before." Not since her own childhood had she felt so strongly that she was capable of predicting in detail the events that would follow this moment. Already her flesh prickled with foreknowledge of the touch that would come ... *now.*

She whirled to stare into the inky eyes of the man who stood beside her, his hand poised lightly on her bare forearm. Yes, he was part of the dream she'd returned to—the long, tormenting dream in which she cried out for wholeness, for decency, and love, only to have the trees close in on her, shutting away the light. "The trees, the trees ..." Margaret murmured. The dream began to fade. She looked down across the packages she held at the dark hand that smoothed the golden hairs on her forearm. *I got those last summer when I swam so much.*

She straightened suddenly as the dream ended, trying to shake off the languor that held her while a strange, ugly man stroked her arm. She managed to jerk away from him, spilling the packages at her feet. He knelt with her to pick them up, his head so close to hers that she smelled his dirty, oily hair. The odor of it conjured up for her *(again?)* the small, cramped room and the bed with the thin mattress that never kept out the cold. Onions were browning in olive oil there over the gas plate. The man standing at the window with his back turned ... *He needed her; nobody else needed her in just that way. Besides, Mama had said to watch over Alberto. How could she leave him alone? But Mama was dead. ... And how could Mama know all the bad things Alberto had taught her?*

"Margaret." Don's voice called her rather sharply out of the dream that had again enveloped her. Margaret's sigh was like a half-sob. She laughed up at her husband, and he helped her to her feet, and gathered up the packages. The strange man was introducing himself to Don. He was Mr. Cravolini, the proprietor. He had seen that the lady was very pale, ready to faint, perhaps. He'd stepped up to assist her, unfortunately frightening her, since his step had not been heard—due, doubtless, to the great depth of the sawdust on the floor. Don, she saw, was listening to the overtones of the apology. If Mr. Cravolini's voice displayed the smallest hint of insolence and pride in the lies he was telling, then Don would grab him by the shirtfront and shake him till he stopped lying and begged for mercy. Don did not believe in fighting. Often while he and Margaret lay warmly and happily in bed together Don spoke regretfully of his "wild kid" days, glad that with maturity he need not prove on every street corner that he was not afraid to fight, glad to admit to Margaret that often he'd been scared, and always he'd been sick afterward. Don approved of social lies, the kind that permitted people to live and work together without too much friction. So Mr. Cravolini had made a mistake. Finding Margaret alone, he'd made a pass. He knew better now. OK. Forget it. Thus Margaret read her husband's face and buried very deeply the sharp, small stab of disappointment. *A fight would have ended it, for good.* She frowned a little with the effort to understand her own chaotic thoughts, her vision of a door that had almost closed on a narrow, stifling room, but was now wedged open . . . waiting.

Don led her down one of the long aisles of trees to where Bonnie and Bruce were huddled beside their choice. Margaret scarcely glanced at the tree. Don was annoyed with her— half-convinced, as he always was, that Margaret had invited the pass. Not by any overt signal on her part, but simply because she forgot to look busy and preoccupied.

"Don't go dawdling along in that wide-eyed dreamy way," he'd said so often. "I don't know what it is, but you've got that look—as if you'd say yes to a square meal or to a panhandler or to somebody's bed."

Bonnie was preening herself on the tree she'd chosen, chanting a maddening little refrain that Bruce would comprehend at any moment: "And Bru-cie did-unt he-ulp. . . ." Already Bruce recognized that the singsong words meant something scornful and destructive to his dignity. His face puckered, and he drew the three long breaths that preceded his best screaming.

Margaret hoisted him up into her arms, while Don and Bonnie hastily beat a retreat with the excuse that they must pay Mr. Cravolini for the tree. Bruce screamed his fury at a

world that kept trying to confine him, limit him, or otherwise
squeeze his outsized ego down to puny, civilized proportions.
Margaret paced up and down the aisles with him, wondering
why Don and Bonnie were taking so long.

Far back at the rear of the store building, where the lights
were dimmest, Margaret caught sight of a display of hand-
made candles. Still joggling Bruce up and down as if she
were churning butter, she paused to look them over. Four pale
blue candles of varying lengths rose gracefully from a flat
base molded to resemble a sheaf of laurel leaves. Very nice,
and probably very expensive. Margaret turned away to find
Mr. Cravolini standing immediately in front of her.

"Do you like those candles?" he asked softly.

"Where is my husband?" Margaret kept her eyes on
Bruce's fine blond hair. *Don't let the door open any more. . . .*

"You're husband has gone to bring his car. He and your
daughter. The tree is too large to carry so far. Why are you
afraid?"

"I'm not afraid. . . ." She glanced fleetingly into the man's
eyes, troubled again that her knowledge of his identity wavered just beyond reality. "Have we met before?" she asked.

"I almost saw you once," Cravolini said. "I was standing at
a window. You were reflected in it, but when I turned around
you were gone. There was nobody in the room but my sister
. . . the stupid cow. . . ." Cravolini spat into the sawdust. "That
day I made a candle for you. Wait." He reached swiftly behind the stacked packing boxes that held the candles on display. He had placed it in her hand before she got a clear look
at it. Sickeningly pink, loathsomely slick and hand-filling. It
would have been cleaner, more honest, she thought, if it had
been a frank reproduction of what it was intended to suggest.
She dropped it and ran awkwardly with the baby toward the
lights at the entranceway. Don was just parking the car. She
wrenched the door open and half fell into the front seat. Bonnie had rushed off with Don to bring out the tree. Margaret
buried her face in Bruce's warm, sweet-smelling neck and
nuzzled him till he laughed aloud. She never quite remembered afterward the ride home that night. She must have been
very quiet—in one of her "lost" moods, as Don called them.

The next morning she was surprised to see that Bonnie had picked one of Cravolini's largest, finest trees, and to discover the tissue-wrapped pale blue candles he had given Bonnie as a special Christmas gift.

Every year after that Margaret promised herself that this year she'd stay at home on the tree-buying night. But something always forced her to go—some errand, a last bit of shopping, or Don's stern injunctions not to be silly, that he could not handle Bonnie, Bruce, *and* the biggest tree in town. Once there, she never managed to escape Cravolini's unctuous welcome. If she sat in the car, then he came out to speak to her. Much better go inside and stick close by Don and the children. But that never quite worked, either. Somehow the three of them eluded her; she might hear their delighted shouts two aisles over, but when she hastened in their direction, she found only Cravolini waiting. She never eluded him. Sometimes on New Year's Day, when she heard so much about resolutions on radio and television, she thought that surely this year she'd tell Don at least some of the things Cravolini said to her—did to her—enough, anyway, to assure the Abbotts never going back there again. But she never did. It would be difficult to explain to Don why she'd waited so long to speak out about it. Why hadn't she told him that first night?

She could only shake her head in puzzlement and distaste for motivations that were tangled in a long, bad dream. And how could a woman of almost forty explain and deeply explore a woman in her twenties? Even if they were the same woman, it was impossible.

When Cravolini's "opening announcement" card arrived each year, Margaret was jolted out of the peacefulness that inevitably built in her between Christmases. It was as if a torn and raw portion of her brain healed in the interim. *But the door was still invitingly wedged open, and every Christmas something tried to force her inside.* Margaret's spirit fought the assailant that seemed to accompany Mr. Cravolini (hovering there beyond the lights, flitting behind the trees), but the fighting left her weak and tired and without any words to help her communicate her distress. If only Don would see, she thought.

If there were no need for words. It ought to be like that. . . . At such times she accused herself of indulging in Bruce's outgrown baby fury, crying out against things as they are.

Every time she saw Cravolini the dream gained in reality and continuity. He was very friendly with the Abbotts now. They were among his "oldest customers," privileged to receive his heartiest greetings along with the beautiful candles and wreaths he gave the children. Margaret had hoped this year that she could convince Bonnie and Bruce to have a different kind of tree—something modern and a little startling, perhaps, like tumbleweeds sprayed pink and mounted on a tree-shaped form. Anything. But they laughed at her bad taste, and were as horrified as if she were trying to bypass Christmas itself.

I wonder if I'll see *her* this year, Margaret thought. Alberto's sister. She knew so much about her now—that she was dumb, but that she had acute, morbidly sensitive hearing—that once she'd heard Cravolini murmuring his lust to Margaret, because that was the time the animal-grunting, laughing sounds had come from the back of the store, there where extra trees lay stacked against the wall. Her name was Angela, and she was very gross, very fat, very ugly. Unmarriageable, Alberto said. Part of what Margaret knew of Angela came from Alberto's whispered confidences (unwanted, oh unasked for!), and the rest grew out of the dream that lived and walked with Margaret there in the crumbling building, beginning the moment she entered the door, ending only with Don's voice, calling her back to sanity and to another life.

There were self-revelatory moments in her life with Don when Margaret was able to admit to herself that the dream had power to call her back. She would like to know the ending. It was like a too-short book that left one hungry and dissatisfied. So this year she gave way to the children, to tradition, and went once again to Cravolini's.

Margaret was aware that she looked her best in the dull red velveteen suit. The double golden hoops at her ears tinkled a little when she walked and made her feel like an arrogant gypsy. She and Don had stopped at their favorite small bar for several drinks while the children finished their shopping.

Maybe it's the drinks, Margaret thought, and maybe it's the

feeling that tonight, at last, I'll settle Mr. Cravolini that makes me walk so jut-bosomed and proud. Don, already on his way with her to Cravolini's, had dropped into a department store with the mumbled excuse that always preceded his gift-buying for Margaret. He had urged her to go on alone, reminding her that the children might be there waiting. For once, Margaret went fearlessly, almost eagerly.

The children were not waiting, but the woman was. *Angela.* Margaret knew her instantly, just as she'd known Alberto. Angela stared up and down at Margaret and did not bother to hide her amusement, or her knowledge of Margaret's many hot, protesting encounters with her brother. Margaret started to speak, but the woman only jerked her head meaningfully toward the back of the store. Margaret did not move. The dream was beginning. *Alberto is waiting, there beyond the stacked-high Christmas trees. See the soft, springy nest he has built for you with pine boughs.* Margaret stirred uneasily and began to move down the aisle, Angela beside her.

I must go to him. He needs me. Mama said to look after Alberto. That I would win for myself a crown in Heaven . . . Did she know how unnatural a brother Alberto is? Did she know how he learned the seven powers from the old, forbidden books? And taught them to me? He shall have what he desires, and so shall I. Here, Alberto, comes the proud, silly spirit you've won . . . and listen, Don and the children are coming in the door.

Margaret found the soft, springy bed behind the stacked trees. Alberto was there, waiting. She heard Don call for her and struggled to answer, struggled desperately to rise to go to him. But she was so fat, so heavy, so ugly. . . . She heard the other woman's light, warm voice answering, heard her happy, foolish joking with the children, her mock protestations, as always, at the enormous tree they picked. Margaret fought wildly and caught a last glimpse of the Abbotts, the four of them, and saw the dull red suit the woman wore, heard the final, flirtatious tinkling of the golden earrings, and then they were gone.

A whole year I must wait, Margaret thought, and maybe next year they won't come. She will see to that.

"My sister, my love . . ." Alberto crooned at her ear.

An SF confection for Christmas,
light as a snowflake.

SANTA RIDES A SAUCER
Donald A. Wollheim

UNDOUBTEDLY IT HAD been a perfect Christmas. An absolutely
perfect Christmas, even down to the last ultimate detail. That
is what bothers me. That is what makes me sometimes lie
awake nights afraid to face my thoughts. That is why I sometimes sit up in bed and stare silently into the darkness just
turning over that perfection in my mind. I don't think I can
stand much more of that kind of thing. I could put it all down
to imagination or hallucination or something save that it was
a perfect Christmas for Betsy and Zack and their mother as
well, asleep as she is in the next bed.

You can't talk that away. It was a perfect holiday for the little ones then, it simply was.

I am, I suppose, what you would call a happy man. That is,
I am comfortably well off, I do the kind of work I like, I have
a wonderful family, and I live in a wonderful old house in the
country. My house is in Montana, away out, far from the
town. It's a lovely old house, spacious as they go in that
country, large rooms, a wonderful old fireplace built by the
original rancher. We hand the kiddies' stockings on that fire-

place every Christmas Eve, in the big living room where the little evergreen is placed.

I suppose you could call me a gentleman astronomer. There are gentleman farmers, so I guess there can be gentleman astronomers. I don't have to depend on my work for my income. My piratical old grandfather stole enough land and cattle to keep all his descendants decently lazy. Not that I'm lazy—I'm an astronomer by profession, even though no one hires me.

My observatory is away from the house, and it's not large. Mainly I do variable-star observing, some planetoid checking, a good deal of speculative writing and theorizing. I've had a number of articles published speculating on life on other worlds. I've measured the heat of the lunar day from my little hillside cabin and I've probed the clouds of Venus with my instruments. I don't claim to have made any great discoveries. I have done little more than add some details to the work of Lowell and Pickering.

Anyway, that Christmas was the year of the flying saucers. Remember them? I didn't pay them very much attention. I never saw one and never expect to see them. The question of visitors from space didn't bother me. I'd come to the conclusion that probably there was life elsewhere in the universe, but I didn't expect it to be concerned with me. The kind of life I believe in outside this earth is concerned with perhaps some hardy conifer forests on Mars and some even hardier lichens in the depths of lunar craters.

Of course, it is true that some Sunday newspaper supplement had given me lurid—and wholly inaccurate—writeups naming me as the world's greatest authority on Martians, as the "Space-life Professor" and all that nonsense. I can't say my work has ever warranted anything like that, but you know reporters must eat.

The special perfection of that Christmas may have been due, in retrospect, to the appearance of the most lurid of these articles only the week before, in a nationally syndicated Sunday supplement that must have found its way into millions of homes. It played up the "mysterious solitude" of my home, labeled me the hermit-professor (a hermit with a wife and two robust kids!), and totally distorted my most recent contribution to a scientific journal wherein I gave some tables of really rather dry statistics on temperature variations of Jupiter's satellites.

Anyhow, that December 24 saw the end of a two-day snowfall, and left our house on Christmas Eve surrounded by a lovely blanket of rolling, soft white. In the distance, the trees stood up on the nearer hillside like scenes from a holiday card. The sky had cleared and the sun shone out of a pale blue sky on this white landscape. We were all snugly at home, didn't bother to dig out a path to the mailbox even. The evening was silent and clear. A half moon threw a deep blue light on the landscape. The stars twinkled sharply overhead. I was almost inclined to go to my observatory to take advantage of the night, but the holiday duties of a fond father quite prevented that.

The kiddies had been tucked into bed with our faithful promise that we'd awaken them early next morn. They had carefully hung their stockings by the mantelpiece over the fireplace, with our solemn assurances that Santa Claus would surely come and fill them. With Betsy and Zack asleep, Edith and I went to work setting up the little tree, decorating it. The presents for the children we had in a closet, ready to be slipped into position before the children awakened.

It takes time to do all this, and by ten-thirty we were both a little tired. Edith and I had ourselves some cake and coffee in the kitchen and then returned to the living room about half past eleven. We sat by the fireplace, chatting a little, resting happy in our home. We were proud of our children, little six-year-old Betsy and four-year-old Zachary. They still believed in the Santa Claus legend, though I wondered how long we could continue to foil Betsy's increasingly inquisitive mind.

I recall that Edith and I talked awhile about the curious Santa Claus legend. It certainly seems strange to believe that someone would come down every chimney of every house at the same time and leave presents. Yet children or many of them, do most positively believe in this. Imagine, I pointed out, an actual supernatural being, physically, in the flesh, coming into one's home. If you think about it as an adult, you can get goose pimples. It is certainly an odd folk notion for an atomic-age civilization to harbor!

Along about five minutes to midnight, I heard whispers up in the children's room. I glanced at Edith. It looked as if they were going to slip down and steal a peak at their Christmas tree at midnight. And we had not yet put their presents into their stockings!

The babes would catch us red-handed if we tried to do it now. Edith rose to the occasion. She was going to go upstairs and shoo the kiddies to bed again. Just then the old chimes clock in the hallway sounded the first stoke of midnight. There were joyful shrieks upstairs and we heard the two little ones' feet come pattering down the stairs, their voices shouting "Merry Christmas!"

It looked like complete disaster. Midnight, no presents distributed yet, and no Santa Claus. But . . .

Well, it was a perfect Christmas after all. We really had all received a wonderful assortment of gifts and we examined them with pleasure, and the kids with screams of delight all Christmas Day.

Among other things, for instance, Betsy had a doll that was so perfectly lifelike it almost fooled you. By pressing it in various ways, it would smile, blink its eyes, wave its hands, kick, squeak in varying tones, and do all but get up and walk. I admit that it also has some odd joints in its body, and it distinctly has six toes delineated on each little foot, but Betsy doesn't seem to mind.

Zachary had wanted some toy soldiers, knights in armor he had specified, for we had been reading to him of King Arthur. He got a set, a large set. They are not really knights, but they do belong to some medieval culture. They have armor of a sort, something like a cross between Old Japanese and Roman; they carry weapons something like halberds, but with little circular saws on top. They have helmets with odd wings and fancy flanges. Their faces are incredibly lifelike albeit a trifle bluish. The figures are about standard toy soldier size, have jointed arms, and I have found by watching Zachary that they are evidently unbreakable. He hit one squarely with a hammer. The floor dented, but the little figure didn't nor did its paint job even chip.

I have a fine new astronomical thermostat, which seems to be incredibly sensitive and whose inner construction I am afraid to meddle with, though I'm quite curious. And Edith has a new necklace of rather large bright beads, the nature of which I am afraid even to speculate on. I shall carry a pistol when I go to town to have it appraised.

The children were in ecstasies. Edith thinks it was something I arranged with a neighbor, and I haven't seen fit to say otherwise. But as for me, I am sitting up nights afraid to face my thoughts.

At the stroke of midnight, just as the children came whooshing down the stairs, there was a noise in the chimney, a sliding noise, and Santa Claus popped out of the fireplace. He was exactly as described. A shortish, plump little man, dressed in red with ermine trim, a white beard, jolly blue eyes, and red stocking cap, and a sack of toys.

While Edith and I stared goggle-eyed, the two children watched him with equal awe. He glanced at us, gave us a broad smile, winked at me, and started to fill the stockings with packages wrapped in green paper he took out of his sack. When he had finished, leaving the two for Edith and me on the mantelpiece itself, he turned, surveyed me steadily for a moment, took a copy of a printed journal out of his sack, handed it to me, bowed, and stepped into the fireplace. He fumbled with something in his clothes, and suddenly rose up the chimney and vanished. We heard a scrambling on the roof and a sudden rushing noise and he was gone.

The two kids recovered first. With screams of sheer joy, they pounced on their stockings and the packages lying in front of the tree. I think it was several minutes before Edith and I recovered our senses.

I am not sure yet what to make of it. I do suppose that Christmas Eve might seem a logical time for interplanetary visitors to pay a visit in a certain disguise to homes they wanted to inspect. The magazine Santa Claus handed me was merely a copy of my latest astronomical article, with certain of my temperature readings corrected in a green-colored ink.

The next morning, looking out of the window, I noticed that there were no tracks in the snow, no signs of automobile tires in the as yet uncleared road, nothing to indicate a visitor except a rather curious large saucer-shaped depression in the snow just outside the porch.

A cyber-Christmas for the whole family.

GRANDFATHER CHRISTMAS

Robert Frazier and
James Patrick Kelly

WE FOUND NICK while we were snooping in Grandma Brewster's attic. It was two days after the funeral and the grownups still weren't paying any attention to us. We could hear them down in the living room, yelling at each other. This time the argument was about Grandma's furniture. Mom claimed nobody would pay $10,000 for the Hepplewhite sideboard, and Aunt Francie said then we'd have to sell off the portrait of sea captain Tristram Olaf Brewster, which Grandma had loaned to the Nantucket Whaling Museum. When Grandma was alive, no one dared raise their voice in this house. Especially on Christmas Eve.

"We shouldn't be doing this," said my cousin Aggie. She sat cross-legged on Grandma's bed, watching entry menus flash across the windowall.

"I know," I said. "That's what makes it fun."

"But what if they find out?"

"They're busy. Listen to them."

"I don't get it. Grandma was rich, so what's the problem?

Besides, if they sell off all her furniture, what are we going to use here?"

I'd tried once before to get into the attic's upper-level files. I tricked the scuzzy driver with the BugUgly utility. I tried patching Dad's Ultrabook through a jumperop cable. I even hit caps-shift-escape with my left hand, enter-alt-home with my right, and F6 with my nose. But it wasn't a hardware problem; I was up against a software encryption lock. Grandma Brewster was old-fashioned about everything but security for her homebrain. She'd encrypted her attic with some kind of public key/private key system.

Of course, Grandma had caught me. She told me little girls shouldn't snoop. I told her I wasn't a little girl anymore but I don't think she was ready to admit that to herself. "You'll just have to wait until you're older, Twilla," she said. "I promise I'll give you complete access someday." Well, I was a freshman in high school now and Grandma was in a bronze urn in the hall closet and I needed to find out what was wrong with her will.

"They'll check the homebrain's log." Aggie was squeamish about bending rules, even for an eighth grader.

"It'll show us playing Witch Cop. I've got it faking moves."

"My mom will ground me until it's *my* funeral," said Aggie. "She's been pretty hard to live with since Dad moved out. And now . . ."

"No offense, Aggie, but your mom's been hard to live with as long as I can remember."

Aggie twisted a strand of her perfect blond hair. "You know, I loved Grandma a lot, and I'm going to miss her and everything . . . but I have this weird feeling." She glanced at me and then back at the windowall. "Like I'm kind of mad at her."

"For dying?"

She nodded.

"Yeah," I said, "especially for when she died. Because from now on, her death is going to be part of Christmas."

I finally reached the attic door. When I tried to open it, the lock icon flashed and Grandma's homebrain prompted

me for the passkey. Obviously, Aunt Francie had been
expecting me. I pulled down the symbol menu and typed
🐚▷✉▷📖♒☺. A silver key appeared next to the
door.

"Hey, where did you get the passkey from?"

"Grandma." I touched my finger to the key and moved it to
the lock icon. "I found it in my secret place, the day we got
here." Each of us had private drop-offs where Grandma
would leave notes and candy and even money sometimes.
Mine was in the blue teapot on the mantel in the Federal parlor. "Here we go." The door opened and we were in. Aggie
moaned as I went to full zoom on the wall.

"See," I said, "most of it is junk." I surfed across the neat
waves of icons. There were to-do calendars that went back to
the last century, tax returns, digitized family pictures, garden
layouts, recipes, lots of old, old E-books. "You ever hear of
Bret Easton Ellis?"

"Twil, this is making my stomach hurt."

"Like when we peeked in the coffin and Grandma's skin
was all droopy like wax?"

"Twil!"

"Look, here's her calendar." I opened it. In the three weeks
she had been in the hospital, Grandma had missed the Christmas Stroll, the Barretts' anniversary party at Chanticleer, and
a concert at the Chamber Music Center. I didn't see any last-
minute meetings with her lawyer, but there *was* one mystery.

"Hey, remember this?"

There was an icon with Nick's face pasted to December 19.
Nicolas Cleary had been Grandma Brewster's second husband, Mom and Aunt Francie's stepfather. He was bald on top
with salt-and-pepper short hair and big sideburns. His pudgy
face was grooved by wrinkles. He had a little white mustache.

I hadn't seen his virt in years. When I was a little kid, she
used to boot him when the whole family flew in for Christmas on Nantucket. It was a tradition, like baking reindeer
cookies with red and green sprinkles and decorating trees on
the windowall and Grandma's inedible sour cranberry sauce.
Then one year she didn't bring him up. She said something
about how he wasn't right. I thought that meant that his pro-

gram was corrupted or decayed. So why schedule him again after all this time? I touched his icon.

First a blur, then his full figure came into focus, frame by slow frame, speeding up so that the image no longer looked like a oozy movement of bees. He was dressed in khakis and a red-and-black flannel shirt. His face was smooth: no wrinkles or mustache.

"Margaret, I need a new compression algorithm," he said. "Feel like I've been sleeping under the dock." He stretched and when he extended a holographic arm out from the wall, I could hear the AV circuits hum. Then he saw me at Grandma's terminal. "Who the hell are you?"

"Twilla."

"Ellen's girl? I thought you were in fourth grade."

I was insulted. "I'm in high school."

"What's the date?"

"December 24, 2019."

"Oh my God, six years." He morphed briefly into the figure from Munch's *The Scream*. "She hasn't booted me for six goddamn years. And who's that, Agatha June?"

"Hi, Gramps." Aggie was beaming. She'd been Nick's pet when he was alive and his virt had continued to spoil her. "I thought you crashed."

"Who said that—not your grandmother? Where is she?"

"Oops," I said softly.

"Something's wrong." His image degraded into the bee swarm and then solidified again, rumpled and out of breath. He looked as if he had just fallen down the front stairs. "I can't get into the rest of the memory. I'm restricted." His hair stood on end, stretched beyond the screen limits of the wall. "Margaret!" He called in a voice almost loud enough for Grandma to hear. "I didn't mean it!"

"Sssh! Nick, keep it down."

"Agatha June Duffbart." Aunt Frances stood in the doorway, a vision of Christmas hell in her red pumps, a dress programmed to holly in a snowstorm, and red wingtip glasses. "What is going on here?"

I said, "We were just playing Witch Cop, and I cast this

opening spell at Sing Sing and all of a sudden we were in . . . in this."

"Is this true, Agatha June?"

I doubted Aggie could stand up to her mother's interrogation for long. "Check the log," I said in our defense.

Nick's face filled the wall completely. "Francie, what's going on here? Something's happened to your mother."

"I'll take care of this." Aunt Francie nudged in front of me, taking my place at the terminal. "Leave the room, you two."

Aggie looked surprised. "What are you doing?"

"Twilla, Agatha June, go now! And shut the door behind you."

If I had known what she planned to do, I would never have left. But I thought we'd have a better chance selling the Witch Cop alibi if we went into good-girl mode. Besides, I didn't want to be there when Aunt Francie broke the news to Nick. It didn't take her long.

"Did he cry?" said Aggie.

"What did you tell him?" I said.

"I didn't tell *it* anything," she said coldly. "I wiped it from the system."

I could not believe this creature was related to me. She had about as much Christmas spirit as a salad fork.

"Y-You . . ." I stammered. "You bitch." I knew it was trouble but I couldn't help myself.

She glared at me. I turned it right back at her, certain that I'd never seen Nick again.

Dad found me on the ledge of the third-floor hall window, staring across the harbor at the beacon of Great Point Light, as it stretched through the night like a white finger. He wriggled through the casing and sat beside me. He didn't say anything at first, just swung his legs in the chilly air and pulled his cashmere sport jacket tight around him. It was the kind of thing only Dad would do. Mom was a worrier; she would've lectured me about how I was risking my life. Aunt Francie probably would've shut the window on me.

"You know," Dad said finally. "Grandma always said she liked winter better than the summer on the island. It wasn't

just that the tourists all went home. She said she could see
things more clearly in cold air."

"Yeah, right. I guess now we can all see a certain person
for what she really is."

"No need to be antagonistic."

"Sorry, but that woman makes me want to puke."

"Okay." He nodded. "But try to look at things from her
point of view. She feels like everything's happening to her at
once. First the divorce, then her mother dies . . ."

"Hey, she was my *Grandma*."

". . . and now she's in a panic over the estate."

"So she gets to yell at us whenever she wants? Dad, she's
ruining my Christmas."

"She's family and she's hurting, okay? We have to make an
effort to get along."

I hated arguing with Dad; he could see the good side to
anything. "So why is she so worried? Is there some problem
with the will?"

"The will?" He looked surprised. "No. Your mom and
Francie split everything down the middle, whatever there is of
it. The problem is that . . . well, your grandma liked to keep
secrets. Which is why her finances are a mess. Poor Francie
feels like *she* has to clean things up."

"Is that what she calls wiping Nick? Cleaning up?"

He sighed, his breath puffing in the cold. "Keep a family
secret?"

I nodded.

"You were too little to realize this, but Francie never had
any use for Nick. Not while he was alive, especially not for
his virt. But she put up with it for Grandma's sake."

"So now I'm supposed to put up with her?" I snorted, then
picked at the laces of my hightops. "She just doesn't like me,
Dad. Remember that time with the candy dish?"

"Is it my imagination or are we freezing to death out
here?" He shivered. "Look, there's a skim of ice on the harbor."

"I'm not groveling to her."

"I wasn't asking you to."

"What are you asking?"

"Just that we eat dinner in peace."

I considered this. "I can stop if she stops."

"Thanks." In the light of a beacon flash, I could see Dad's smile. "Oh, I guess I was supposed to do something about your . . . um . . . choice of language."

I stiffened. "Like what?"

He patted me on the back. "Francie made Grandma's special sour cranberry sauce. I want you to take some."

"I am *not* eating that . . . stuff."

"Then push it around a little," he said. "Just having it on your plate is punishment enough." As he wiggled back into the hallway, his jacket snagged on the head of a nail and ripped a pocket. "Wouldn't you know it?" he said.

The Fabfood cranked out the same dinner we'd had every Christmas Eve since forever: turkey with gravy, allnut stuffing, both sweet and mashed-flavored potatettes, butter broccoli bits. But everything else was different. I kept counting all the people who weren't there. Grandma, of course. Uncle Tom, Aggie's dad, who used to burp wisps of black smoke after dinner because of his enzyme problem. And flickery old Nick, who I hadn't missed for years.

I tried to be polite. Maybe Aunt Francie did too, but if you ask me she didn't try halfway hard enough. I think it had become a Brewster Christmas tradition that the two of us fight. Meanwhile Aggie was busy being sullen—no help there. Mom wanted to tell stories about when she and Franice were girls living on the island, which always seemed to end with Francie saving the day. Dad talked about the food, the weather, the elections, and all the boring shows he'd seen on the Archeology Channel.

As dinner was winding down, Aunt Francie really got into it. She insisted that Aggie and I account for every nanosecond we'd been in the attic.

"And you're sure you didn't erase anything?" she asked.

"I'm sure," I said. "Are you? After all, it was *your* finger on the delete key."

"Well," she said to my mom huffily, "they're not in any

memory I can access. I was sure she'd tucked them somewhere in the attic."

"What are you looking for?" I said. "Maybe I can help."

Aunt Francie looked back at me, squinting as if I were
some germ she was seeing through a microscope. "Just some
financial files we need to clear up Grandma's estate," she
said.

"Oh," I said, "you mean really important stuff I'm too stupid to understand?"

"We think she must've hidden her assets," said Mom.
"There's no way she could have afforded to live on what
we've found so far."

Aunt Francie went back to picking on Aggie. "I still don't
understand why you didn't buzz us immediately."

"What's immediately mean?" I interrupted her.

"As soon as he appeared. It's not your business to talk to
him."

"Not my business?" said Aggie. "He was my grandpa."

"Mine, too!" I said.

"I've told you before, Aggie," said Aunt Francie icily.
"Your grandfather was Grandpa John. My father."

"Who none of us ever knew," I said.

Mom and Aunt Francie exchanged glances. "Aggie," said
Aunt Francie, "we've just buried your grandmother. We're in
the middle of trying to settle her business. And we're having
a hard enough time without that . . . that graphical bigmouth
distracting us." When she frowned, I could see little lines
around her mouth, like someone had yanked a purse string
tight. Aunt Francie was six years older and twelve times
meaner than Mom. "Nick is dead," she said. "A virt is software, not a person. It shouldn't make demands."

"The truth is," Mom said, "that he—the virt—was driving
Grandma crazy." Mom pushed a glob of purple cranberry
sauce across her plate. "He claimed he really was Nick. He
wanted to be left on all year long, said he needed a virtual address, network access, everything. He . . . it preyed on her
memories until finally she told me that she never what to see
it again as long as she lived. She decided not to boot him and
she had every right to do it. He belonged to her."

"Then why didn't *she* erase him?" I said. "Why did she put him back on her calendar?"

"Ellen, would you please control your daughter?" Aunt Francie fixed me with a withering stare. "All this back talk is a bad influence on Aggie."

"Look," said Mom, "we've all be under a lot of stress. . . ."

"Maybe that's your excuse," I said, "but your big sister has been bullying this family for years."

Aunt Francie's eyes bulged.

"Speaking of dressing . . ." Dad passed his plate.

"I do not bully people."

"No?" I said with dramatic pause. "Then tell us why you've blocked incoming access to the house?"

That pricked up Dad's ears. "Is that true, Frances? My contract with the firm says twenty-four hours on call, no exceptions."

"It can't be helped. We can't have anyone trying a file recovery on that virt."

I said, "What?"

Francie pointed at Mom. "I think your daughter stole the passkey. My guess is that she had outside help. I'm not letting her or any of her criminal friends tinker any further with our affairs."

I waited for Mom to stand up for me; I might as well have been waiting for a present from the King of England.

"Francie," said Dad, "for Christ's sakes."

I picked up my plate; we were eating off Grandma's best china. I was thinking of using some of it to express just how much I enjoyed these cozy family reunions when Aggie swooped by. She took the plate, slid it under hers, gathered my silverware and stacked it carefully on the pile of dishes.

"Twilla promised to help me with my hair after dinner." She kicked my chair hard. "We can get *out* to the net, can't we?"

I looked to Aunt Francie. She grumbled, "Yes."

"Then I'm finished."

Mom nodded. "We'll trim the tree in the morning."

We were dismissed. I knew that Aggie had saved me just

in time. I could feel steam in my ears, poison beading under my nails.

Mom was right about one thing. Grandma's death had been a strain on us all. She could be just as headstrong as Aunt Francie but, like Mom, she listened when you talked to her. She had glued the two halves of the family together. So I thought it was strange when nobody cried at the funeral except Aggie. I kept waiting for Mom to cry, so I could. She was probably waiting for Francie; Mom wasn't herself when she was with her big sister.

I said as much to Aggie. We were sitting on the edge of the four-poster in the kids' room looking at ourselves mirrored on the windowall. We had linked the homebrain to HairNet and were trying on new styles.

"Yeah," said Aggie. "I don't know what's gotten into my Mom either. Believe me, she's usually not wound this tight. I mean, remember last Christmas? When she had the silly stocking cap on and she was dancing around the living room with a holo of some old movie guy . . ."

"Tom Travolta."

"Yeah, and everyone was laughing at her. She was laughing too, remember?"

"Grandma put that hat on her."

We sat there for a moment thinking about all the differences between this Christmas and last. On the windowall a cartoon hairdresser turned Aggie's hair candy-cane red.

"Want to see what Grandma left in *my* secret place?" said Aggie. She offered me a pair of dangle earrings, sculpted into a cascade of silver water. The bubbles in the cascade looked like tiny diamonds.

I held them up to the light. "They're really beautiful." I was jealous.

"Yeah," she said, "and they make me feel really guilty. I've been thinking maybe I should turn them over to Mom. Maybe they're worth something."

I arranged them on the bedspread in front of her. "Grandma left them to *you*."

"It's not like I really need more earrings." She picked them up. "Or any of this moldy old furniture either." She poured them from one hand to another. "But Twil, they wouldn't sell Grandma's house, would they?"

"They wouldn't dare," I said, but it felt like a lie. Selling your favorite place in the whole world was exactly the kind of thing grown-ups did to kids. I wanted to say something to cheer Aggie up, but I didn't know what.

Sitting in that room made me remember summer nights when Grandma used to tell me bedtime stories. She'd always change the main character to me. Twilla and the Beanstalk. Or she would make stories up. Brave Little Twilla and the Elephant Boy of Oz—I'd been astonished. Twilla's Christmas Wish. I'd be tucked right in this very bed, the sea murmuring outside, the foghorn bleating out on Brant Point. I brushed my hand across the patchwork quilt she had made before I was born and realized I wanted it for myself. I wanted to take it home and pull it around me when the wind howled through the streets of Boston. Whenever I needed to remember how my Grandma Brewster loved her best little girl.

"Your eyelighter is running." Aggie pulled a Kleenex. "Left side."

I took it. "Thanks."

"You better watch out," said the hairdresser on the windowall. "You better not cry. You better not pout, I'm telling you why." The cartoon morphed into Nick. "You-know-who is coming to town."

"Gramps!" said Aggie.

"Ho-ho-ho!" he said.

"How did you survive?" I would've hugged him, only how do you hug a electron pattern on a windowall?

"That was just an alias file Francie erased. When you told me I'd been archived so long, I dumped my real self into Worldnet and ran. But I've got problems, girls. The failsafes on the net are snooping after me and if they catch me, I'm dead as last year's batteries. I need a place to hide out. And there's no place like home for the holidays."

"Aunt Francie has shut down all incoming to the house," I said. "All we can get is read-only."

"Sánta taught me a couple new tricks." He twirled his mustache. "If you can just get me Francie's private key code, I'll edit everything out of the log."

I turned to Aggie.

"Oh, no," she said. "We'll get in trouble again."

I stared an icicle at her.

"Okay, okay, never mind." She pushed me away. "Just go away while I enter it?" I stood by the window and listened to the clack of keys. "Voice override on the com port two," she said, "revert to default for three seconds and then undo revert." Then for my benefit, she muttered, "So what if I spend high school chained to a doorknob?"

The wall shimmered like the surface of the harbor in a light breeze. Then Nick was standing between us, a filmy hologram projected from the windowall. He was wearing a Santa suit and was carrying a sack. "Thanks." When he moved, he trailed rainbows. "For a minute I was afraid you were going to tell me there was no room at the inn."

He put the sack down and started rummaging through it, muttering to no one in particular. "I have something." He brought a photo in a gold frame to the top of the bag. "No," he said, as if reminding himself, "this is for Frances." I only saw it for a second; it looked like some bride and groom standing in a garden. "Something else. Where the hell did I . . . oh, want to see what I got for Twilla's dad? He's the archeology nut, right?" He showed us a cube with a lion sculpted on it. "Opens into a scale model of Persepolis. All the palaces, temples, tombs, treasure-houses, even furniture." He reached deeper into the bag. "Tidings of comfort and joy," he sang under his breath, "comfort and . . . *ah*!" He came up with a handful of icons and threw them in our direction. They passed through us and rang like coins as they hit the windowall and stuck there. All the latest vids: *Great Red Spot, Gertie and the Virties, Street French, Girls Live Girls, Bobby Science Down Under.*

Aggie touched the lump on Bobby Science's neck reverently. She had been in love ever since he'd had his larynx replaced with a twenty-thousand-voice synthesizer.

"You like this stuff?" said Nick. "I was lurking on some empty tracks in a recording studio and it just stuck to me."

"It's great," I said, "but how did you pay for them?"

"I'd better find a place to bed down." He yawned and stretched. "In case someone comes looking for me."

"Try Grandma's recipes," said Aggie. "There are lots of dead files to hide in."

Nick's face lost expression for a moment. "Dead files? Guess that's appropriate."

I said, "Nick, you did *pay* for those vids."

He picked up the sack, slung it over his shoulder. "Ssh! What's that?" He gaped at us in astonishment. I froze, expecting the data cops or Aunt Francie to kick in the door. "Listen." He pointed at the ceiling.

"I don't hear anything." Aggie flattened herself against a wall so she could peek out the dormer window. "Where?"

"On the roof. Sounds like . . . *reindeer*." And then he was gone, his faint *ho-ho-ho* echoing into silence.

"He's such a lunatic," said Aggie. She was laughing as she went to the terminal to make hard copies of the vids for herself. I wonder if she might be right. Maybe some of his files *had* been corrupted.

Or maybe he was the one who was corrupt.

I knew Aggie was asleep because she started making that little clicking sound in the back of her throat when she breathed. But as soon as I eased the covers off, Grandma's house started scolding me. Bedsprings creaked, floorboards moaned, doorknobs rattled, hinges squealed. It took me almost ten minutes to get upstairs to Grandma's bedroom without waking everybody up. It would have been quicker to use one of the downstairs terminals but I needed the privacy.

"Nick," I whispered.

He wandered onto the windowall in an old-fashioned night-shirt and a stocking cap. He was carrying a candle and his eyes were all squinchy, like he'd been asleep. I knew better; he was software.

" 'Twas the night before Christmas," he said, "when all through the house, not a creature was stirring, except Twilla the mouse."

"The louse," I said. "Twilla, the louse who let you in. Who are you?"

He brought the candle closer, as if to see me better. "I'm your Grampa Nick."

I shook my head. "It's okay to pretend with Aggie, she's still a kid. You're not Nick. The question is, are you really his virt?"

"How would I know so much about you all if I wasn't?"

"Virts don't steal stuff."

"I didn't steal anything," he said calmly. "I paid good money for those presents."

"Virts don't buy stuff either. Virts are like home videos. You're supposed to watch them and remember with them and feel good and that's all. They don't mess with your life."

"Look, Twilla. Your Grandpa Nick knew about the cancer for a long time. He spent the last three years of his life getting ready to be dead. Making me. Cost him a fortune. He recorded hundreds of hours of reminiscences, loaded every experience he could simulate into the attic. The recipes, for example. His investment strategies. All his books. He wrote down his dreams every night. He didn't want to be just another ornament to be tucked away with the Nutcracker on the Saturday after New Year's. He wanted to cram as much of his mind into this attic as possible. He wanted to be conscious, to be himself."

"Did it work?"

He considered. "No." He shrugged, then closed his hand around the candle, which disappeared. "I'm not going to lie to you. I'm conscious all right, but I'm not exactly Nicolas Cleary." The nightshirt morphed into a business suite; the windowall changed into a mirror image of Grandma's bedroom. Nick's bedroom. "There's too much missing, spaces I have to fill in my own way. As I do, I become someone new. Or at least I would if that goddamned woman hadn't put me on a shelf for six years." He settled on the edge of the bed.

I was angry with him, with Grandma, my family and all their secrets, this whole rotten Christmas. "So what am I supposed to do with you?"

"Nothing, tonight. We'll sort this out in the morning. I'm

working on a plan. So get some sleep, sweetheart. Do you know what time it is?"

"Half past my bedtime?"

He winked. "Merry Christmas." And switched off.

I punched him back up.

"What plan?"

"I need to work on the Grinch, find a way to keep her from stealing Christmas."

"Aunt Francie? She hates you."

"And I've never understood why. Your Grandmother loved me, your mom. I took good care of them all—just look at this house."

"This is Grandma's house."

"Fa-la-la-la-la-la-la-la-la." He shrank himself into a Christmas star. "Whose side are you on, Twill?" He twinkled and began to drift slowly off the wall.

I let him go. It was a good question.

The kids' ornament time was a Brewster tradition that supposedly stretched back to the days of Captain Tristram. Before we opened presents on Christmas morning, the youngest member of each family brought a new ornament to put on the tree. We sat around the huge windowall in the living room, a screen fourteen feet tall and twenty feet wide. Dad set the program on auto. The graphic built slowly. The trunk pushed up from the floor and branched out limbs which sprouted needles. Lights blinked, tinsel glittered and the boughs bent under the imaginary weight of ornaments we had already hung. The homebrain breathed the scent of crushed balsam through the heating vents. Mom and Aunt Francie *ooed* and *awwed* like silly little girls as piles of soft presents appeared under the tree beside the hard presents scattered in front of the wall.

I hadn't gotten enough sleep and so I was pretty cranky when Dad began his speech. "Okay, you all know what today is. Christmas is a time when we put aside our personal differences."

"Got that, Aunt Francie?" I said.

"Twilla." I could tell Dad was disappointed in me.

"I think we should get on with it," said Aunt Francie, "Aggie, do you have something for us?"

Aggie stood and went to the wall. She held up one of the dangle earrings. "This was Grandma's. She gave it to me." She turned, picked a spot high on the tree, and held the earring to it long enough for the homebrain to make a copy.

"Twilla?" said Mom.

I stalked up to the wall and flattened my palm against it. Grandma had given the earrings to Aggie, the attic passkey to me. The way I figured it, she must have wanted me to find the icon she had pasted onto December 19. "Now, Nick," I said. When I pulled my hand away, his icon hung from the tree.

Aunt Francie tried to stand but Mom forced her back down with a firm push on the shoulder. Aggie's eyes were as big as sugar cookies. Dad looked grim.

"You forgot somebody." I watched as the icon expanded into Nick, then projected out as a hologram pacing the room. He was wearing his Santa suit again and he had his bag of presents. He was paler than he'd been yesterday; his colors needed more saturation. He looked about as tense as I felt.

"I'm sorry to barge in like this," he said. "I spent last night hiding in Margaret's sour-cranberry-sauce recipe, trying to think of what to say to you all. We have to talk."

He walked toward Aunt Francie, then right through where she sat on the couch. She twitched. "No, we don't."

"Yes, we do," said Aggie. I was proud of her.

Nick walked into the end table that held our glasses and a pitcher of eggnog. The pitcher fell. Mom went to catch it and then froze as it passed through her hands and disappeared. The real pitcher stayed in place on the table. "You see, I need a place to stay, a permanent place. I don't want to be shut down anymore and I need access to the net. That's all. And I'm willing to pay my way."

Aunt Francie snorted. "With what?"

"Your mother and I always kept our money separate, Frances. She insisted, even though she was not a rich woman. Before I died I set up a trust and named her as sole beneficiary. She had complete use of the income for as long as she lived, although she couldn't touch the principal. Now that she's dead, I intend to make use of the trust."

"You can't," said Aunt Francie. "You have no legal status. In fact, as part of mother's estate, you belong to us. We own you."

He swelled into a giant; his head slipped in and out of the chandelier as he nodded. "Me, but not my trust. The trustees are instructed to dissolve it and donate the proceeds to charity should my master file be lost or corrupted."

"So that's how she could afford to keep this place," said Mom. "God knows what she spent all her own money on, but at least she could count on Nick's trust. Otherwise she would've had to sell Brewster House years ago."

"I knew it." I was furious at her. "You are going to sell this house."

"Mom," said Aggie, "Grandma promised that someday I could bring *my* kids here in the summer."

"This isn't a cottage, Aggie." Aunt Francie slumped dejectedly against the couch. "It's a mansion. After we get done paying the estate taxes . . ."

"Which brings me to my proposal." Nick shrank back to normal size. "Or should I call it my Christmas present? What if I cover the tax, pay you rent, and live here in the attic? You own the house; use it whenever you want. I'll manage my portfolio and stay out of your way, although I'd like permission to visit the girls. Oh, and one of you will have to act as my agent since I can't enter into contracts or make transactions by myself."

"It's not fair." Aunt Francie muttered, almost as if she were talking to herself. "There's nothing left, nothing but the house. She should've warned me she'd spent all her money. Maybe I could've done something."

"Nick's got the answer," said Mom. "It works, Francie."

"Nick," Aunt Francie said. "It's always *Nick* to the rescue, isn't it? He bought his way into this family, you know. You were too little to understand but I was there. Dad wasn't even dead a year, less than a goddamned year, when he moved in."

"Francie." Mom put an arm around her. I wasn't sure

whether she was comforting her or holding her back. The rest of us just watched, speechless.

"Well, it's true." Her voice was very small. Wounded. Then it was as if she realized what she had just said, because she covered her face with her hands and broke down. I had never seen Aunt Francie cry; it was scary. For the first time I realized that grown-ups are nothing but big kids with jobs. Nick, plain Nick in a gray suit, cocked his head and stared out at all of us with an odd choked smile. I wished I were on the other side of the wall with him.

"You're right, Francie," said Mom. "I never knew Dad. I wish I had. But Nick was a good father to me." I was stunned; I never would have expected my mom to save the day. "I think we should accept his present. It's Christmas, after all. Time to put differences aside." Maybe when Aunt Francie shrank, she made more room for Mom.

All told Aunt Francie allowed herself about three nanoseconds to feel her feelings. Then she drew her hands slowly down her face, fingertips digging the tears out of the wrinkles. When she looked at us she was Mom's big sister again. The head of the Brewster family. "I agree" was all she said.

What we were supposed to do next was open presents. So we did, grateful to be saved from ourselves by Christmas tradition. There's nothing like unwrapping a truckload of new stuff to make you forget your troubles. They gave me four shirts, two sweaters, and a nice skirt, which I probably won't ever wear because no one wears skirts at my school. Plus 3DTress, the fashion AI, and fifty hours on Worldnet. Aunt Francie gave Aggie the same Bobby Science vid that she'd gotten from Nick, but she didn't say anything. She seemed even more pleased than when Nick gave it to her. Dad's favorite present was his model of Persepolis; he was still playing with it during the Notre Dame game on New Year's Day. I thought we were going to have another disaster when Nick gave Aunt Francie his present. It was a wedding picture of Grandma and Grandpa John, Mom and Francie's father. Aunt Francie glanced at it and smiled and thanked him and then quickly reached for another package. I could tell that she was either touched or upset at herself for being touched, but she had shown us all the emotion we were going to see from her that day—or maybe that decade.

When we were finished, the floor was scattered with enough paper to wrap the ferry and Nick had been squeezed into 2D by a landslide of blinking icons. Our family had single-handedly saved the Massachusetts economy once again. Aunt Francie and Dad went off to the kitchen to program lunch.

"Jesus, Mary, and Joseph!" Nick staggered backward across the windowall, merging with the tree. "So that's what she did with it."

"Who?" said Mom. "What?"

"I've just found the rest of Margaret's money. Or rather, it has found us."

"Great," I said.

"Maybe not." He looked like someone who had just seen a ghost. "Someone release the restriction on incoming data, please. Oh, that woman did love her secrets."

Mom went to the terminal and set it to revert to default. Part of the wall started to sparkle; it looked like a diamond the size of a door.

"It's about time you let me into my own house," said the sparkle. Then it resolved into a person. "Where's my sauce? We always have my sour cranberry sauce."

"Hi, Grandma!" Aggie squealed.

"Well, Margaret?" said Nick.

"Oh, Nick," Grandma said.

"Twilla," said Mom, her voice brittle as a glass angel. "Would you please ask your aunt to step in here?"

You figure it out.

The Outpost Undiscovered by Tourists

A Tale of Three Kings and a Star for This Sacred Season

Harlan Ellison

THEY CAMPED JUST beyond the perimeter of the dream and waited for first light before beginning the siege.

Melchior went to the boot of the Rolls and unlocked it. He rummaged about till he found the air mattress and the inflatable television set, and brought them to the cleared circle. He pulled the cord on the mattress and it hissed and puffed up to its full size, king size. He pulled the plug on the television set and it hissed and firmed up and he snapped his fingers and it turned itself on.

"No," said Kaspar, "I will not stand for it! Not another night of roller derby. A King of Orient I are, and I'll be *damned* if I'll lose another night's sleep listening to those barely primate creatures dropkicking each other!"

Melchior glowed with his own night light. "So sue me," he said, settling down on the air mattress, tidying his moleskin cape around him. "You know I've got insomnia. You know I've got a strictly awful hiatus hernia. You know those *latkes* are sitting right here on my chest like millstones. Be a person for a change, a *mensch*, it couldn't hurt just once."

Kaspar lifted the chalice of myrrh, the symbol of death, and shook it at Melchior. "Hypochondriac! That's what you are, a fake, a fraud. You just like watching those honkytonk bimbos punching each other out. Hiatus hernia, my fundament! You'd watch mud wrestling and extol the esthetic virtues of the balletic nuances. Turn it off . . . or at least, in the name of Jehovah, get the Sermonette."

"The ribs are almost ready," Balthazar interrupted. "You want the mild or the spicy sauce?"

Kaspar raised his eyes to the star far above them, out of reach but maddeningly close. He spoke to Jehovah: "And this one goes ethnic on us. Wandering Jew over there drives me crazy with the light that never dims, watches institutionalized mayhem all night and clanks all day with gold chains . . . and Black-is-Beautiful over there is determined I'll die of tertiary heartburn before I can even find the Savior. Thanks, Yahweh; thanks a lot. Wait till *you* need a favor."

"Mild or spicy?" Balthazar said with resignation.

"I'd like mine with the mild," Melchior said sweetly. "And just a *bissel* apple sauce on the side, please."

"I want dimsum," Kaspar said. His malachite chopsticks materialized in his left hand, held far up their length indicating he was of the highest caste.

"He's only being petulant," Melchior said. "He shouldn't annoy, Balthazar sweetie. Serve them cute and tasty ribs."

"Deliver me," Kaspar murmured.

So they ate dinner, there under the star. The Nubian king, the Scrutable Oriental king, and the Hebrew king. And they watched the roller derby. They also played the spelling game called *ghost*, but ended the festivity abruptly and on a rancorous note when Balthazar and Melchior ganged up on Kaspar using the word "pringles," which Kaspar contended was *not* a generic but a specific trade name. Finally they fell asleep, the television set still talking to itself, the light from Melchior reflecting off the picture tube.

In the night the star glowed brightly, calling them on even in their sleep. And in the night early warning reconnaissance troops of the Forces of Chaos flew overhead flapping their leathery bat-wings and leaving in their wake the hideous car-

barn monoxide stench of British Leyland double-decker
buses.

When Melchior awoke in the morning his first words were,
"In the night, who made a ka-ka?"

Balthazar pointed. "Look."

The ground was covered with the permanent shadows of
the bat-troops that had flown overhead. Dark, sooty shapes of
fearsome creatures in full flight.

"I've always thought they looked like the flying monkeys
in the 1939 MGM production of *The Wizard of Oz*, special effects by Arnold Gillespie, character makeup created by Jack
Dawn," Kaspar said ruminatively.

"Listen, Yellow Peril," Balthazar said, "you can exercise
that junkheap memory for trivia later. Unless the point is lost
on you, what this means is that they know we're coming and
they're going to be ready for us. We've lost the element of
surprise."

Melchior sighed and added, "Not to mention that we've
been following the star for exactly one thousand nine hundred
and ninety-nine years, give or take a fast minute, which unless they aren't too clever should have tipped them off we
were on the way some time ago."

"Nonetheless," said Kaspar, and fascinated by the word he
said it again, "nonetheless."

They waited, but he didn't finish the sentence.

"And on that uplifting note," Balthazar said, "let us get in
the wind before they catch us out here in the open."

So they gathered their belongings—Melchior's caskets of
Krugerrands, his air mattress and inflatable television set,
Kaspar's chalice of myrrh, his Judy Garland albums and
fortune-cookie fortune calligraphy set, Balthazar's wok, his
brass-bound collected works of James Baldwin and hair-
conking outfit—and they stowed them neatly in the boot of
the Rolls.

Then, with Balthazar driving (but refusing once again to
wear the chauffeur's cap on moral grounds), they set out
under the auspices of power steering, directly through the perimeter of the dream.

The star continued to shine overhead. "Damnedest thing I

ever saw," Kaspar remarked, for the ten thousandth time. "Defies all the accepted laws of celestial mechanics."

Balthazar mumbled something.

For the ten thousandth time.

"What's that, I didn't hear?" Melchior said.

"I said: at least if there was a pot of gold at the end of all this . . ."

It was unworthy of him, as it had been ten thousand times previously, and the others chose to ignore it.

At the outskirts of the dream, a rundown section lined with fast food stands, motels with waterbeds and closed circuit vibrating magic fingers cablevision, bowling alleys, Polish athletic organizations and used rickshaw lots, they encountered the first line of resistance from the Forces of Chaos.

As they stopped for a traffic light, thousands of bat-winged monkey-faced troops leaped out of alleys and doorways with buckets of water and sponges, and began washing their windshield.

"Quick, Kaspar!" Balthazar shouted.

The Oriental king threw open the rear door on the right side and bounded out into the street, brandishing the chalice of myrrh. "Back, back, scum of the underworld!" he howled.

The troops of Chaos shrieked in horror and pain and began dropping what appeared to be dead all over the place, setting up a wailing and a crying and a screaming that rose over the dream like dark smoke.

"Please, already," Melchior shouted. "Do we need all this noise? All this *geshrying*! You'll wake the baby!"

Then Balthazar was gunning the motor, Kaspar leaped back into the rear seat, the door slammed and they were off, through the red light—which had, naturally, been rigged to stay red, as are all such red lights, by the Forces of Chaos.

All that day they lay siege to the dream.

The Automobile Club told them they couldn't get there from here. The speed traps were set at nine miles per hour. Sects of religious fanatics threw themselves under the steelbelteds. But finally they came to the Manger, a Hyatt establishment, and they fought their way inside with the gifts, all tasteful.

And there, in a moderately-priced room, they found the
Savior, tended by an out-of-work cabinetmaker, a lady who
was obviously several bricks shy of a load who kept insisting
she had been raped by God, various shepherds, butchers, pet
store operators, boutique salesgirls, certified public accoun-
tants, hawkers of T-shirts, investigative journalists, theatrical
hangers-on, Sammy Davis, Jr., and a man who owned a whip-
pet that was reputed to be able to catch two Frisbees at the
same time.

And the three kings came in, finding it hard to find a place
there in the crowd, and they set down their gifts and stared at
the sleeping child.

"We'll call him Jomo," said Balthazar, asserting himself.

"Don't be a jerk," Kaspar said. "Merry Jomomas? We'll
call him Lao-Tzu. It flows, it sings, it soars."

So they argued about that for quite a while, and finally settled on Christ, because in conjunction with Jesus it was six
and five, and that would fit all the marquees.

But still, after two thousand years, they were unsettled.
They stared down at the sleeping child, who looked like all
babies: like a small, soft W.C. Fields who had grown blotchy
drinking wine sold before its time, and Balthazar mumbled,
"I'd have been just as happy with a pot of gold," and Kaspar
said, "You'd think after two thousand years someone would
at least offer me a chair," and Melchior summed up all their
hopes and dreams for a better world when he said, "You
know, it's funny, but he don't look Jewish."

An extraordinary discovery
and an unusual gift.

Diesel Dream
Alan Dean Foster

WHATTHEHELL. I MEAN, I know I was wired. Too many white
crosses, too long on the road. But a guy's gotta make a living,
and everybody *else* does it. Everybody who runs alone, anyway. You got a partner, you don't have to rely on stimulants.
You half a married team, that's even better. But you own, op-
erate, and drive your own rig, you gotta compete somehow.
That means always making sure you finish your run on time,
especially if you're hauling perishables. Oh sure, they bring
their own problems with 'em, but I'd rather run cucumbers
that cordite any day.

Elaine (that's my missus), she worries about me all the
time. No less so than any trucker's wife, I guess. Goes with
the territory. I try to hide the pills from her, but she knows I
pop the stuff. I make good money, though. Better'n most in-
dependents. Least I'm not stuck in some stuffy little office listening to some scrawny bald-headed dude chew my ass day
after day for misfiling some damn piece of paper.

Elaine and I had a burning ceremony two years ago. Mort-
gage officer from the bank brought over the paper personal

and stayed for burgers and beer. Now there's a bank that *understands*. Holds the paper on our place, too. One of these days we'll have another ceremony and burn that sucker, too.

So I own my rig free and clear now. Worked plenty hard for it. I'm sure as hell not ready to retire. Not so long as I can work for myself. Besides which I got two kids in college and a third thinking about it. Yep, me. The big guy with the green baseball cap and the beard you keep seein' in your rearview mirrors. Sometimes I can't believe it myself.

So what if I use the crosses sometimes to keep going? So what if my eyesight's not twenty-twenty every hour of every day? Sure my safety record's not perfect, but it's a damnsight better than most of these young honchos think they can drive San Diego–Miami nonstop. Half their trucks end up as scrap, and so do half of them.

I know when I'm getting shaky, when it's time to lay off the little mothers.

Anyway, like I was gonna tell you, I don't usually stop in Lee Vining. It's just a flyspot on the atlas, not even a real truck stop there. Too far north of Mammoth to be fashionable and too far south of Tahoe to be worth a side trip for the gamblers. A bunch of overinsulated mobile homes not much bigger than the woodpiles stacked outside 'em. Some log homes, some rock. Six gas stations, five restaurants, and one little mountain grocery. Imagine; a market with a porch and chairs. Lee Vining just kind of clings to the east slope of the Sierra Nevada. Wouldn't surprise anyone if the whole shebang up and slid into Mono Lake some hard winter. The whole town. The market sells more salmon eggs than salmon. Damn fine trout country, though, and a great place to take kids hiking.

Friendly, too. Small-town people always are, no matter what part of the country you're haulin' through. They live nearer nature than the rest of us and it keeps 'em respectful of their humanity. The bigger the country, the bigger the hearts. Smarter then you'd think, too.

Like I was saying, I don't usually stop there. Bridgeport's cheaper for diesel. But I'd just driven nonstop from LA with a quick load of lettuce, tomatoes, and other produce for the casinos at Reno and I was running on empty. Not Slewfoot:

she was near full. I topped off her tanks in Bishop. Slewfoot's my rig, lest you think I was cheatin' on Elaine. I don't go in for that, no matter what you see in those cheap films. Most truckers ain't that good-lookin', and neither are the gals you meet along the highway. Most of them are married, anyway.

Since diesel broke a buck a gallon I'm pretty careful about where I fill up. Slewfoot's a big Peterbilt, black with yellow and red striping, and she can get mighty thirsty.

So I was the one running on empty, and with all those crosses floating around in my gut, not to mention my head, I needed about fourteen cups of coffee and something to eat. It was starting to get evening and I like to push the light, but after thirty years plus on the road I know when to stop. Eat now, let the crosses settle some, drive later. Live longer.

It was just after Thanksgiving. The tourists were long gone from the mountains. So were the fishermen, since the high-country lakes were already frozen. Ten feet of snow on the ground (yeah, feet) but I'd left nearly all the ski traffic back down near Mammoth. U.S. 395's easier when you don't have to dodge the idiots from LA who never see snow except when it comes time for 'em to drive through it.

The Department of Transportation had the road pretty clear and it hadn't snowed much in a couple of days, which is why I picked that day to make the fast run north. After Smokeys, weather's a trucker's major devilment. It was plenty cold outside; cold enough to freeze your BVD's to your crotch, but nothing like what it would be in another month or so. It was early and the real Sierra winter was just handing out calling cards.

Thanks to the crosses I kind of floated onto the front porch of a little place called the Prospector's Roost (almost as much gold left in those mountains as trout), twenty percent of the town's restaurant industry, and slumped gratefully into a booth lined with scored Naugahyde. The window behind me gave me something besides blacktop to focus on, and the sun's last rays were just sliding off old Mono Lake. Frigid pretty. The waitress gave me a big smile, which was nice. Soon she brought me a steak, hash browns, green beans, warm rolls with butter, and more coffee, which was better. I started to mellow as my stomach filled up, let my eyes wander as I ate.

It's tough to make a living at any one thing in a town the size of Lee Vining. If it don't take up too much floor space, some folks can generate an extra couple of bucks by operating a second business in the same building.

So the north quarter of the Prospector's Roost had been given over to a little gift shop. The market carried trinkets and so did the gas stations, so it didn't surprise me to see the same kind of stuff in a restaurant. There were a couple of postcards, film, bare-necessity fishing supplies at outrageous prices, Minnetonka moccasins, rubber tomahawks for the kids, risk-kay joke gifts built around gags older than my uncle Steve, Indian turquoise jewelry made in the Philippines. That sort of thing.

Plus the usual assortment of local handicrafts: rocks painted to look like owls, cheap ashtrays that screamed MONO LAKE or LEE VINING, GATEWAY TO YOSEMITE. T-shirts that said the same, (no mediums left, plenty of extra-large).

There was also a small selection of better-quality stuff. Some nice watercolors of the lake and its famous tufa formations, one or two little hand-chased bronzes you wouldn't be ashamed to set out on your coffee table, locally strung necklaces of turquoise and silver, and some wood carvings of Sierra animals. Small, but nicely turned. Looked like ironwood to me. Birds and fish mostly, but also one nice little bobcat I considered picking up for Elaine. She'd crucify me if I did, though. Two kids in college, a third considering. And tomorrow Slewfoot would be thirsty again.

The tarnished gold bell over the gift-shop entrance tinkled as somebody entered. The owner broke away from his kitchen and walked over to chat. He was a young fellow with a short beard and he looked tired.

The woman who'd come in had a small box under one arm, which she set gently on the counter. She opened it and started taking out some more of those wood carvings. I imagined she was the artist. She was dressed for the weather and I thought she must be a local.

She left the scarf on her head when she slipped out of her heavy high-collared jacket. I tried to look a little closer. All those white crosses kept my eyes bopping, but I wasn't as sure about my brain. She was older than I was in any case, even if I'd been so inclined. Sure I looked. It was pitch black out now and starting to snow lightly. Elaine wouldn't have minded . . . much. A man's got to look once in a while.

I guessed her to be in her mid-fifties. She could've been older but if anything she looked younger. I tried to get a good look at her eyes. The eyes always tell you the truth. Whatever her age, she was still a damn handsome woman. Besides the scarf and coat she wore jeans and a flannel shirt. That's like a uniform in this kind of country. She wore 'em loose, but you could still see some spectacular countryside. Brown hair, though I thought it might be lighter at the roots. Not gray, either. Not yet.

I squeezed my eyes shut until they started to hurt and downed another swallow of coffee. A man must be beginnin' to go when he starts thinking that way about grandmotherly types.

Except that this woman wasn't near being what any man in his right mind would call grandmotherly, her actual age notwithstanding. Oh, she didn't do nothin' to enhance it, maybe even tried hiding it under all those clothes. But she couldn't quite do it. Even now I thought she was pretty enough to be on TV. Like Barbara Stanwyck, but younger and ever prettier. Maybe it was all those white crosses makin' gumbo of my thoughts, but I couldn't take my eyes off her.

The only light outside now came from a gas stations and storefronts. Not many of the latter stayed open after dark. A few tourists sped through town, fighting the urge to tromp their accelerators. I could imagine 'em cursing small towns like this one that put speed limits in their way just to keep 'em from the crap tables at Reno a little longer.

I considered the snow. Drifting down easy, but that could change. No way did I need that tonight. I finished the last of my steak and paid up, leaving the usual good tip, and started out to warm up Slewfoot.

The woman was leaving at the same time and we sort of ended up at the door together, accidental-like. Like fun we did.

"After you," she said to me.

Now, I was at least ten years younger than this lady, but

when she spoke to me I just got real quivery all through my body, and it wasn't from the heavy-duty pharmaceuticals I'd been gulping, either. She'd whispered, but it wasn't whispering. I knew it was her normal speaking voice. Now, I've had sexier things whispered to me than "After you," but none of 'em made me feel the way I did right then, not even those spoken on my fourth date with Elaine, which ended up in the back of my old pickup truck with her telling me, "Whatever you want, Dave."

Somebody real special has to be able to make "After you" sound like "Whatever you want." My initial curiosity doubled up on me. It was none of my business, of course. Here I was a married man and all, two kids in college and a third thinkin', and I oughtn't to be having the kinds of thoughts I was having. But I was running half an hour ahead of my schedule, and the snow was staying easy, and I thought, Well hell, it don't hurt nothing to be friendly.

"You local?"

She smiled slightly, not looking up at me. It got darker fast when we stepped outside and those damn crosses were making like a xylophone in my head, but damned if I didn't think she was so pretty she'd crack, despite the fine lines that had begun to work their way across her face. She pushed her jacket up higher on her body and turned up the sheepskin collar.

"It's cold, and I've got to go." I shivered slightly, and it wasn't from the snow. "Nothing personal. I just don't believe in talking to strangers."

What could I say, how could I reassure her? "Heck, I don't mean no harm, ma'am." I think maybe that got to her. Not many folks these days say heck and ma'am, especially truckers. She glanced up at me curiously. Suddenly I wasn't cold anymore.

"Where are you from?"

"I asked you first."

"All right. I live here, yes. You?"

"LA right now, but me and my wife are from Texas. West Texas. The back o' beyond." Funny how Elaine had slipped into the conversation. I hadn't intended her to. But I wasn't sorry.

"Nice of you to mention your wife." She'd picked up on

that right away. "Most men don't. That's why I try to come
into town around dark. You'd think an old lady like me
wouldn't have that kind of trouble."

"No disrespect intended, ma'am, but I've never set eyes on
an old lady looked like you do." I nodded toward the cafe/gift
shop. "You do those woodcarvings?"

"Yes. Do you like them?"

"I've seen a lot of that kind of stuff all over the country,
and I think yours stack up real well against the best. Real
nice. Good enough to show in a big gallery somewhere.

"Willie's place is good enough for me." Her voice was honey
and promise. "This is my home now. The people up here leave
you alone and let you be what you want to be. I'm happy."

"You married?"

"No, but I have friends. It's enough that they like me for
what I am. I've been married before, more than once. It never
worked for me."

The snow was coming down heavier.

"I'm sorry." She must have seen the concern on my face.
"Got far to go?"

"Reno and on to Tahoe. Groceries for them folks that are
trying to make it the easy way. Can't let the high rollers go
hungry." Her smile widened slightly. It made me feel like I'd
just won a new rig or something.

"No, I guess you can't." She tossed her head slightly to her
left, kind of bounced a little on her feet. "It's been nice talking to you. Really."

"My name's Dave."

"Good meeting you, Dave."

"You?"

She blinked away a snowflake. "Me what?"

"What's your name?"

"Jill," she said instantly. "Jill Kramer." It was a nice name,
but I knew it was hollow.

"Nice meeting you too, Jill. See you round, maybe."

"See you too, Dave."

That's what did it. She didn't so much say my name as sort
of pucker her lips and let it ooze out, like a little hot cloud.
She wore no lipstick. She didn't have to.

White crosses. White crosses and bennies and snow. Damn it all for a clear head for two lousy minutes!

I tried to think of something to say, knowing that I had to glue my eyes to the blacktop real soon or forget about driving any more that night altogether. I couldn't afford that. Nobody pays a bonus for brown lettuce and soft tomatoes.

"I thought you were dead," I finally blurted out. I said it easy, matter-of-fact, not wanting to startle her or me. Maybe the crosses made me do it; I don't know. She started to back away, but my country calm held her.

"I knew I shouldn't have talked to you this long. I try not to talk to anyone I don't know for very long. I thought by now ..." She shrugged sadly. "I've done pretty well, hiding everything."

"Real well." I smiled reassuringly. "Hey, chill out. What you've done is no skin off my nose. Personally I think it's great. Let 'em all think you're dead. Serves 'em all right, you ask me. Bunch of phonies, the lot of 'em."

She still looked as if she wanted to run. Then she smiled afresh and nodded. "That's right. Bunch of phonies. They all just wanted one thing. I spent all my time torn up inside and confused, and nobody tried to help. Nobody cared as long as they were making money or getting what they wanted. I was just a machine to them, a thing. I didn't know what to do. I got in real deep with some guys and that's when I knew that one way or another, I had to get out, get away.

"Up here nobody cares where you come from or what you did before you got here. Nice people. And I like doing my carvings. I got out of it with a little money nobody could trace. I'm doing fine."

"Glad to hear it. I always did think you were *it*, you know."

"That wasn't me, Dave. That was never me. That was always the problem. I'm happy now, and that's what counts. If you live long enough, you come to know what's really important."

"That's what me and Elaine always say."

She glanced at the sky and the light from the café fully illuminated her face. "You'd better get going."

"How'd you work it, anyway? How'd you fool everybody?"

"I had some friends. True friends. Not many, but enough.

They understood. They helped me get out. Once in a while they come up here and we laugh about how we fooled everyone. We go fishing. I always did like to fish. You'd better get moving."

"Reckon I'd better. You keep doing those carvings. I really liked your bobcat."

"Thanks. That one was a lot of work. Merry Christmas, Dave."

"Yeah. You too . . . Jill."

She turned away from me, knowing that I'd keep her secret. Hell, what did I have to gain from giving her away? I knew how she must feel, or thought I did. About the best thing you can do in this mean world is not step on somebody else's happiness, and I wasn't about to step on hers. It's too damn hard to come by and you might need somebody else to do you a similar favor sometime. It doesn't hurt to establish a line of credit with the Almighty.

I watched her walk away in the falling snow, all bundled up and hidden inside that big Western jacket, and I felt real good with myself. I'd still make Reno in plenty of time, then pop over to Tahoe, maybe get lucky and pick up a return load. My eyes followed her through the dark and white wet and she seemed to wink in and out of my sight, dreamlike.

White crosses. Damn, I thought. Was she real or wasn't she? Not that it really mattered. I still felt good. I sucked in the sharp, damp air and made ready to get back to business.

That's when she sort of hesitated, stopped, and glanced back at me. Or at least, whatever I saw there in the Sierra night glanced back at me. When she resumed her walk it wasn't the stiff, horsey stride she'd been using before but a rolling, rocking, impossibly fluid gait that would've blasted the knob off a frozen thermometer. I think she'd did it just for me. Maybe it was because of the season, but I tell you, it was one helluva present.

Not knowing what else to do, I waved. I think she waved back as I called out, "Merry Christmas, Norma Jean." Then hurried across the street to the parking lot to fire up Slewfoot.

A deal with Santa.

SANTA CLAUSE
Robert F. Young

"STATE YOUR BUSINESS," the Adversary said, when the smoke had cleared away. "I haven't got all night!"

Ross swallowed. He hadn't really thought the pentagram would work. He debated on whether to stand up in the Inimical Presence, or to go on sitting behind his desk. He decided on the latter procedure: The Adversary, he was sure, wouldn't be in the least impressed by protocol.

"Well?"

Ross swallowed again. "I—I want there to be a Santa Claus."

"I see. . . . For everyone, or just for yourself?"

"Just for myself, naturally," Ross said. "I wouldn't stand to gain a thing if everyone cashed in on the deal. Why, there'd be inflation as sure as Ford made green Edsels."

"You've got a point there." The Adversary scratched the back of his neck reflectively with the tip of his tail. "And I must say, your request is original. No one ever thought about *that* angle before . . . There are considerations, of course."

"I expected there would be," Ross said.

"Don't be in such a hurry to show off your cynicism. By 'considerations' I mean that I can't subdivide childhood fantasy. If you want there to be a Santa Claus, you'll have to take everything that goes with him—and live by the rules."

An octet of reindeer pulling a red sleigh pranced through Ross's head. Imagination wasn't one of his strong points. "Sounds all right to me," he said.

"Fine!" The Adversary pulled a mimeographed contract from beneath his robe, punctured a vein in his wrist, and filled in the pertinent blank spaces. He handed it to Ross. "You'll find the terms generous, I think."

"I doubt it," Ross said, running his eyes down the page, paying particular attention to the fine print. Abruptly he gasped. "What's this here? For *life*?"

"That's right. I'm waiving the time limit in this case. Better sign before I change my mind."

Ross took the pen, punctured one of his own wrist veins, and dashed off his name. "But *why*?" he asked.

The Adversary leered. "You'll find out," he said. There was the usual puff of smoke, the usual odor of brimstone, followed by the usual empty space. . . .

Ross had fun writing his letter to Santa Claus that year. He came right to the point. *Dear Santa,* he wrote: *Please send me a 1959 Cadillac de Ville, a beautiful 40-24-40 Mansfield, 52 cases of top-shelf liquor, 365 cases of Schlitz, a year's subscription to* Whisper—The list was quite imposing, and he didn't really think he'd get *all* he'd asked for; but even if he only got the first three items, he felt that his afterlife would have been invested profitably.

Santa, however, came through with everything. On Christmas morn, Ross found himself the possessor of—in addition to the aforementioned items—a completely stocked deep freeze; a solid chrome refrigerator; three gin mills; a Buick-red living room suite; a terra-cotta bedroom suite; the complete works of the Marquis de Sade; a 24" blond TV console; a *Sputnik* wall clock with a little dog that popped out every hour and barked what time it was; an electric organ, together with a book entitled, *You Too Can Play the Organ—In Six*

Easy Lessons!; a chrome bathroom ensemble; a uranium mine; a large economy-size Laurence Welk record album; 365 Brooks Brothers shirts; a woodworker's do-it-yourself kit; a South Sea island; a deluxe edition of the current best-seller *What's in it for Me?*; six gross of Miltowns; an electric train; a *Sputnik* cigarette lighter that went *beep beep!* when you flicked it; a chalet in the Swiss Alps; and a solid gold bottle opener.

The Cadillac did wonders for his ego. For the first time in his life, he felt like a whole man. As for the Mansfield, whose name was Candace, he took one look at her and proposed, she was that irresistible. She said yes, of course—he'd specified in a P.S. that she should fall in love with him at first sight—and that very afternoon they were married by an out-of-state justice of the peace.

Back in the apartment, Ross took his Christmas present in his arms. This, he thought, kissing her, was worth all the empty Christmas stockings he'd ever gotten up to. And it was only the *first* Santa Claus Christmas. The thought of all the things he could ask for on the forthcoming ones made his head swim, and he made a mental note to start work on his next list early, so that he'd be less liable to forget anything.

Presently Candy drew away. "Good night, darling," she said.

"I'll 'good night' you!" Ross said, grabbing her and kissing her again.

She responded as a good blonde should—up to a point. When he passed that point, she disengaged herself and headed for the bedroom. Ross followed. She paused in the doorway. "Good night, darling," she said again, and closed the door in his face. There was a tantalizing little click as the lock slipped into position.

Ross stared disbelievingly at the pink panels. Then he started pounding on them. When Candy opened the door a crack, he roared: "What in hell's the matter with you? This is our *wedding* night!"

"I know it is, darling. Haven't I let you kiss me twice already?"

"Sure you let me kiss you twice. What of it? I didn't marry you just so I could kiss you!"

She gasped at him. "Then why on earth *did* you marry me?"

Before he had a chance to answer he found himself confronted by the pink panels again. He resumed pounding, but this time he got no response. After a while his hands started to hurt, and he desisted.

He went over to the liquor cabinet and poured himself four fingers of I.W. Harper's. He gulped them down, poured four more. He gulped them down, too. Suddenly he became aware that someone—or something—was tapping on the window. He stepped across the room and threw up the sash. A small, pale man was sitting in the bos'n's seat, just beyond the sill. He had a silver pail in one hand and a putty knife in the other.

"This is a hell of a time for maintenance!" Ross said. "Just what is it you're doing, anyway?"

"Why I'm putting frost on your window, of course," the pale man said. "What did you think I'd be doing on a cold night like this?"

For a moment Ross couldn't speak, he was so furious. Then: "What's your name?" he demanded. "I'm going to report you to the management!"

"The management, ha ha,". the pale man said. 'The management, ha ha!"

"I'll 'ha ha' you if you don't tell me your name!"

"Why I'm Jack Frost, you idiot. Who else would be putting frost on your window?"

Ross stared. "Jack *Frost*!"

The pale man nodded. "Himself."

"For Pete's sake, d'you think I'm a kid? There's no such person as Jack Frost."

"Isn't there, now. First thing you know, you'll be telling me there's no such person as Santa Claus!"

Ross slammed the window shut. He returned to the liquor cabinet and poured himself four more fingers of I.W.; then he went over and sat sullenly on the sofa.

He tried to think. What was it the Adversary had said? That he couldn't subdivide childhood fantasy? That in order to make Santa Claus real, he had to make everything that went with Santa Claus real, too?

Jack Frost?

Well why not? Wasn't Jack Frost an integral part of childhood fantasy?

Nonsense, Ross thought. I'll be damned if I'll believe it!

He tossed off his drink and threw the empty glass into the fireplace. He stared glumly at the bedroom door. Suddenly he had a feeling that there was someone standing behind him, and he turned angrily. Sure enough, there *was* someone—a tall, lanky individual wearing a white cowboy suit, armed with a set of silver six-guns, and carrying a golden guitar. A halo, like a circular fluorescent tube, scintillated over his sombrero; a chrome star, with the letters "G.A." stamped on it, glittered on his breast; and a pair of pin wings sprouted from his shoulders.

Ross sighed. "All right," he said wearily. "Who are *you*?"

The winged cowboy struck a throbbing golden chord. "I'm your G.A.," he drawled.

"My *what*?"

"Your Guardian Angel."

"Whoever heard of a Guardian Angel wearing a cowboy suit and carrying a guitar!"

"Got to keep up with the times, podner. I'd look a mite silly, wouldn't I, wearin' a white robe and carryin' a harp?"

Ross almost said that he looked a mite silly, anyway. But he didn't. For some reason he didn't feel much like talking. He looked around the room a little desperately, noticed that there were still a few fingers remaining in the I.W. bottle. After chug-a-lugging them, he returned foggily to the sofa and lay down. The G.A. got blankets from somewhere and tucked him in for the night.

After a while the Sandman came in, carrying a little red pail, and threw sand in his eyes.

After a week of dead-end kisses and arguments that got him nowhere, of nightly visits by Jack Frost and the Sandman, Ross was ready to tie on a good one. The season was appropriate, and New Year's Eve found him, Candy, and the

G.A. ensconced in a dim corner of one of the gin mills Santa had brought him.

Candy, as might have been expected, drank like a bird. Ross was disgusted. Next time he put a Mansfield on his Christmas list, he told himself bitterly, he'd be sure to specify what *kind* of a Mansfield. If the old boy in the red flannel suit didn't understand the facts of life, it was high time he learned.

It was a wretched evening—from Ross's point of view. Candy, though, seemed to enjoy herself—in a Milquetoast kind of way—and the G.A. had a ball. He strummed his guitar incessantly and sang song after song in a treacly voice, and every so often he got up and danced around in a little circle, employing a peculiar sideways step. The fact that no one saw or heard him, save Ross and Candy, didn't seem to bother him a bit.

Around eleven o'clock, Ross noticed an old man with a scythe wandering among the tables. No one paid any attention to him, or, for that matter, seemed to see him. For a while Ross was puzzled; then, at twelve on the dot, the old man walked out and a rotund little boy, wearing nothing but a sash, walked in.

"Nuts!" Ross said. "Let's go."

Jack Frost was merrily at work on the window when they entered the apartment, and Ross glimpsed the Sandman lurking in a shadowy corner. The G.A. went over and started making up the sofa. Candy slipped out of her pastel mink and stood provocatively in the middle of the room.

"I'm ready for my good-night kiss," she said.

In mid-January, after a long drawn-out battle with his G.A., Ross visited a divorce lawyer. "I want my marriage annulled," he said.

"Calm down a little," the lawyer said. "We'll get it annulled for you—if you can show sufficient cause."

"Cause! Why, I can show enough cause to annul twenty marriages! My wife will only let me kiss her!"

"That's no justification for an annulment—or a divorce, either. What do you expect her to do?"

Ross felt his face burn. "What do you think I expect her to do?"

"I can't imagine."

"Look, I'm in no mood for a hard time. I'll break it down for you just once, and I'll be damned if I'll draw you a picture. When *you* kiss your wife, does she run away from you and lock you out of the bedroom?"

"Naturally not! But that has nothing to do with you. You're different."

"*Why* am I different?"

The lawyer looked bewildered. "I—I don't exactly know," he said. "You—you just are."

"Oh for Pete's sake!" Ross said. He stomped out of the room, slammed the door behind him.

Five divorce lawyers later, he gave up.

Late in February, Candy started knitting. Little things. She dropped her eyes demurely when Ross confronted her. "I'm going to have a baby," she said.

For a while, Ross couldn't speak. The occasion demanded a careful choice of words, and it was some time before he found the one he wanted. It filled the bill nicely:

"*Whose?*" he said.

She stared at him. "Why yours, of course. You're my husband, aren't you?"

"I guess that's what you'd call me."

"Then what a silly question to ask! You don't think I'd let anybody else kiss me, do you?"

Ross sighed. "No, I guess you wouldn't at that," he said.

He didn't really believe she was going to have a baby, of course. But he decided to humor her. As the weeks passed, she was happier than he'd ever seen her before, and her knitting, pointless or not, seemed to give her a direction in life that had previously been lacking.

He continued to humor her even after she started buying maternity dresses. If she wanted to retreat completely from reality, it was all right with him. He had to admit, though, that she *was* putting on weight; however, that wasn't too surprising when you considered how much she ate.

The G.A. continued to hang around, strumming his guitar,

singing, and polishing his six-guns. Jack Frost was on hand almost every evening, with his putty knife and pail, and the Sandman never missed a night. But, while the situation was predominantly dark, it did have its brighter aspects.

For instance, early in March Ross had to have a tooth pulled, and remembered, when he saw the dentist about to drop it into the waste can, that teeth, in childhood fantasy, had a monetary value. So he asked the dentist for the tooth back, and that night he placed it under his pillow. Sure enough, next morning a shiny coin reposed where it had been. Hmm, he thought . . .

That afternoon he visited a nearby novelty store and bought two dozen sets of toy false teeth at twenty-five cents apiece, and that night, before he went to bed on the sofa, he put one of the sets under his pillow. Twenty teeth, at the current rate of fifty cents apiece, he reasoned should bring him a total of ten dollars—if the Tooth Fairy fell for the scheme. The Tooth Fairy did, and next morning Ross was $9.75 to the good. He was in business again.

And then there was the time on Chocolate Rabbit Sunday when he talked the Easter Bunny into leaving golden eggs instead of the conventional hard-boiled variety. He really hauled in the loot that day—and if he'd had any kind of wife at all, she'd have fallen all over him and given him anything he wanted. Candy didn't. She just kept right on knitting, and when ten o'clock came, stood up and said: "Well aren't you going to kiss me good night, dear?"

June, and girls in summer dresses . . . Ross started looking around. No man, he told himself, had ever had more justification. But the G.A. didn't see it that way at all, and Ross had no sooner made his first pass when he felt a heavy hand on his shoulder and heard a sonorous voice in his ear:

"The dirtiest critter riding the plains is the critter who steps out on his missus. I aim to keep you clean, podner. Clean. Y'hear me?"

"Go home and get up a game of pinochle with the Sandman and the Tooth Fairy," Ross said. "I'm busy."

"Clean, podner. Clean," the G.A. repeated, and to prove he

meant business, he picked Ross up, carried him home, and put him to bed.

Ross stared miserably at the ceiling. What did you do, he asked himself, when the wife you'd got for Christmas turned out to be a dud, and the Guardian Angel you'd got along with her turned out to have the morality of a Zane Grey range rider?

Answer (general): You ordered another wife.

Answer (specific): You wrote, *Dear Santa: Please send me a new wife,* and by so phrasing your request, automatically guaranteed the cancellation of the first wife when the second arrived.

Certainly, in the world of childhood fantasy, a man couldn't have *two* wives!

Ross began to feel better. He started to work on his Santa Claus letter the next day. He worked on it all summer and into the fall, dedicated to the proposition that Santa Claus wasn't going to make a fool out of him two times running. No one bothered him except the Sandman, who persisted in throwing sand in his eyes the minute he began to nod. (Jack Frost had stopped coming around with the advent of warm weather.)

On Halloween, he interrupted his work long enough to steal a besom from a feeble old witch, to catch a crippled leprechaun and make it reveal its treasure's hiding place, and to talk two teenage brownies into doing his housework for the forthcoming fantasy-year. But the next day he was right back at it again.

Late one November night he heard a tapping on the window. He had just entered item no. 6,002 on his list and was debating on whether to treat himself to a brandy or a Scotch and soda. Candy had retired early, saying that she wasn't feeling well.

When the tapping continued, he got up and went over to the window. It was a cold night, and at first he thought that Jack Frost had come back, and he raised the sash, intending to give the pale man a piece of his mind. Then he saw that it wasn't Jack Frost after all.

It was the Stork.

* * *

It was also the last straw. Ross slammed the window shut, ran over to his desk, got out pencil, paper, and ruler, and went to work on another pentagram.

The Adversary, when he appeared some minutes later, was his usual leering self. "Well," he said, a little tiredly, "what is it this time?"

"I want there *not* to be a Santa Claus," Ross said, "and I want there *not* to be a Sandman and a Jack Frost and a G.A. But most of all, I want there *not* to be a Stork!"

"I see . . . For everyone, or just for yourself?"

"Just for myself, naturally. It's *my* soul I'm selling. . . . Besides, they don't exist for everyone."

"They do in a way," the Adversary said, "An eventuality which underlines the 'considerations' I mentioned during our first meeting. My inability to subdivide childhood fantasy applies to my eliminating it as well as to my materializing it— and my eliminating it would involve taking away not only its present reality, but the normal residue remaining from your childhood as well. To accomplish that, I'd have to go all the way back to your formative years and alter your original attitude. There could be complications—"

"You're not getting through," Ross said.

The Adversary flicked his tail in exasperation. "All I'm trying to bring out," he said, "is the fact that, while the concept of the Stork may seem ridiculous to you now, a long time ago it made a phase of your life bearable and enabled you to grow up retaining the illusions on which the love life of your particular culture is based."

"I don't need illusions for *my* love life," Ross said. "All I need is good old reality."

"Then you shall have it!" The Adversary produced another mimeographed contract, punctured a vein, and began filling in the pertinent blank spaces. He spoke each word aloud as he wrote it down. "Signing of this agreement invalidates the original agreement . . . elimination from life of signer all belief in any and all aspects of childhood fantasy . . . term of agreement: life."

"Again?" Ross asked.

"I'm in another generous mood," the Adversary said, handing him the pen and the contract.

Ross hesitated a moment. For some reason, the life clause failed to reassure him this time. Then he thought of Candy sleeping virginally beyond the impenetrable pink panels, of the Stork waiting outside the window. Hurriedly, he punctured one of his own veins and scrawled his name. He handed the pen and the contract back.

"See you later," the Adversary said.

When the smoke had cleared away, Ross looked around the room. The corner where the Sandman usually lurked was empty. He glanced over his shoulder: the G.A. was gone. He listened: the tapping on the window had ceased.

He looked contemplatively at the bedroom door.

For some reason the pink panels left him cold.

But he got up, anyway, and walked over and knocked. "Come in," a warm voice said. "Come in darling."

He reached out, touched the knob. He knew that this time the door wouldn't be locked. Suddenly he thought of Candy sprawled on the sweaty bed, shameless, with vast naked udders . . . Loathing rose up in his throat, almost choked him. His hand fell away from the knob and he turned and ran from the apartment.

Filthy Creature! he thought. He hated her so much he couldn't stand it.

He hated her almost as much as he hated his mother.

A Christmas fruitcake.

GRANDMA BABKA'S CHRISTMAS GINGER
Ken Wisman

CHRISTMAS BEGAN AT Thanksgiving.

When we were done with dinner and Father waddled away to sleep the meal off and Mother was busy cleaning, Grandma Babka would call Sister and me into the kitchen to construct the Christmas house of ginger. From the age of two we helped gather up the implements and ingredients necessary, participating in the tradition each year to our seventh.

That was the year that our story takes place—the year the bad luck came.

"Brother, bring scissors!" Grandma Babka said, whipping us into action. "Sister, fetch spatula and knife!"

Grandma Babka was brusque. And spoke her mind. And did not ask but barked her orders.

"Sister, eggs! Brother, flour!"

She had the face of a withered monkey with wens and warts and moles with hairs protruding so that it looked like tiny animals had taken residence on her face.

"Baking pans, Brother! Pastry bag, Sister!"

Once full-bodied and robust, she had shrunken in on herself

and her actions were spare. ("I remove all my water," she once whispered mysteriously to Sister and me. "Like salted fish, it preserve me.")

"Sugar, gumdrops, peppermint sticks, pistachios!"

But Sister and I loved Grandma Babka better than waking to a snowfall on a schoolday morning. Better than Christmas candy.

When the kitchen was at the proper stage of chaos with flour clouds swirling, pans banging, and cooking implements bouncing on the floor, Grandma Babka announced: "Shuttup!"

Sister and I watched as she went through the ritual of laying out. Like the serving master at a Japanese tea ceremony, she arranged each tool and ingredient according to a rigid and preconceived plan. Then and only then did the construction of the ginger house truly begin.

Now, each year Grandma chose a new type of house, so that one year she had a chalet, another a bungalow, still another a Queen Anne with delicate trimming. That year was to be a house from "the old country."

First, she mixed the walls made, of course, of ginger. While these baked she made the icing.

"Cement," she called it.

Which was concocted of egg whites and cream of tartar and confectioner's sugar.

Halfway into the process, Mother came in. She was humming a strange song, and she looked wistfully after Sister and me. She retired without a word.

Then Grandma Babka took out the ginger walls, raising them in her hands with the reverence of a priest raising the host in consecration. The walls went up pasted down on cardboard. The windows went in on either side. (Clear as glass and made of sugar crystals, Sister and I called them our "peeking-in windows.")

When the roof was going up, Father woke and came in.

"Don't keep them up too late," he growled.

He didn't like Grandma Babka much. When she was in the house, his authority was in question.

She ignored Father. She would be ready when she was ready.

Father slunk off to bed.

The decorations went on, each gumdrop heart placed with care, the icing snow with fastidiousness, the sugar-melt icicles with a particular attention to detail. Last on was the door made from a Social Tea Biscuit and put on paper hinges so that it swung in and out.

Then Grandma Babka took a tiny bag hung on a band around her neck. She procured a pinch of blue powder and sprinkled it on the threshold.

The blue powder smelled like fresh milk, sheets dried in sunlight, wind off a lake filled with summer.

"What's it made of?" Sister asked.

"Spring," Grandma answered arcanely.

"Why do you use it?" I asked.

"You think Leshy stupid? Want to stay out winter in cold? Reminds Leshy of warm days in forest." She stood back to admire the cottage—all ginger and gumdrops, peppermint and icing. "Is remind me old country." A tear squeezed forth from that salt dried, wizened body. "Must go this year."

Sister and I protested.

"Will see you Christmas," Grandma Babka said. Then she picked up the cottage and carried it out on the back porch that overlooked the forest beyond our house.

It was traditional for Grandma to "read" Sister and me bed-time stories after the ginger house was made—though the hour was past midnight. Our room looked out on the forest and our window was just above the porch. We three kept vigil.

"I read this one." Grandma Babka said, grabbing a book at random. She sat in the rocking chair near the window, and with the book upside down pretended to read.

"Blue moon rise in black sky. Is shine on far fields covered in snow. And now moon opens a blue hole in drifts. Grandma is walking with sister and brother and they fall into blue hole through blue light into land called Baboosh."

"Where is Baboosh?" Sister asked.

"Next to Ziloptka," Grandma Babka said annoyedly.

"Shuttup now to listen." And she took us into Baboosh and there we had adventures.

After the story, Grandma Babka rocked. Over her creaking we heard the approach of a train through the morning.

"Is Death-Train," Grandma Babka said.

Sister and I shivered.

"You hear clickety-clack?"

Sister and I nodded in the dark.

"Is Shmertsh himself snapping fingers to make train go faster. Don't like stay on earth too long."

Grandma Babka said you knew by the sound of the whistle where the train was bound. If it was a wailing like all the mourners that ever mourned it was bound for Pee-eckwo. If it was a sound like choirboys singing, raising their voices in rejoicing, it was bound for Nyeh-bo.

The last note of the Death-Train trembled like the breath in a lark's breast and was gone. Sister and I fought sleep, drifting in and out of dreams: Grandma Babka rocking across the Milky Way, sprinkling her powder, which became blue stars filling empty space.

Between three and four we heard walking across the moon night, the silence of a second hand ticking . . .

click

click

click

                   . . . around the ginger house. Then voices—silver bells tinkling in the wind; laughter—pure and brittle like hail against ice.

"They're in."

Grandma Babka rose. She went downstairs and tiptoed out on the porch, where she carefully lifted the ginger house. By the time she brought it inside, Sister and I were asleep.

The following day the ginger house rested on the table in the living room.

It was even more impressive in the daylight. Against the ginger slabs were red pistachio nuts mortared with icing into walls of brick. A roof of Nabisco Shredded Wheat thatched the roof, which in turn was covered with a coating of white icing heaped into drifts. Icicles hung in sugar melts from the eaves.

The barest of wisps of colored smoke curled from the chimney (made of mortared gumballs), the first indication that the Leshy were ensconced inside.

"Pine," Sister said, smelling the smoke.

"Peppermint," I said, sniffing.

And we smelled all the special scents of Christmas—orange sauce and incense, red wine and candle wax, duck and lemon whiskey—until Grandma Babka chased us away.

"Don't bother Good Luck Leshy," she hissed. "If upset could mean—" She left the sentence hanging.

"What?" I asked.

"They move out."

"And?"

"Bad luck move in."

We were given a time (at sundown) when it was okay to peek.

And in the particular year (our seventh) of which we tell, we observed a family of five. It wasn't easy to tell the sex of Leshy. Each had a beard—the grown-ups blue ones, the children white. But the family seemed composed of a father, mother, sister, brother, and a tiny grandmother.

A fire burned on their hearth, but not a flame of the ordinary kind. Leshy fire was a bright, sparkling light of changing colors—blue fading gold fading silver—which produced the spiced odors in the chimney.

Sister and I can vouch for the luck we had when the ginger house was occupied by Leshy. Thanksgiving to Christmas (though the ginger house stayed until spring) was especially fortuitous.

Winter was the time Father got promotions and raises. Which meant more gifts and presents. And overall we were in the best of health—while everyone around us caught colds and flus and we went apple-cheeked and healthy.

But this year was to be different.

Three days after Thanksgiving Grandma Babka was boarding a plane and saying good-bye to Father, Mother, Sister, and me.

"Sister, Brother, guard ginger house," she whispered.

We nodded, determined to fulfill our responsibility.

"No bad luck," Grandma Babka mouthed, and disappeared inside the big plane on her way to the old country.

A week passed. Aunt came over with Uncle and their son Ricky J who was eight.

Ricky J was the kind of boy who was polite and always said "thank you" or "excuse me"—as long as a grown-up was around. But when we were alone he'd get nasty and call us names.

"What about that stupid gingerbread house," Ricky J said when we were alone in the living room. "You got to eat it is all."

He made advances on the ginger house, but when he saw that Sister and I were serious in guarding it, he slunk away.

Before bed, we got Mother to put the house up on the mantel between the clock and candlesticks. And when everyone was asleep, Sister and I snuck down and built the fire in the hearth and stood vigil. But between three and four our eyelids drooped as low as pine branches ladened with snow.

We slept.

When we awakened, the fire in the hearth was cold ashes. A ladder stood against the mantel. The gumball chimney was snapped off at the top. Several bites in the snow roof exposed the shredded wheat. And a missing candy cane in the corner left the cottage precariously leaning.

Sister and I stared at the ginger house with dread. We saw smoke curling from the ruined chimney. And climbing the ladder, we sniffed.

"Sewer water," Sister said.

"Wet dog," I confirmed.

We peeked into the special windows and something with red eyes stared back. Later, Ricky J was found in bed with a stomachache, his belly filled with a terrible flatulence.

The effects in our house were gradual.

Christmases past, Mother would set up scenes on the windowsill: cotton laid down for snow with a pocket mirror

placed for a pond of ice, and little skaters made of lead and
brightly lacquered blue and gold. Sister and I would watch
these scenes with the hot radiator air rising, smelling of snow
and white sheets.

Christmases past, Father would hang lights in strings
around the outside windows: the bulbs melting little, blue
caves in the drifting snow, warm places we imagined curling
up in and falling asleep.

And the tree. Mother said we should dress it like a lady
come out to dance: her gown silver, stars on her arms, and a
string of tiny flames around her waist.

And Grandma Babka's baubles from the old country, made
of glass as fragile as an egg. Seven went on our lady. And the
sparkle of candle flame reflected on chalets depicted with
foot-thick roofs of snow—country scenes from Baboosh and
Ziloptka.

And, oh, the hours of adventures, stories forgotten like patterns faded on a quilt, the half-remembered pages of a dream.

Instead of the usual joy that went with the weeks before
Christmas, a heaviness settled.

This terrible year Mother and Father were distracted and
cross. They quarreled over the least triviality, avoided each
other, refused to do anything until the other apologized.

No lights went up; no windowsill scenes. The house didn't
smell of butter cookies cut in the shape of Santa and snowmen. But these were only portents of coming things.

Two weeks before Christmas, Father was fired. He took it
hard and grew sullen. One week before Christmas, Mother
got sick. First a cold, then a flu with fevers that rose every
day. She took to her bed.

Father withdrew into drinking, sitting long hours at the dining table throwing back whiskey to hold back the fear. Day by
day the ginger house changed—its roof turned gray, its corners round until it looked like a mushroom cap.

Sister and I peeked in at the window to see red eyes huddled before a red fire.

Yet, we held on to hope. For Grandma Babka promised she
would be back. Then on Christmas Eve the telegram came.

Sister and I answered the door (Mother and Father were that far gone). And it said that Grandma Babka was dead.

Darkness flowed down the chimney, put out the fire, dimmed the lights. Shadows rose in every corner—visions of Mother in the hospital, pale, cold dead; of Father wandering, found frozen in an alley; of Sister and me orphaned, alone.

We tiptoed into the dining room where Father sat drinking whiskey. The room was dark and we could see his eyes, like the red glowing eyes of the Leshy.

Then we tiptoed into Mother's room filled with candles. She stared out the window. And the wind whispered.

Doomed.

The whole house was enveloped in a dark flame.

We went to weep in our room.

Sister and I fell into a fitful sleep. But it was between the hours of three and four that we awoke and heard the mournful sound—like babies crying with no one to comfort them, like a mouse caught in an owl's talon.

Sister threw open the window.

I called out her name—"Grandma Babka!"—three times.

Shmertsh screeched as the engine ground to a halt. Then we heard the *chuff, chuff, chuff* of his angry impatience.

She came. Gliding through the forest, enveloped in a blue egg of light, up the porch steps and into the house.

"You failed!" Grandma Babka said.

There was no use in making excuses; we had failed.

"Can we save Mother?" I asked.

"Can we save Father?"

"Is too late." Grandma Babka stared at the ginger house. The round cap roof grew on a sickly stem. Two red eyes peeked from the one remaining window at the top. "Unless—"

"Yes?"

"Answer questions. What is Christmas meaning?"

Sister and I searched through our heads. All the while the fungus expanded before our eyes; the gloom thickened.

Ornaments and snow and Santa, I thought.

Roast duck and stockings and peppermint sticks, Sister thought.

"Gifts!" I said.

The mushroom grew a little; stench filled the room.

"Giving!" Sister seconded.

Laughter issued from the window in the mushroom cap.

The blue plasma egg around Grandma Babka erupted in streaks of lightning that popped like firecrackers. Two blue balls of lightning flew tumbling from her eyes and pinned us with terror.

"What is the greatest gift can give?" Grandma Babka roared. She produced a long bladed knife.

Our thoughts melted together and we saw Father frozen in the dining room, a drink at his lips, and Mother in the bedroom wasting away.

"Ourselves!" we cried. "Take us instead!"

"Sacrifice," Grandma Babka said. And grabbing our hands she slashed deftly down our thumbs, nail to knuckle, and held the bleeding fingers over the stinking fungus. Steam hissed off the slippery surface, the mushroom shrank, and inside the Leshy shrieked.

"Blood of innocents," Grandma Babka said.

The toadstool withered down to nothing.

"Is okay now," Grandma Babka said. "Father get job back tomorrow. Mother have miracle recovery."

A mournful wail—like an animal in pain—sounded from the back of the house.

The blue plasma egg that was Grandma Babka bulged toward the door. "Shmertsh impatient."

"Where will you go?" Sister and I asked.

"Made deal with Death. He let me come back; I go with him to bad place."

"Pee-eckwo!" we wailed.

And we tried to hold Grandma Babka, but our arms wrapped around blue air. She glided through the door.

Sister and I rushed to our room and the window to get a last glimpse. The forest had mysteriously disappeared, leaving a far field covered with snow. Bisecting the field were tracks upon which was a black locomotive with two red eyes glaring from the rear. A line of black cars stretched across the horizon.

Grandma Babka glided over the landscape. And as we watched, the moon peeked out from the clouds and opened a blue hole in the snow. Grandma Babka turned one last time to wave farewell and, seeing the hole, hopped in—straight to Baboosh.

And there she had adventures.

DEATH IN THE CHRISTMAS HOUR
James Powell

As THE LAST magical stroke of midnight sounded high over the snowy city that Christmas morning, a Welsh corgi named Owen Glendower was leading a young man on a leash past the houseware windows of McTammany's department store. Austin W. Metcalfe, as this young party called himself, possessed a round face cluttered with glasses and a short-stemmed, fat-bowled pipe whose operation he had not yet mastered. A burgundy muffler was tucked up neatly under his chin. His hands and feet were warm in fleece-lined leather. Every button of his dark blue overcoat was buttoned. He moved with the sedate and serious air of a second assistant curator of the Metropolitan Museum of Toys.

In other words—as Owen Glendower would be the first to admit—Metcalfe was a very, very pompous personage. The dog looked back over its shoulder as if about to unload a considerable burden of complaint, which it quite certainly could have done since, during the first hour of Christmas morning, toys come to life and animals possess the power of speech. Yes, poor square Metcalfe really needed his corners knocked off. The dog hoped some young woman would come along crazy enough to take a liking to him and do the job before it was too late. Recently Metcalfe had met a girl who seemed to fill the bill. Owen Glendower had used his considerable powers of thought transference to inspire a phone call. (Half the good ideas humans get come from their pets. Owen Glendower didn't know where the other half came from.) But the young stick-in-the-mud wouldn't make the move. The dog turned to mutter at a hydrant. What the hell!

Though the wind was picking up, Metcalfe waited patiently in the falling snow, conscious of being a kindly and, he was sure, a beloved master. He'd have enjoyed dwelling on that but his pipe went out again and he had to struggle to relight it. Meanwhile, around the corner and just ten feet from where he stood, the occupants of the largest of McTammany's toy windows had come to life. The Dick and Jane dolls were in the middle of a fashion show displaying their extensive wardrobes to an appreciative audience of frogs in frill collars, pigs in dresses, and a variety of robots, those metal facsimiles of humanity who beeped, hummed, and flashed their approval, which was amazing since batteries were not included.

When Owen Glendower was ready to move on, he gave a warning cough. The toys froze in their tracks. (If people ever found out about the Christmas Hour the annual chance to socialize and blow off a little steam would become one big media event with trundling television cameras and microphones in every toy face.) Then the dog led the young man around the corner to let the whole window see what an honest corgi had to put up with all year long. Metcalfe knew this window well. His museum had loaned its popular toy display and the young man's personal creation, "A Victorian Christmas," to McTammany's for the holidays. Metcalfe came every evening to admire his handiwork, which was on exhibit one window over. But he always stopped here first. His antique toys never suffered from the comparison.

When Owen Glendower felt he couldn't interrupt the toys' fun any longer, he gave another warning cough and led the way to Metcalfe's window. The young man's design featured a small alabaster fireplace in a Victorian living room. To the left of the fireplace stood a Christmas tree hung with brightly painted wooden ornaments and topped by a caroling angel. In front of the tree was a music-box ballerina on tiptoe and a blue and yellow jack-in-the-box. On the hearth rug sat two fine Punch and Judy hand puppets and their simple theater. To the right of the fireplace was a wing chair upholstered in green. On its matching hassock stood a most elegant Victorian dollhouse whose porcelain mistress waited at the door in a plum-colored hoop skirt. At the hassock's base a nutcracker captain of hussars with fierce grin and drawn saber led a formation of toy soldiers in scarlet coats and bearskin hats.

At least this was how Metcalfe had laid out the exhibit. But tonight the soldiers were nowhere to be seen. The hussar and the rest of the toys stood in a circle in front of the jack-in-the-box staring down at Judy lying on the red Turkey carpet, looking limp and forlorn like a hand puppet from which the hand had been withdrawn forever.

And there was more uncanniness. Sure, the jack-in-the-box was out and nodding on its spring. But traffic vibrations sometimes triggered the box latch. And the hussar seemed atremble as though it had just snapped to attention. Still, that might have been Metcalfe's imagination. But where did that Sherlock Holmes doll come from? And why did Metcalfe have the distinct impression the little detective was on the verge of pointing an accusing finger?

Then he saw the teddy bear at Holmes's side, and the light dawned. Miss Tinker, the department-store window dresser who'd helped him set up the museum display, said she always put her teddy in one of the toy windows at Christmas and please couldn't she sit him there on the wing chair? Using the arch laugh he'd developed to heap scorn on things, Metcalfe had explained how every toy, ornament, and piece of furniture in the display was an authentic Victorian artifact. But teddy bears were Edwardian. With bad grace she had accepted his compromise that she wrap up the bear and put it in with the other presents under the tree. Why, he wondered, were the pretty ones all so featherheaded? On the other hand, he hadn't been completely honest with her. The museum didn't have a Victorian Christmas-tree angel. Mr. Jacoby, their toy-repair-

and-reproduction wizard, had fashioned this one from an
Amelia Earhart doll from a bygone "Toys Conquer the
Clouds" display. For several days afterward Metcalfe had
been sorely tempted to call her up and confess. Now he was
glad he hadn't. A Sherlock Holmes doll, indeed! Metcalfe
relit his pipe and rocked back and forth on his heels, puffing,
with his hands clasped behind his back. Yes, he would defi-
nitely have to speak to the young lady about this. And about
how the teddy bear got there, too.

Metcalfe might have stayed there for some time, fuming,
imaging his righteousness at this confrontation. But Owen
Glendower gave a sigh of tedium and led him away from the
window and back to their apartment.

As for where Teddy had come from, the answer was the
Midwest. Miss Ivy Tinker had brought him with her as a mas-
cot when she moved East to take the job with McTammany's.
For Teddy, mascoting was a kind of lonely, fallow time. He
was anxious for Miss Ivy Tinker to get married and have children so he could get back to toying again.

Teddy had spent his first Christmas Hour out East alone,
pacing up and down with his forepaws in his pockets and
nothing to do but kick at the corner of the rug. To insure that
wouldn't happen again he'd furrowed his brow and directed
his powers of thought transference at Miss Ivy Tinker's sleeping head behind the bedroom door. The next morning she announced through toast that she'd dreamed she'd included him
in one of her Christmas-toy windows. And why not? The perfect cachet for a Tinker-dressed window. The stuffed bear
wasn't surprised a bit. (Half the good ideas humans get come
from their toys. Teddy didn't know where the other half came
from.)

Teddy hadn't spent a boring Christmas Hour since. Last
year he'd been right in the middle of McTammany's stuffed-
animal window. On the stroke of midnight, in clopped the
team of stuffed Clydesdales, the kangaroo pulled the spigot
out of his pouch and told the one about Australian beer being
made out of kangaroo hops, and a damn good time was had

by all. Teddy'd worn a hangover and a lopsided grin for the rest of the year.

And now it was Christmas Hour again. Stretching at the first rush of vital power, Teddy felt some constricting bond and heard the crinkle of paper. His paw quickly found the seam in the wrapping, located the end of the velvet bow and gave it a yank. With the toll of midnight sounding dimly in the distance he emerged and found himself standing among a pile of presents under a Christmas tree. Farther out in the room he could see other toys coming to life. He was just about to join them when the sound of a muffled violin made him stop. Teddy laid his ear to each of the gay presents around him until he found the source. He stripped back the paper. The lid illustration on the box depicted night and fog and a doorway from another era. The number was 221 B. The name on the lamppost was Baker Street. Large bright letters declared: "The Original Sherlock Holmes Doll. Another wonderful creation from Doyle Toy." Teddy opened the box. The doll inside wore a deerstalker's cap and a coat with a cape. In addition to its violin and bow, which the doll now lay aside with a smile, the other accessories included a hand glass, a calabash pipe, and a Persian slipper stuffed with shag. "Thank you, my dear sir," said Sherlock Holmes, taking Teddy's poffered paw to help himself out of the box. "I spent I don't know how many Christmases wedged down behind a radiator in the toy-department stockroom. I'm the sole survivor of an unpopular and long-forgotten line of dolls. I don't know who to thank for being here."

"Miss Ivy Tinker needed more boxes for under the tree," explained Teddy. Then he introduced himself.

Holmes looked the bear up and down. "*Ursus arctus Rooseveltii?* I hardly think so," said the detective. "And I did publish an anonymous monograph on stuffed animals." Reaching for his hand glass, he examined Teddy carefully. "Your eyes are French glass manufactured by Homard et Fils. Your seams are a double stitch called English nightingale because like that bird it is only found in England east of the Severn and south of the Trent. Homard et Fils supplied only one company in that area, Tiddicomb and Weams. That firm produced stuffed bears only once. On the birth of Queen Victoria's son Prince Leopold in 1854, Tiddicomb and Weams presented the royal child with a papier-mâché replica of the House of Lords complete with twelve stuffed bears dressed in stars and garters and full pontificals to represent the lords spiritual and temporal. This wonderful toy the teenaged prince later donated to an auction in aid of the victims of the great Chicago fire and it disappeared from sight in America. You, Teddy, are a Bear of the Realm."

Teddy's chest swelled with pride and his voice grew husky. "We stuffed animals have notoriously short memories. When Miss Ivy Tinker said I was a teddy bear I believed her."

"Well, come along, old fellow," said Holmes, taking his arm. "It's the Christmas Hour. The game's afoot."

Teddy needed no urging. They strolled from under the tree together, walking to the beat of the carol being sung by the silver-voiced angel atop the tree who, in the nature of Christmas-tree angels, preferred to spend the hour singing hymns of joy and praise.

Suddenly a captain of hussars blocked their way, a dozen red coats at his back. The officer raised a suspicious eyebrow and laid the point of his saber against Teddy's hairy breast. "Well, you ain't no alligator but you could be a rat in disguise," said the hussar, gnashing his teeth in a most threatening manner.

Teddy knocked the saber aside and growled as a Bear of the Realm might. "What I am is a bear."

Impressed by this lack of meekness, the officer said, "You mean one of those stuffed-animal chappies? Then welcome aboard. Captain Rataplan here. We can use anyone with spunk enough to stand beside us in this damn business."

"And just what business is that, Captain?" asked Holmes.

"Let's save that for over refreshments once we've got the perimeter secure," said the hussar. "I see old Punch has opened for business."

Holmes followed the officer's finger to the hearth rug, where the two hand puppets were converting their stage into a bar, Punch polishing the counter with a rag while Judy set up the bottles and glasses.

But Teddy's eyes couldn't get past the music-box ballerina only a few feet away. She had the dancer's classic features, small head, large eyes, and long legs. "A fine figure of a woman, that," agreed Captain Rataplan, giving Teddy an elbow in the ribs. "That's Allegretta. Gretta, we call her. Likes to play hard to get, don't you know. Well, I don't mind that in a woman. Faint heart ne'er won fair lady, eh?" He snorted fiercely and marched his men away.

Holmes and Teddy headed off across the carpet in the direction of the bar. As they passed the closed jack-in-the-box, Holes remarked, "Jack seems to be a slugabed."

Then they stopped and introduced themselves to the ballerina, who sat nursing a foot in her lap. "Come and join us for a drink," urged Teddy. *"Tempus fugit."*

"I'll be right along, okay?" she said through chewing gum. "Boy, are my dogs barking."

"After a year on tiptoe, dogs that didn't bark would be quite a clue indeed," observed Holmes with a smile. Then they crossed to the bar, where Punch greeted them with a "What'll it be, gents?" in a squeaking, batlike voice.

"Something with a splash of the old gasogene, Landlord, if you please," said Holmes. "A Scotch whiskey, I think."

"Make mine a gibson," said Teddy. The cocktail was very popular among creatures who only came to life for one hour a year.

"So be it, gents," squeaked Punch. But as the hunchback reached for the Scotch he shouted over his shoulder, "Judy, where you off to?"

"An olive," squeaked his female partner, waving an ice pick.

"Onions for gibsons, old hoss," scolded Punch, stopping Judy in her tracks. The bartender mixed their drinks and served them. Judy supplied the pickled onion from a jar with the point of her ice pick. "Your health, gents," declared Punch, raising his own mug of beer. As they clinked their drinks Punch turned once again to Judy and demanded, "Where now, old hoss?"

"An olive," she said. "Here comes Captain Rataplan for his martooni."

But the hussar heard her and shook his head. "My men

come first. Twelve mugs of the nut brown ale." Judy put the ice pick in the pocket of her smock and obediently set to filling the mugs. Turning to Holmes and his bear companion, Captain Rataplan said, "Getting back to the alligator situation, the damned things feed on sewer rats all year round. So come Christmas Hour we're a delicious change of pace and they swarm up and make a try for us. No problem. We can give as good as we get. Alligators are a stupid, musclebound crew. But then there's the rats. Cowards, of course. But smart as whips. Gentlemen, one of those years the rats are going to talk the alligators into an alliance. What I see coming against us is an army of alligators each with a rat riding on its neck whispering orders in its ear. Mark my words, when that day dawns toydom will vanish from human memory and dogs and cats won't be far behind."

"A grim prospect," said Holmes gravely. "Let's hope the rats never get the idea."

As Rataplan left with his mugs of ale on a tray, some of the gloom from his words went with him. After a few pulls at his drink, Holmes leaned back with elbows on the bar and said, "Rat masterminds astride alligators or not, Teddy, it's great to be alive again. I only miss one thing: a mystery to be solved. No, I'm a liar, Teddy. Two things."

"And what's the other, Holmes?" asked Teddy, chewing the onion from his gibson.

Sherlock Holmes did not answer. He straightened up. "Speak of the devil!" he exclaimed. "Excuse me, old man, won't you?" Taking off his cap, the detective strode across to the hassock, where a woman stood smiling down at him from the dollhouse doorway. Not a woman, but *the* woman. "Can it be you, Miss Alder? I mean, Mrs. Godfrey Norton." For that indeed was the married name of the heroine of *A Scandal in Bohemia.*

"Good morning, Mr. Sherlock Holmes." The woman smiled, allowing the detective to help her down onto the rug. "And it is Irene Adler. I assumed my professional name again when my husband's death obliged my return to the operatic stage."

"Allow me to offer you my arm, Miss Alder," urged the detective. "Let us walk a bit apart. I must know how you come

to be here. I was just telling my friend Teddy that there were
only two things I miss: Miss Irene Adler and a good mystery."

"In that order, Mr. Holmes?"

"Indeed," insisted the detective.

Irene Adler laughed gaily at the lie. Then they picked out a
design in the carpet to use as a path and walked together toward the big window. "I'm from the Diva series of dolls," she
explained, "each a replica of a famous prima donna. The museum has us all displayed on the stage of a Victorian-doll opera
house. Well, last year there was that terrible business when the
alligators came bursting in on us right at the start of the Christmas Hour, all shouting in their vile sewer language. If it hadn't
been for Captain Rataplan and his thin red line of soldiers
which bestrode the aisle and Punch who backed them up with
his club none of us would have had time to find high ground.
The rest of the Victorian Christmas people sought refuge up on
the hassock. But in the excitement Lady Gwendolyn, the mistress of the dollhouse, fell over the edge and into the midst of
the alligators and was swallowed up in a single gulp."

Holmes and the woman had reached the window. They
stood in silence, contemplating the darkness beyond the glass
and watching the wind swirl the snow beneath the streetlights.
Then Irene Adler said, "The second assistant curator chose
me to take Lady Gwendolyn's place. I'm glad he did. The
Diva Christmas Hours were oppressive with all the ladies trying to upstage each other. Personally I've always preferred the
company of men." Then she said, "But come, tell me how
you come to be here."

But before the detective could answer Teddy came running
up behind them. "I say, Holmes," he said in a voice which
had become progressively more British since he'd learned of
his ancestry, "something terrible's happened. Judy's been
murdered."

Judy was quite dead. There was evidence of a severe contusion under her hooked chin. But death had come another way.
Concealed within the folds of the voluminous smock hand
puppets wear was the ice pick which had found her heart.

Holmes rose from his examination of the corpse and sur-

veyed the horrified toys who stood around it, including a
newcomer, a young man in a cap with bells and a particolored
suit. This would be Jack. His box stood wide open and empty
behind him.

Irene Adler had turned pale. "And are we toys capable of
murder?" she asked.

"Yes," said Holmes grimly. "And of seeing that justice is
done, as I assure you it will. Now, what happened here?"

Gretta said, "Judy came running up to Jack's box, giggling
like a goose and squealing something about olives, okay?
Next thing I know, whacko!, out pops Jack."

Jack said, "I guess she was leaning over the box and the lid
caught her under the chin." Bells tinkled as he shook his head
sadly. "A nasty rap, Mr. Holmes. But I thought it only knocked
her out. I sent Gretta for a wet cloth to put on the contusion."

The ballerina nodded. "Punch came running back with me.
We found Captain Rataplan bending over her. He jumped up
quick and started yelling at Jack."

"I thought the scoundrel'd struck her, Mr. Holmes," said
the hussar. "I accused him right to his face. Not that it surprised me. The man's an utter coward. He proved that last
year, lurking in his box when there were alligators to be
driven off. And yes, by thunder, I lost my temper and tried to
throttle him. I admit it. But Punch pulled me off."

"When Punch leaped up from tending Judy the wet cloth
fell off her chin," said Gretta. "I was putting it back on when
I saw the ice pick. That's when your stuffed friend came running up."

"I was on the hassock getting some tables and chairs for
the ladies," said Teddy. "I saw the fight from up there and
came on the double."

"We'd all warned the dumb old hoss not to carry the ice
pick around in her pocket," said Punch.

"This was no accident," said Holmes. He paused for a
thoughtful moment. Then he turned to Jack. "After Allegretta
ran off for the wet cloth, did you examine Judy? Was she still
alive?"

Jack hung his head. "I was so upset by what I'd done I just
stood there."

"And you, Captain Rataplan," asked Holmes, "could you swear Judy was alive when you bent over her?"

"I didn't look farther than the mark on her chin and flew off the handle," admitted the fierce hussar. "This jack-in-the-box fellow's an upstart."

"You can say that again," mused Holmes.

"I mean the fellow's trouser legs don't even match," said Rataplan. "And yet he had the brass to have his eyes on Lady Gwendolyn, who lives in the big house on the hassock. Last year I slew three alligators and left them as dead as luggage. And only the brave deserve the fair. But I would never, never have aspired to the hand of so fine a lady." Rataplan paused to clear his throat. "Of course, my heart is elsewhere," he said. Here, like many brave men, he was overcome by emotion and averted his eyes. Holmes was quick to observe that it was the ballerina's unsympathetic stare the captain of hussars was avoiding. With only one brief hour of life each year toys were as quick to show their emotions as young people in wartime.

Holmes looked at Punch. "Landlord, was Judy alive or dead when you leaned over her?"

"Search me, guv," said the hunchback. "I mean, the fracas broke out right away."

"And yet you were certainly attached to Judy."

"A strictly professional relationship," insisted Punch. "I mean, did you ever see the snoot on her?"

"You're rather well endowed in that department yourself," observed Holmes.

"But I don't have to look at me, you see," said Punch quickly. "And while we're on the subject, you've got something of a beak yourself."

Holmes turned to confront Jack. "And just what was your relationship with the deceased?" he demanded.

"We all need someone, Mr. Holmes," said Jack.

"But why do you in particular need someone?"

"I don't understand."

Holmes made an exasperated noise and said, "Must we reconstruct the crime?"

Jack turned white. He laid a hand on the detective's arm and murmured, "Could I have a word in private, Mr. Holmes?"

"If you'll be more straightforward than you have been up to now," replied Holmes.

The bells in Jack's cap jingled as he swore he would be. When they had moved off a bit from the others Jack said, "I'm sure you realize that I can't trigger my lid latch from the inside."

"I am quite familiar with the Wunderbar jack-in-the-box mechanism," said the detective.

"But the others aren't, Mr. Holmes," said Jack. "When Christmas Hour comes I can't even get out of my box myself. That's a humiliating situation for a grown toy. That's my dark secret. Oh, sure, my first Hour here in the Victorian Christmas exhibit I was lucky. A passing subway train triggered my latch. But I couldn't count on that happening again. I had to tell my secret to someone. I chose Lady Gwendolyn because she was so kind and good." Jack gave a sad little smile and shook his head, remembering.

Then he continued, "Every Christmas Hour after that she'd slip over here first thing and let me out. But last year she fell to her death. In fact I'd still be in the damned box if Rataplan hadn't come storming over after the alligators turned tail. He called me a coward and beat on the lid with his bloody saber until he accidentally triggered the latch. Well, with Lady Gwendolyn dead I needed somebody else to let me out of the box for Christmas Hour. Since Judy'd always been a bit soft on me, I took the chance of explaining things to her. Hey, she was glad to help. She even came up with the olive business. You see, Rataplan's martooni was always the first drink of the night. So she gave me the olives to keep in my icebox."

"Your secret has cost the lives of two people," said the detective. "I cannot believe that to be a coincidence. Come, let us settle this matter."

They returned to the waiting circle of toys, where Holmes said, "Ladies and gentlemen, Judy's murderer is a very resourceful and decisive person who has committed a perfect crime."

"Come now, Holmes," protested Teddy, "don't tell us you're baffled."

"Consider my dilemma," said Holmes. "There are four suspects: Jack, Captain Rataplan, Punch, and Gretta. All had the opportunity to kill. There is no clue to tell us which one did it. Ergo, a perfect crime."

"And so justice will not be done, Mr. Holmes?" said Irene Adler.

"Ah, but it will be, Miss Adler," said Holmes. "It will, indeed. Our murderer's mistake was to kill once too often. You see, Lady Gwendolyn's tragic death last year was no accident. She was pushed from the hassock by a jealous hand. And her murderer would have escaped discovery except for killing again. Judy's murder, perfect though the crime was, points the unerring finger of guilt at Lady Gwendolyn's killer. Let us consider the events of last year's Christmas Hour. Rataplan and Punch were fighting the alligators. Jack was in his box. And two toys had found refuge with Lady Gwendolyn up on the hassock. Judy was one of them. Clearly the murderer of Judy and Lady Gwendolyn is . . ." Holmes was about to point the accusing finger when a corgi coughed.

The Christmas tree angel fell silent and the toys froze in their places. The figure of an owlish, self-satisfied young man loomed on the other side of the window glass.

Under his breath Teddy whispered, "It's the second assistant curator from the toy museum, Holmes. Met him once. Something of a royal stuffed shirt, don't you know. Miss Ivy Tinker has spoken of him most severely to me."

"He looks invincibly square, old fellow," whispered Holmes, venturing a glance. "I'd say she's got her work cut out for her." After what seemed to be forever the human beyond the glass was led away by the corgi.

Holmes's accusing finger pointed. But as quick as a cat Gretta snatched the astonished Rataplan's saber away from him and knocked the captain of hussars to the floor with the flat of it. When Punch made a grab for her she wounded him in the arm. Jack turned pale and popped down into his box and couldn't get out again.

"There are soldiers at all the exits. You can't escape, you know," said Holmes calmly.

"We'll see about that," said the ballerina. She held them at bay with the saber and moved slowly backward in the direc-

tion of the Christmas tree. Leaving Irene Adler to tend to
Punch, Holmes and Teddy kept pace as close as Gretta would
allow.

"Yes, I killed them both," she boasted. "When fate and the
second assistant curator brought Jack into my life I knew I'd
found the toy for me. There was a crazy electricity about the
way he dressed and how he'd pop out of the box when you
least expected it. I fell for him hard and swore to myself I'd
kill anybody who came between us."

The ballerina was directly under the tree now. "I knew Jack
had something going with Lady Gwendolyn," she continued.
"I wasn't born yesterday. I saw them whispering. And whenever she came to visit he'd always pop right out of his box.
He never did that for me. When the alligators broke in I saw
my chance and took it." She shook her head with disbelief.
"But right away he got pally with Judy. Judy, can you imagine that? So tonight when she came waltzing over to the box
I saw red and applied my foot to the small of her back. She
hit the latch on Jack's box face first and out he popped. I'd
only meant to warn her off. But later when I saw I could get
away with it I said what the hell and slipped in the ice pick."

"And now the game's up, Gretta," said Holmes.

With a contemptuous laugh the woman put the saber between her teeth, leaped up into the tree and disappeared from
sight inside the evergreenery.

"But surely she doesn't think she can get away, Holmes?"
said the amazed bear.

"There's only one way to find out, old fellow," answered
the detective, clambering up the tree trunk.

"Onward and upward, then," said Teddy, who was stuffed
with excelsior.

But pursuit wasn't easy. As Gretta fled up the tree she cut
the strings on the wooden ornaments and sent them crashing
down on her pursuers, obliging them to seek frequent shelter.
And the dancer's excellent physical condition enabled her to
leap from branch to branch like a monkey. She soon left them
far behind. "Adios, okay, Mr. Holmes?" she shouted trium-
phantly.

"I've been a blind fool, Teddy," said the detective, ducking to avoid a falling ornament. "She's going to hijack the angel and make it fly her to the Cuban Mission to the United Nations."

"Political asylum?" puffed Teddy.

"A lot more than that!" shouted Gretta from the top of the tree, where she was holding the blade of the saber across the angel's throat. "Before this Christmas Hour is done I'll have told the rats in the Cubans' basement everything. When you all come to life next year an army of alligators with rat riders will be there to greet you. Pleasant dreams. Hell hath no fury like a scorned toy!" With this cry she vaulted onto the angel's back and slapped the creature's thigh with the flat of the saber. The angel flapped its wings and launched them both into space. It circled the top of the tree in a wide arc and then executed a barrel roll Amelia Earhart would have been proud of. Gretta fell headfirst the long distance to the floor.

The Victorian Christmas exhibit has been returned to the museum, where it continues to attract crowds. Metcalfe replaced Gretta with a Bo Peep with a velvet bow on her crook and brought the broken music-box ballerina to Mr. Jacoby for repairs. ("Listen, Metcalfe," said the overworked Mr. Jacoby, laying the doll in a small cardboard box and fastening the lid with a stout elastic band, "this goes on the shelf in the closet. If I get to it in twenty years I'll be lucky.") And a new, less timid Judy has been found. They say it gives Punch as good as it gets. And sitting in the wing chair wearing the full regalia of a Knight of the Garter is Teddy. A card nearby informs the world that it is in the presence of a rare Bear of the Realm on loan to the museum from Miss Ivy Tinker.

Mr. Metropolitan, the generous Armenian who was the museum's director and major endower, was delighted with the Bear of the Realm acquisition and congratulated his second assistant curator on recognizing so rare a toy. Metcalfe did not tell him how his righteous indignation over Miss Ivy Tinker's tampering with his window display had left him so unsettled that first hour of Christmas morning that he'd been obliged to read himself to sleep, choosing an old unsigned monograph on stuffed toys he'd picked up in a secondhand bookshop.

Later, when the holidays were over and he arrived at
McTammany's for his confrontation with Miss Tinker, his indignation vanished when he noticed Teddy's English nightingale stitching and glass Homard et Fils eyes. Excited, he
begged her to loan the priceless antique to the museum. She
did not agree at once. They had to return to the subject over
several dinners and during numerous cultural events about
town. One night, as an illustration of the point she was making about the dangers of extremism on matters of authenticity,
Miss Tinker observed that even though the Irene Adler doll
was Victorian while the Sherlock Holmes doll was a contemporary piece they somehow went up together wonderfully.
Metcalfe was foolish enough to heap scorn on this idea with
that arch laugh of his. As a result Miss Tinker refused to loan
Teddy to the museum or set eyes on Metcalfe again until the
two dolls in question were standing side by side in the dollhouse doorway in the Victorian Christmas exhibit.

Of course Miss Tinker retained visiting rights to Teddy.
Sometimes when she and Metcalfe came to the museum after
closing time they brought Owen Glendower along. (The corgi
rather liked her. The young woman hadn't knocked off all
Metcalfe's corners yet but she was well on the way.) And
sometimes all three of them would stop in on the late-working
Mr. Jacoby. One evening, in the middle of a discussions, Mr.
Jacoby set his teacup down on the workbench, stroked his cat,
and said, "Speaking of authentic, Mr. Metcalfe, we can always find another place for Amelia Earhart. But that Judy
hand puppet somebody worked over with an ice pick, it's Victorian. What say I make it into a Christmas-tree angel for
your exhibit?"

Metcalfe gestured enthusiastically with his pipe. "Honestly,
Mr. Jacoby," he said. "I just don't know where you come up
with all your ideas."

No one noticed Mr. Jacoby's cat and Owen Glendower exchange glances.

A Christmas ghost story.

THE BOXING DAY SPECTRE
Kit Reed

WHEN DAVE AND Jane chose a middle Victorian with a widow's walk and surrounding porches instead of buying one of the upscale architects' houses going up in Governors' Grove outside New Haven, Jane's mother tried to talk them out of it.

"What are my friends going to think," she began, infuriating Jane, who snapped:

"They're going to think it's none of your business."

"They're going to think you couldn't afford a new house."

Dave said quietly, "Why should you care what people think," but it was an empty effort, rather like spitting into the whirlwind.

"I had so hoped you'd get a modern house," said Mother, whose house was brand new the day she moved in as a bride after World War II. Because she was loaning them the down payment, they'd been compelled to make the ritual pilgrimage to Levittown to break the news.

"Modern isn't very interesting, Mother." Jane was too polite to add: It dates pretty fast.

"Old is so *inconvenient*. Now I have my built-in air-conditioning, and my built-in microwave ..."

Pragmatic Dave said, "Twice the space at half the cost."

"But Victorian. It's so—spooky." Social anxiety made Mother craven; she appealed to Jane's little boys. "Don't you think it's spooky, kids?"

"Spooky?" Struggling out of one of Grandmother's matched Barcaloungers with some difficulty, Davy looked at her through the thicket of Hummel figurines she kept on her Fabulous Fifties room divider, a saccharine assortment of elves, gnomes and rosy, smug little fat kids holding cute things. "Not really."

Bobby thought Grandmother's thick shag rug and her gold brocade upholstery were spooky, but was too polite to say so. "I love it."

"An old house," she said with a fastidious little shudder. "You don't know *who's* done *what* there ..."

Jane said stiffly, "The owners were descended from retired bankers and judges, they're moving to Florida ..."

By that time even the boys were too angry to pick up their grandmother's sinister hint. "... or what they've left behind ..."

"... because they won the lottery."

"Moving in after other people. I don't know," she said in a final stab. "It's like wearing somebody else's clothes."

Jane said grimly, "Just wait until we have it fixed up."

The place was a beauty; a little Victorian gem. She and Dave spent months restoring it, going through unfinished rooms at night after the contractors left, choosing wall colors and where to hang extra lights and installing shutters in the long windows where heavy draperies had hung. They prowled Ada's Antiques, picking up furniture that would look right with the carved staircase and the dentil moldings and when their confidence flagged, hardy Ada bucked them up, tucking her thumbs in the pockets of her khaki coverall. "Place like that—it's a beauty. Your own little bit of the past."

It was going to be beautiful; they reveled in the sense of space, spinning giddily in empty rooms. Davy and Bobby would have the two back bedrooms upstairs and the ornate, heavily decorated dining room would be painted white and turned into a family room—TV and kids' projects exorcising ghosts of stuffy dinners past. Their favorite room was the second parlor with the big bay window where, everybody agreed, they would put the Christmas tree.

Good, generous Ada brought an octagonal vitrine with mirrored shelves to go into the second parlor—her housewarming present; it glistened in the corner and Jane and her family made private decisions to give each other Christmas presents that would sit well on the mirrored shelves.

They moved in at Thanksgiving. Their first night was wonderful; they loved the noises—banging shutters, floors creaking, the hum of the giant furnace; it was like settling into a ship.

On the second night, Mother came. Flushed with ownership, Jane ushered Mother into the front hall. "Well, how do you like it?"

"It's lovely," Mother said in a thin voice. "I just wish it could be a little—*newer*."

"You mean like those glass boxes in Governor's Grove."

"Just something a little more—contemporary," Mother said. "These high ceilings, and your *fixtures* . . ."

"Oh Mother, come see the second sitting room."

"Your brother Mitchell has bought Patsy a beautiful new condo in Florida, with a completely sunken bathroom and terazzo floors, I've shown the picture to my friends . . ."

"Look, we have a bay window."

". . . and my friends think Mitchell's a huge success."

"And Ada gave us this beautiful case for ornaments . . ."

But Mother wasn't listening. "Eeeek!"

"Mother, what's the matter?"

"Over there!"

"I don't see anything."

"Of course not. That's the whole thing." Mother clenched Jane's arm and her voice dropped. "Something brushed past me in the hall!"

Was there something there? Sunny afternoon in the late twentieth-century—not likely. "This is an old house, Mother," Jane said. "It's drafty."

She said in a squeaky whisper, "Old houses have ghosts."

"It's your imagination."

And Mother? She said, "You wish."

Upstairs, she bypassed the guest room, where Jane had put out fresh towels, and went into the master bedroom and threw her coat and hat on Dave's pillow. "This is a nice room," she said grudgingly. "But isn't that a fresh crack running along the wall behind the bed?"

Jane suppressed wishful visions of an apparition seeping out to scare Mother in the night, or a steel-clawed hand snatching her into the crack. *Nightmare on Elm Street?* Not a prayer. "You see too many movies Mother," she said, leaving her to unpack by herself.

Mother's voice trailed after her. "If this place is haunted, you'll have to move."

Dave was not altogether thrilled that he and Jane were going to be spending the holidays in the guest-room double bed, but when Jane pointed out that it was only for the holidays he shrugged and grinned suggestively. "Well then, I guess we'll have to make the most of it."

Jane got to bed late because the unfamiliar kitchen slowed her down and it was midnight before she finished her Thanksgiving pies; Dave was already asleep. It might have been fatigue or the narrow bed or the wind rising around the house but she slept poorly, waking before dawn in a tightly sealed room with thick carpeting that eliminated drafts. What had waked her? Something cold across her face: a breeze, or was it a hush? A . . . presence. She was sure of it.

Riveted, she waited for more: outlines of a shape, a few words, anything, but sometime between then and sunup, consciousness blurred. When she woke again, Dave had opened the curtains; sunlight crashed into the room and the presence, if there had been a presence, was gone.

It was a mercy that Ada came to Thanksgiving dinner; when Mother launched her recital on the joys of Mitchell's condo, Ada distracted her, drawing her into the second parlor to read her palm. "You are too caught up in appearances," Ada said soberly, while behind Mother's back, Jane and her loved ones exchanged secret smiles.

It was pleasant in the second parlor even at this hour, when premature darkness drew black squares in the windows, which gave back reflections of the lovely room. Looking up from the inlaid table where her mother's palm was spread for Ada's scrutiny, Jane tried to decide: Had she seen some part of the reflection moving? Something more than the mirrored activities of her restless kids? She didn't think so, but there was something extra in the air tonight—a gentle movement, rather like a sigh.

Then over dishes Ada said matter-of-factly, "I passed your ghost on the way to the bathroom."

"Our ghost!"

"She's very sweet."

"I wish you hadn't told me," Jane said.

"You don't look like the kind of person who's afraid of ghosts."

"It's Mother. She'll kill us with terminal I-told-you-so."

"But it's a *nice* ghost . . ."

But Jane's worries outstripped her. "If she finds out she won't let up."

". . . and it's only a little sad. She won't mind this ghost," Ada said, wiping her hands on her khaki coverall and picking up a dish towel. "It's only a little girl."

"You don't know Mother. She'll make us move."

Ada said dryly, "Maybe you need to get rid of your mother."

"It would be easier to get rid of our ghost!" As soon as Jane spoke, the water in the old sink bubbled regretfully, filling Jane with remorse. "Oh, please don't get upset, I didn't mean to hurt your feelings," Jane said.

"Feelings? Whose feelings?" Unbidden, Mother barged in.

"Nothing, Mother. It's this wretched drain."

"That's old houses," Mother said unfeelingly. "I think I'll get a train back tomorrow, if it's all the same to you. This old place is too drafty for me."

On the way to the station she laid out her agenda: the inconvenience, the risky investment; "What's more, there's something shady going on. That thing I saw in the hall."

"Mother, you didn't see anything."

"Don't tell me what I didn't see. It's *creepy*. It's unsafe for children and unwholesome," she said, leading up to her ultimate threat. "When I come back for Christmas I'm going to be on the alert. If there is a ghost, you're moving, for the sake of my grandchildren, and if you won't move, I'm going to take my money out."

Back at the house, Jane and Dave called Ada to consult. She arrived with something in a bowling bag. It turned out to be her crystal ball, which she set up on the inlaid table in the second parlor. "You want to get in touch with your ghost?"

"If Mother sees her, it's curtains. We have to warn her to hide."

"Easier said than done."

Dave said, "You don't think she'd just stay out of the way?"

Ada squinted. "Depends on what her problem is."

"I mean, she's already invisible."

Ada's voice dropped. "Invisible now."

Dave said, "Is that such a big thing to ask?"

"Depends," Ada said, "Ghosts have their priorities too."

"Oh please, Ada. We don't have much time. Mother's due back on Christmas Eve."

Ada rolled up her sleeves. "Let's see what we can do." They gathered in the second parlor on the first in a series of desperate evenings in which they tried to contact their resident spirit, first with Ada's crystal ball, which really worked, although not in these circumstances, and then with a hastily contrived ouija board. Nothing seemed to work.

Meanwhile Mother was spending the between-holiday hiatus in Mitchell's ultramodern waterfront palazzo in Florida. She sent eight-by-eleven color enlargements of herself and Patsy and Mitchell in front of Mitchell's place, a spanking glass brick number on a sandy spit in a Florida bay created so recently by dredges and piledrivers that it was too raw for ghosts. The three of them were wearing trendy beach gear and squinting into the camera, grinning as the gestured at the ultimate latest—the business end of an outdoor-indoor swimming pool; you dove in outdoors, next to the breezeway, and came up indoors, in the living-room conversation pit. And Mitchell's children? Unlike Jane's wiry, introverted, thoughtful pair, they looked tanned, blond, smug and modern, *modern* with their blond heads and dazzling grins and their matching scuba gear. The photos came with a card with an all-too-predictable message: WISH YOU WERE HERE.

Jane telephoned: "Mother, you look so comfortable, maybe you'd rather do Christmas down there with Mitchell, where you'll . . ." Never find out we have a ghost? ". . . be warm."

"Oh no," Mother said, "I wouldn't miss Christmas in New England for the world, and besides . . ." She left the rest unspoken. In the silence, it sounded like a threat.

Jane thought she could supply it: If I can expose your ghost, I can make you move. Right now it wouldn't be hard to prove; manifestations were clearer and more frequent as the holidays approached.

Using a fast setting on his camera, Dave caught a white blur that looked like a white skirt flickering around the corner into the second sitting room. Every time Jane came into the house with another armful of Christmas packages, something followed her upstairs and into the master bedroom, where she hid presents until it was time to wrap. The kids said they kept running into Tillie, which is what they named her, in the halls.

But no matter what ruses Jane and Dave and the kids employed, no matter how Ada sweet-talked her, they couldn't trap Tillie in conversation or convince her to answer by knocks, whistling or any other signs, the pressing questions they wanted to pose: Who are you? Why are you still here after all these years? And, most pressing: What do you want?

Three days before Christmas Eve—and Mother's arrival— Jane locked the bedroom door and got out the packages she had to wrap: comic avengers for Davy and Bobby, games, books, everything a boy could want; she got out the sweater, the gold cuff links and the record albums for Dave and the (groan) crocheted scarf for Mother, along with the china ornament she'd paid too much for and hated so much she hadn't even bothered to take it out of its box; she hardly noticed when this second package for Mother fell off the bed. She wrapped everybody's presents from Mitchell, who always sent a check, and then she wrapped the plaid hunting cap for

Ada and the dozens of other trinkets and tidbits she kept adding until each person's pile of presents looked right. She was about to finish when she had to find a sweater because her hands were shaking with cold; then she realized why. Going deliberately from dresser to bed she sat down, accidentally kicking the present for Mother under the bed where it would lie until Boxing Day, when she finally remembered it. Then without turning around she said to the presence behind her, "Tillie?"

That's not my name.

"Then what is it?"

No answer.

"Well," Jane said because this was, after all, only a child, "then it's just going to have to do. Listen, Tillie," she said, collecting herself. "My mother's coming back and I need a favor."

Although she didn't answer, Tillie was still there. Jane was certain she saw her flickering at the end of the bed.

"Dave and I like you and all, and after all it's your house too, but listen . . ."

There was a little hush in which Tillie drew in her breath—if she still drew breath.

"I need you to, ah—*hide?*—until she's gone. She's hell on wheels and if she can prove we have a ghost she's going to make us move out." Jane paused for emphasis. "OK, Tillie, OK?"

I can't.

Instinctively, as if she could grab Tillie and shake her for emphasis, Jane wheeled. "But you have to."

Tillie was gone; at least Jane thought she was.

Only her words trailed after her, spinning into the room and hanging there like smoke. *I never got what I wanted,* Tillie said.

Because she'd been a mother for so long, Jane took Tillie's point. She phoned Ada, who came at once. "I heard her!"

"She spoke to you?"

"She said, 'I never got what I wanted.' Poor thing!"

And good old Ada said immediately, "Right! She died of something, poor little thing got carried off by disease or disappointment right after the Christmas when she didn't get what she wanted. That should have been the end of it, but her wish was too big to go away."

"And it's still around."

"Exactly. And so is she. Now that it's Christmas again, you're going to see her a lot."

"Not if I can help it," Jane said.

"She won't go away until she gets what she wants."

"That's the whole thing," Jane said. "I think I know what to do."

Ada said quietly, "I don't suppose you'd give me a clue."

"Shh," Jane said, bending close in case Tillie turned out to be eavesdropping. "I don't want her to know."

Jane knew exactly what to do; she shopped. Heaven knows she shopped; she bought dolls and dishes and doll clothes in little doll trunks; books she bought, and toys and perfume and stationery with flowers on it and on the off chance that this Victorian child was ahead of her time, toy trains and cap pistols and a toy doctor kit—an enormous pile of presents for Tillie, which she wrapped and sneaked up to lay out in the attic with a placard with TILLIE written on it which on second thought she removed and replaced with a sign that read, DEAR GHOST, THIS IS FOR YOU. Then she left the door to the attic ajar so their little girl ghost would see it and go up.

She could not be certain, but she thought it worked. In the last few days before Christmas there was not a sign of Tillie, and when Mother walked in on Christmas Eve with her antennae out even she remarked that the house wasn't nearly as gloomy as she remembered it, for whatever that was worth. There were no strange shadows in the corridors, no unseemly flashes of white and no suspicious drafts.

Christmas was quiet and pleasant and it passed uneventfully. Ada brought Mother a new silver kid bag from the mall as a present, which was just as well, as in the flurry of shopping and wrapping the presents she'd hidden for Tillie, Jane had completely forgotten Mother's second gift and all she got was the crocheted scarf. The rest of present-opening was fine; the boys loved their presents and so did Dave, who'd bought Jane an antique pearl brooch that delighted her because it went with the house. Dinner was fine and the pies were fine and when Mother came out to the kitchen, she had to admit Christmas in the old house had worked out all right after all.

Jane and Dave went to bed congratulating themselves. Too soon.

They were waked by a rustle and clatter overhead—Tillie opening her presents? That too was fine, Jane thought, snuggling deep. In the next second the room shook so violently that she was jolted out of bed. The bed shook; the floor shook; the windows shook; the house shook, and foolhardy Jane, who had imagined she could satisfy their ghost with a few little presents, heard a spectral voice going higher and higher, in concentric vibrations strong enough to wake Mother and disturb the dead: *I never get what I want!*

And poor Jane, lying on her belly on the rug carpet, rolled over, crying, "I tried, Tillie. I tried!" As she struggled to rise, she collided with a box caught in the dust ruffle: Mother's other present! Oh fine, she thought bitterly. A lot of good this will do.

She came down the next morning to find her mother fully dressed and sitting on a pile of suitcases in the front hall. "I'm leaving now. Dave can drive me to the train."

"Oh please, have a little breakfast first."

"I'd be afraid to eat. And you might as well get ready to move. The place is haunted . . ."

"Could have been an earthquake?"

". . . and you'll be hearing from my bank."

Dave said desperately, "We live over a fault." Behind him, an entire stack of dishes clattered into the sink.

"Earthquake, hell! I'm taking my money out."

"Let's talk about this later," Jane said.

"If she wants to go let her go," Dave growled. "I'll take her."

"I'll call you from Mitchell's," Mother said.

"Oh, wait!" Desperate, Jane remembered the forgotten present. "Right now, let's have some coffee while Dave gets dressed."

"After I get my coat."

"In here," Jane said, dragging her into the second parlor. "I have an extra present for you." There was a stirring just outside the circle of her vision.

"A present?"

A present?

"Something special." Oh Tillie, Jane thought. You wouldn't touch it with a stick.

I never get what I want.

Mother said grudgingly, "All right."

The second parlor was brilliant in the morning sunlight, which beggared the colored lights on the Christmas tree, and yesterday's presents shifted slightly, as if in a subtle breeze. For the moment even Mother seemed mollified, sitting on the Victorian love seat with Jane's package in her lap, slitting the ribbon with one varnished nail and opening the paper carefully, so it could be reused. "Oh Jane," she said. "It's beautiful. Just what I always wanted."

"I'm so glad you like it," Jane said, swallowing distaste: the one Hummel her mother didn't have. It was the Hummel little boy with his pink bottom showing and his china pants pulled down over his rosy china knees.

"Time to go," angry Dave said brusquely, sweeping in like an avenging angel, tucking Mother's luggage under one arm and with the other, stuffing her into the coat. Before Jane could even say good-bye he had her by the elbow and was hustling her out. "Jane, say 'Good-bye, Mother.' Mother, say 'Good-bye, Jane.' "

When he slammed the door the house shook.

There was an immediate hush and in the next second the whole place trembled in a departure as swift and powerful as a tidal wave; it was Tillie! She was leaving! She was . . . she was . . .

"She's going with Mother!" Jane cried.

. . . gone. Then Jane's head filled with unspoken thanks: Tillie's final manifestation before she left them forever and took up residence on a higher plane:

All I ever wanted was a Hummel, Tillie said.

In which a little girl saves the world.

THE TOY MILL
David Nickle and Karl Schroeder

I
Emily Gets Her Wish

THE MAN IN the Moon's smile began to slip. It turned into a leer. Then, breaking from the rim of the moon came a shape of crystalline hardness, led by eight bobbing points. Emily, perched straddling the peak of her auntie's home with the cold shivering through her spine, counted those points three times, and whispered aloud:

"Comet, Cupid, Donner, Vixen." She mouthed the rest of the verse, to hide that she didn't remember the other names.

The procession cut behind a black smear of cloud, and Emily scrambled higher on the roof, her back pressed against the frozen brick of the chimney. The winter air made a frost in her throat and she clutched her pink parka over her chest. The sleigh was gone. She'd missed it—if it had ever been there.

Emily turned away, filled with a deep and despairing sense of abandonment. The moon turned darker.

Iron runners hissed past inches above her head, and a

breath of stratospheric cold made her shiver. For a moment all she could see was the swollen underbelly of the sleigh, like the black bottom of a cauldron. Then the thing was landing, with unctuous delicacy, on the virgin snow of the roof.

The ski tracks began near enough to Emily that she could touch them, and that is what she did, even though they steamed with a black substance like the burnt drippings from an overcooked roast. The tracks were wider than her hand, and packed down so hard as to make the snow into a sheet of perfect, polished ice.

At the ends of those tracks, great iron skis whose ends spiraled four times glowed with tiny red embers from treetops brushed too closely, and creaked around the thick rivets that held the sleigh together.

She couldn't see the reindeer for the bulk of the sleigh. But Emily could clearly see her own tracks through the deep wet snow of the roof; they were the only disturbance in its blued perfection other than the tracks of the sleigh.

She forced herself to stand up, and cautiously sidled around the edge of the sleigh. The roof was steep here and she wanted to hold the sleigh for support, but she was afraid to touch it.

Her heart in her mouth, she peered up the steep side of the monstrous car and said, "Santa?"

For a moment nothing happened. Then, a creaking sound like frozen leather, and a hand whiter than the moon appeared, to clutch the rail of the sleigh.

It seemed as though the entire rooftop swayed, but it was only a shifting of runners on the sharp-peaked roof. The fingers, long and dexterous as only a toymaker's can be, bent back at the third joint with the effort of movement. Santa Claus grew over the rail like a thunderhead over mountaintops.

His hair was whiter than his flesh. Thick whorls of ice embedded his beard in icicles like a January cataract. More separated the thick hairs of his eyebrows into individual daggers, pushed back by the yuletide winds of the stratosphere so that they radiated from the bridge of his narrow, blue-tinged nose. Wisps of pale hair scattered from beneath his red cap, over his small pink ears. His eyes were tiny too, pink-rimmed and black at their iris; and looking, searching the eaves troughs, the darkened windows, the empty playground three streets down, questing hungrily and never blinking once in an endless hunt for girls and boys.

"Ahem," said Emily in her politest voice.

Santa's little eyes narrowed even more, but still he didn't see her. He leaned out a long way from the sleigh, his breath coming in slow steady rasps like a dry bellows. Finally Emily screwed up her courage and reached up to pluck his sleeve.

He jerked back like a puppet, and his eyes widened impossibly as he saw her. For a second she thought he was angry, then maybe no, he was scared. But breaking past all those things came a kind of smile. It sent the icicles around his mouth into a macabre dance.

"Oooh," he said at last. "A *child*."

His voice was a high tenor, with breathy overtones. Emily could not see how such a vast and disordered bulk could produce a voice like that.

"Hello," she said.

"Well." He raised a trembling hand to clink the strands of his beard. "Well. Indeed. Yes, hello, hello, little thing. You are a little thing, aren't you?"

"Santa," she said with all of her eight years' determination, "I want to be an elf."

He didn't answer, just stared at her.

A wind curled up from the street below, sending a twist of cutting snow into Emily's eyes. A tiny part of her was crying, the same part that cried when she was six, when her parents went away and Auntie told her she could have the room with the grandfather clock that had stopped.

"I want to be an elf, Santa," she repeated, and stomped her foot on the frozen rooftop.

"Please!"

There was another shudder from inside the sleigh, and Santa gave a lurch and rose five more feet over the house of Emily's aunt. He gripped the sleigh's rim with a white-knuckled fist.

In his other hand, he held a box, wrapped in blue shiny pa-

per with a ribbon so red that it could only have been spun by
elves. Santa Claus lifted that arm high, and suddenly bent at
his waist so that his face was inches from Emily's.

Ice crumbled in crystalline avalanches as his smile widened
and his narrow tongue darted across his blue, thin lips.

"A child," he breathed, sending a frosty wind at Emily that
made her blink. "Yes, a good, good child, a child who is
never naughty; never ever *bad*. Only one thing for this child."

Santa pulled away from Emily and his great head whipped
toward the front of the sleigh, to the unseen reindeer.

"Isn't that right, Rudolph!" he shrieked. Emily clapped her
hands over her ears and nearly lost her balance.

And then, as fast as the echoes of Santa's cackling cheer
died in the neighborhood, the shiny-wrapped box was trembling before Emily, Santa's right hand gripping it carefully so
as not to damage the wrapping. His face hovered five inches
behind it, and his tiny black eyes watched her with anticipation. The ice-bound eyebrows twinkled invitingly. The box,
Emily saw, was doll-sized.

"No," she said firmly, and repeated her request slowly—in
case Santa was hard of hearing:

"I! Want! To! Be! An! Elf! Please!"

He looked puzzled. Then he drew the present back, and
with hurried, savage moments, tore the box up. He dangled a
limp doll in front of her face, eyeing her with fixed concern
over the back of his hand.

Emily shook her whole head, and her upper body too for
good measure.

"Doesn't want the dolly," muttered Santa through an uncomprehending frown. "Don't want the dolly?" He tugged at
his beard. Then with a quick decisive movement he stuffed
the doll into a fold of his great red coat.

"Where's the, where—" He turned and scrabbled about in
the back of the sleigh. "Aha. Here." He brought out an ornate
snuff box and opened it. Taking out a pinch of powder, he
tossed it at Emily.

Golden, shimmering dust settled about her with a sound
like tinkling chimes.

"There. Saalaa, kaboom. You're an elf now." He turned away and grabbed the reins. Then he looked back.

Tears rolled down Emily's cheeks. She looked up at him resentfully.

"What?" he said, taken aback.

"I said, I want to be an *elf*. I want to go to the North Pole and make toys and sing with the other elves and see the reindeer and Rudolph and his nose and all the toys and be Christmas all year round!" she wailed. Then she was past words.

"You *want* be *my* elf?" Santa stroked his beard, and a thoughtful glint appeared in the outside corner of his left eye. Santa's uncertain lips twitched back into a smile. "Make toys? Go away"—he sniggered wetly through his nose—"go away . . . with Santa?"

Emily thought of her auntie and her room with the silent clock that loomed all night long, and about long division and detentions. "I want to be an elf," she repeated.

"All right then," he bellowed, and, reaching down with a long, branchlike arm, hoiked her over his lap into the seat beside him.

Emily fought to right herself as he drew up the reins and flipped them mightily. *"Gowan!"* he screamed.

She heard the sound of tiny hooves scrabbling in the deep snow. Emily righted herself in time to see eight impossibly tiny reindeer, hauling with all their might, fall in pairs off the edge of the roof.

With a crunch of iron against ice, the sleigh fell. Emily screamed as the ground rushed up—then they were plummeting, not down, but sideways between the tall houses. They continued to fall, higher and higher, into the sky.

II
A Night To Remember

The stars stood still above them, as Emily and Santa flew the world over. Emily had never been happier. It was a Christmas of frantic scrambling down chimneys behind Santa, whose great skeleton snapped and crunched to fit the tiniest aperture, some of which were too narrow for even Emily to pass. At the bottom of the larger chimneys, Emily watched Santa as his bones knitted and he painfully lurched to the base of a glittering tree and spewed gifts there from a great sack of green burlap that undulated with shifting boxes. Each box he would then arrange with a meticulous care, whispering, "A truck, Jimmy Thorne, see how you like *that*," or "You thought I'd finished with you after last year's dollhouse, Jacqueline Jones," and a terrific cackle over a pink-wrapped box bigger than Emily. And then it would be the next house.

Now the houses were all behind them. The runners drew white contrails like cuts across the deep blue sky, and she dreamily traced those lines away and over the horizon, thinking of the vast web of such lines she and Santa had made over the entire globe.

The forests fell behind, replaced with glimmering ice. The sleigh careered over a range of saw-toothed mountains, then into a deep valley of black tundra patched with snow. At the center of this bowl rose a vast building.

"The North Pole!" shrieked Santa, sending his whip twitching over the raw, foaming backs of his reindeer. The sleigh rocked as the reindeer scrambled madly against the frozen air, and for a moment they were all Emily could see, their wide and terror-struck eyes twisting in their emaciated sockets.

"No!" Santa bellowed, whipping again. "Down! To the Pole!

"Down to the Toy Mill!"

The reindeer disappeared as they arched downward, and Emily felt a roller-coaster lurch as the massive sleigh descended into free fall. Emily clutched at Santa's deep red greatcoat and stared ahead, down at Santa's workshop.

The building filled Emily's vision. Seven great smoke-stacks, black as the tundra where the fumes had cooked the brickwork, grew like spikes from the structure, which itself sprawled under green metal roofing into long and labyrinthine additions. Tarmac lots surrounded the buildings. The sleigh leveled out, and one of the smokestacks suddenly loomed before them. Above, a plume of soot climbed high into the Arctic night and a volcanic rumbling grew louder by the second.

"Damn you!" Santa screamed, and his whip cracked like a thunderbolt. *"Up!"* Snap! *"Higher!"* Snap! *"Away!"*

The sleigh was enveloped in black smoke. It got into Emily's eyes and made her cry, but when she breathed it for another sob it became impossible even to weep. The blackness passed, and she blinked away the filth.

The runners hit hard against tarmac with a butchershop crunch. They were in a space bounded by high walls, at the top of which ice-choked green metal eaves frowned over dark windows. Higher still, the aurora borealis sputtered and died.

The sleigh skidded to a halt in a shower of blue sparks, describing a twisting half-circle around the stationary reindeer and pulling three of them to the ground. There was a terrible shrieking and then silence, broken only by the distant hum of machinery.

Santa Claus leaned close to Emily and grinned a ghastly grin into her eyes.

"Welcome to the North Pole, little elf." He giggled in a small and girlish voice. "Merry Christmas, yes. Merry, merry Christmas."

With a frantic scrambling and pattering of small feet, a mob of elves surrounded the sleigh. Santa reared high in his seat, and glared at them.

The crowd parted and three of the elves approached. One held a shabby blue towel; Santa grabbed it and mopped his face, where the icicles were starting to droop. The second elf held out a fat brown cigar and the third a blue silk smoking jacket.

With a flourish Santa threw aside his greatcoat, blinding Emily. She pushed the smelly cloth away, and Santa reappeared, wrapped in blue. He bent and touched the end of his cigar to one of the smoking runners. Then, contentedly, he drew a deep breath and exuded a vast miasma of gritty gray smoke.

Santa Claus swatted his three helpers away with a broad arc of his palm, making even Emily duck involuntarily. But Santa's arm wheeled back and he snatched one of Emily's new ears between two fingers. He took a long, choking drag on his cigar and grinned down at her. Smoke rolled from his nostrils as he spoke.

"Well, little elf. Christmas year-round, eh? Ha ha! Christmas year-round is just what you'll get!"

Santa turned to the other elves, who were backing surreptitiously clear of his impressive reach. He snarled at them. "Yes, elves! Move off, back to work! One new elf doesn't mean long lunches for you lot! No, no, no! Back to the lines! Back to the shifts, by damn!"

The elves, who had been moving that way anyway, now turned and ran, their thin, bent legs carrying them in terrified sprints. Santa clamped his teeth around his cigar and strode in the opposite direction, dragging Emily behind him.

They made a jog to the left between a pair of tall buildings, walked down a narrow alleyway choked with icicles as wide as Emily, and finally emerged in a wide courtyard. This was lined with sheet-metal huts protruding from the brickwork. At the end was a wall with a single, gigantic doorway.

The roar of the mill was deafening.

Santa quickened his pace, pausing only once to drop his spent cigar, and soon they were at the door. *"Christmas all the time!"* Santa bellowed as the door swung open. His cackling was cut short by a tide of oily smoke. Emily held the greatcoat to her face, but it did little good. Through tears and acid coughs, she beheld the Toy Mill.

Dazzling light and knife-edged shadows cut through a vast space filled with huge machines in rows, like headstones. Coils of cable drooled down from catwalks festooned with pipes and valves. The catwalks crossed and recrossed, up and up in successive layers until they were hidden in darkness, a great iron spiderweb.

"This is it!" Santa waved proudly. "Your new home! What do you think of it, eh little elf?"

"It's dreadful."

"Yes!" The melting icicles in Santa's beard sparkled in the radiance of his glowing pride. "And it's just what you wanted!"

III
A Matter of Correspondence

The letters had been separated into boxes, which were labeled by the age and nationality of their young authors. They rose in mountainous, teetering stacks beyond the rafters of Warehouse 12. Sometimes, one of those stacks would begin to wobble, and from the celestial gloom above a dozen or more boxes would plummet, bursting like ill-bound volumes on the cracked cement floor and spewing their multicolored contents through the narrow canyons. Some of those canyons were all but impassable, blocked to twice the height of an elf with jaggedly torn envelopes and the crayoned, penciled and—rarely—neatly typed lists.

"Put her to work!" Santa had screamed into the dark as he clutched the brass door handles and pulled the great metal-wrapped doors shut on the Correspondence Hall.

"Are all the letters from all the boys and girls in the world here?" Emily asked, wide-eyed, of the dark elf who led her deep into the maze.

"Yawm," drawled the elf. It darted a suspicious look at her. "Ah-whee, that's em innit."

"What?"

"Twirl yer gams, Miss Hoitee Toitee." The elf grabbed a long-handled broom up from the floor. "Sortenem's the way."

She clutched the broom, staring at the concrete labyrinth that stretched off into smog-hazed distance. "Please, Mr. Elf, are my letters here? Did Santa read them?"

"Read?" The elf wrapped his wizened lips around the word as though he had never heard it before. "Who reads?" He made brisk shoving motions with his hands. "Sortem. Day, month, time, pla'. Sortem all." He made the shoveling motion again.

"You mean he didn't see my letters?" she asked tremulously. "He didn't read them?"

"Readem? Ach-eh, wot daftness be ye onit?"

Pouting, Emily dragged the broom along the floor, looking back every two or three steps at the elf. He tapped his foot impatiently, and after a while she stopped looking back.

Emily shoveled the fallen paper into heaps, which other elves picked over, tossing the correspondence into boxes that, paradoxically, were passed up to the tops of the stacks again. The operation seemed endless.

She gamely tried to keep up. After all, Emily was an elf now, and that was a very special and important thing to be. And elves were industrious, and never ever tired. But she did tire, and the letters blurred together before her eyes. She tried to stop reading all the letters that she swept up. But even after the lists, the painstaking explanations of why Donnie or Sue or Millie had been good this year, all faded together into one big "Please!" in her mind, she kept seeing the words, over and over:

Dear Santa.

"Dear Santa," said the boys and girls of America. "Dear Santa," said England. "Dear Santa, Dear Santa, Dear Santa," said all the little children of the world. The words swirled around her; they were piled into quivering ziggurats above her, sprawled into a swelling maze in which, finally, she was lost.

Emily stopped pushing her broom, sat down, and began to cry.

Who *did* read these letters, anyway? The elves here didn't—Emily had begun to doubt they could speak properly, let alone read. And Santa? Emily tried to remember the last time Santa Claus had brought her something she'd asked for, and found that she couldn't. The only time he'd done anything she wanted was when she'd demanded it, face-to-face.

Emily wiped the tears from her eyes. "That's the problem," she said aloud. "Santa doesn't know!"

A heap of letters rustled beside her and the elongated soot-damaged face of an elf appeared. He glanced only briefly at Emily before hefting a watermarked carton to his shoulder and shuffling indifferently into the dark. Emily didn't care. "Santa doesn't know," she repeated. "He doesn't know what girls and boys really want! That's why it's so dreadful at the North Pole!"

Emily continued with similar exclamations for the remainder of her shift, but for all the gravity of her revelation, she did not sit idle. She scrabbled through the papers on the floor in search of an intact box, and although she could not find one entirely undamaged, she was able to repair one of the broken ones with the help of the tape gun that dangled from her tool belt. Then she set about filling her new box with letters.

The elves in the Correspondence Hall didn't try to stop her as she reached up and pulled down the brass handle on the great doors. Perhaps, thought Emily, they are secretly with me. As the doors opened and a whirl of wind-borne ice slipped inside, Emily turned to her coworkers as they huddled together in the gloom.

"Don't fear!" she shouted. "Santa will make things right!"

And then she turned with her box and stepped into the chill. Behind her, the great doors creaked shut.

Santa's quarters were on the roof of the Mill. There, amid an expanse of drifted snow, squatted a high-peaked penthouse with gargoyled corners and tall, jaded glass windows. The Arctic night cradled it and the whole Mill in icy grayness. Emily dragged the box up to the tall, bronze door to the building and tried to knock. Her tiny fist made no sound on the metal.

The door did respond to her push, though. She slipped gratefully into the dark warmth of Santa's Penthouse. She dusted the snow from her boots and said, timidly, "Santa?"

Firelight glowed through a wooden archway. Emily put the box down by the arch and looked through it.

Santa's vast living room was lit solely from the fireplace. Silhouetted elves heaped logs bigger than themselves onto the fire, which was already spilling out onto the stone hearth. The heat was blistering.

A corpulent white bathtub had been wheeled to within a foot of the fire. Santa, wreathed in suds, reclined in the tub, shooting jets of smoke up from his cigar.

"More wood!" he bellowed, sweeping one arm over the high side of the tub. The elves avoided him adroitly, and ran for the wood box.

"Santa?" Emily asked timorously.

He frowned, glanced over, and said, "Zounds elf! Aren't you working?" Sudsy bubbles rose from behind his head, to be withered into ash by the incandescent flames.

Emily bravely brought the box out. "Santa, there's something I think you should know."

"Nonsense." He sank slowly down, until only his cigar and eyes appeared above the rim of the tub. "I have no reason to know anything."

"These letters." She held them up. "Have you read them?"

"Read them? What an idea." He crossed his eyes to look at the tip of his cigar. "What do they have to do with me?"

"They—it's because—" Emily wiped away a tear, and sniffled. He hadn't read them! "Because Santa, these are all the letters from all the boys and girls of the world, and they're all about what all the boys and girls want for Christmas!"

"Is that so?" His eyes slid half-closed. He dropped lower in the tub. "Never really thought about it, I guess." His eyes opened a bit. "What they want? What do you mean, what they want?"

"Santa!" Emily put her hands on her hips. She couldn't believe this. "Every girl and boy writes letters to Santa at Christmastime—"

"I know. It's *such* a nuisance."

"But they're telling you that they've been good all year, and they're asking you for presents!"

"Really?" His eyes opened wide, flicking suds away. He propped his chin on his hand, frowning and puffing madly. "Never would have thought . . ."

"But Santa! What did you think all these letters were?"

"Show me." One hand appeared, fingers snapping, above the mountain of suds. Emily moved closer to the blasting heat, and stretched out to hand him a letter. Santa held the paper up.

"Dear Santa," he read aloud. " 'From Billy.' Who in hell is Billy? Um um, 'I have been very very good'—have you, Bill my boy?—um, um . . . 'I wish I had a truck . . . I wish . . .' " Santa squinted and sloshed forward so that he loomed like a vulture over the letter. "By the Devil's flaming anus!" Santa sat up suddenly, splashing water everywhere. Blinding steam hissed up around him.

" 'I wish my sister was dead!' "

Santa's red, bedraggled face emerged from an inferno of crackling flame and billowing steam. His gaze was beatifically calm. "Emily my good girl, I think you're on to something."

IV
Christmas Dinner

Emily did not see Santa Claus for some time after their fateful meeting, but that is not to say that his gratitude was unfelt.

"No more, my sweet pernicious little elf, will you crouch over your broom with no dreams to move you beyond your station," he had crooned, eyes half-closed and a towel concealing the bulk of his white, mottled skin. "Your sweeping-up days are behind you, now that you are at the helm of our mighty design, oh yes oh my oh yes. Your only task now, oh Emily mine, is to find me—" As he spoke, Claus bent and snatched from a steaming puddle the soaked and fast-streaking requests of angry young Billy. "—find me more like him!"

Santa shook the letter over Emily's head, and she ducked back as Claus repeated: *"More like him!"* She was out the door and beyond the arch in no time. *"Do y'hear me, Emily! More! By Christmas, by Christ! More!"*

Starting back into work at the Correspondence Hall, Emily couldn't help but feel as important as Santa seemed to think she was. She started as Executive Elf in Charge of Correspondence at half past January, and by February she thought she was already beginning to see the light at the end of the tunnel. At least that is what she told the elves she had alphabetizing the stacks and repairing the scaffolding: "We are beginning to see the light at the end of the tunnel, people. Soon it will be Christmas the way it was meant to be."

By a quarter to March, Emily and her three assistants began compiling her first quarterly report for Santa. Emily had made her elves separate all of the gift requests into categories: *Ani-*

mals, which included such things as ponies, doggies, kitties, and baby brothers and sisters, as well as more exotic pets such as boa constrictors and Nile crocodiles; *Machinery* was a broad category including automobiles, aircraft, munitions ranging from pellet guns to M-16s and AKMs, and chain saws; and then there was the broader-still category that she had simply dubbed *Situations*. This last one often gave Emily an upset stomach. Billy's final Christmas wish fit the category, as did a plethora of others. One little boy named Albert wanted his whole town to catch incurable syphilis because he had been excluded from marching in the Santa Claus parade—"Let their noses rot off and see how they like that then," Albert had written in his awkward, boyish scrawl.

There were over fifty requests from little girls to be changed into mice or birds; a hundred and twelve little boys who wanted their driver's license; and thousands, tens of thousands it seemed, of requests from orphaned little girls and boys to have their dead parents returned to them.

But upset stomach or no, Emily pressed on. She worked through March, April, May, all the summer months and much of the autumn with scarcely a wink of sleep. Yet as far as she could tell, she didn't need sleep. Not when the true spirit of Christmas was at stake.

It wasn't until five to December that she was called away from her high, sloped desk. She did not get a very good look at the elf who brought the notice, nor did she recognize the script on the single milky-white card proffered to her so mysteriously. Though it was unsigned, the words on the card were unmistakable, and they buoyed her spirit every time she re-read them.

A Christmas dinner would take place, the first of December, at the reindeer stables. And Emily, it appeared, had been invited.

On the appointed evening, Emily made her way to the stables. She knew in a general way where they were, but had never been to them because her responsibilities kept her so busy. To get to them, she had to pass through the darkest pulsing foundries of the Mill, past shrieking boilers and

pounding triphammers, and up out into the vast, cold waste-
land of the Pole.

Much of the land around the Mill consisted of tarmac run-
ways periodically covered and unmasked again by twisting
dunes of snow. At the end of the longest runway, a brave
stand of spruce trees sprang from the tundra. Like sickly
guards, they encircled a long low building of gingerbread
construction. A thin coil of smoke came from the stout stone
chimney above one end of the stable. Lights shone in the windows there.

Despite the cutting wind and the barrenness of the plain,
Emily was warm with curiosity and anticipation as she approached the place. It was only as she neared the door itself
that she realized hers were the only footprints leading here.

"Perhaps I'm the first guest," she said to herself, and
knocked. No one opened the door, but she thought she heard
a faint voice, bidding her enter. Emily hoisted the iron latch
and let herself in.

"Hello?" She unwrapped herself from her scarf, and turned
to close the door. Then she raised her head to look at the
party scene.

After her months in the grayness of the Mill, Emily had
hoped for brightness and warmth here, among the reindeer at
Christmas. And, indeed, it was bright; candles glowed everywhere: on side tables, in sconces in the walls, on wagon-
wheel chandeliers and the long, long dinner table. They even
flickered in unsteady ranks along the floor itself. And it was
warm; a dry, pressing warmth that Emily felt in her sinuses.

The dinner table had been set for at least thirty. It was a
great slab of wood, wide enough to sleep on. All along both
sides were high chairs and low chairs, thrones and stools,
with place settings before each.

All were empty.

As Emily took her first steps into the room, a vapor of dust
rose up around her. She sneezed, and along the tabletop, a
wave of dust rose, tingled in midair for a moment, then settled down again onto the still, pale plates and saucers.

"Come in, child," said a dry, listless voice. A figure at the
far end of the table moved. Emily gasped.

It was a woman. A tall, stately creature, she sat in the lesser of two vast thrones at the head of the table. The lunar oval of her face held empty sadness. Dried mistletoe tangled her gray hair. Her green gown shimmered with highlights from the candle flames, except on her shoulders where it was dull with dust. On the table before her were a plate full of withered unidentifiable things, and a gold goblet overflowing with mold.

When she spoke, her eyes fell half-shut with a terrible weariness. "I have heard, child, of the work you have done for the Claus."

"Who are you?" Emily stepped carefully around the stalagmites of wax dotting the floor. "Am I early for the party?"

"You are . . . on time," said the ethereal woman. 'I am Mrs. Claus."

Emily stopped, thunderstruck. She had approached to within a few feet of the woman. Now she could see that the throne next to Mrs. Claus's was as dusty and old as any alongside the table. A fork had been jammed into the arm of the throne, and stood like a single mute protestor on the silent lawn of the upholstery.

"I . . . I'm honoured to meet you, ma'am," Emily remembered to curtsy. "Will . . . will Mr. Claus be joining us for dinner?"

"No . . ." A kind of animation entered the woman's eyes. "No. Sit down here." A delicate hand rose from her lap to point to a stool at her right. Emily sat.

"No one will be joining us, Emily," sighed Mrs. Claus. "No one will come." She seemed to withdraw into herself, gazing out over the silent place settings. Then, as if unbidden, words came from her lips.

"You have done an evil thing, dearest Emily. Long are the years that silence and peace have reigned here. Long has it been since the Claus has troubled us." She blinked slowly. "The Claus is not a messenger of good. Perhaps once . . . before the rot of years took their toll upon him, things were different. Although even I, I must confess, can barely recall." Mrs. Claus's hands trembled in the dust of her lap. "Now as his great sleigh takes to the sky, it flies not on the faerie dust of goodwill, but is driven by the engines of his wrath. His gifts are wholly malicious, Emily. Or so . . . he has believed."

She turned her dull eyes toward Emily. "For many decades I have kept from the Claus the knowledge that his efforts have failed. He did not know that the children of the world welcomed his visits. I told him the letters contained complaint, that the children of the world begged him not to continue his cruel dispensation. Now you have told him the truth."

Emily thought about the letters Santa had told her to find. The ones whose young authors wished their parents dead, or for their schools to be swallowed up by cyclones.

Mrs. Claus bent forward, her sad, dark eyes wide. "Do you understand," she whispered, almost inaudibly, "what Claus is going to do with the truth?"

Emily did not, but she was afraid of how she would feel if she did. She looked down and kicked her feet.

"Something must be done," Mrs. Claus continued in her whisper. "For the first time in centuries, more is at stake than even Christmas."

V
Best of the Season

Emily wore a fuschia-dyed, ermine-lined greatcoat to the Christmas Inspection, and although it kept much of the Arctic chill from her narrow elvish bones, she shivered as the doors to Claus's administration building opened and she filed along with the nineteen other supervisory elves outside, across the ice-strangled courtyard and into the Toy Mill proper.

As they arrived they were led to a raised podium, decorated with bright red velvet and green crepe-paper streamers. Emily was at once struck by the difference between the Toy Mill she had entered nearly a year ago and the one in which she now sat.

Where previously scaffolding, ductwork, deafening, sparking machinery had dominated every imaginable view, now every spot was hung with dark, impenetrable curtain. A year ago, the lighting was flickering and sporadic, but now fresh new fluorescents hummed brilliantly overhead, the new light not altogether flattering to the upturned faces of the assembled elves. The air smelled not of oil and ozone and rusty water, but something else that made Emily's nose wrinkle. It smelled like fresh pine, or soap.

A spotlight came on, and swept its luminous circle across the crowd and up the nearest wall. As it moved, a loudspeaker crackled deafeningly. The walls shook as a giant finger tapped thunderously on a microphone.

"Welcome!" Claus boomed through the Toy Mill. "Welcome all, welcome to the twenty-first century!"

A collective "Oooooh" rose up from the assembled elves.

Emily followed the spotlight to where it stopped, at a catwalk three stories up. There it oscillated back and forth, until it finally speared a lone figure, made tiny by the distance.

Claus, wearing a neat white shirt and narrow blue tie underneath a freshly pressed greatcoat, leaned forward and squinted through the light at the thing his Toy Mill had become. In one hand, he held his cigar, in the other a glittering cordless microphone.

"Wishes," thundered Claus into his microphone. "Who would have thought, eh elves? Who would have thought that the key to our recovery, yes, to our very salvation, could be based upon so simple a principle?"

At that, Claus snapped his fingers and Emily very nearly lost her hearing. The echoing had not yet died when a well-dressed elf handed Claus a clipboard with a wide sheaf of paper on top.

"I should have thought of it long ago," said Claus, his eyes scanning down the first of 152 pages on the clipboard—it had been 151, but Emily had seen that the 152nd was added this morning.

"Give the children what they want, and that shall be their undoing! What a principle! What a motto, eh? And we've put it to work for us, haven't we, elves?" Santa snapped his fingers again, and this time the curtains that covered the Toy Mill began to part.

"Look now, upon the fruits of our labors," said Santa, as the needle-pointed, serrated-edged totality of the Toy Mill's

GNP was revealed. "It has taken us a year, and I would say we have worked harder and faster at it this year than in our entire three hundred years of production. By hell, I wouldn't even be able to remember where each of these were to go, even what they all are, I've seen so many requisitions cross my desk this year!"

The mass of toys was certainly daunting, and Emily wouldn't have believed Santa Claus could fit them all onto a hundred sleighs if she hadn't flown with him a year ago. The toys had been stacked in the same categories she had divided the wishes into. There were the *Animals*, horses and dogs and cats and babies, what seemed like a million babies, all drugged and stacked in cords like firewood; *Machinery*, filled with monster trucks and Sherman tanks and bazookas and chain saws, guns and knives and hand grenades.

Situations contained objects that were harder to identify, but Emily knew their significance. There was a rack of glass ampoules, filled with a neurotoxin developed in July by the Toy Mill's R&D wing to leave no trace in an autopsy—Claus would deliver those personally, injecting brothers, sisters, former best friends and even parents depending on the specified wishes of the good little girls and boys. And Emily could make out the larger containers, in a portable refrigeration unit. In September, R&D had developed an incurable strain of syphilis, but there were strict rules as to the temperature of its storage. They had been about to develop an inoculant, but little Albert's wishes did not include immunity for himself, so the project had been filed away with the World Peace serum, abandoned in late November as too difficult for this year.

Claus went through them all, wish by wish. "Lot 543," he would call, and an elf would bring forward the weaponry or the twitching zombie of a recently deceased parent or the working submarine with four torpedo tubes. Claus would inspect it carefully from his perch, sometimes ordering the elf to turn it upside down or around backward so he could be certain the wish matched specifications. Then he would read off the next lot number.

Finally, he came to the bottom of the list.

"Lot 10761," said Claus. There was an uncomfortable silence. Claus repeated himself.

"Lot 10761, I said.'

Still nothing. Claus tapped the microphone again. "Did you hear me?" he roared. "Where is my last wish?"

There was movement among the elves then. Emily saw it before Claus did because the woman below stayed shrouded in relative darkness until she had risen. When the spotlight hit her, Mrs. Claus was at her full height, towering over the assembled elves like a twisted Halloween tree. She wore a fuschia greatcoat like Emily's, and she held a small black metal box in her hand.

"By the thunder of hell's reindeer!" Santa's eyes were wide red orbs. *"What brings the moribund back from perdition?"*

Mrs. Claus spoke, but she was drowned out by the shrieking feedback that followed Claus's shocked outburst. She repeated herself.

"The final lot," she said, her own voice filling the mill only by its own power, "is on its way. You need not fear, Claus. It will be here when it is needed."

Santa's elves began a worried muttering among themselves.

The loudspeaker hissed and crackled with Claus's sputtering rage.

"What do you mean with this, woman?" Claus sneered. "Do you think you can come *begging* to *me*, now in my moment of greatest triumph?" He gestured with his cigar, a trail of embers underlining his contempt. "Back to the stables, hag, with the other sows."

Mrs. Claus shook her head. "You were always too slow, Claus. Even when it's spelled out for you, you just can't keep up."

Claus was about to say something, but Mrs. Claus pressed a button on her box.

"Here's your final lot," she said. "It's for a little girl named Emily. You'll find her Christmas wish destructive enough, I'd wager."

The Toy Mill rocked with a distant explosion.

* * *

Claus went pale under the spotlight. "What is this?" he roared. "What Christmas wish is this?"

"The one you missed, Claus," said Mrs. Claus. "Once again, you were sloppy. And once again, you stopped reading the wish lists that came across your desk, in your eagerness to fulfill them all. So it was easy to add one last wish. . . ." Her voice was lost in a thunderous *whump* that shook the mill and brought a shower of dust down from the ceiling. Claus looked up with alarm.

Emily could contain herself no longer. She broke free from the crowd and ran to the open space below Santa's catwalk. "I wish your Christmas would never happen!" she yelled at him. "I wish it would all just stop! And I wish you would never, ever get to have Christmas your way again!"

The lights flickered and went out. Another explosion rocked the mill, and a tongue of blue flame licked through a sudden rent in the wall above Claus.

"By the blighted wastes 'neath Satan's sphincter!" Spittle trailed like broken scuds to the Toy Mill floor. *"Woman, you are my undoing!"*

The elves panicked as one. Eyes rolling, they broke into frenzied motion, racing for the giant rolling doors to the outside. Emily cowered in the darkness, listening to the shrieking and continuing blasts, until a light hand descended on her shoulder.

Mrs. Claus led Emily out into the red-lit night. The Mill collapsed, eaten from its heart by multicolored fires. The insensate machinery tore free of its moorings, smashing blindly through wall and pillar, window and cable. As the ceiling collapsed, great gouts of smoke poured out from ground level.

Emily and Mrs. Claus ran across the tarmac. Elves were scattering away in all directions.

A low ominous rumbling sound began. A weird flickering blue glow reflected across the frozen landscape. Emily stopped, pulling free of Mrs. Claus, and turned to look.

The core of the Mill turned into a pillar of electric fire, like the northern lights set loose. A fierce wind picked up, blowing into the heart of the fire. And silhouetted by the glare, his long crooked shadow darting across the snow at her, was Claus.

He battled against the hurricane, taking step after tortured step to follow Emily. His frozen eyes flashed with northern blue and his mouth opened in a noiseless scream. His great-coat flapped out behind him like a raven's wings.

Over Emily's head, Mrs. Claus said, in tragic resignation, "Oh, Claus."

Claus slipped, and slid back ten feet. He grabbed a spire of ice, but it snapped in his hand. For just a moment, he stood poised, his icy hair flaring up around him like lightning.

"Merry Christmas," he bellowed. *"Merry Christmas, you ungrateful bastards!"*

And then the vortex had him, and he was swept into flailing snow, and burning blue light, and was gone.

Mrs. Claus turned away, a single gilded tear sliding down her cheek.

But Emily could not look away from the sight. For the Toy Mill had been her home, terrible as it was, and now it was gone.

Mrs. Claus touched Emily's chin, and lifted it up so that their gazes met. Mrs. Claus's eyes held a measured kind of triumph, but their weariness was in no way diminished by that fact. The old woman's lips quivered like shreds of ribbon in a breeze.

"So young," she whispered. "So young."

Mrs. Claus held Emily's face in such a way for a long time. The explosions had finished, the wind was dead, and thick white flakes began to fill the polar air. But they were not snowflakes—Emily didn't even have to put her tongue out to know that. They were ashes; and if Emily and Mrs. Claus stood there for long, they might well be buried in them.

Wordlessly, Emily took Mrs. Claus's hand and let her back to the reindeer stables.

Emily was sick for Christmas, and had to stay in bed the whole day through. Her auntie hadn't time to buy her presents. Emily had only arrived back from the North Pole Christmas Eve, and it was all Auntie could do to take her inside,

call the doctor, and tell the police that Emily had come back.
The police had wanted to talk to Emily, but Auntie had put
her foot down—"Not until after Christmas," she'd said, "and
that's final." Then Auntie had given Emily a great big hug,
and put her to bed, and made her hot soup that was the best
soup Emily had ever tasted.

Auntie spent most of Christmas Day with Emily in the
room with the grandfather clock that didn't work, and went to
bed only after Emily had seemed to fall asleep.

But Emily was only pretending. When her auntie had shut
off the light and closed the door, Emily crept over to her window and looked out.

The moon was in a quarter-phase, and cloud patterned the
sky like wallpaper in a child's bedroom. If a sleigh ever
crossed such a sky, it would do so empty of toys, and fly so
quietly that Emily would never know it had passed.

A new Christmas myth.

THE HUNDRED-YEAR
CHRISTMAS
David Morrell

❄

"ABOUT SANTA CLAUS?" the young girl asked.

"That's right," the father said. "Now pull your blankets close. It's cold tonight."

"A story about Santa Claus?" the other child, a young boy, Matthew, asked. He snuggled in the other bed.

The father thought about it, nodding. "Yes, he's sometimes known as Father Christmas, and he has a friend named Father Time."

"Who's *he*?" the first child, Sarah, asked. "Who's Father Time?"

"Does he bring presents, too?" Matt asked.

"No, not exactly. Not the kind you'll find beneath the tree tomorrow morning. But he lets us have one special gift."

"What is it?" Sarah asked.

The wind howled past the bedroom window. The snow fell thickly.

"Christmas will be white this year," the father said.

"The present. What's the present?" Matthew said.

"It's something Santa gives us, too. The best gift of them all. At least, that's what the story claims."

"Then tell it. Tell the story," they insisted, both at once.

The snow kept falling.

"What you have to understand is there've been many Santas."

"At one time?"

"No, in a row. First one, and then another, then another. Each was human like ourselves, and each was asked if he would like the job. Each Santa lasts a hundred years, and when his time is up, he has to look for his replacement."

"But what happens to the old one?"

"Christmas Eve of his last year, he has to go away."

"To where?"

"The story tells us. See, where Santa lives isn't marked on any map. Not *this* North Pole. You'd never find it in the Arctic. It's beyond the Arctic, farther north than north, beyond all other places. It's invisible. From outside, you can't see it. But from inside, it's a peaceful valley, beautiful, surrounded by steep hills. Santa has a big, old, pleasant house. A stream flows past it. There are willow trees and maple trees and pine trees. There are rabbits, squirrels, and chipmunks. There are fields of waving grass. The seasons change as ours do. When it's summer here, it's also summer there. And when it's winter here, it's also winter there."

"You mean it's snowing there right now?"

"I bet it is. But what I'm going to tell you isn't happening right now. It happened last year and the year before. It starts on New Year's Eve, the end of Santa's ninety-ninth and the beginning of his hundredth year. He has to look for his replacement. First he also has to say good-bye."

"To who?"

"His good friend Father Time."

"You haven't told us who he is."

"Well, Father Time is special, just as Santa is. Each New Year's Eve, a baby's born. No, not exactly born. He doesn't have a mother or a father. What he does is . . . he appears as if from nowhere. Santa finds him sleeping in a cradle, wearing a diaper. Santa takes care of him. At the start, the child is called the New Year's Baby. Mostly, even as a baby, though, he's known as Father Time."

"That's silly. Babies can't be fathers."

"All the same, that's what he's called. Though Santa has a hundred years, this baby has just *one* year. His whole life lasts only that brief time. He ages very quickly. By the end of January, he's already eight, and by the end of February, he's sixteen. That's eight years every month. By June, he's forty-eight. And by December, well, he's ninety-six. In fact, the last day of the year, his birthday, he becomes one hundred. Then he has to go."

"To where?"

"The same place Santa has to go. Up the hill. The biggest hill. The one that faces toward the north. No matter what the season, summer, winter, even if there's snow, a path leads toward that hill. A winding path that's brown and narrow, like the kind you find in summer when the grass gets trampled and the earth shows through. No one made it. No one uses it but Father Time each New Year's Eve—and Santa every hundred years. Regardless if the snow stands five feet high, the path is always there. It points the way."

"What's on the other side?"

"Well, that's the strangest part of all. Nobody knows. Not Santa and not Father Time. All they know is when their time is up they have to walk along that path. They have to climb the hill and then go down the other side."

"If I was Santa, I'd explore."

"And so would I. But Santa can't. That breaks the rules. He's not supposed to climb that hill until he has to. When his time is up. Besides, the hill is scary."

"Now you're getting to the good part."

"There's a mist behind the hill. A pure-white mist that hides whatever's waiting there. The mist is high, like clouds on mountains, and it glows as if a blinding light is at its center. Sometimes, too, it glimmers—and it flashes."

"Gosh, I wouldn't want to go there."

"Nor does Santa. Nor does Father Time. But when their time is up, they have to leave."

"What happens if they don't?"

"I'm not sure *what* would happen. No one's ever disobeyed the rule. Each New Year's Eve, although he doesn't want to, Father Time walks up that hill. And every hundred years—he doesn't want to either—Santa also goes. They're nervous. They're afraid. No matter what, they go."

"I'm sad. Is this a sad part?"

"One of them."

"I hope it doesn't make me cry."

"Then maybe I should stop."

"No, tell the story. Tell the story."

"Well, it starts two New Year's Eves ago—December thirty-first. The sun is setting: brilliant crimson off the knee-deep snow. The sky is clear, the air is cold, and Santa's outside near his house. He wears his warm red coat with the thick, white, fleecy wool at the cuffs and collar and the bottom of his coat. He has his red wool pants, his wide black belt, his high black boots. Of course, his long red tassel cap. He leans against a fence and squints in the sunset toward his reindeer. You remember their names? Dasher, Dancer, Prancer, Vixen. Comet, Cupid, Donder, Blitzen. They worked hard on Christmas. Now they rest, pawing the snow to nibble the grass beneath. The reason Santa squints, though, isn't the sunset glinting off the snow. He's crying. Tears roll from his eyes, trickling down his ruddy cheeks. At first, the tears are warm. But then the cold air changes them. They turn to ice on his long white beard. His eyes ache, and his throat feels tight."

"But why is Santa crying?"

"That's exactly what the reindeer want to know. They frown. They nuzzle at his beard to cheer him up. He sniffles, and he pats them, but he stiffens when he hears a sound behind him, from his house. The front door opens—then it closes. Santa hears the steps come toward him, slow and weary, scraping on the snowless path. He shuts his eyes and bites his lip. The steps come nearer, making a different sound as they leave the path and crunch through the snow that leads up to the fence. They echo in the cold. They stop, and in the winter evening's quiet, Santa turns. He wipes his tears and sees an old, old man, much older than your grandpa, old and tall and very thin. It's Father Time. He stoops from age. He has a long white beard."

"Like Santa's?"

"Just as white, but even longer, hanging to his chest. He wears a dark gray robe that droops in folds on his body, dangling to his feet. The hood clings over his forehead, but beneath it Santa sees his wrinkled cheeks and his glowing eyes. The old man holds a scythe."

"What's *that*?"

"A long curved knife on a pole. It once was used for cutting down hay. They call that 'reaping.' Father Time, when he gets old, is sometimes called the Reaper. The Grim Reaper."

"What does he cut down?"

"Well, that's another story. I think I'd better save it for a few more years."

"His eyes glow, and he carries that big knife? I thought this was a sad part, but he's scary."

"It depends on what you're used to. Santa isn't scared. He's crying. He's good friends with Father Time."

"I'm ready." Father Time's voice quivers. "Ready as I'll ever be."

"I hate to see this happen." Santa's chest feels tight. His heart aches.

"It's the rule."

"I understand. But I don't have to like it," Santa says. "Good friend, I'm going to miss you."

"I'll miss *you*. I'm worried. What's beyond the hill? What's waiting in the mist?"

"I've always wondered. All these years, I've watched the other Father Times walk up that hill. I watched the Santa who selected me walk up that hill. I'm still not used to it. Each time I feel more sad. And lonely. Much more lonely."

"There's the baby. He will keep you company."

"He hasn't come yet. Not until you're out of sight, over the hill. But even then, I know in a year he'll have to take his own walk. I'll raise *him* as I raised *you*. But next year I'll be going. Next year *my* time ends as well."

"Perhaps I'll see you then. Perhaps I could be waiting for you."

"Yes, I'd like that. On the other side."

They face the northern hill. The sun sinks low, now orange instead of crimson, faint instead of brilliant. But the mist beyond the hill grows radiant.

The old men hug each other, weeping.

Father Time says, "I'm afraid."

"I'll walk with you. Till you reach the hill."

They leave the fence, shuffling through the knee-deep snow. They step down on the frozen path. The hill appears to grow as they approach it. With an arm around each other, they walk bravely forward.

Father Time says, "I don't think you ought to come this far. You're not supposed to see what's on the other side. Until you take your own walk."

"Just a few more steps."

But then the path begins its upward slope. The hill looms high above them.

Santa stops. "I love you."

"*I* love *you*. I still remember how you sang to me when I was young and how you used to take me fishing. Maybe one day . . ."

". . . we'll go fishing once again."

They nod and kiss each other's tear-wet cheeks. As Santa sadly watches, Father Time walks up the hill. The snow lies deep beside the path. The sun turns pink now, almost gone, but there's still light enough for Santa to continue watching as his friend plods upward wearily. The mist glows. Father Time stands outlined at the top, his gray robe stark against the mist, his scythe in profile. Father Time peers down the other side. He turns, afraid, and waves good-bye. Weeping, Santa waves as well. Then Father Time walks toward the mist. First, Santa cannot see his feet and legs. Then Santa cannot see his waist and back. The stooping shoulders and the gray hood disappear. The last thing Santa sees is Father Time's bright curving scythe, the blade held high above his good friend's head.

"And then what?"

"Santa stares up till the sun is gone. The darkness makes him sadder. But he can't wait any longer. Wiping at his tears, he has to walk back to his house. The lights are on. White smoke drifts from the chimney. He goes in and takes off his hat and coat and gloves and boots, putting on his furry slippers. In his red shirt, he walks through the living room. It looks like Grandma's living room—a soft old sofa and a rocking chair before the fireplace, a cat curled on another chair beside a reading lamp. Santa doesn't stop, though. He keeps going toward the bedroom next to his, the one that Father Time used. Santa turns the doorknob, pushing gently, walking in. The room is dark, but faint light creeps in from the living room. He holds his breath and listens to the silence. In a corner, Santa sees what he expected."

"It's the New Year's Baby!"

"Right. You'd think that Santa would get used to what he finds. Sure, he expects to see the baby, but although each New Year's Eve the baby's always waiting for him, nonetheless he's still surprised. Because the baby is a miracle, and with a miracle, regardless of how many times you see it, you can't quite believe it. Each year, Santa wonders if the miracle will come again, and when it does, he feels a tingle. Santa peers down at the crib. The baby's cute and tiny, curled up, sucking at his thumb, asleep.

"Santa covers him with a blanket. Then he knows he'd better heat the baby's milk. But first he has a more important job to do. On a table, there's an hourglass."

"What's that?"

"Two cones. Like the kind you put a scoop of ice cream in. Except, these cones are made of glass. The narrow ends point toward each other. They're supported in a frame, and one cone's filled with sand. The sand drains from the top cone to the bottom one, and when the bottom one is filled, you turn the bottom to the top and let the sand drain down again. It takes an hour for the sand to drain. That's why the cones are called an hourglass. When clocks and watches hadn't been invented, people used an hourglass to know what time it was. The sand in this glass drains much longer than an hour, though. It drains for one full day. And now the sand has almost reached the bottom. Santa turns the cones, so the sand falls from the top again."

"What happens if he doesn't, if the sand stops draining?"

"Time stops. Everything comes to an end."

"You mean the world?"

"That's right. Ourselves and everything around us."

"Gosh."

"That's Father Time's job. To make sure the cones are turned and the sand keeps draining."

"What if he gets sick?"

"Then Santa does it."

"What if Santa's working? What about at Christmas?"

"That's why Father Time is so important. Santa can't always be there to turn the glass, so he depends on Father Time. We all do. But on New Year's Eve, Father Time is still a baby. Santa turns the glass for him, then tiptoes from the bedroom toward the kitchen. In a while, the baby starts to cry. When Santa comes back with the warm milk in a bottle, he discovers the baby needs his diaper changed."

"Oh, yuck."

"I did the same for you, Matt. One day you'll change diapers, too."

"I still say yuck."

"Then Santa carries the baby to the living room and settles in the rocking chair to feed him. As the fire crackles, Santa thinks about the Father Time who disappeared within the mist beyond the hill. He thinks about the year ahead of him, his last year, when he'll have to find another Santa. But for now he feels exhausted after his hard work at Christmas, and he has to watch the baby, so he shuts his worries from his mind. The baby finishes the bottle. Santa burps him. Don't say yuck, Matt. Then the baby sighs with pleasure, snuggles close to Santa's chest, and, sucking a finger, goes to sleep. The fire's heat relaxes Santa. Stretching out his legs, he tilts back in the rocking chair. The cat comes over, sniffing at the baby, curling under Santa's legs, and as the night's frost makes wild patterns on the window, Santa starts to snore."

"That makes me sleepy, Dad."

"You *should* feel sleepy. Gosh, I didn't realize how late it was. You need your rest. Tomorrow will be busy."

"First, the presents in the morning!"

"Then we'll go to church. A little later, we'll see Grandma."

"Is she feeling better?"

"Quite a bit. She's anxious to see both of you and hear about your presents."

"I hope she likes what we're giving her."

"You bet she will. And Grandpa can't wait to take you sledding. A busy day for sure. I'll see you early."

"But what about the story? Aren't you going to finish it?"

"You said it made you sleepy."

"Just when Santa started snoring. I'm awake now."

"Well, I guess a few more minutes couldn't hurt. I'd better whisper. Mom said not to keep you up late."

"Mom won't mind. I bet she'd like to hear the story, too."

"She's reading it. You're right, though. She won't mind. Tonight is special."

The snow fell harder.

"Santa has a busy January—heating bottles, changing diapers. Every day he bathes the baby. Every night, when the baby cries, Santa holds him in his arms and, rocking, sings to him. By January fifteenth, halfway through the month, the child is out of diapers. He's already four. He's learned to walk, and he starts getting into mischief, pulling dishes out of cupboards, spilling milk."

"I used to do that. Not anymore."

"He pulls the poor cat's tail."

"I never did."

"Yes, Santa has to keep a close watch on that boy, I'll tell you. But then January ends. The boy is eight, and he likes skating, sledding, building snowmen. February rolls around, the midpoint of the month, and Father Time is twelve. He has to start to do his job, to make sure the sand keeps draining. Santa talks to him about the rules—how, if he doesn't turn the glass, then Time will end. The boy gets scared. He's never had a grown-up job. He promises he won't forget; he won't make Santa disappointed. Then the boy gets big enough to help take care of Santa's reindeer, brushing them and picking ice balls from their hoofs and making sure that they have lots of hay. These reindeer are good-natured. Santa lets the boy take rides on them, and Santa lets the boy throw snowballs at him. Everything is like a game for Father Time."

"It sounds like fun."

"Then something awful happens."

"What?"

"One night when Father Time's asleep, Santa tiptoes in to smile at him. As Santa turns to leave, he sees the awful thing."

"The sand!"

"The boy forgot to turn the glass. The moonlight glimmers through the window, toward the time-glass on the table, and the last few grains have almost fallen to the bottom. They drop quickly. You could pinch what's left between two fingers. Then not even that much. Ten grains. Five. The room begins to shudder. Four more seconds, and the world will end. The room will vanish."

"Hurry, Santa!"

"And he does. He scrambles toward the table, lunging at the glass, and as the last small grain of sand slips toward the bottom, Santa flips the glass. Again the sand is where it should be. At the top. A full cone pouring toward the bottom."

"That was close. If all the sand fell . . . Santa saved us just in time."

"And Santa knows it. Outside, freezing wind claws at the window. In the bedroom, Santa sweats, though. Trembling, he clutches the table, his knees so weak he's afraid he'll fall. His heart pounds. He can't breathe. He turns in anger toward the boy."

"He isn't going to spank him, is he?"

"What would you do?"

"I'd get angry, sure. The boy did something bad. Much worse than bad. But Dad, it's like last summer when you told me not to kick my football in the street. I kicked it anyhow and broke poor Mrs. Murphy's window. That was bad."

"You bet. For sure, Mrs. Murphy thought so."

"What about me? The time you told me not to climb that maple tree in our front yard. You said the branches were too thin. I climbed it anyhow and broke three branches. That was bad. I still feel sorry for the tree."

"You disobeyed. You broke the rules."

"And you were angry."

"I sure was."

"But Dad, you didn't spank me. Oh, you shouted at me, and you scared me. Then you made me earn the money to replace the window."

"And with me, you made me cut the branches into pieces. You made me paint that black stuff on the tree trunk where the branches used to be. You wouldn't let me play outside for three whole days."

"Three days. Three branches. It seemed fitting."

"But you didn't spank me."

"Nor does Santa spank the boy."

"I'm glad."

"He almost wakes up Father Time and shouts at him, but then he realizes he's too angry, so he grits his teeth and leaves the room."

"That's all?"

"Not quite. The night is long. He rocks before the fire, brooding. In the morning, when the boy comes out to eat his breakfast, Santa pours some milk and cereal for him, then sits across from him and sips a cup of coffee. As the boy gulps down his breakfast, Santa tells him how Time nearly stopped last night.

"You didn't turn the glass."

The boy quits chewing. Looking sick, he almost chokes. "I must have—"

"What?"

"Forgot. My gosh, I'm sorry."

"That's not good enough. I trusted you. You gave your word."

"I didn't mean to break it."

"But you broke it all the same."

"I promise. I'll try harder."

"No, do more than try. Today's the first of March. You're not a child now. You're sixteen. You have to do your duty. No excuses, no apologies. You have to be a man."

"I'll never let you down again."

"I hope. There's something I must tell you. I've been waiting till you're old enough to understand."

"What is it?"

Santa tells the boy about the hundred years—how this is

Santa's final year and how he soon must journey south to find a brand-new Santa. "While I'm gone, I'm not sure I can trust you here alone to do your job. You might forget again, and then there won't be any world or brand-new Santa. Everything will end. Because you're not responsible."

"I promise."

"Keep your promise. Please don't disappoint me. Let the world have another Christmas."

"Then you'll climb that hill?"

"That's right. On Christmas Eve."

The boy begins to cry. "I'll miss you."

Santa frowns. "There's something else I have to tell you. Six days later, New Year's Eve, another baby takes your place. Like me, you have to climb that hill."

"You mean ... ? I live *only* for a year?"

"That's right."

"I'm *scared*."

"An insect called the mayfly lives only for a day. That's all the time it knows, but for that mayfly, one day has to be enough. For you, one year must be enough. It's not a hundred years, but everything is relative. In my hundred years, I've seen a hundred times more sadness than you'll know."

"You've also seen a hundred times more happiness."

"But in the world, they have a saying. *Grant me the wisdom to change what I can change and to accept what I must accept.* What matters isn't how long we live but how we *use* the time we have. In your case, Time itself is your responsibility. It's why you're here. You have to do your duty. Be a man."

"Does Father Time forget again?"

"He keeps his word. But Santa watches him. He checks the glass each night to make sure Father Time remembers. Soon the boy turns twenty. By the end of March, he's twenty-four. He's tall and strong and handsome. Though he wants to play, he does the heavy work for Santa. He helps out—he's useful. Truly he's a man now. But he laughs less. He looks worried. Santa hates to see this change in him. He notices how Father Time spends many hours frowning at the draining sand inside the glass. Then spring comes, and the snow begins to melt. One evening, Santa goes to him and says, 'Tomorrow is the first of May. I have to start my journey. I don't know how long I'll be.' And Father Time replies, 'However long you need. I won't forget to turn the glass. Good luck.' But Santa only answers, *'Pray.'* "

"For what?"

"For wisdom. Santa has his own responsibility. Suppose he picks the wrong man to replace him. What would happen if the brand-new Santa didn't like the job and didn't care enough to make each Christmas special? Think of all the boys and girls who'd wake up Christmas morning and find nothing under the tree. Imagine all the disappointment."

"Gosh, I didn't realize."

"Sure, we depend on Santa, but we never think he'd let us down. We take his generosity for granted. What if he was lazy and unloving, though? Or what if he got lonely for his friends back in the world? Suppose he quit the job?"

"But he can't do that."

"Yes, he can. No one forces him to keep the job. He has to *want* to keep it. If he ever decides to go back to the world, all he has to do is journey south and stay there."

"Who'd be Santa then?"

"Well, if he didn't take the time to find another Santa, then there wouldn't be one. And in fact, that almost happened. Many years ago. But the Santa I'm telling you about, he doesn't quit. He keeps the job and prays for guidance as he journeys south for his replacement."

"Does he use his sled and reindeer?"

"Not in May. There won't be snow. Besides, he only needs the sled to carry all the presents when it's Christmas. On this search, he goes alone. He knows he'd draw attention in his Santa suit. He takes it off and puts on clothes that won't look strange. A jacket and a tie seem too darn formal. But he figures he'll fit in if he wears jogging clothes. A lot of people wear them. Santa guesses he'll look normal. Then he shuts his eyes and concentrates. Inside his mind, he sees a park that's in the middle of a giant city. Huge high buildings soar around the park. He sees a lake and paths and many trees, people riding bikes or jogging. It's a sunny day. As Santa concentrates, he feels the warm spring air. And poof! He disappears. He hears a roaring wind. And then the far-off blare of traffic and the nearby song of birds, the whir of bikes, the rush of joggers. He decides to look. Of course, he's in the park."

"I bet it's *Central* Park."

"Exactly. Someone almost hits him with a bike. He has to jump away before two joggers knock him over. Sheltered by a tree, he wipes his brow and glances all around. The park is massive. But he barely takes a moment to admire it. He's got a job to do. . . . That evening, Father Time sits in the kitchen when he hears a moan from Santa's bedroom. Going in, he frowns at Santa sprawled across the bed, unconscious, groaning from a nightmare. Santa's jogging suit is torn. His face is bruised. His brow feels warm. He twists at a crumpled newspaper, looking so weary that, instead of waking Santa, Father Time undresses him and covers him with a blanket and holds his hand to soothe him through the night. When Santa wakens, he groans, frightened. Squinting at Father Time, he shivers."

"You look like you've seen a ghost."

"A monster." Santa's face turns pale. He tries to swallow, but his throat won't work.

"Here, drink this glass of water."

Santa drains it in three swallows. Drops roll down his beard. He wipes them. "Thanks. I don't know what I'd do without you."

"You took care of me when I was young. It's my turn now to care for you. What happened?"

Santa shudders. "Everything's changed. The newspaper . . ." Santa fumbles around him. "I was sure I brought it with me."

"Here. I found you twisting it as if you wanted to destroy it."

"Did you read it?"

"While I watched you."

"Then you know. The bad things people can do to one another. I wasn't prepared."

"The world was different when you lived there? Long ago, a hundred years, before you came here to be Santa?"

"*Very* different. But at Christmas, I've always been too busy to notice the changes. I don't understand what happened. Things have gotten worse. The world seems smaller, faster, louder. Everything's gray. The people all look desperate. New inventions should have made the world content. Instead they've made the world less satisfied. The wars are worse. I'm frightened. Something bad is going to happen."

"Then you might not find another Santa?"

"I don't know. There must be someone. Somewhere there must be a person worthy to be Santa."

"You need rest."

"It's almost June. I should have started looking earlier."

"You still have many days. A hundred years have tired you. You need your strength. I'll cook some soup."

"I couldn't eat it."

"Try? For me?"

". . . I'd do anything."

"Does Santa get his strength back?"

"Father Time takes care of him. Indeed it seems that Santa's a baby now and Father Time is actually a father. Santa soon gets well enough to search again for his replacement. He goes everywhere, to all the different countries, all the cities in the world. No matter where he goes, he can't find anyone to take the job. The people don't have faith. They don't believe in Christmas spirit. They're not generous. Through June, July, and August, Santa searches. Father Time grows older. Soon he's forty-eight, then sixty-four. October comes. He's eighty, with his long white beard, his long gray robe, his wrinkled cheeks and glowing eyes, his scythe. But Santa hasn't been successful. Christmas will arrive, and there'll be no one to deliver presents."

"What about the elves?"

"Yes, Santa's helpers. Two feet tall with pointed ears and turned-up noses. In a workshop close to Santa's house, they make the toys that Santa gives on Christmas. But the elves can't work without him. They need Santa's guidance. In November, when he comes back from another unsuccessful search, the elves explain to him why he can't go away again. The toys aren't ready. Everything's disorganized. If Santa doesn't stay to help, there won't be any presents for a brand-new Santa to deliver. Santa frowns. He goes to Father Time to seek advice."

"You've got a problem, all right." Father time looks older every moment. "If you go away to search for your replacement, you can't stay to prepare for Christmas. If you stay to prepare for Christmas, you can't go away to search for your replacement. Even *you* can't do two things at once, and yet you have to do them both."

"I need your help. Your wisdom."

"Time's your problem. You don't have enough of it."

"But even you can't give me more of it."

"That's true. I guard Time. I can't lengthen it. I can't create it. Christmas Eve, you have to climb that hill. Have you forgotten, though? At Christmas, people act their best."

"I don't know what you mean."

"Do one job, then the other. First, prepare for Christmas. After, when you've got the presents ready, use your last few days to search for your replacement. Since the people act their best at Christmas, you in turn will have your best chance to find someone to replace you."

Santa smiles. "I understand. Yes, I'll work extra hard to make the presents. If I find another Santa, this'll be the greatest Christmas of them all. The best. The finest. People will remember it forever. And if . . ."

"Yes? Go on."

"And if I'm not successful in my search, the presents will be wasted. There'll be no one to deliver them. There won't be any Christmas."

"No! There has to be a Christmas!"

"Through November, Santa and his elves work night and day. They stack the shelves with toys. They paint the sled. They brush the reindeer, tying jingly bells around their neck. The reindeer tremble. Everything is ready. Santa doesn't bother changing clothes. December twentieth. A few more days. He shuts his eyes. He concentrates. And poof! Again he disappears."

"But will tomorrow be another Christmas?"

"Listen as the story ends. The last days before Christmas Eve go quickly. Father Time waits anxiously. Each night, he turns the glass. He sits before the fireplace and worries. Three more days. Then two more days. Then one. What's keeping

Santa? What's gone wrong? December twenty-fourth arrives. The sun comes up. It passes through the sky and starts to set. But still no Santa. Something awful must have happened. Father Time peers out the window toward the last rays of the sun. It's Christmas Eve, and there's no Santa. Darkness thickens. Father Time stops hoping. All at once, the air begins to crackle. The room gets bright, and poof! Abruptly Santa reappears, alone, collapsing in the rocking chair. 'I tried my best. I failed. I couldn't find another Santa.' "

"No! You mean tomorrow won't be Christmas?"

"Wait, and you'll find out. You see, what Santa discovered is that people like receiving more than giving. Everybody said, 'A hundred years as Santa? What do *I* get in return?' And Santa answered, 'You receive the joy of giving.' But that answer wasn't good enough. The people snorted and complained about the hard work that they'd have to do for others. 'Everybody benefits but us,' they said. 'Let someone else be Santa. We don't want to lose our presents.' "

"If he came to me, I'd take the job."

"I wonder. Think about it. No more presents for you."

"Gosh, you're right. I didn't think. I don't know what I'd do if I was asked. If everybody felt that way, there wouldn't be a Christmas. Dad, that's awful."

Santa can't wait any longer. Wearily he stands to take his walk.

"But," Father Time says, "if you leave, tomorrow won't be Christmas. Stay."

"I can't. The rule is clear. No matter what, I have to climb that hill. I told you—no excuses, no exceptions."

"It's not you who failed."

"What is it then?"

"The other way around. The world failed you. It failed itself."

"I couldn't make it understand. The world failed, but I failed as well. It's time to go. For me, the end of time."

They sadly leave the house. They face the darkness.

Santa stops. "There's something I forgot." He goes back in the house, returning with a bag of toys. "I don't know what

I'll find inside the mist. There might be someone who deserves these presents."

Sobbing, they walk toward the hill—an old man in a gray robe with a scythe across his shoulder, and another old man in a red suit with a sack of toys across his shoulder. Santa's reindeer watch them leave. They feel the sadness, and they frown. The night is cold. The snow lies deep beside the path. A fir tree stands alert, its branches spread as if in blessing. Through the dark, the old men reach the hill. The mist glows brilliantly. It waits.

"I should feel frightened," Santa says. "Instead I'm disappointed that I didn't do my job. After all the other Santas, I'm the one who ended Christmas."

"Are you sure you can't turn back?"

"I'm late already. Friend and son, I'll miss you."

"I'll miss *you*."

As tears roll down their cheeks, they kiss each other. Santa climbs the hill. It's steep. He gasps for breath. Regardless, he plods higher, sad, the final Santa and the end of Christmas.

At the top, he rests. The mist glows brighter, close before him. Glancing toward the bottom of the hill, he takes his final look at Father Time. If only there was someone . . .

"You!" he shouts to Father Time.

"What is it?"

"*You* can give the presents!"

"I'm not Santa."

"It doesn't matter! There's no rule against it! Who says only Santa can give presents? What's important is that *someone* does! The world can have this final Christmas! Take my place!"

"But how?"

"The reindeer know the way! If you try hard—with love—you can't go wrong! A special gift to everyone! Another Christmas! Please? For me?"

". . . I'd do anything."

Abruptly Santa feels the warmth of happiness flow through him. With a sigh, he smiles and turns to face the mist. He's ready. There won't be another Santa, and in years to come, there won't be other Christmases. But *this* year . . .

He steps forward, blinded by the mist.

From the bottom, Father Time stares up. He sees his friend and father disappearing. First he can't see Santa's boots and pants, and then he can't see Santa's coat. At last, he only sees that bulging sack of toys and Santa's long red tassel cap.

Father Time frowns.

Why has Santa stopped? The mist surrounds him, but his head and shoulders are still visible.

Now Santa turns this way, and Father Time feels stunned by the smile on Santa's face, a smile more brilliant than the mist. Santa's eyes are radiant as if what waits in the mist is overwhelming—wonderful and beautiful. He lifts an arm to wave farewell. With joy, he turns to face the mist once more. He takes a step.

And he is gone.

"Did Santa go to heaven?"

"You could say that."

"Is he happy there?"

"Completely. After all his years of giving, he received the happiness he wished for others."

"And does Father Time do what he promised?"

"He runs to the house and turns the time-glass. Then he quickly hitches the reindeer to the sleigh. He sets the bag of toys in back. He scrambles in and grabs the reins. The bells on the reindeer jingle. 'Dasher! Dancer! Prancer! Vixen! Comet! Cupid! Donder! Blitzen!' As he shouts each name, the reindeer tug. The sleigh begins to move. The reindeer pull it harder, and the sleigh streaks through the snow. Its blades hiss. Snow flies. Suddenly the sleigh takes off. Eight reindeer and an old man form a silhouette against the winter moon. Abruptly they zoom high out of sight."

"He took just one bag of toys. That's not enough."

"The bag is never empty. It holds every toy that Santa and his helpers made. When Father Time takes out one toy, another toy will fill its place."

"But how can Father Time reach every home before the children wake on Christmas Day? The night's too short."

"But like the bag of toys, it always seems to last. In every home, in each apartment and each house, wherever there are people, Father Time leaps from the sleigh and hurries with his bag of toys."

"He really goes down chimneys?"

"Sometimes. Or else doors and windows open for him. Sometimes he just walks through walls. He realizes that on Christmas Eve he can do anything."

"And doesn't anybody see him?"

"No. Children fall asleep when he arrives. On rare occasions, parents see him, but their minds get clouded, and they don't remember seeing him. A night of miracles. Of wonders. He brings more than toys. He brings the Christmas spirit. People wake, and they feel joyous. Fathers who have been away come home. And mothers who've been sick get better. Everyone feels loved. On Christmas morning, church bells ring their message—peace, goodwill to everyone. That Christmas is the greatest. Truly extra special. Father Time works harder than he ever dreamed. He's more successful than he ever hoped. The sun comes up. The reindeer bring him home. He leans back in the sleigh and sighs, exhausted. But then he smiles, and then he laughs. Because, although the world is far away, he still can hear the joyful echo of the people laughing and the church bells ringing merrily. Those distant sounds of happiness are his reward. He frees the reindeer from the sleigh. He pets and brushes them. He gives them lots of fresh sweet hay. They kick their hooves and frolic in the snow. At last, he rests. And then remembers he's alone. Six short days go by. On New Year's Eve, he turns the glass. The final time. He stays until the sun has almost disappeared. He takes his last look at the house, then walks along the path, and climbs the hill."

"But wait. When Father Time is gone—"

"The New Year's Baby will arrive."

"Who will watch the baby?"

"No one."

"Who will turn the time-glass?"

"No one. When the sand stops draining—"

"Time will stop? The world will end?"

"Because people wanted to receive instead of give. Because nobody cared enough, was generous enough, to want to be the brand-new Santa."

"They'll be sorry now."

"But Father Time feels awful. As he climbs the hill, he wishes his old friend were back. He weeps, not for himself but for the world. If people understood. If people had another chance. He pauses on the hilltop, squinting toward the mist. He wants to stay, to save the world. He hears the New Year's Baby crying in the house. He almost turns to go to it. But rules are rules. They can't be broken. That's the lesson Santa taught him. Wincing as the baby cries, he forces himself to step ahead. The mist waits, flashing. But if only . . . Suddenly he feels a blinding burst of heat. He's fat. He wears a red suit. And a tassel cap. He's—"

"Santa!"

" *'Go,'* a voice booms from the mist. *'Despite temptation, you obeyed the rule. You're worthy. Give the world this priceless gift, although the world does not deserve the gift. A hundred years of Christmas. And the time to learn to love.'* The mist goes silent once again. The brand-new Santa weeps with gratitude. His heart swells, filled with thanks. He turns and walks back down the hall. The New Year's Baby cries much harder. But there's someone to watch over him. And someone to watch over Time, to turn the glass, to make the sand keep draining. Santa laughs with joy. He starts to run."

"Tomorrow is another Christmas?"

"Now. Today. It's after midnight. Gosh, I don't know where the time went. You two better get some sleep."

"But I was hoping I'd see Santa."

"You remember what I told you? If by chance you catch a glimpse of him, he'll cloud your mind. You won't know that you've seen him. Hey, the snow has stopped. The wind is gone. Tomorrow will be perfect."

"A white Christmas."

"The beginning of another hundred years. I hope the world makes use of Santa's gift. I hope it learns to love. A kiss for you. And one for you. I'll see you in the morning."

"Merry Christmas."

"And to you. The best. We're all together. What more could we want? Yes, Merry Christmas."

A bad boy meets Santa.

SANTA'S TENTH REINDEER
Gordon Van Gelder

BILLY AVENDIL DIDN'T go to sleep on Christmas Eve. He lay awake in bed, watching the minutes tick off his clock. He was nervous, he was excited, he was anxious, he had something up his sleeve.

He waited until he felt he had waited long enough, then he tiptoed out of his room, taking precautions in case somebody was still half awake. He slid down the banister to avoid the squeaky stairs and because it was fun.

He instantly went to work, setting up his trap, testing it, making sure that everything was right. He considered setting a fire in the fireplace for the twelfth time, and for the twelfth time he decided that Santa would see the fire in time. Especially if his doubts were correct. But that was what he was doing all this for.

Then came the waiting. He sat down behind the tree, chewing his nails. He got up, started pacing, considered taking a cigarette from his mother's pocketbook, decided against it, paced some more, and was getting up for the cigarette when he heard noises on the rooftop.

Ho ho ho jingle jingle. The sound of hoofs beat against the roof. Billy raced to his spot behind the tree and gripped the pole nervously. He wondered about the reindeer, for if his theory was right, then the reindeer would be different, but he didn't have time to follow up on the thought.

Ho ho ho ugh ugh damn oof ugh. Santa was on his way down. Billy wondered if he should have stuck a knife in the chimney.

Ah phew ho ho whooooa oof! Santa emerged from the fire-place, stepped onto the skateboard, and went flying into the tree. Billy pushed the angel off the tree, and it struck Santa on the head with a crash. Then Billy hit Santa on the head with the pole. Santa fell to the floor, unconscious.

Billy tied Santa's hands to the tree, and lashed the feet together. Then he confirmed his theory, and took a picture for proof. He waited for Santa to awaken.

Santa came to with an awful headache. He realized where he was, and he swore, a long string of curses too terrible to repeat. When his "speech" was over, he said, "Why'd you do this, Billy? If it's my presents you want, take them. I don't give a damn. It just means that a lot of kids are going to be disappointed."

"Take you presents and stuff them up your fat rear, one at a time. I don't want your presents. All I wanted was proof of who you are, and I've got it," said Billy.

"All right, son, you've caught me."

"Get lost. My father's upstairs, with enough drugs in him to put an elephant to sleep. I know who you are."

"Damn, I think that you do know."

"That's right, Santa. I know why you always wear red, and it's not because it matches your nose. That was a pretty good joke, with the switch of the names. I liked it."

"I'm thrilled," said Santa unemphatically.

"Aww. Why so sad, Prince? Sad that the cat's out of the bag, along with all the other stuff you've got in there?" asked Billy.

"Do you know what a pain in the, uh, neck you are, Billy? I have stuff to do, and you're keeping me from doing it," said Santa.

"Aww, that's too bad. The Prince of Evil worried that he won't give out enough presents? Tsk tsk."

"You're the snottiest kid I know, and I think that all kids are snotty," said Santa.

Billy made a disgusting noise in response to Santa's statement. "Could you tell me something?" asked Billy. "Why do you do it? Why give out presents, and eggs on Easter, and love on Valentine's Day, why?"

"Take a guess," said Santa dryly. "Are you going to let me loose?"

"Not until I get answers, that's for sure. Why do you do it?" he repeated.

"You're evil, you're clever, figure it out."

"If I could've figured it out, I wouldn't have asked. Tell me."

"More hate comes through love than any other way," said Santa.

"Bull. That ruins the definition of love."

"Really? Think about it. What are half the murders? Husband and wife. How do best friends become best enemies? By chasing after the same person. Don't you see? Love and hate go hand in hand, like life and death. Are you going to release me?"

Billy was considering everything Santa had said. "I see your point, Santa, but there are still things I don't understand. Why give out presents?"

"They go with evil, too. Haven't you ever seen two kids fight over who gets the better present? Just think about the things you ask, and you'll get answers."

"No. True, presents do cause some evil, but they spread a lot of love. So does Valentine's Day, so does Easter, so do all your holidays."

"The world cannot exist without opposites—love and hate, life and death, day and night, and so on. Nobody can do anything without opposites occurring. I try to cause evil, and some good comes of it. Same with you, same with what everyone does. Are you going to let me go?"

"I think I see what you mean. Do I have an opposite?"

"Of course. Everybody does. You'll probably marry her.

But I have some bad news for you. Your plan isn't going to work. The picture you took won't convince anybody."

"Yeah, sure, like I'm really going to buy that."

"It's true. They won't accept Santa as something else. It's the opposite theory again. The people think that Santa is good. Believe me. Other people have tried what you're going to."

"You mean, all I've done is going to go to waste?"

"No. I've found out that you're evil, and that's important. You're so evil, in fact, that I have an offer to make to you. How would you like to become a helper of mine, a cupid, or maybe a bunny?"

"No thanks. I couldn't stand it. I'm fine as I am right now."

"You don't want to be an elf, huh? Well, how about a personal assistant? I could make my former one an elf, and let you have the job."

"Very tricky. Then when somebody new comes along, I'm an elf. No thanks. I'm fine as I am."

"I'll level with you. There is a time when certain people have to be removed from the world, or else they would wreak too much havoc. No matter what you say, a good soul is going to change places with you. You may as well get as good a position as you can."

"I don't believe a single word you've said. Take your proposition and shove it."

"That's it." Santa stood up, rearing himself to his towering full height, hands and feet free by some unknown means. His eyes twinkled—with evil and not merriment.

"That's it, Billy. You've had your chance, and you shoved it. No longer shall I ask, I shall *do*. From now on, you will be my helper. One night a year, you will tow me around the world with nine others as evil as you. You will learn what it feels like to be whipped, and what it feels like to freeze on rooftops. For three hundred and sixty-four days, you will live in the Arctic and eat moss. I shall deprive you even of death. Your life will become a living hell, no pun intended." He smiled at the horror in Billy's eyes, and made a motion with his hands . . .

. . . And Billy changed. His smile softened, his eyes filled

with awe at the sight of Santa. Santa put out the presents for
the Avendil family, winked at the new Billy, and hustled up
the chimney, hoping the tenth reindeer would make up for the
lost time.

"Ho ho ho! Move, boys! On Donner, on Blitzen, on Vixen!
Get your rear in gear, Billy! Merry Christmas to all, and to all
a good night!"

**How can we have Christmas
unless we know when it is?**

TICK
M.J. Engh

"THERE'S SOME PEOPLE here that want to celebrate Christmas."

"So?" The Timekeeper looked up, deep-set eyes like things moving in underwater crannies.

The clerk grimaced apologetically. "So they want to know when it is."

The Timekeeper's eyes reverted to the datasphere humped like a large translucent pudding on the desk. The clerk scratched the side of her nose and waited. She'd get an answer eventually. In due time.

The Timekeeper prodded the datasphere with one finger. "Tell them I'll work on it."

"Oh," said the clerk.

"Did you think it would be easy?"

That was exactly what the clerk had thought. "So fine, I'll tell them." She shrugged her shoulders and dropped through the floor.

Ketral aun Tso slid smooth as a lecturer's lightpencil out of the maintenance hatch and into his wife's playful chant of welcome. "Here comes Ketter-Ket! Here comes Ketter-Daddy! Give him a Paddy-hug!"

"Wait till I get this off," Ketral said. "It's—whoops!—slippery."

Paddeen had launched himself like a small, excited probe unit, collided with Ketral in a starburst of laughter, and slid off the smooth surface of his coverall. Ketral caught him by the wrist and hauled him back into the promised hug. Paddeen's little body slithered against the nonfriction fabric, but he managed to plant a brusque kiss on his father's cheek before he was squirted out of the embrace.

"I get one, too?" his wife demanded. She pressed herself into a slithery hug. "Love you," she sang, that light, unrefusable lilt he knew so well.

"Love you, Tso," Ketral said into her hair.

And in spite of all that, it wasn't going to be a good two point seven hours. Ketral could tell by the way she pulled away from him as soon as her hug had taken effect.

"We just came by to say hello," Tso observed lightly, "because we won't be seeing you for a while. Tell where we're going, Paddeen."

"Going to church," Paddeen said, bouncing a bubbleball on his palm.

Disappointment turned Ketral limp. "I have to be at work again in two point six eight."

"So?" Her eyebrows lifted.

"I was hoping we could spend the time together." He began pulling off his coverall—pointless now, but something to do with his hands. Paddeen instantly dropped the ball and reached to help him, tugging at a tab.

"I had hoped that too," Tso said. "But since you consider the church an object of ridicule, I think Paddeen and I had better keep that part of our life separate. I don't want you making fun of him."

"Huh?" Ketral pushed his fingers through his hair. "I went to the Timekeeper's Office with you, didn't I—you and your church friends?"

"Yes, you did, apparently to laugh at us—to announce to

the Expedition that we're silly. I think 'silly' was the word you used."

Ketral searched his memory. "I said I felt silly. That's all."

Tso laughed. "Yes, well, I wouldn't want you to feel silly."

"Move your foot, Daddy, move." Paddeen was yanking at the coverall that now lay pooled around his father's feet. Absently, Ketral stepped out of it. He knelt and put one arm around Paddeen, who was busy wadding the coverall into its self-pocket.

"Come on, son, we'll be late to church if we don't hurry," Tso caroled.

Paddeen dropped the coverall and wrapped his arms around Ketral's neck, enthusiastically but briefly. Then he snatched up the coverall again, presented it to Ketral with a flourish that started it spilling out of its pocket, and bounded to his mother's side. She was already turning away.

"Don't forget your ball, Paddeen," Ketral called after them.

This church thing, Ketral reflected gloomily, had never been a problem—no more, at least, than any other of Tso's fads—until some of the church people got the idea of reviving ancient traditions. Now it seemed they were always finding differences between themselves and the rest of the Expedition. He'd gone with the delegation to the Timekeeper's Office because Tso had begged him to, and because he'd thought it was a way they could be together.

And he had messed it up. Ketral tightened his fists in his pockets as he stepped into a pedestrian chute and slid along with downcast eyes. He should have kept his mouth shut. But Tso had asked him right there in the Timekeeper's Office how he felt, and he'd said, in front of all the office staff and the people waiting, "I feel a little silly." Stupid, stupid. And in a few days he'd be back in the Timekeeper's Office, doing a maintenance check on their matter-interpenetration equipment.

At the other end of the pedestrian chute, Ketral paused at a notice board and scanned the public schedule, looking for something fun to do. There: communal and individual swim coming up in fourteen hours plus. Tso would like that, and

Paddeen would go wild. He touched his left wrist to activate the personal schedule he always carried there, and watched the duties and times scroll past. Sector D-six air cycler check in twelve point six four (point six three as he thumbed the wrist display off) and nothing after that for a good three hours. He punched in the swim on his personal schedule and went on, whistling softly.

Paddeen liked low-gravity walkways, and Tso was in a motherly mood, so that was the route they took home. He liked to drag himself from one handhold to another along the netting that lined the walls and ceiling. It had been a good swim—maybe not as good as Ketral had hoped, but you took what you got.

A young woman with a long braid of pale reddish hair grabbed at the netting to stop herself in midstride. She aimed her hand at them, forking her fingers to point. "You're some of the Christmas people, aren't you?" They all stopped.

"Yes, we are," Tso said. "I'm Tso aun Ketral. I'm one of the people who started the idea. This is my husband and my son Paddeen." She stroked Paddeen's head, which was bobbing up and down at her hip level.

Paddeen bounced higher, staring curiously at the redhead. Ketral recognized her—a clerk in the Timekeeper's Office. "Say hello," he admonished Paddeen.

"Hello," Paddeen said. "We went swimming." He shoved off and bounced away down the walkway, aiming high kicks at both walls.

"Yah, I saw you at the office the other day," the clerk said. There were small flecks of pigment in the pale skin of her face, mostly across her nose and cheekbones. "The Timekeeper's working it out. I didn't think it would take so long." She looked at her wrist. There were freckles there too. "Been almost a hundred hours already."

"Look at me," Tso raged, "just look at me when I'm talking! If you'd just meet my eyes when I'm speaking to you, maybe I'd hope we could talk things out."

"I'm meeting your eyes," Ketral said. "Talk."

"Good. Maybe now I won't have to shout so loud."

Ketral bit the inside of his lip. "What exactly do you want to talk out?" He couldn't remember where the argument had started, but it had covered most of the details of their life. He was tired; he wanted to sleep.

"If you think Paddeen doesn't meet your supposedly high standards of courtesy, why don't you try to set a good example for him instead of ordering him around in public? He's your son, not your slave."

"You mean I shouldn't have told him to say hello when I hadn't said hello myself. You're right, Tso. I've already said you're right, I've already apologized, I've already said it was stupid. Now can I go to sleep?"

"You usually do." She laughed her sudden throaty laugh, the sound that could still, in the right circumstances, stir him to the roots. "Maybe that explains why you do these things."

"Why?"

"Because they're stupid." She rolled over onto him, gurgling with laughter. "Love you," she crooned. Her fingers plucked at his ears and hair, little mischievous tugs. "Is the mean daddy still mad?"

"I can't switch it off and on, Tso. Just let me sleep for now. I have to be at work in four hours." But half against his will he felt his body rousing. He groaned and hugged her against him resentfully.

"Love you," she chuckled. Ketral made an inarticulate noise. At least this time she had called Paddeen his son.

"Maintenance check," Ketral announced, and offered his hand for identification.

The Timekeeper's clerk swept his palm with her ID brush and nodded. "Ventilator?"

"No, your interpenetrator. Any trouble with it?" That was an unnecessary question. If there'd been any trouble, he'd have heard. But there was something about the clerk's casual friendliness that made him want to say unnecessary things.

"Nah, works fine." She laughed. "It used to scare me, going through the ceiling like that." She gestured upward. "You get used to it, and then you think you can walk through walls."

"I know what you mean." Ketral lifted the interpen plate from the floor beside the clerk's desk and began checking its underside. "I'd like to take my little boy on one of these, but I don't know—" There he went again, always talking about Paddeen.

"You're afraid he'd get too scared?"

"Paddeen? No!" Ketral laughed. "I'm worried he'd be try-ing to *run* through walls—and jump through ceilings."

"I could tell he's a lively kid." She wrinkled her forehead. "I suppose you're wondering why the Timekeeper still hasn't come up with an answer on your Christmas thing."

"It's not mine," Ketral said, with more force than he'd intended—and heard himself adding, "I hope the answer turns out to be 'impossible.' "

The clerk made a face. "Not your style, huh?"

"I'm not one of them," Ketral said. "I just came along with my wife. It—I don't know, some of it worries me. As far as I can tell, it's all about something that happened on Earth—I don't mean Earth now, I mean Earth way back off schedule. My wife says they want to know *when* it happened."

The clerk grimaced. "You mean when it's going to hap-pen?"

"No, when it happened. When, off schedule."

"That's crazy," the clerk said tolerantly. "Either it's going to happen, and the schedule tells you when, or it's off sched-ule and it doesn't matter."

"I know," Ketral said. He was suddenly embarrassed. "I have to check the penetrable plate." He pointed at the ceiling. "Can I go through for about eighty seconds?"

The clerk sucked her lower lip thoughtfully. "You want to talk to the Timekeeper?"

"No, that's not necessary. I just need to make a few mea-surements."

She shrugged. "Suit yourself. I thought as long as you're here, I could maybe get you a few minutes to talk about the Christmas thing. If you're really worried. I don't think the Timekeeper knows anybody's worried about it."

"Does the Timekeeper care?" Ketral's voice sounded sour to his own ears.

"Oh, yah. That's part of the assessment for scheduling anything. Especially anything new."

Ketral finished fitting the interpenetration plate back into the floor and straightened slowly. "Well—"

The clerk grinned. "No promises. I'll see what I can do. The Timekeeper's nice, really. You'll be surprised." She stepped onto the plate, flicked her activator, and was lifted through the ceiling.

Ketral felt her going as a sudden drag that pulled at something inside him. What could a maintenance technician say to the Timekeeper of the Expedition? What he'd already said to the clerk was stupid, probably.

In a little she descended, her soft braid swinging. "Timekeeper's in a good mood. Take as long as you want." She winked and offered the interpen plate with a gesture.

Rising into the Timekeeper's presence was like sinking into one of the underwater galleries in the swimming complex— the sense of entering another world, slower and darker and more awesome, with always that unvoiced hope that your gill-kit had been properly maintained. The Timekeeper sat, or loomed, at a broad desk whose central bowl cradled a datasphere almost half a meter wide. "I have just a few things to check," Ketral said, and bent at once to make his measurements.

"By all means." The Timekeeper's deep-chested voice was resonant. "I trust that you will keep to your schedule. But I understand that you have a concern to discuss with me. Please do so; I value your input. This matter of the Christmas event demands careful assessment. When you have completed your measurements, feel free to be seated."

Ketral repocketed his recorder and sat down in the one vacant seat, facing the Timekeeper across the datasphere. "I don't know what to say exactly. My wife is one of the people who asked you about Christmas. I don't know what could be wrong with putting it on the schedule—I guess what bothers me is, this whole Christmas thing is from something off schedule, something that happened back on Earth. And I don't really understand what they're asking you to do. It's not just putting it into the schedule, is it? It's figuring out when it *is*—whatever that means."

The Timekeeper made a warm, purring sound. "Let me explain to you the concept of date."

That was the trouble, Ketral thought, with these high-toned specialists: they were always using words nobody else had ever heard of. "All right."

"I shall proceed to do so. In many ways the Expedition reproduces, or at least reflects, the life of humans on Earth. But there is one basic difference."

The Timekeeper paused for so long that Ketral decided an answer was called for. "Uh, yes, I know."

"Do you?"

Ketral stirred uneasily. "Well, I thought you meant the Expedition is an artificial, closed environment. That's the difference they teach you in school." He cleared his throat and added, "My wife is a teacher." The Timekeeper made him nervous.

The Timekeeper sighed audibly. "Yes, in a sense that is a significant difference, although I doubt that it greatly impacts the ordinary life of most people. No, I referred to a societal difference. Earth has history; the Expedition has schedules."

Ketral's forehead creased. Another new word. "What's history?"

"Ah." The Timekeeper's voice was satisfied. "To begin with the more familiar, what are schedules? Have you considered what, in fact, they do?"

"They tell you what's going to happen when," Ketral said.

"More exactly," the Timekeeper corrected, "they tell us the anticipated time interval between the present and an expected future event."

How else could you do it? Ketral wondered; but all he asked was "Don't they have schedules on Earth?"

"From time to time various Earth cultures have used schedules of a sort, and our latest information shows them still employing some schedules, though of a radically different type from ours." The Timekeeper's large hand waved slowly back and forth. "But let us discuss history." The Timekeeper frowned for several seconds. "This is difficult to explain, difficult to grasp. You are, of course, familiar with the Data Archives. Imagine a sort of archive in which what is stored is not data but a record of the events from which data could be derived."

"That's—awfully inefficient, isn't it?"

"Distressingly inefficient. Such a record is a history. Now, Christmas, the subject of our present concern, is an event in Earth's history."

"But—" Ketral stopped, baffled.

"Quite," said the Timekeeper. "Perhaps an example can make this comprehensible. Take the next item on your personal schedule."

Ketral consulted his wrist. "Meet my wife at her school, two point one eight hours."

"And the following item."

"Maintenance check, pedestrian chutes, sector C-six, ten point three nine."

"Good. So the interval between the two events is eight point two one hours."

"Yes, that's my off-shift."

"And that interval will remain the same," the Timekeeper continued inexorably, "even as time passes. Correct?"

"I suppose so."

"We can therefore say that the first event takes place at Moment One, the second event at Moment One plus eight point two one hours." The Timekeeper leaned forward portentously. "We have given the two events *dates*."

"What good does that do?"

"Try to think of it as an educational exercise," the Timekeeper said with asperity. "The point I want to make is that dates, unlike schedules, do not change. Three hours from now, the dates of our dated events will still be Moment One and Moment One plus eight point two one hours."

"But—"

"Kilodays from now, they will still be Moment One and Moment One plus eight point two one hours."

"No, they won't," Ketral protested. "They'll be all the way off schedule. They won't exist."

"They would exist," the Timekeeper said, "historically. A date remains the same, whether it is future, present, or off schedule. Any event can be given a date. All that is required is a starting point to which it can be compared, and a unit—a standard interval—with which to make the comparison. Let the starting point be called Moment One, and the unit be called tick."

"Called what?"

"Tick," the Timekeeper repeated testily. "From the sound generated by a primitive timekeeping mechanism. Tick tick tick tick. It may represent the movement of a spring-powered ratchet, the human heartbeat, the oscillation of a cesium atom, or any other repeating event. Repeating event, and hence interval between any two proximate occurrences of the event. Do you understand?"

"I think so," Ketral said. "You mean that's what an hour is, a kind of tick."

"Just so. On the Expedition we use our ticks to make schedules, which are constantly changing. But they could also be used to establish dates, which never change. A history is a collection of off-schedule dates."

"And what good—well, sorry." There was nothing else Ketral could think of to say.

"What good indeed? I myself believe that Earth could have achieved interstellar travel far sooner without the burden of these histories cluttering their archives, misdirecting their research, and retarding their educational processes—not to mention the blighting effect of histories on social development. Significantly, the Expedition remains, so far as we know, unique—the first, and still the only, serious interstellar mission. The few other spacecraft that we know to have left the Solar system have been merely probes of the nearest stars, designed to collect information and return it to Earth." The Timekeeper nodded ponderously. "The burden of history is the suppression of imagination."

Ketral frowned. "How did we get rid of all that?"

"Fortunately, the Expedition has had the incentive of limited storage capacity, so that we early discarded all such histories and adopted a forward-looking schedule system. We still transmit our reports to Earth, or at least in the direction of the Solar system, and people there are quite competent to make histories of them if they wish. But we ourselves, for the most part, are not interested in what we have done, only in what we will do."

Ketral nodded. He felt a bit queasy. "Except—"

"Yes, except for your delegation of church people with their intriguing curiosity about the date of Christmas. You say this troubles you. I confess that it troubles me."

Ketral sat forward. "There's something wrong with it, isn't there? What is it that's so wrong?"

" 'Wrong' is perhaps too judgmental a term. Certainly it is not incorrect to suppose that Christmas can be assigned a date, at least in theory. But consider." The Timekeeper sighed heavily. "What is time?"

"Time is what schedules measure," Ketral said.

"Well put, if not entirely comprehensive. Time is a measurement, and measurement implies a unit, and units imply rhythm. Please note. Rhythm"—the Timekeeper lifted a finger magisterially—"makes time; time does not make rhythm."

"What does that mean?"

"Rhythm is the basis of all timekeeping. On Earth, both human physiology and external environment altered rhythmically, following a pattern of three superimposed but incommensurate cycles."

"Like a maintenance schedule," Ketral said. "Most things get checked on a regular cycle, but the cycles are different lengths, and they don't come out even very often."

"Exactly. The three Earth cycles to which I refer are the day, the month, and the year."

"They had days on Earth?"

"Not like ours. The original Earth day was the planet's period of rotation."

Ketral nodded. That was comprehensible, at least. "And what were the other things you said?"

"Month: the period of revolution of Earth's one moon. Year: the planet's own period of revolution. You perceive, perhaps, the inherent flaw in all these as units of time measurement."

"They sound pretty inconvenient," Ketral said.

"Inconvenient and worse. Any unit based on planetary motion must change as orbits and velocities evolve. One year does not equal another year, nor one day another day. But in terms of human perception and human lifetimes, especially at a low level of civilization, the changes are slight and can be ignored."

"I suppose it would work," Ketral said, "if you didn't have anything better."

"Just so. At first, all human timekeeping consisted of more or less unsuccessful attempts to reconcile these three cycles. Then, with the dawn of experimental science in the age of Galileo and Einstein, a new concept emerged as the basis of a new timekeeping—a precise, reproducible base unit, in practice the wavelength of certain species of atomic radiation. Again, a rhythm, a natural cycle, but a far more useful one."

"Well, yes," Ketral said. "Naturally."

"This type of unit is the basis of Expedition timekeeping. It gives us our second, in terms of which the hour and the day are defined. Yet it has not entirely freed us from the rhythm of planetary movement. We remain vulnerable; we could fall victim once again to the enslavement of history. That is the danger of this Christmas project."

"I don't see how," Ketral said. He stole a glance at his wrist schedule.

"Life on Earth," said the Timekeeper, "was not so much a process as a series of recurrences. Anniversaries, if I may use the technical term. Just as we have certain expectations and certain customary patterns of activity for each day's meal periods and work shifts, so Earth-dwellers would have expectations and activity patterns for, let us say, the month of January or the rainy season. An individual's life span was divided into years and tens of years, marked off in many cultures by 'birthdays,' so called because they celebrated that point in the cycle of the year at which the individual had been born. Education, socialization, maturation were all conceived of and measured in year units. Sexual behavior, exercise of one's profession, recreation, almost any human activity might be regulated in terms of the interval elapsed since birth."

"That's bizarre!" Ketral burst out.

"So it would seem. And yet we carry within us a certain propensity to respond to cycles. Circadian rhythms are built into a wide variety of human physiological processes, and hence the day has remained an important macrotemporal unit for the Expedition. Other Earth cycles, the month and the year, were clearly irrelevant and have dropped out of use, replaced by the more meaningful hectoday, kiloday, et cetera. Our cycles, based on a single tick, are all commensurable. And they are uniform. One day, as a time interval, equals any other day. That is the theory."

In Ketral's experience, when somebody said *That's the theory,* they meant, *It doesn't really work that way.* But he wasn't sure if that applied to the Timekeeper. "Does it work?"

"No." The Timekeeper's brooding face hovered above the datasphere. "Or, let me say, it works very well but not perfectly. Constant calibration is the price of uniformity. On Earth, years, months, and days were regularly recalibrated by reference both to changing planetary movements and to the presumably unchanging atomic frequencies—a continual cross-check between different systems of measurement. But what of the Expedition? Without the inconvenience of planetary motions, we are also without their assistance as calibration tools."

"I can see why Earth cycles would need calibration," Ketral said.

The Timekeeper regarded him reprovingly. "But you are not sure that the Expedition does so. Indeed, in a closed environment, what more is necessary for time measurement than a starting point and a tick? And if the length of the tick is not always identically the same, what harm is done? Even atomic frequencies fluctuate within imperfectly understood limits. But consider. The first ten ticks of a series may be equivalent to the following nine ticks—or ninety. For most purposes the self-contained tick system is altogether adequate. But for the Christmas people, as my clerk calls them"—the Timekeeper's voice settled into its habitual darkness—"the lack of external verification is most unfortunate. Without it, they cannot connect their Christmas celebration to the Earth date it commemorates. Yet there is hope. What, I ask you, is the Expedition's purpose?"

Ketral blinked. "The Expedition's purpose is to find a habitable body and there establish a colony."

"And to put that colony in communication with Earth—just as another part of our mission is to maintain our own communication with Earth, however useless that may appear. And in the event—the highly probable event, let me inform you—that the Expedition continues after the founding of the first colony, we are to remain in communication both with the colony and with Earth. The possibility exists, therefore, of an eventual network of communications uniting the Solar system, and us, with colonies scattered across the galaxy; perhaps even"—the Timekeeper's voice lowered—"with other Expeditions. And since every node in that network will have its own frame of reference, all in continuous relative motion, some form of calibration is indeed essential."

"I—see," Ketral said. "So what do we do?"

The Timekeeper beamed. "We do the virtually impossible. There can be no simultaneity between distant points. Do you understand what I mean?"

Ketral squinted. "You mean we don't have any way to tell if something happens on the Expedition at the same time as something else happens on Earth."

"Ah, more than that. We might know on exactly what Earth date we left the Solar system. We might know exactly how long we have been traveling. But even with that information in hand, we could not answer the question, 'What is the date on Earth at this moment?' Do you understand why not?"

"No," Ketral said helplessly.

"Because the question is meaningless. Between the Earth and the Expedition there is no 'at this moment'—no simultaneity. This was a question of the type 'Which is longer, a second today or a second tomorrow?' There is no means of comparison, no common measuring stick. And yet"—the Timekeeper leaned forward—"the Expedition carries an invaluable cargo, a precious jewel—I speak now metaphorically—that can serve this purpose. It is called the date verification system."

"I never heard of that," Ketral said.

"And I have never used it. The occasion has never before arisen in my time. Its only ongoing use is to date the reports we send to Earth."

"What is it?" Ketral asked curiously. Hard to imagine there was a system on the Expedition he knew literally nothing about.

"It is complex. But in essence it is simply a double clock. One part of the system patiently counts ticks, recording the time elapsed since our departure from the Solar system. The other is our calibrator, measuring time as it is presumed to be passing on Earth. Inaccuracies are inevitable, unmeasurable, and probably great. Nevertheless, it is the one thing that attaches our frame of reference conceptually and computationally to that of Earth. You see, therefore, why I refer to it as a precious jewel, the single most important item to be transferred to our future colonies. Of course," the Timekeeper added modestly, "I speak as a Timekeeper."

"So without the date verification system," Ketral said, working it out at last, "you couldn't schedule Christmas."

"On the contrary, I could schedule Christmas as I can schedule any other Expedition event. But I could not *date* Christmas."

"I'm not sure it would be Christmas, then," Ketral said. "Not the way my wife talks about Christmas."

The Timekeeper thrust a long finger into the datasphere and made slow, stirring motions. "First, then, I must establish a date. After that, it will be possible to enter Christmas into the general Expedition schedule. Your misgivings, and mine, are not adequate reasons to deny the request of a group of Expedition members. Besides"—a smile softened the Timekeeper's face—"the computational problem is very intriguing. I want to thank you, Ketral aun Tso, for an interesting discussion."

"See?" the clerk said. "Timekeeper's not so bad. I go up there sometimes just to talk."

Ketral rubbed his forehead and grinned. "My brain has had a workout."

"Yah, that happens. Interpen all right?"

"Perfect," Ketral said.

He wanted to walk—really stretch his legs, not just ease along a low-grav walkway or give himself up to the inert glide of a pedestrian chute—so he stepped into the nearest panorama corridor. This was one he didn't often use. Tso had never liked it. It was a vista in browns and rosy beige—skin tones, when you thought about it. Like caressing a multitude of friendly bodies with your eyes—a quiet crowd that stretched off into a far distance, overlapping and shifting as you moved, the curved and angled shapes never quite resolving into a free-fall tangle of buttocks and knees. Tso's favorite was the corridor in sector B-five, with curtain beyond curtain of green and yellow and a towering colonnade that stretched away to nothingness. Paddeen's favorite was the meteor-swarm corridor in B-seven, where rocky shapes hurtled and twisted as far as you could see. Maybe, Ketral thought, they could walk that one after Paddeen's next school shift. He'd take a look at the next notice board, see what there was to go to in B-seven.

There was a show on the latest planetary system, perfect for a family outing. Paddeen loved everything about it—putting on the mask, steering his probe among the virtual trajectories, swooping through a methane atmosphere into the wild heart of a gas giant. Ketral made his own tour quickly, laughing with the feeling of freedom and control. It wasn't real, of course; you could only go where the system was ready for you. He pulled off the mask and grinned at Tso, who was just pulling off hers. Even now, they pulsed together sometimes.

Paddeen, still masked and deep in the glory of flight, crowed with laughter. A moment later he was jiggling his controls angrily, trying to break out of a trajectory that refused to take him where he wanted to go. That was the pain, Ketral thought; finding the limits, making the cruel decision of when to stop trying to break through. Paddeen's face cleared as he found a path and swooped his way back, planet by planet to an imaginary docking in the Expedition's outer hull. He yanked off his mask and turned to his parents. "Can I do that again?"

"Not this time," Ketral said. "Run and check out a toy, if you want one." Paddeen galloped across the observation room to the display of planetary toys, said to be educational.

"This was so good," Tso said. "I love it when we do something as a family. And Paddeen learns so much at this kind of show. Flying among the planets of an alien sun—it certainly beats reading about them."

"More fun, at least," Ketral said. They were swinging their clasped hands between their two seats, blessedly easy. "I always worry a little about these things; they seem so realistic, but they're not. I'm afraid he's learning the wrong ideas about distance and velocity and what a planetary system is like."

Tso made a dismissive noise, but her fingers were gently massaging his. "How could he be? It *is* realistic. It's all from actual probe data."

"Yes, extrapolated and enhanced and edited. But the way they put it together is as much for entertainment as for information. You couldn't get into a real probe and just go zip, zip from one planet to another like that."

"Oh, maybe not. But it's the feel of it that counts."

"That's what I mean," Ketral said.

Paddeen had made his choice, pressed first his palm and then his personal schedule chip against the toy vendor's sensor/printer, and now came running back with a fuzzy "planet" the size of his head, orbited by multicolored rings and a fist-sized moon. "Look, Mama!"

"Ooh, beautiful! I bet you flew to one like that."

Paddeen nodded emphatically. "Look at it, Daddy!"

Ketral set the rings spinning. "That's great. When is it due?"

Paddeen thrust his personal schedule at his father and let it drop again, dangling by its cord from his belt. Ketral laughed and snatched it back. "Wait, I didn't see. A hundred hours. That's good. We can renew it if you decide you want to keep it longer."

"Let's take a chute," Tso suggested. They strolled out, waving their greetings to friends.

"That was a good star," Paddeen pronounced with authority. "That's the best star I ever saw."

"God did that," Tso said brightly. "God made all the stars."

"And the planets?"

"Yes, God made the planets."

"Did God make the whole Expedition?" Paddeen pursued. "Did God make the probes?"

"People made the probes," Tso said. "And even the whole Expedition. But God made people so they *can* do things like that."

Ketral's forehead wrinkled, but he said nothing. Maybe he worried too much about Paddeen getting wrong ideas of the physical universe. And anyway, he knew by experience there was no use arguing when Tso mentioned God. They stepped into a pedestrian chute, and Paddeen immediately began hopping backward, trying to stay in one place as the chute moved under him.

"You're so big!" Tso caroled. She laughed as she tried to lay her hand on Paddeen's bouncing head.

"You're bigger!" He slammed the planet toy against the chute wall, and it responded with a mellow booming sound and leaped away in multicolored random hops. Paddeen pursued it, squealing with joy and rage.

"He *is* big, compared to how little he was," Tso said fondly. "Remember, Ketter-Daddy?"

"I remember." Ketral mimed rocking a baby in his arms.

"Remember the day he was born?"

"Yes, I do. I was called off work shift—the only time that's ever happened to me."

"You were called off work shift! I had to miss a whole decaday. Remember what you were doing when you got called off?"

"No," Ketral confessed.

"I remember everything about that day," Tso said. "I was wearing my old green jersey, barely big enough to stretch around me—remember? You came in with some kind of equipment still in your hand—"

"Did I?"

"Boombadoom!" whooped Paddeen. He raced past them in

the other direction, his rush countering the movement of the chute floor, and caromed off Ketral's legs as he followed the toy's wild trajectory.

"You know one of the things I was scheduled to teach that day?" Tso said. "Reproduction." She dissolved in chuckles. They linked arms companionably. "But also I remember I was teaching nutrition the day before, and my class was scheduled for a visit to a food center. And one of the children wanted to know why you can't just recycle food inside you and save a lot of trouble. I remember a thousand little things from Paddeen's birth-time. Don't you remember things like that?"

Ketral laughed, following Paddeen's noisy progress with his eyes. "No, not really."

"Yes, you do. Think about it. What were you doing when you were called off shift? What was your work schedule?"

Ketral thought. "There wasn't anything special. Just the normal maintenance schedule."

"And what's the normal maintenance schedule? Tell me about it."

She wasn't often like this. He felt his memory rise and strengthen to her coaxing. "Well, I know I was checking the pedestrian chute control system. That's one thing."

"How often is that scheduled?"

"Every hectoday. There are so many things that can go wrong with it."

By the time they reached their homespace, he was babbling about the art and science of maintenance, the things that had to be done on a complex intermeshing of cycles and the things that had to be done irregularly, the loneliness and beauty of it, the tedium and surprises. "And how many times have you done that since Paddeen was born?" Tso kept asking, and he found that sometimes he could give her an answer. He remembered other things, too, things beneath the surface of this or any conversation—all the times when the thought of her name had been enough to rouse him, painfully and longingly: *Tso, Tso,* a sighing breath, a one-word song. All the times she had been music to him, as she was now.

But at the homespace door she kissed him and tapped her wrist schedule. "I have a class. I'll see you later."

"What? Do you have to? This is your rest shift."

"It's a new class on anepochal dysphoria I want to take. Is that all right, big husband? Am I free to do that?"

Ketral slumped in the open doorway. "Why not?" Tso was always taking courses in subjects Ketral had never heard of. He'd tried to keep up with her at first, taking some of them himself, asking her about what she was learning.

"You don't understand, do you?" Tso said. The music had drained away from her, and there was a sudden desolation in her face that wrung his heart. She touched his cheek with one finger. "If you were a Christian. If you only knew what it means to hope for the Coming of the Lord." Her hand went out toward Paddeen, who stood now staring up at them with a troubled face. "We could be a family again."

"We are a family," Ketral said, straightening. He tried to put his arms around her, and she shrugged away from him.

"Bye-bye, Pad-Pad." She bent to catch Paddeen in a hug, but he slithered loose, tossing his toy and leaping to snag it in midair. It gave a melancholy boom. Ketral shepherded him inside and closed the door behind them.

"Look, Daddy, I'll show you what my boombadoom can do. Look!" Paddeen sent the toy ricocheting through the homespace. It bounced off Ketral's chest, a touch as light and quickly gone as Tso's caresses. "Look, I'll show you, I'll show you how to catch it!" Paddeen leaped, batted the falling planet into renewed vigor, chased, crouched in ambush, and finally smothered it against the floor. "I want to be a probe pilot," he declared with conviction.

Ketral squatted beside him. "That would be fun. But you know something? Probes don't happen very often. Only when the Expedition comes close to a star."

"How often?"

"Oh, kilodays—myriadays."

The vast numbers didn't mean anything specific to the child, Ketral could see that, but they did mean *big*. Paddeen's face clouded. "Are you sure?"

"Pretty sure," Ketral said gently.

Paddeen's face twisted resentfully. "How do you know? Mama says you're just a maintenance technician."

Ketral took a breath and let it out. "You knew that already. Remember what I told you a maintenance technician does?"

"Fixes things before they break." Paddeen balanced carefully, rubbing the outside of one foot against the opposite knee. "So they *won't* break."

"That's right." Ketral studied his son. "So what's wrong?"

"Mama says that's not important. Dumb people can do it."

Ketral's hands bunched into fists. Seconds passed before he trusted himself to move or speak. "It would be really bad if nothing ever worked, wouldn't it? It would be dark all the time—like when you go to sleep, only it would be that way *all* the time. We couldn't ride the chutes or the speed cars. There wouldn't be any schedules. Pretty soon there wouldn't be anything to eat, and then there wouldn't be any air to breathe and we'd all die. That's what would happen if there weren't any maintenance technicians to keep things working. So I think maintenance technicians *are* pretty important. They get to access the Archives and the control systems, too. Not many people can do that." He took a slow breath. "And they can't be *too* dumb, or they couldn't do the work right. But tell me this, Paddeen: What's so bad about being dumb?"

"I don't know." Paddeen's gaze dropped.

"It's nice to be smart, like it's nice to be strong or fast, because it helps you do things. That's all. It's nothing special." He touched his son's face. "I'm a lot stronger than you are, Paddeen, but that doesn't make me any better or more important."

Paddeen bounced reflectively on the balls of his feet. "I want to be a maintenance technician," he announced.

Tso crying in the dark, laughing in the dark, warm in the dark. Tso in his arms, whispering, "I feel so alone, so alone." He would never leave her, it was stupid to think of that—or at least not now, not yet, not while she needed him. And he couldn't take Paddeen away from her, and he couldn't leave Paddeen.

Besides, dissolving a marriage was a serious thing. People wondered, with good reason, what was wrong with you. Nobody had to get married; if you chose to do it and then couldn't make it work, it was like failing a qualification test. Maybe you'd do better next time; but maybe you wouldn't. Probably there wouldn't be a next time.

"Bet you don't know what I know." They were in bed with the light on—better that way, sometimes—and Tso was sitting upright and naked, combing her hair. Ketral lay on his back with his hands clasped behind his head and watched her. Her wide mouth pursed for an expectant moment, challenging him to riddles, games, kisses.

Ketral grinned. "Not till you tell me." She had been glowing with something since she came home, behind schedule and brushing off all questions. Something about Paddeen, from the way she'd cooed over him. Now she was ready to announce her triumph.

Tso arched her brows and straightened her neck proudly. "Paddeen is five years old."

He tried to make sense of the words. The Timekeeper had talked about years. "I give up. What's that mean?"

"It's not a riddle. Paddeen's birth has been off schedule for five years—more than five, I think."

"Is something wrong with him?" That was parental anxiety for you; if you heard anything you didn't understand involving your child, right away you were worried.

"I give up! Listen." She bent over him. "I went to see the Timekeeper."

"Right," Ketral said. Sometimes she forgot he already knew something.

"I'm not talking about the church delegation! *I* went to see the Timekeeper—myself alone."

"What for?" He couldn't keep the worry out of his voice, and that was a mistake. Now she'd feel insulted, and he'd have to work through a lot of noise to find out what had happened and why. He added quickly, "Did you get in?"

"You think they'd talk to a church delegation but not to me? That's a real statement of respect!" She laughed, holding him up to her own ridicule, putting on a show for herself.

"What did you talk about?" He hadn't told her about his

own conversation with the Timekeeper. Maybe that was a mistake, too.

She turned away from him to lay down her comb, offering the smooth barrier of her back. "I don't think it's relevant to you, anyway." She faced around with a hard stare. "You don't really want to know. You're just afraid I've done something to embarrass Ketral the true-blue atheist maintenance technician."

"Look, if you don't want to tell me, nobody says you have to. If it's going to embarrass me, I'll know soon enough. And if it—"

"So, so, so, Ketral does care!" She crossed her ankles and clasped one with each hand, singing her laughter, her breasts swaying between her arms. "Ketral doesn't hide it very well when his itty-bitty dignity is threatened." She leaned close over him. "I went to see the Timekeeper because—no, never mind." She straightened away from him before his reaching hand could close on her breast. It had been a halfhearted attempt.

"And what did the Timekeeper say?" Ketral asked conversationally. Sometimes a little change of tone was all it took.

"I got the idea when I was talking to you." She shone at him, offering a measured share of whatever secret glory she carried. "And from things our minister has told us at church. He's quite an expert, you know. Though even he doesn't realize—" She chuckled, and bent toward Ketral. "Do you know what a year is?"

Ketral tucked his hands under the back of his head again. "It's Earth's planetary revolution period."

"Yes, but that doesn't matter. Did you know it can be expressed as a certain number of days?"

"I hadn't thought about it."

"Well, I have! The Timekeeper has. There's a certain number of days between each Christmas and the next one. And a certain number of days between now and the day Paddeen was born."

Ketral grimaced. Going backward, measuring time off-schedule—it was all as abstrusely theoretical as the Timekeeper's lectures. He spoke to what he more nearly understood. "How many of these things are you going to do?"

Tso laughed, all scorn and incredulity. "Did you think there was only one Christmas? Or only five, or sixteen, or whatever? It's not something anybody can number, Ketral. There's one Christmas after another, and always will be." Her voice turned solemn. Her face was still as gold. "Always, until Christ comes again. Christ," she said. "Whose birth we celebrate."

There was a note on the message board just inside the homespace door: *Gone to visit friends. Love you.* Ketral stared at it a long time before he blanked it. His fingers were shaking. Just *friends*, so he wouldn't know who, so he couldn't join them. And they couldn't have been gone long; Paddeen's school shift was barely off the schedule. She must have hurried to get out of the homespace before Ketral got here.

All right. She had gone to some of her church friends, probably, or some of the other people she knew and he didn't—other teachers (though she didn't talk much about them anymore) or people she'd met at hobby classes. Tso was always making new friends, to replace the ones she'd worn out. She'd expect him to stay here, forlorn and angry, hoping for them to come back. Or to search for them, calling one name after another from the church membership list, something guaranteed to embarrass him and make her furious. Or maybe just to sleep, or go to a show, or look up some of his own friends—he still had some of those, the few he hadn't given up for Tso's sake.

Well, he could do better than that. Until now, he'd always been very circumspect with church people, not wanting to say or do anything that might reflect ill on Tso, and not sure what that might be. But hadn't the minister told him, "Drop by and chat any time you're not busy"? He sat down to the datasphere and ran his fingers over the surface, calling up the minister's status. In his homespace, active. All right.

"You know I'm an ecopsychologist," the minister said. "I bring my own preoccupations to my church work, as we all do. But it was really your wife who had the idea of reviving Christmas."

"She's smart," Ketral said. "She has lots of ideas." It gave him a glow, even now, to say things like that.

"Yes, it emerged at one of our meetings, where we'd read something about Christmas celebrations on Earth. Tso immediately suggested we could do the same, and I must admit it fell in with my own interests. You see, I think there's something missing in our environment."

Ketral shook his head. "We're fully supplied. With the new regeneration system, it will be gigadays before there's any measurable chance of running out of anything."

The minister raised his hand apologetically. "I don't mean a shortage of elements. Everyone knows the Expedition has enough matter and energy, and adequate means of manipulating them. Rather, it's the structure of our environment that has a harmful effect on some people—and, I suspect, on our whole society."

There was a sort of coldness in Ketral's chest and a stillness in his fingers. Somehow this was what he'd come to hear—what doom had fallen on Tso, what doom awaited the Expedition. But that was stupid. "How can that be?" he demanded. Fighting it for Tso's sake and his own; for Paddeen's sake. "Everything on the Expedition is designed for health and comfort."

"Yes, it is," the minister said. "Health, comfort, and functionality. But those things turn out to be very complex. Everybody knows that human beings can only function within certain ranges of environmental parameters. If the temperature is too high or too low, we die. And as we approach those extreme limits, our efficiency and comfort decrease."

"Yes," Ketral said. "And atmospheric pressure and composition, and electromagnetic radiation, and all of that. It's all been worked out. It's all been taken care of."

"A great deal has been worked out and taken care of," the minister said. "And did you know that quite a bit of it has been worked out by trial and error on the Expedition? We're still learning."

Ketral was startled. "Didn't they know, back on Earth? Couldn't they tell what people need?"

"It's not all as obvious as temperature and air. Remember, humans evolved into a ready-made environment—the Earth environment, enormously complex. And humans are adaptable. The questions were, which factors of the Earth environment were essential for optimal human functioning; which, if any, were superfluous; and could any of them be improved upon? Just as a general example, the Earth environment was full of fluctuations—regular and irregular changes in temperature, humidity, and such. It's obvious—now—that we can survive without such changes. But that couldn't have been predicted a priori. For some Earth organisms, certain fluctuations were essential for survival; the same might have been true for humans."

The twinge or chill or whatever it was that Ketral had felt was gone now. He grinned. "Well, we *are* surviving. We must be doing it right."

"Yes, we do the survival part very well. But if we want more than simple survival—if we want optimal functioning, not only physical but mental and emotional—"

"We have that," Ketral protested. "Well, pretty close. Better than Earth, they say."

The minister chuckled agreeably. "Yes, pretty close. I don't doubt that the Expedition's environment is more wholesome than Earth's in many ways. But we do have to pay attention to parameters besides the obvious ones. After all, why do we have the panorama corridors?"

"They're relaxing," Ketral said. "They improve your eyesight and make you feel better."

"Yes, they do. That was already known before the Expedition left the Solar system. People need vistas—long-distance fields of vision—for optimal physical and mental health. I imagine they first tried simulations of scenes from Earth. But those have long since been replaced by the present more abstract style, for which we can probably be grateful." The minister smiled. "Still other things we've found out for ourselves. For example, nobody on Earth seemed to have realized that a lifetime of touching only smooth surfaces results in neuromotor and perceptual problems. We had to put texture back into our lives."

Ketral fingered the shoulder of his jersey, then the alternately slick and grainy panels on the side of his chair. "I didn't know that."

"I wouldn't know it if it weren't part of my job." the minister said. "If babies and children aren't exposed often enough to different textures, they never develop the neural networks for tactile discrimination. I imagine that in the Expedition's first few generations there was quite an epidemic of tactile disorders—people who couldn't tell what they were touching. Would you care for a little incense?"

"Thanks, that would be nice."

The minister adjusted the odor spectrum of his censer and nudged the flow control with one finger. The little box hummed once (machine noises were part of the environmental design too, Ketral knew that from his own work) and emitted a gentle flow of scent, sweet and cool in the nostrils. "My point is," the minister went on, "we've learned a lot about how certain sensory input can help keep people healthy and happy and generally functioning well. But I'm beginning to think we've overlooked a major area."

Ketral breathed deep, fending off the fear that still hovered somewhere behind his shoulders. "Time?"

The minister looked surprised, as if he wasn't used to people understanding his points so fast, or at least hadn't expected it from Ketral. "Yes, something about time. Those of us in the profession of ecopsychology have identified a condition that we call anepochal dysphoria."

"I think I've heard of that," Ketral said, "but I don't know what it is."

"It's a term that wasn't found in the Archives," the minister said, "until we put it there. To tell the truth, we're not sure the condition exists—or rather, we're sure about the condition, but we're not sure we've given it the right name and explanation. You've probably heard people talk about a growing malaise in our society."

"Yes," said Ketral. "And other people saying there's no more malaise now than there's always been."

"Well, that's the thing," the minister said. "There's no way to tell, really. And of course some unhappiness and dysfunctional behavior has other causes—many causes. But we're all children of evolution, Ketral. Earth's environment made us what we are. Our bodies and minds are built to receive and respond to cyclic input, because we evolved in a cyclic world. If we don't receive that input—or not enough of it, or not the right kinds of it—we may not be able to function to our full capacity."

"If that were true," Ketral said, "we'd be better off sitting around in dirt, picking parasites out of each other's hair and eating them. Just because we evolved in one situation doesn't mean we can't do better in a different one."

The minister laughed. "I see you know your evolutionary biology. Let me put it a better way. When we don't get the kind of input we evolved to deal with, then there are at least two things that can happen. Our response systems for that type of input may become inactive—possibly atrophy—or they may look for alternative input, something for the hardware to work with. My guess is that both those things happen to us, with the particular mix varying widely from one individual to another. But I think that all of us, to some extent, are hungry for a food we've never tasted. And for some of us, that hunger is a gnawing ache in the vitals, so fierce that we chew ourselves from the inside out." The minister laughed again. He didn't look like a man who had ever been hungry in his life, let alone chewed himself from inside. "I'm afraid that metaphor didn't come out as well as I had hoped, but I trust you see what I'm saying." He inhaled deeply. "That's what we mean by anepochal dysphoria."

Ketral squinted. Never mind the theory. What was important was Tso and Paddeen. "You think Christmas will help?"

"Yes, I do. I think that we—and here I'm speaking especially of Christians—will benefit from Christmas in several ways. Most simply and obviously, it's a return to our roots, a reminder of the origin of our faith. Christianity is a time-based religion; it deals with real events—individual, unique events, not just data such as we find in the Archives, separated from the events that generated them. Christmas celebrates the birth of a particular individual at a particular moment of time—this is difficult to explain—"

"A date," Ketral suggested.

"Why, yes." The minister smiled. "I forget that Tso must have talked to you about this."

"Not very much," Ketral said.

"Well, then. Since you understand the concept of date, I think you can appreciate another benefit I foresee. This Christmas celebration will be only the first of a long series. And here's the important part, the exciting part: *We mean to keep count.*"

Ketral was puzzled. "Count of what? There's only one Christmas at a time, isn't there?"

"Only one at a time, but many times. Christmas Number One, Christmas Number Two, Christmas Number Three—it can go on indefinitely. And once the Timekeeper provides us with a method of dating our Christmas—our Christmases—then we'll have a cycle, a new cycle, very much like the Earth cycles we've lost." The minister laughed. "I see you're shaking your head. It *is* strange."

"I just don't see what practical effect that could have."

"No, it's not obvious. But think about this: People will have, in effect, *permanent* schedules to refer to. Can you imagine what that would be like? I confess I can't. But I can see parts of it. People will be able to say things like, 'Last Christmas we went to a party in sector D-twelve,' or 'We plan to get married at Christmas Number Fifteen,' or 'Our baby was born three Christmases ago.' Do you see?"

Cold clamped down in Ketral's chest, like a weight of ice compressing his heart and lungs. "Maybe," he said. "Maybe I see a little." His voice sounded choked to him, but the minister seemed to take no notice. "That sounds like what the Timekeeper calls 'years.' "

"Yes, that's it," the minister said. "I don't understand the mathematics of it—I don't *quite* understand how a year relates to a Christmas—but that's the principle, and I can visualize the results. It's the difference between drifting in a low-gravity corridor with no nets to hold on to, and sitting here in the one g we evolved for. I think it will make a real difference in how we live."

"Yes, I guess so," Ketral said. "It would be like—like everybody is measured all the time. Like specifications and tolerances. You're five years old, with a tolerance of plus or minus so many days. Why does anybody want to know that?"

"Oh, your wife has already thought of some good reasons. A fair and convenient way of sorting people, children especially—in schools, for example—and a standard for measuring their progress. Has this child learned what's appropriate for her year-group—and if not, what remedy is needed? That sort of thing."

"This date thing," Ketral said. "Do you really have to have that? I mean, can't you just do a Christmas when you feel like it? When you're ready?"

"Yes; yes, I think we could," the minister said. "But then we wouldn't have the cycle, the standard, the way of sorting. You see, when our church voted to consult the Timekeeper for the date of Christmas, most people simply thought of it as a nice added touch, a little extra authenticity. But when I realized that a dated Christmas could give us the very thing we've been missing—that yearly cycle, that gravitational field to keep us balanced—well, I confess I became quite an enthusiast. Your wife has been a strong partisan for it from the beginning. But simply to celebrate Christmas—no, we don't need a date, not really."

"Good," Ketral said.

He took a speed car home, suddenly eager. Tso would be there. They would bruise each other with words and heal with touches. And Paddeen would be there.

But they were not there. The message board was empty, and he realized with a pang that he had forgotten to leave a note. He could hear Tso's voice in his mind: *I knew you'd come home, because you'd blanked my note. But you didn't leave any note for Paddeen and me, so I knew you didn't care about us.*

He paced through the homespace, seeing it as if someone else lived here, people he barely knew. Paddeen's private space was a mess—clothing and toys, scraps of food and unidentifiable debris scattered randomly. Wherever else he looked, he saw something of Tso's—books and projects, the unfinished sculptures, the charts for redecorating the homespace and reorganizing the Expedition, unused makeup and medications, religious trinkets. He paused at the datasphere; he might just check. Tso's status was *active, out*. No surprise there. He tried another. *Active, office*. Didn't the Timekeeper ever rest?

At the message board, he left a note: *Gone to visit friends*. After a pause, he added, *Love you*.

"You need not apologize," said the Timekeeper. "I receive many requests, but few visitors. Furthermore, I believe I know why you are here."

"I came to ask you something," Ketral said.

"So I have assumed. You know that I welcomed the inquiry concerning the date of Christmas. But I have received a related inquiry that troubles me." The Timekeeper paused ponderously, gaze fixed on Ketral. "An inquiry seeking to relate the date of Christmas and the birth of an Expedition member."

"I don't understand," Ketral said.

"Your wife," said the Timekeeper, "wants to know if your child was born on Christmas."

Ketral stared blankly. "But—what does that mean? Christmas isn't even on the schedule yet."

"You are right. The date verification had not been completed. I have, however, finished all the other calculations." The Timekeeper touched the datasphere caressingly. "When Tso aun Ketral visited me, I was engrossed in studying correlations between the Expedition day and the hypothetical Earth year—I say 'hypothetical' for reasons probably beyond your immediate interest—"

"That's right," Ketral said hastily.

The Timekeeper looked resigned. "Yes. I made a casual reference to a three-hundred-and-sixty-two-day year—"

"What's that?"

"Merely a manner of speaking, a rather loose manner in actuality. The datasphere had just given me that roughly esti-

mated ratio of the day as we know it to the Earth year as we
may presume it to have developed. Somewhat to my dismay,
she seized upon this figure with enthusiasm. I attempted to
explain that it was neither a precise nor an unchanging quan-
tity, and indeed not an accurate one, but I am by no means
sure that she absorbed or accepted my explanation."

"I'm sorry," Ketral said; "I still don't understand what
'born on Christmas' means."

"Your wife strongly believes that her son's birth was simultaneous with an earlier Earth Christmas. She hopes for—
indeed, she almost demands—confirmation."

"But you said," Ketral objected, "there's no such thing as
simultaneous between distant points, like Earth and the Expedition."

"Profoundly true. As I also told you, we have a pragmatic
substitute in the date verification system. For your wife's purposes, for most purposes, it is, if I may put it so, good
enough. She has already ascertained, to her own satisfaction
though not entirely to mine, the approximate number of days
that have passed since the birth of your son—a very rough ap-
proximation, based upon remembered maintenance schedules."

"I see," Ketral said. He felt flattened, a balloon's sense of
betrayal. She had inflated him for this.

"She then applied to me for information concerning the interval between successive Christmases. I was not aware, when
I mentioned the length of the year in days, that she was cal-
culating your son's age."

"Age?"

"The interval between his birth and the present. As a mathematical concept, what one might call off-schedule duration.
Now, with the information you and I have severally given her,
she prefers to express that duration in years."

"You mean when she says Paddeen is five years old. That's
what I came to ask you about."

"Exactly so." The Timekeeper's heavy head swayed from
side to side. "I regret that I ever undertook to find the date of
Christmas. I cannot imagine a greater detriment to progress

than measuring ourselves, our lives, our doings from fixed points in the past."

"Then why do it? You could have said no, couldn't you?"

"I too," the Timekeeper said, as if revealing a gloomy secret, "am human. I could not—or, more precisely, did not—resist the challenge of the problem."

"Then what about the Council?" Ketral said. "Can't they stop it?" You didn't often think about the Council doing something—you didn't often think about the Council at all, except when they coopted a new member, or the Expedition reached a new planetary system. Like maintenance schedules, all the Expedition's processes ran themselves without much supervision.

"I have submitted the proposal to the Council, with my reservations," said the Timekeeper, "and the Council has judged my reservations inadequate. Christmas has been approved for scheduling—not once but repeatedly."

Ketral touched his wrist schedule, eyeing it thoughtfully. "How much longer will it take to get it scheduled?"

"Several hours only."

Ketral stood up, moving his arms restlessly. "Do you know what Christmas is, exactly? I mean, what would it mean for somebody to be born on Christmas?"

The Timekeeper waved one hand slowly, wafting the question aside. "It is one of the many annual religious festivals that have flourished on Earth, more or less complexly connected to seasonal cycles. I am not cognizant of its exact significance for those who participate. Perhaps your wife could enlighten you."

"Yes," Ketral said. "Perhaps she could."

In the room below, the red-haired clerk smiled at him. "I think I saw your kid checking out a toy at the show the other day. Looked for you and your wife, but there was such a crowd."

"Yes, we were on the other side of the room." He felt her friendliness like a warm bath washing over his tight muscles. "Paddeen loves that toy. He calls it his boombadoom. That's from the noise it makes."

The clerk laughed. "I'll have to tell my husband that. He'll think it's funny."

Ketral hung silent for a moment, startled by disappointment. How cold it was, the little lump of knowledge. Stupid, he thought, stupid. He hadn't asked her name, hadn't considered that she might be married, hadn't noticed he was building reasons to care if she was or not. It wasn't only a husband she had, but a whole life that he knew nothing about. Maintenance people, Christmas people, the necessities and the oddities of Expedition life—what could they be for the Timekeeper's clerk but objects of friendly tolerance? Stupid, stupid.

He took a speed car, not to waste more time. The minister was surprised to see him again so soon. "Ah, Ketral aun Tso. Did you forget something?"

"Yes," Ketral said. "I forgot to ask you something about Christmas."

The minister beamed. "Well, come in. I'm delighted that you're so interested. Would you care for a little incense?"

"No, thanks. I just wanted to ask— You said Christmas is about the birth of an individual. Who?"

"Christmas," the minister said with grave satisfaction, "commemorates the birth of Christ."

"And"—Ketral groped, remembering what he'd heard from Tso—"Christ is your god?"

"Well, in a sense. We worship God in three Persons: God as Parent, God as Child, God as Spirit. Christ is the incarnation of God as Child—God born as a human being, living a human life. We believe that at the end of time Christ will come again. Please do sit down and make yourself comfortable. I'll be glad to explain everything I can."

"No, thank you." Ketral looked blankly at his wrist schedule, as if he were reading it. "I have to go home."

Paddeen was in his private space, engrossed in a lap game. He greeted his father offhandedly, without looking up.

"Where's your mother?" Ketral demanded.

"I don't know."

"Where have you been today?" He had to ask twice before he got a response.

"I don't know. What's wrong with that?"

What's wrong with that? It was a phrase he had picked up from his parents' arguments, and he used it, anxiously, to query any uncomfortable situation. Ketral looked around. "Listen, Paddeen. You can finish your game, and then I want you to clean up your private space. All right?"

Paddeen did not answer. Ketral laid a hand on his son's shoulder. "Look at this mess, Paddeen. You see it? You see all these things in the wrong places? It's time to clean them up. Just as soon as you finish—"

Paddeen's face turned up to him, scrunched with anger, eyes brimming with tears. "I don't have to do that. Mama says!"

"Why don't you have to?"

"Because Mama says! Tso says!"

Ketral sluiced aside a surge of anger. He squatted to meet Paddeen's gaze on a level. "Why does she say you don't have to?"

Paddeen shifted restlessly. "Because we're Christians."

"But, honey, you still need to keep your own space neat. Everybody has to do their own work, or the whole Expedition would get messed up. Don't you think so?"

Paddeen's face had unkinked. He waved his hands as he tried to explain. "Yes, but, but, Christians are special, and, and, and I'm special. Mama says."

From the front of the homespace Ketral heard the sound of the door opening and closing. He stood up and went to meet his wife.

"Well!" she greeted him sardonically. "So you decided to come home." She turned to scan the message board, and blanked his note with delicate deliberation.

"Paddeen doesn't want to clean his space." Ketral waited for a moment. Just in case.

But Tso turned to face him with a little, rolling swagger in her movement and open challenge in her eyes. "Was it too much for you to do? Beyond your abilities?"

"I want him to do his share. He needs to learn what will make things better for him later on."

"You're right. If he were going to be a corridor cleaner or a maintenance technician I could see the value of teaching him to clean up messes."

"Everybody needs to clean up their own messes, Tso. And we don't know what Paddeen's going to be."

"I do." Her face flared with certainty. "You don't—that's obvious—but I do."

Sooner or later he always took her bait; it might as well be now. "Do you? What's he going to be, then?"

"A leader," she sang. "Something you can't even conceive of. You don't understand."

Maybe it was a tone in her voice, a flash of music, that tumbled something over inside him. She had radiated that music often when she first joined the church. "I think maybe I do understand," Ketral said gently. "You want to be something unique, and you want everybody to know about it." He moved toward her. "But you don't have to worry about that, Tso. Just being you is good enough."

"You don't seem to think so."

"I mean people can like you and respect you and love you even if you're not a superbeing."

She turned away. "I've figured out what's wrong with you," she said flatly. "You're jealous."

Ketral brushed his hands on his jersey. So here they went again. "Who am I jealous of this time?"

"Of me, and of the church, and especially of my son. I didn't realize that, till after I had the Christmas idea. But you've been jealous ever since I got involved with the church."

"Not jealous. I just don't believe what you believe."

"I don't mean your lack of faith. I mean you've never distinguished yourself in any way, shape, or form, and it bothers you to see people paying attention to what I say. It especially bothers you to think that my son could be someone—'unique,' as you put it."

"Paddeen is Paddeen," Ketral said. "I don't like you trying to make him into something else."

She whirled on him. "And I won't let you deprive him of his heritage!"

"What is his heritage?"

Her face glowed with a light and sweetness that were not for him. "Oh," she said, throaty and soft. "Wait. Christmas is coming."

Ketral looked at her, wordless. Then he swallowed. "Are you going to be here for a while?"

"I have an appointment in three point two. Until then I don't plan to leave my son."

"You just did."

Instantly she was in a rage. "A few hundred seconds, that's all! Paddeen was tired, and I had one more short visit to make."

"Who are all these friends you're suddenly visiting?"

"They're friends! Do you know what friends are? I want to be sure they know about Christmas."

"It isn't even on the schedule yet. What is there to know?"

"That it's coming. That I've been to see the Timekeeper. I want to be sure they watch the schedule." Momentarily she chuckled. "It's coming."

"Fine," Ketral said. "I'm going. I'll see you later."

"Wait a minute! Where are you going?"

"I have work to do," he said, and the door closed behind him.

He chose one of the maintenance cubicles least likely to be in use and locked himself in. He wanted privacy, and it was only from a maintenance datasphere that he could get at the control systems. There were security blocks to prevent tampering, of course; but they had to be maintained too, which meant there were ways for a good maintenance technician to get through them without even signaling an alert.

It was all here, in the master maintenance map—the Expedition's substrate, everything that could be expected ever to need maintenance, which meant everything. Ketral fingered the datasphere, massaging one system after another to the surface. Where was that general map index? There ought to be an index to the indexes. Ah, there it was. Now, something with "date" in it; there couldn't be many of those.

There! Date verification, a subsystem of schedule punctuation, which was one of the more obscure timekeeping routines. A double clock, the Timekeeper had called it. He hadn't expected so many connections, ramifying through archival input functions in every sector of the Expedition. But that was good—any malfunction would be that much harder to trace. He wasn't going to damage anything really, just turn it off for a minute.

He finished in plenty of time, and went out of his way to walk the brown-beige panorama corridor. There was an uneasy feeling from the back of his head all the way down his spine. What kind of a maintenance technician was he?

Tso was waiting for him at the door. She had changed her clothes and reshaped her hair. "Was this a test?" she greeted him. "Did you want to see if I'd leave my child alone? Or did you just want to make me late?"

"You won't be late. I've kept an eye on the schedule."

"How do you know what I might want to do on the way? Never mind." Paddeen watched silent from the entrance to his private space. She went to him, bending for an embrace. He squirmed away. "See you soon, Christmas boy," she crooned. At the door she told Ketral icily, "I'm going to the Timekeeper's office. I don't know when I'll be back."

"Tso—"

"Good-bye, Paddeen!" she shouted, and rushed past Ketral. He watched her step into an upchute and rise slantingly away from him, the translucent chute walls melting her image. After a little he turned back inside.

"Come on, Paddeen!"

"Where are we going?"

That was a detail to be worked out. "We're going to find a new place to live," Ketral said.

"Wait. I have to get my boombadoom." Paddeen threw an anxious look at his father and darted back into his private space.

"Come on!" Ketral shouted. But Paddeen was right, they'd better take what was dearest to them. He looked around the homespace indecisively. No, there was nothing here he couldn't cheerfully leave to Tso. How had he lived here so long and made so little of it his own?

Paddeen came dashing back with the toy tucked under one arm, and Ketral took his hand. No, he wouldn't leave a note. If he could have explained to Tso, he would have done it by now. "Let's go," he said, and led his son out."

"Can we go through the meteor shower?"

"What? Yes, that's where we'll go." They would go where the panorama corridor took them, and access the change-of-quarters system from a public datasphere. Tso could claim as much as she liked that Paddeen was born on Christmas—it would always be a meaningless statement. And the Timekeeper wouldn't have to worry about people measuring themselves from fixed points in the past. The past had been cut off—off schedule, where it was supposed to be.

Paddeen held his father's hand firmly, content for once to match his pace to an adult's. He did not pull away until they reached the panorama corridor. Then he raced ahead into the half-lit dark, hurling his toy at the images of meteors that streamed past on all sides. It rebounded with mournful boomings from unseen walls.

"Ketral aun Tso!" The voice thrummed like music overamplified; it seemed to resound at Ketral from all directions. He turned, his gaze sweeping through unreal distances, and was face-to-face with the Timekeeper—anomalous without desk and datasphere, like a wrinkle in the Expedition's fabric. For a moment Ketral did not even notice Tso at the Timekeeper's side. Her face was clenched with strain.

"The date verification system," the Timekeeper said, and was resonantly silent.

"Yes," Ketral said. Glancing down the corridor, he saw Paddeen turn back and approach them in short hops, looking uneasily from one to another of them.

"What did you *do*, Ketral?" Tso shouted.

"Have you understood," the Timekeeper said, "the effect of, let us say, a radical malfunction of that system?"

Ketral squared himself. "I think so." Sparkling motes

swirled around the Timekeeper's head. Ketral focused on Tso's face. "It means you can't fix a date for Christmas."

The Timekeeper made a large, vague gesture with both hands, like something between a spasm of pain and a threat of violence. "It means, Ketral aun Tso, that we can never fix any date—that the messages we send to Earth are no longer anchored in Earth's frame of reference; that we, and all our ultimate colonies, are forever disconnected."

Paddeen tugged at his father's leg. "What's wrong with that? Dad? What's wrong with that?"

Ketral looked down. "I don't know what's wrong with it. I really don't." He raised his eyes to the Timekeeper's dark stare. "I don't see that it matters till we find a place to set up a colony. That can't happen for myriadays, and it may never happen. And anyway, the system is running now."

The Timekeeper made a sound like a groan. "Running, but running wild. The connection is broken."

Ketral took Paddeen's hand. A dark illusion of mass swept over them, so close it was hard not to cower. The Timekeeper turned away. Tso took a step to follow. Then she swung back wildly, and Ketral saw her tormented face. "Do you know what you've done? Do you know?"

"Your minister says you don't need a date for Christmas—"

She gave a guttural cry, inventing a language for her pain, and flung her arms out as if she were hitting invisible attackers. Paddeen edged behind Ketral's leg. "Yes! I need it! For Paddeen! I want, want— You don't understand!" Her shriek shattered into weeping, and he caught at her shoulder, trying to pass some touch of comfort to her.

"No, I don't understand. Tell me, Tso."

She sobbed against his shoulder for an instant, then tore away. "I want something, something to know. Something to hold to. Is that so bad? Is that so hard to understand?"

"Tso—"

He watched her stumbling among the meteors, out of the corridor, out of his line of sight, and Paddeen watched beside him. It was the first time, he thought, that he had ever destroyed anything.

A Christmas revolution.

Merry Gravmas
James P. Hogan

It is a fact that Sir Isaac Newton was born on December 25 (in 1642). I mentioned this one evening when Jackie and I were with a group of friends in a Sonora bar. After some debate, we decided that the date is too much to be a coincidence: Providence is trying to tell us something.

We finally agreed that the time has come for a change. We're all part of Western scientific civilization, after all, and things have been dominated for too long by traditions rooted in ancient Palestinian mysticism. In future, therefore, we have decided that as far as we are concerned, the customary holiday season celebrates the birthday of the intellectual founder of mathematical, analytical method. Further, to commemorate the formulation of his famous universal law, the name of the feast shall be changed from "Christmas" to "Gravitational mass," or, more simply, "Gravmas."

Who knows?—the whole thing could spread like wildfire. Two thousand years from now, it might form the basis for the philosophy and worldview of a whole, new global culture, which by that time may revolve around a dominant race of supertech, spacegoing Chinese. . . .

"Is that you, Li?" Cheng Xiang called, looking up from the notescreen propped against his knee. He had been amusing himself with a few tensor integrals to clear his mind before taking his morning coffee.

The sounds of movement came again from upstairs. Moments later, his ten-year-old son appeared, floating down the staircase on an anti-g disk. "Good morning, Father."

"Merry Gravmas."

"And to you." Li hopped off the disk and stood admiring the decorations that the family robot had put up overnight. There were paper chains hanging in hyperbolic catenary curves and sinusoids, Gaussian distribution bells, and pendulums wreathed in logarithmic spirals. In the corner opposite the total-sensory cassette player, there stood a miniature apple tree with binary stars on top, a heap of gaily wrapped gifts around its base, and its branches adorned with colored masses or various shapes, a string of pulsing plasma glows, and striped candies shaped like integral signs. "It looks nice," Li said, eyeing the presents. "I wonder what Santa Roid has brought this year."

"You'll have to wait until your brother and sister get here before you can open anything," Xiang told him. "What are they doing?"

"Yu is sending off a last-minute Gravmas present to a schoolfriend over the matter transmitter to Jupiter. Yixuan is helping Mother program the autochef to cook the turkey."

"Why does everyone in this family always have to leave everything until the last minute?" Xiang grumbled, setting down the screen and getting up. "Anyone would think it wasn't obvious that the ease of getting things done varies inversely as the square of procrastination."

Li walked over to the window and gazed out at Peking's soaring panorama of towers, bridges, terraces, and arches, extending away all around, above, and for hundreds of meters below. "How did Gravmas start?" he asked his father.

"Hmph!" Xiang snorted as he moved to stand alongside the

boy. "Now, isn't that typical of young people today. Too wrapped up in relativistic quantum chromodynamics and multidimensional function spaces to know anything about where it came from or what it means. It's this newfangled liberal education that's to blame. They don't teach natural philosophy any more, the way we had to learn it."

"Well, that kind of thing does seem a bit quaint these days," Li said. "I suppose it's okay for little old ladies and people who—"

"They don't even recite the laws of motion in school every morning. Standards aren't what they used to be. It'll mean the end of civilization, you mark my words."

"You were going to tell me about Gravmas. . . ."

"Oh, yes. Well, I presume you've heard of Newton?"

"Of course. A newton is the force which, acting on a mass of one kilogram, produces an acceleration of one meter per second per second."

"Not *a* newton. *The* Newton. You didn't know that Newton was somebody's name?"

"You mean it was a person?"

Xiang sighed. "My word. You see—you don't know anything. Yes, Newton was the messiah who lived two thousand years ago, who came to save us all from irrationality. Today is his birthday."

Li looked impressed. "Say, what do you know! Where did this happen?"

"In a quasi-stable, in a little town called Cambridge, which was somewhere in Britain."

"That's in Europe, isn't it?" Li said.

"Oh, so you do know something."

"My friend Shao was in Europe last year," Li went on distantly. "His parents took him on a trip there to see the ruins. He said it was very dirty everywhere, with the streets full of beggars. And you can't drink the water. It sounds like a strange place for a civilization like ours to have started from."

"Strange things happen. . . ." Xiang thought for a while. "Actually, according to legend, it didn't really start there."

"What?"

"Gravmas."

"How do you mean?"

"Supposedly it was already a holiday that some ancient Western barbarian culture celebrated before then, and we stole it. It was easier to let people carry on with the customs they'd grown used to, you see. . . . At least, that's how the story goes."

"I wonder what the barbarian culture was like," Li mused.

"Nobody's quite sure," Xiang said. "But from the fragments that have been put together, it seems to have had something to do with worshiping crosses and fishes, eating holly, and building pyramids. It was all such a long time ago now that—"

"Look!" Li interrupted, pointing excitedly. Outside the window, a levitation platform was rising into view, bearing several dozen happy-looking, colorfully dressed people with musical instruments. The strains of amplified voices floated in from outside. "Carol singers!" Li exclaimed.

Xiang smiled and spoke a command for the household communications controller to relay his voice to the outside. "Good morning!" it boomed from above the window as the platform came level.

The people on board saw the figures in the window and waved. "Merry Gravmas," a voice replied.

"Merry Gravmas to you," Xiang returned.

"May the Force be proportional to your acceleration."

"Are you going to sing us a carol?" Xiang inquired.

"But of course. Do you have a request?"

"No, I'll leave it to you."

"Very well."

There was an introductory bar, and then,

"We three laws of orbiting are,
Ruling trajectories local and far.
Collisions billiard,
Particles myriad,
Planet and moon and star.
O-ooo . . ."

THE NUTCRACKER COUP
Janet Kagan

MARIANNE TEDESCO HAD *The Nutcracker Suite* turned up full blast for inspiration, and as she whittled she now and then raised her knife to conduct Tchaikovsky. That was what she was doing when one of the locals poked his delicate snout around the corner of the door to her office. She nudged the sound down to a whisper in the background and beckoned him in.

It was Tatep, of course. After almost a year on Rejoicing (that was the literal translation of the world's name), she still had a bit of trouble recognizing the Rejoicers by snout alone, but the three white quills in Tatep's ruff had made him the first real "individual" to her. Helluva thing for a junior diplomat *not* to be able to tell one local from another—but there it was. Marianne was desperately trying to learn the snout shapes that distinguished the Rejoicers to each other.

"Good morning, Tatep. What can I do for you?"

"Share?" said Tatep.

"Of course. Shall I turn the music off?" Marianne knew that *The Nutcracker Suite* was as alien to him as the rattling

and scraping of his music was to her. She was beginning to
like pieces here and there of the Rejoicer style, but she didn't
know if Tatep felt the same way about Tchaikovsky.

"Please, leave it on," he said. "You've played it every day
this week—am I right? And now I find you waving your
knife to the beat. Will you share the reason?"

She *had* played it every day this week, she realized. "I'll
try to explain. It's a little silly, really, and it shouldn't be
taken as characteristic of human. Just as characteristic of
Marianne."

"Understood." He climbed the stepstool she'd cobbled together her first month on Rejoicing and settled himself on his
haunches comfortably to listen. At rest, the wicked quills
adorning his ruff and tail seemed just that: adornments. By local standards, Tatep was a handsome male.

He was also a quadruped, and human chairs weren't the
least bit of use to him. The stepstool let him lounge on its
broad upper platform or sit upright on the step below that—in
either case, it put a Rejoicer eye to eye with Marianne. This
had been so successful an innovation in the embassy that they
had hired a local artisan to make several for each office.
Chornian's stepstools were a more elaborate affair, but
Chornian himself had refused to make one to replace "the
very first." A fine sense of tradition, these Rejoicers.

That was, of course, the best way to explain the
Tchaikovsky. "Have you noticed, Tatep, that the further away
from home you go, the more important it becomes to keep
traditions?"

"Yes," he said. He drew a small piece of sweetwood from
his pouch and seemed to consider it thoughtfully. "Ah! I
hadn't thought how very strongly you must need tradition!
You're very far from home indeed. Some thirty light-years, is
it not?" He bit into the wood, shaving a delicate curl from it
with one corner or his razor-sharp front tooth. The curl he
swallowed, then he said, "Please, go on."

The control he had always fascinated Marianne—she
would have preferred to watch him carve, but she spoke instead. "My family tradition is to celebrate a holiday called
Christmas."

He swallowed another shaving and repeated, "Christmas."

"For some humans Christmas is a religious holiday. For my family, it was more of . . . a turning of the seasons. Now, Esperanza and I couldn't agree on a date—her homeworld's calendar runs differently than mine—but we both agreed on a need to celebrate Christmas once a year. So, since it's a solstice festival, I asked Muhammed what was the shortest day of the year on Rejoicing. He says that's Tamemb Nap Ohd."

Tatep bristled his ruff forward, confirming Muhammed's date.

"So I have decided to celebrate Christmas Eve on Tamemb Nap Ohd and to celebrate Christmas Day on Tememb Nap Chorr."

"Christmas is a revival, then? An awakening?"

"Yes, something like that. A renewal. A promise of spring to come."

"Yes, we have an Awakening on Tememb Nap Chorr as well."

Marianne nodded. "Many peoples do. Anyhow, I mentioned that I wanted to celebrate and a number of other people at the embassy decided it was a good idea. So, we're trying to put together something that resembles a Christmas celebration—mostly from local materials."

She gestured toward the player. "That piece of music is generally associated with Christmas. I've been playing it because it—gives me an anticipation of the Awakening to come."

Tatep was doing fine finishing work now, and Marianne had to stop to watch. The bit of sweetwood was turning into a pair of tommets—the Embassy staff had dubbed them "notrabbits" for their sexual proclivities—engaged in their mating dance. Tatep rattled his spines, amused, and passed the carving into her hands. He waited quietly while she turned it this way and that, admiring the exquisite workmanship.

"You don't get the joke," he said, at last.

"No, Tatep. I'm afraid I don't. Can you share it?"

"Look closely at their teeth."

Marianne did, and got the joke. The creatures were tommets, yes, but the teeth they had were not tommet teeth.

They were the same sort of teeth that Tatep had used to carve
them. Apparently, "fucking like tommets" was a Rejoicer
joke.

"It's a gift for Hapet and Achinto. They had *six* children!
We're all pleased and amazed for them."

Four to a brood was the usual, but birthings were few and
far between. A couple that had more than two birthings in a
lifetime was considered unusually lucky.

"Congratulate them for me, if you think it appropriate,"
Marianne said. "Would it be proper for the embassy to send
a gift?"

"Proper and most welcome. Hapet and Achinto will need
help feeding that many."

"Would you help me choose? Something to make children
grow healthy and strong, and something as well to delight
their senses."

"I'd be glad to. Shall we go to the market or the wood?"

"Let's go chop our own, Tatep. I've been sitting behind this
desk too damn long. I could use the exercise."

As Marianne rose, Tatep put his finished carving into his
pouch and climbed down. "You will share more about Christmas with me while we work? You can talk and chop at the
same time."

Marianne grinned. "I'll do better than that. You can help
me choose something that we can use for a Christmas tree, as
well. If it's something that is also edible when it has seasoned
for a few weeks' time, that would be all the more to the spirit
of the festival."

The two of them took a leisurely stroll down the narrow
cobbled streets. Marianne shared more of her Christmas customs with Tatep and found her anticipation growing apace as
she did.

At Tatep's suggestion they paused at Killim the glassblower's, where Tatep helped Marianne describe and order a
dozen ornamental balls for the tree. Unaccustomed to the idea
of purely ornamental glass objects, Killim was fascinated.
"She says," reported Tatep when Marianne missed a few cru-

cial words of her reply, "she'll make a number of samples and you'll return on Debem Op Chorr to choose the most proper."

Marianne nodded. Before she could thank Killim, however, she heard the door behind her open, heard a muffled squeak of surprise, and turned. Halemtat had ordered yet another of his subjects clipped—Marianne saw that much before the local beat a hasty retreat from the door and vanished.

"Oh, god," she said aloud. "Another one." That, she admitted to herself for the first time, was why she was making such an effort to recognize the individual Rejoicers by facial shape alone. She'd seen no less than fifty clipped in the year she'd been on Rejoicing. There was no doubt in her mind that this was a new one—the blunted tips of its quills had been bright and crisp. "Who is it this time, Tatep?"

Tatep ducked his head in shame. "Chornian," he said.

For once, Marianne couldn't restrain herself. "Why?" she asked, and she heard the unprofessional belligerence in her own voice.

"For saying something I dare not repeat, not even in your language," Tatep said, "unless I wish to have *my* quills clipped."

Marianne took a deep breath. "I apologize for asking, Tatep. It was stupid of me." Best thing to do would be to get the hell out and let Chornian complete his errand without being shamed in front of the two of them. "Though," she said aloud, not caring if it was professional or not, "it's Halemtat who should be shamed, not Chornian."

Tatep's eyes widened, and Marianne knew she'd gone too far. She thanked the glassblower politely in Rejoicer and promised to return on Debem Op Chorr to examine the samples.

As they left Killim's, Marianne heard the scurry behind them—Chornian entering the shop as quickly and as unobtrusively as possible. She set her mouth—her silence raging—and followed Tatep without a backward glance.

At last they reached the communal wood. Trying for some semblance of normalcy, Marianne asked Tatep for the particulars of an unfamiliar tree.

"*Huep*," he said. "Very good for carving, but not very good for eating." He paused a moment, thoughtfully. "I think I've put that wrong. The flavor is *very* good, but it's very low in food value. It grows prodigiously, though, so a lot of people eat too much of it when they shouldn't."

"Junk food," said Marianne, nodding. She explained the term to Tatep and he concurred. "Youngsters are particularly fond of it—but it wouldn't be a good gift for Hapet and Achinto."

"Then let's concentrate on good *healthy* food for Hapet and Achinto," said Marianne.

Deeper in the wood, they found a stand of the trees the embassy staff had dubbed gnomewood for its gnarly, stunted appearance. Tatep proclaimed this perfect, and Marianne set about to chop the proper branches. Gathering food was more a matter of pruning than chopping down, she'd learned, and she followed Tatep's careful instructions so she did not damage the tree's productive capabilities in the process.

"Now this one—just here," he said. "See, Marianne? Above the bole, for new growth will spring from the bole soon after your Awakening. If you damage the bole, however, there will be no new growth on this branch again."

Marianne chopped with care. The chopping took some of the edge off her anger. Then she inspected the gnomewood and found a second possibility. "Here," she said. "Would this be the proper place?"

"Yes," said Tatep, obviously pleased that she'd caught on so quickly. "That's right." He waited until she had lopped off the second branch and properly chosen a third and then he said, "Chornian said Halemtat had the twining tricks of a *talemtat*. One of his children liked the rhyme and repeated it."

"*Talemtat* is the vine that strangles the tree it climbs, am I right?" She kept her voice very low.

Instead of answering aloud, Tatep nodded.

"Did Halemtat—did Halemtat order the child clipped as well?"

Tatep's eyelids shaded his pupils darkly. "The entire family. He ordered the entire family clipped."

So that was why Chornian was running the errands. He *would* risk his own shame to protect his family from the awful embarrassment—for a Rejoicer—of appearing in public with their quills clipped.

She took out her anger on yet another branch of the gnomewood. When the branch fell—on her foot, as luck would have it—she sat down of a heap, thinking to examine the bruise, then looked Tatep straight in the eye. "How long? How long does it take for the quills to grow out again?" After much of a year, she hadn't yet seen evidence that an adult's quills regenerated at all. "They do regrow?"

"After several Awakenings," he said. "The regrowth can be quickened by eating *welspeth*, but . . ."

But *welspeth* was a hothouse plant in this country. Too expensive for somebody like Chornian.

"I see," she said. "Thank you, Tatep."

"Be careful where you repeat what I've told you. Best you not repeat it at all." He cocked his head at her and added, with a rattle of quills, "I'm not sure where Halemtat would clip a human, or even if you'd feel shamed by a clipping, but I wouldn't like to be responsible for finding out."

Marianne couldn't help but grin. She ran a hand through her pale white hair. "I've had my head shaved—that was long ago and far away—and it was intended to shame me."

"Intended to?"

"I painted my naked scalp bright red and went about my business as usual. I set something of a new fashion and, in the end, it was the shaver who was—quite properly—shamed."

Tatep's eyelids once again shaded his eyes. "I must think about that," he said, at last. "We have enough branches for a proper gift now, Marianne. Shall we consider the question of your Christmas tree?"

"Yes," she said. She rose to her feet and gathered up the branches. "And another thing as well. . . . I'll need some more wood for carving. I'd like to carve some gifts for my friends, as well. That's another tradition of Christmas."

"Carving gifts? Marianne, you make Christmas sound as if it were a Rejoicing holiday!"

Marianne laughed. "It is, Tatep. I'll gladly share my Christmas with you."

* * *

Clarence Doggett was Super Plenipotentiary Representing Terra to Rejoicing and today he was dressed to live up to his extravagant title in striped silver tights and a purple silk weskit. No less than four hoops of office jangled from his belt. Marianne had, since meeting him, conceived the theory that the more stylishly outré his dress the more likely he was to say yes to the request of a subordinate. Scratch that theory. . . .

Clarence Doggett straightened his weskit with a tug and said, "We have no reason to write a letter of protest about Emperor Halemtat's treatment of Chornian. He's deprived us of a valuable worker, true, but . . ."

"Whatever happened to human rights?"

"They're not human, Marianne. They're aliens."

At least he hadn't called them "Pincushions" as he usually did, Marianne thought. Clarence Doggett was the unfortunate result of what the media had dubbed "the Grand Opening." One day humans had been alone in the galaxy, and the next they'd found themselves only a tiny fraction of the intelligent species. Setting up five hundred embassies in the space of a few years had strained the diplomatic service to the bursting point. Rejoicing, considered a backwater world, got the scrapings from the bottom of the barrel. Marianne was trying very hard not to be one of those scrapings, despite the example set by Clarence. She clamped her jaw shut very hard.

Clarence brushed at his fashionably large mustache and added, "It's not as if they'll *really* die of shame, after all."

"Sir," Marianne began.

He raised his hands. "The subject is closed. How are the plans coming for the Christmas bash?"

"Fine, sir," she said without enthusiasm. "Killim—she's the local glassblower—would like to arrange a trade for some dyes, by the way. Not just for the Christmas tree ornaments, I gather, but for some project of her own. I'm sending letters with Nick Minski to a number of glassblowers back home to find out what sort of dye is wanted."

"Good work. Any trade item that helps tie the Rejoicers into the galactic economy is a find. You're to be commended."

Marianne wasn't feeling very commended, but she said, "Thank you, sir."

"And keep up the good work—this Christmas idea of yours is turning out to be a big morale booster."

That was the dismissal. Marianne excused herself and, feet dragging, she headed back to her office. " 'They're not human,' " she muttered to herself. " 'They're aliens. It's not as if they'll *really* die of shame. . . . ' " She slammed her door closed behind her and snarled aloud, "But Chornian can't keep up work and the kids can't play with their friends and his mate Chaylam can't go to the market. What if they starve?"

"They won't starve," said a firm voice.

Marianne jumped.

"It's just me," said Nick Minski. "I'm early." He leaned back in the chair and put his long legs up on her desk. "I've been watching how the neighbors behave. Friends—your friend Tatep included—take their leftovers to Chornian's family. They won't starve. At least, Chornian's family won't. I'm not sure what would happen to someone who is generally unpopular."

Nick was head of the ethnology team studying the Rejoicers. At least he had genuine observations to base his decision on.

He tipped the chair to a precarious angle. "I can't begin to guess whether or not helping Chornian will land Tatep in the same hot water, so I can't reassure you there. I take it from your muttering that Clarence won't make a formal protest."

Marianne nodded.

He straightened the chair with a bang that made Marianne start. "Shit," he said. "Doggett's such a pissant."

Marianne grinned ruefully. "God, I'm going to miss you, Nick. Diplomats aren't permitted to speak in such matter-of-fact terms."

"I'll be back in a year. I'll bring you fireworks for your next Christmas." He grinned.

"We've been through that, Nick. Fireworks may be part of your family's Christmas tradition, but they're not part of mine. All that banging and flashing of light just wouldn't *feel* right to me, not on Christmas."

"Meanwhile," he went on, undeterred, "you think about my offer. You've learned more about Tatep and his people than half the folks on my staff; academic credentials or no, I can swing putting you on the ethnology team. We're shorthanded as it is. I'd rather have skipped the rotation home this year, but . . ."

"You can't get everything you want, either."

He laughed. "I think they're afraid we'll all go native if we don't go home one year in five." He preened and grinned suddenly. "How d'you think I'd look in quills?"

"Sharp," she said and drew a second burst of laughter from him.

There was a knock at the door. Marianne stretched out a toe and tapped the latch. Tatep stood on the threshold, his quills still bristling from the cold. "Hi, Tatep—you're just in time. Come share."

His laughter subsiding to a chuckle, Nick took his feet from the desk and greeted Tatep in high-formal Rejoicer. Tatep returned the favor, then added by way of explanation, "Marianne is sharing her Christmas with me."

Nick cocked his head at Marianne. "But it's not for some time yet. . . ."

"I know," said Marianne. She went to her desk and pulled out a wrapped package. "Tatep, Nick is my very good friend. Ordinarily, we exchange gifts on Christmas Day, but since Nick won't be here for Christmas, I'm going to give him his present now."

She held out the package. "Merry Christmas, Nick. A little too early, but—"

"You've hidden the gift in paper," said Tatep. "Is that also traditional?"

"Traditional but not necessary. Some of the pleasure is the surprise involved," Nick told the Rejoicer. With a sidelong glance and a smile at Marianne, he held the package to his ear and shook it. "And some of the pleasure is in trying to guess what's in the package." He shook it and listened again. "Nope, I haven't the faintest idea."

He laid the package in his lap.

Tatep flicked his tail in surprise. "Why don't you open it?"

"In my family, it's traditional to wait until Christmas Day to open your presents, even if they're wrapped and sitting under the Christmas tree in plain sight for three weeks or more."

Tatep clambered onto the stool to give him a stare of open astonishment from a more effective angle.

"Oh, no!" said Marianne. "Do you really mean it, Nick? You're *not* going to open it until Christmas Day?"

Nick laughed again. "I'm teasing." To Tatep, he said, "It's traditional in my family to wait—but it's also traditional to find some rationalization to open a gift the minute you lay hands on it. Marianne wants to see my expression; I think that takes precedence in this case."

His long fingers found a cranny in the paper wrapping and began to worry it ever so slightly. "Besides, our respective homeworlds can't agree on a date for Christmas. . . . On some world *today* must be Christmas, right?"

"Good rationalizing," said Marianne, with a sigh and a smile of relief. "Right!"

"Right," said Tatep, catching on. He leaned precariously from his perch to watch as Nick ripped open the wrapping paper.

"Tchaikovsky made me think of it," Marianne said. "Although, to be honest, Tchaikovsky's nutcracker wasn't particularly traditional. This one *is*: take a close look."

He did. He held up the brightly painted figure, took in its green weskit, its striped silver tights, its flamboyant mustache. Four metal loops jangled at its carved belt, and Nick laughed aloud.

With a barely suppressed smile, Marianne handed him a "walnut" of the local variety.

Nick stopped laughing long enough to say, "You mean, this is a genuine, honest-to-god, *working* nutcracker?"

"Well, of course it is! My family's been making them for years." She made a motion with her hands to demonstrate. "Go ahead—crack that nut!"

Nick put the nut between the cracker's prominent jaws and,

after a moment's hesitation, closed his eyes and went ahead. The nut gave with an audible and very satisfying craaack! and Nick began to laugh all over again.

"Share the joke," said Tatep.

"Gladly," said Marianne. "The Christmas nutcracker, of which that is a prime example, is traditionally carved to resemble an authority figure—particularly one nobody much likes. It's a way of getting back at the fraudulent, the pompous. Through the years they've poked fun at everybody from princes to policemen to"—Marianne waved a gracious hand at her own carved figure—"well, surely you recognize *him*."

"Oh, my," said Tatep, his eyes widening. "Clarence Doggett, is it not?" When Marianne nodded, Tatep said, "Are you about to get your head shaved again?"

Marianne laughed enormously. "If I do, Tatep, this time I'll paint my scalp red and green—traditional Christmas colors—and hang one of Killim's glass ornaments from my ear. Not likely, though," she added, to be fair. "Clarence doesn't go in for head shaving." To Nick, who had clearly taken in Tatep's "again," she said, "I'll tell you about it sometime."

Nick nodded and stuck another nut between Clarence's jaws. This time he watched as the nut gave way with an explosive bang. Still laughing, he handed the nutmeat to Tatep, who ate it and rattled his quills in laughter of his own. Marianne was doubly glad she'd invited Tatep to share the occasion—now she knew exactly what to make *him* for Christmas.

Christmas Eve found Marianne at a loss—something was missing from her holiday and she hadn't been able to put her finger on precisely what that something was.

It wasn't the color of the tree Tatep had helped her choose. The tree was the perfect Christmas-tree shape, and if its foliage was a red so deep it approached black, that didn't matter a bit. "Next year we'll have Killim make some green ornaments," Marianne said to Tatep, "for the proper contrast."

Tinsel—silver thread she'd bought from one of the Rejoicer weavers and cut to length—flew in all directions. All seven of the kids who'd come to Rejoicing with their ethnologist parents were showing the Rejoicers the "proper" way to hang tinsel, which meant more tinsel was making it onto the kids and the Rejoicers than onto the tree.

Just as well. She'd have to clean the tinsel off the tree before she passed it on to Hapet and Achinto—well-seasoned and just the thing for growing children.

Nick would really have enjoyed seeing this, Marianne thought. Esperanza was filming the whole party, but that just wasn't the same as being here.

Killim brought the glass ornaments herself. She'd made more than the commissioned dozen. The dozen glass balls she gave to Marianne. Each was a swirl of colors, each unique. Everyone ooohed and aaahed—but the best was yet to come. From her sidepack, Killim produced a second container. "Presents," she said. "A present for your Awakening Tree."

Inside the box was a menagerie of tiny, bright glass animals: notrabbits, fingerfish, wispwings.... Each one had a loop of glass at the top to allow them to be hung from the tree. Scarcely trusting herself with such delicate objects of art, Marianne passed them on to George to string and hang.

Later, she took Killim aside and, with Tatep's help, thanked her profusely for the gifts. "Though I'm not sure she should have. Tell her I'll be glad to pay for them, Tatep. If she'd had them in her shop, I'd have snapped them up on the spot. I didn't know how badly our Christmas needed them until I saw her unwrap them."

Tatep spoke for a long time to Killim, who rattled all the while. Finally, Tatep rattled too. "Marianne, three humans have commissioned Killim to make animals for them to send home." Killim said something Marianne didn't catch. "Three humans in the last five minutes. She says, Think of this set as a—as an advertisement."

"No, you may not pay me for them," Killim said, still rattling. "I have gained something to trade for my dyes."

"She says," Tatep began.

"It's okay, Tatep. That I understood."

Marianne hung the wooden ornaments she'd carved and painted in bright colors, then she unsnagged a handful of tinsel from Tatep's ruff, divided it in half, and they both flung it onto the tree. Tatep's handful just barely missed Matsimoto, who was hanging strings of beads he'd bought in the bazaar, but Marianne's got Juliet, who was hanging chains of paper cranes it must have taken her the better part of the month to fold. Juliet laughed and pulled the tinsel from her hair to drape it—length by length and *neatly*—over the deep red branches.

Then Kelleb brought out the star. Made of silver wire delicately filigreed, it shone just the way a Christmas-tree star should. He hoisted Juliet to his shoulders and she affixed it to the top of the tree and the entire company burst into cheers and applause.

Marianne sighed and wondered why that made her feel so down. "If Nick had been here," Tatep observed, "I believe he could have reached the top without an assistant."

"I think you're right," said Marianne. "I wish he *were* here. He'd enjoy this." Just for a moment, Marianne let herself realize that what was missing from this Christmas was Nick Minski.

"Next year," said Tatep.

"Next year," said Marianne. The prospect brightened her.

The tree glittered with its finery. For a moment they all stood back and admired it—then there was a scurry and a flurry as folks went to various bags and hiding places and brought out the brightly wrapped presents. Marianne excused herself from Tatep and Killim and brought out hers to heap at the bottom of the tree with the rest.

Again there was a moment's pause of appreciation. Then Clarence Doggett—of all people—raised his glass and said, "A toast! A Christmas toast! Here's to Marianne, for bringing Christmas thirty light-years from old Earth!"

Marianne blushed as they raised their glasses to her. When they'd finished, she raised hers and found the right traditional response: "A Merry Christmas—and God bless us, every one!"

"Okay, Marianne. It's your call," said Esperanza. "Do we open the presents now or"—her voice turned to a mock whine—"do we *hafta* wait till tomorrow?"

Marianne glanced at Tatep. "What day is it now?" she

asked. She knew enough about local time reckoning to know what answer he'd give.

"Why, today is Tememb Nap Chorr."

She grinned at the faces around her. "By Rejoicer reckoning, the day changes when the sun sets—it's been Christmas Day for an hour at least now. But stand back and let the kids find their presents first."

There was a great clamor and rustle of wrapping paper and whoops of delight as the kids dived into the pile of presents.

As Marianne watched with rising joy, Tatep touched her arm. "More guests," he said, and Marianne turned.

It was Chornian, his mate Chaylam, and their four children. Marianne's jaw dropped at the sight of them. She had invited the six with no hope of a response and here they were. "And all dressed up for Christmas!" she said aloud, though she knew Christmas was *not* the occasion. "You're as glittery as the Christmas tree itself," she told Chornian, her eyes gleaming with the reflection of it.

Ruff and tail, each and every one of Chornian's short-clipped quills was tipped by a brilliant red bead. "Glass?" she asked.

"Yes," said Chornian. "Killim made them for us."

"You look magnificent! Oh—how wonderful!" Chaylam's clipped quills had been dipped in gold; when she shifted shyly, her ruff and tail rippled with light. "You sparkle like sun on the water," Marianne told her. The children's ruffs and tails had been tipped in gold and candy pink and vivid yellow and—the last but certainly not the least—in beads every color of the rainbow.

"A kid after my own heart," said Marianne. "I think that would have been my choice too." She gave a closer look. "No two alike, am I right? Come—join the party. I was afraid I'd have to drop your presents by your house tomorrow. Now I get to watch you open them, to see if I chose correctly."

She escorted the four children to the tree and, thanking her lucky stars she'd had Tatep write their names on their packages, she left them to hunt for their presents. Those for their parents she brought back with her.

"It was difficult," Chornian said to Marianne. "It was dif-

ficult to walk through the streets with pride but—we did. And
the children walked the proudest. They give us courage."

Chaylam said, "If only on their behalf."

"Yes," agreed Chornian. "Tomorrow I shall walk in the
sunlight. I shall go to the bazaar. My clipped quills will glitter, and *I* will not be ashamed that I have spoken the truth
about Halemtat."

That was all the Christmas gift Marianne needed, she
thought to herself, and handed the wrapped package to
Chornian. Tatep gave him a running commentary on the habits and rituals of the human Awakening as he opened the
package. Chornian's eyes shaded and Tatep's running commentary ceased abruptly as they peered together into the box.

"Did I get it right?" said Marianne, suddenly afraid she'd
committed some awful faux pas. She'd scoured the bazaar for
welspeth shoots and, finding none, she'd pulled enough
strings with the ethnology team to get some imported.

Tatep was the one who spoke. "You got it right," he said.
"Chornian thanks you." Chornian spoke rapid-fire Rejoicer
for a long time; Marianne couldn't follow the half of it. When
he'd finished, Tatep said simply, "He regrets that he has no
present to give you."

"It's not necessary. Seeing those kids all in spangles brightened up the party—that's present enough for me!"

"Nevertheless," said Tatep, speaking slowly so she wouldn't
miss a word. "Chornian and I make you this present."

Marianne knew the present Tatep drew from his pouch was
from Tatep alone, but she was happy enough to play along
with the fiction if it made him happy. She hadn't expected a
present from Tatep and she could scarcely wait to see what it
was he felt appropriate to the occasion.

Still, she gave it the proper treatment—shaking it, very gently, beside her ear. If there was anything to hear, it was drowned
out by the robust singing of carols from the other side of the
room. "I can't begin to guess, Tatep," she told him happily.

"Then open it."

She did. Inside the paper, she found a carving, the rich
wine-red of burgundy-wood, bitter to the taste and therefore
rarely carved but treasured because none of the kids would

gnaw on it as they tested their teeth. The style of carving was
so utterly Rejoicer that it took her a long moment to recognize the subject, but once she did, she knew she'd treasure the
gift for a lifetime.

It was unmistakably Nick—but Nick as seen from Tatep's
point of view, hence the unfamiliar perspective. It was Looking Up At Nick.

"Oh, Tatep!" And then she remembered just in time and
added, "Oh, Chornian! Thank you both so very much. I can't
wait to show it to Nick when he gets back. Whatever made
you think of doing Nick?"

Tatep said, "He's your best *human* friend. I know you miss
him. You have no pictures; I thought you would feel better
with a likeness."

She hugged the sculpture to her. "Oh, I do. Thank you,
both of you." Then she motioned, eyes shining. "Wait. Wait
right here, Tatep. Don't go away."

She darted to the tree and, pushing aside wads of rustling
paper, she found the gift she'd made for Tatep. Back she
darted to where the Rejoicers were waiting.

"I waited," Tatep said solemnly.

She handed him the package. "I hope this is worth the
wait."

Tatep shook the package. "I can't begin to guess," he said.

"Then open it. *I* can't stand the wait!"

He ripped away the paper as flamboyantly as Nick had—to
expose the brightly colored nutcracker and a woven bag of
nuts.

Marianne held her breath. The problem had been, of
course, to adapt the nutcracker to a recognizable Rejoicer version. She'd made the Emperor Halemtat sit back on his
haunches, which meant far less adaptation of the cracking
mechanism. Overly plump, she'd made him, and spiky. In his
right hand, he carried an oversized pair of scissors—of the
sort his underlings used for clipping quills. In his left, he carried a sprig of *talemtat*, that unfortunate rhyme for his name.

Chornian's eyes widened. Again, he rattled off a spate of
Rejoicer too fast for Marianne to follow ... except that
Chornian seemed anxious.

Only then did Marianne realize what she'd done. "Oh, my God, Tatep! He wouldn't clip your quills for *having* that, would he?"

Tatep's quills rattled and rattled. He put one of the nuts between Halemtat's jaws and cracked with a vengeance. The nutmeat he offered to Marianne, his quills still rattling. "If he does, Marianne, you'll come to Killim's to help me choose a good color for *my* glass beading."

He cracked another nut and handed the meat to Chornian. The next thing Marianne knew, the two of them were rattling at each other—Chornian's glass beads adding a splendid tinkling to the merriment.

Much relieved, Marianne laughed with them. A few minutes later, Esperanza dashed out to buy more nuts—so Chornian's children could each take a turn at the cracking.

Marianne looked down at the image of Nick cradled in her arm. "I'm sorry you missed this," she told it, "but I promise I'll write everything down for you before I go to bed tonight. I'll try to remember every last bit of it for you."

"Dear Nick," Marianne wrote in another letter some months later. "You're not going to approve of this. I find I haven't been ethnologically correct—much less diplomatic. I'd only meant to share my Christmas with Tatep and Chornian and, for that matter, whoever wanted to join in the festivities. To hear Clarence tell it, I've sent Rejoicing to hell in a handbasket.

"You see, it does Halemtat no good to clip quills these days. There are some seventy-five Rejoicers walking around town clipped and beaded—as gaudy and as shameless as you please. I even saw one newly male (teenager) with beads on the ends of his unclipped spines!

"Killim says thanks for the dyes, by the way. They're just what she had in mind. She's so busy, she's taken on two apprentices to help her. She makes 'Christmas ornaments' and half the art galleries in the known universe are after her for more and more. The apprentices make glass beads. One of them—one of Chornian's kids, by the way—hit upon the bright idea of making simple sets of beads that can be stuck on the ends of quills cold. Saves time and trouble over the hot glass method.

"What's more—

"Well, yesterday I stopped by to say 'hi' to Killim, when who should turn up but Koppen—you remember him? He's one of Halemtat's advisors? You'll never guess what he wanted: a set of quill-tipping beads.

"No, he hadn't had his quills clipped. Nor was he buying them for a friend. He was planning, he told Killim, to tell Halemtat a thing or two—I missed the details because he went too fast—and he expected he'd be clipped for it, so he was planning ahead. Very expensive *blue* beads for him, if you please, Killim!

"I find myself unprofessionally pleased. There's a thing or two Halemtat *ought* to be told. . . .

"Meanwhile, Chornian has gone into the business of making nutcrackers.—All right, so sue me, I showed him how to make the actual cracker work. It was that or risk his taking Tatep's present apart to find out for himself.

"I'm sending holos—including a holo of the one I made—because you've got to see the transformation Chornian's worked on mine. The difference between a human-carved nutcracker and a Rejoicer-carved nutcracker is as unmistakable as the difference between Looking Up At Nick and . . . well, *looking up at Nick.*

"I still miss you, even if you do think fireworks are appropriate at Christmas.

"See you soon—if Clarence doesn't boil me in my own pudding and bury me with a stake of holly through my heart."

Marianne sat with her light pen poised over the screen for a long moment; then she added, "Love, Marianne," and saved it to the next outgoing Dirt-bound mail.

Rejoicing
Midsummer's Eve
(Rejoicer reckoning)

Dear Nick—

This time it's not my fault. This time it's Esperanza's doing. Esperanza decided, for *her* contribution to our

round of holidays, to celebrate Martin Luther King Day.
(All right—if I'd known about Martin Luther King I'd
probably have suggested a celebration myself—but I
didn't. Look him up; you'll like him.) And she invited
a handful of the Rejoicers to attend as well.

Now, the final part of the celebration is that each person in turn "has a dream." This is not like wishes,
Nick. This is more on the order of setting yourself a
goal, even one that looks to all intents and purposes to
be unattainable, but one you will strive to attain. Even
Clarence got so into the occasion that he had a dream
that he would stop thinking of the Rejoicers as "Pincushions" so he could start thinking of them as Rejoicers. Esperanza said later Clarence didn't quite get the
point but for him she supposed that was a step in the
right direction.

Well, after that, Tatep asked Esperanza, in his very
polite fashion, if it would be proper for him to have a
dream as well. There was some consultation over the
proper phrasing—Esperanza says her report will tell
you all about that—and then Tatep rose and said, "I
have a dream . . . I have a dream that someday no one
will get his quills clipped for speaking the truth."

(You'll see it on the tape. Everybody agreed that this
was a good dream, indeed.)

After which, Esperanza had her dream "for human
rights for all."

Following which, of course, we all took turns trying
to explain the concept of "human rights" to a half-
dozen Rejoicers. Esperanza ended up translating five
different constitutions for them—*and* an entire book of
speeches by Martin Luther King.

Oh, god. I just realized . . . maybe it *is* my fault. I'd
forgotten till just now. Oh. You judge, Nick.

About a week later Tatep and I were out gathering
wood for some carving he plans to do—for Christmas,
he says, but he wanted to get a good start on it—and he
stopped gnawing long enough to ask me, "Marianne,
what's 'human'?"

"How do you mean?"

"I think when Clarence says 'human,' he means something different than you do."

"That's entirely possible. Humans use words pretty loosely at the best of times—there, I just did it myself."

"What do you mean when you say 'human'?"

"Sometimes I mean the species *Homo sapiens.* When I say, Humans use words pretty loosely, I do. Rejoicers seem to be more particular about their speech, as a general rule."

"And when you say 'human rights,' what do you mean?"

"When I say 'human rights,' I mean *Homo sapiens* and *Rejoicing sapiens.* I mean any *sapiens,* in that context. I wouldn't guarantee that Clarence uses the word the same way in the same context."

"You think I'm human?"

"I *know* you're human. We're friends, aren't we? I couldn't be friends with—oh, a notrabbit—now, could I?"

He made that wonderful rattly sound he does when he's amused. "No, I can't imagine it. Then, if I'm human, I ought to have human rights."

"Yes," I said. "You bloody well ought to."

Maybe it is all my fault. Esperanza will tell you the rest—she's had Rejoicers all over her house for the past two weeks—they're watching every scrap of film she's got on Martin Luther King.

I don't know how this will all end up, but I wish to hell you were here to watch.

Love, Marianne

Marianne watched a Rejoicer child crack nuts with his Halemtat cracker and a cold, cold shiver went up her spine. That was the eleventh she'd seen this week. Chornian wasn't the only one making them, apparently; somebody else had gone into the nutcracker business as well. This was, however, the first time she'd seen a child cracking nuts with Halemtat's jaw.

"Hello," she said, stooping to meet the child's eyes. "What a pretty toy! Will you show me how it works?"

Rattling all the while, the child showed her, step by step. Then he (or she—it wasn't polite to ask before puberty) said, "Isn't it funny? It makes Mama laugh and laugh and laugh."

"And what's your mama's name?"

"Pilli," said the child. Then it added, "With the green and white beads on her quills."

Pilli—who'd been clipped for saying that Halemtat had been overcutting the imperial reserve so badly that the trees would never grow back properly.

And then she realized that, less than a year ago, no child would have admitted that its mama had been clipped. The very thought of it would have shamed both mother *and* child.

Come to think of it . . . she glanced around the bazaar and saw no less than four clipped Rejoicers shopping for dinner. Two of them she recognized as Chornian and one of his children, the other two were new to her. She tried to identify them by their snouts and failed utterly—she'd have to ask Chornian. She also noted, with utterly unprofessional satisfaction, that she *could* ask Chornian such a thing now. That too would have been unthinkable and shaming less than a year ago.

Less than a year ago. She was thinking in Dirt terms because of Nick. There wasn't any point dropping him a line; mail would cross in deep space at this late a date. He'd be here just in time for "Christmas." She wished like hell he was already here. He'd know what to make of all this, she was certain.

As Marianne thanked the child and got to her feet, three Rejoicers—all with the painted ruff of quills at their necks that identified them as Halemtat's guards—came waddling officiously up. "Here's one," said the largest. "Yes," said another. "Caught in the very act."

The largest squatted back on his haunches and said, "You will come with us, child. Halemtat decrees it."

Horror shot through Marianne's body.

The child cracked one last nut, rattled happily, and said, "I get my quills clipped?"

"Yes," said the largest Rejoicer. "You will have your quills clipped." Roughly, he separated child from nutcracker and began to tow the child away, each of them in that odd three-legged gait necessitated by the grip.

All Marianne could think to do was call after the child, "I'll tell Pilli what happened and where to find you!"

The child glanced over its shoulder, rattled again, and said, "Ask her could I have silver beads like Hortap!"

Marianne picked up the discarded nutcracker—lest some other child find it and meet the same fate—and ran full speed for Pilli's house.

At the corner, two children looked up from their own play and galloped along beside her until she skidded to a halt by Pilli's bakery. They followed her in, rattling happily to themselves over the race they'd run. Marianne's first thought was to shoo them off before she told Pilli what had happened, but Pilli greeted the two as if they were her own, and Marianne found herself blurting out the news.

Pilli gave a slow inclination of the head. "Yes," she said, pronouncing the words carefully so Marianne wouldn't miss them, "I expected that. Had it not been the nutcracker, it would have been words." She rattled. "That child is the most outspoken of my brood."

"But—" Marianne wanted to say, Aren't you afraid? but the question never surfaced.

Pilli gave a few coins to the other children and said, "Run to Killim's, my dears, and ask her to make a set of silver beads, if she doesn't already have one on hand. Then run tell your father what has happened."

The children were off in the scurry of excitement.

Pilli drew down the awning in front of her shop, then paused. "I think you are afraid for my child."

"Yes," said Marianne. Lying had never been her strong suit; maybe Nick was right—maybe diplomacy wasn't her field.

"You are kind," said Pilli. "But don't be afraid. Even Halemtat wouldn't dare to order a child *hashay*."

"I don't understand the term."

"*Hashay?*" Pilli flipped her tail around in front of her and held out a single quill. "Chippet will be clipped here," she said, drawing a finger across the quill about halfway up its length. "*Hashay* is to clip here." The finger slid inward, to a spot about a quarter of an inch from her skin. "Don't worry, Marianne. Even Halemtat wouldn't dare to *hashay* a child."

I'm supposed to be reassured, thought Marianne. "Good," she said aloud, "I'm relieved to hear that." In truth, she hadn't the slightest idea what Pilli was talking about—and she was considerably less than reassured by the ominous implications of the distinction. She'd never come across the term in any of the ethnologists' reports.

She was still holding the Halemtat nutcracker in her hands. Now she considered it carefully. Only in its broadest outlines did it resemble the one she'd made for Tatep. This nutcracker was purely Rejoicer in style and—she almost dropped it at the sudden realization—peculiarly *Tatep's* style of carving. Tatep was making them too?

If *she* could recognize Tatep's distinctive style, surely Halemtat could—what then?

Carefully, she tucked the nutcracker under the awning—let Pilli decide what to do with the object; Marianne couldn't make the decision for her—and set off at a quick pace for Tatep's house.

On the way, she passed yet another child with a Halemtat nutcracker. She paused, found the child's father, and passed the news to him that Halemtat's guards were clipping Pilli's child for the "offense." The father thanked her for the information and, with much politeness, took the nutcracker from the child.

This one, Marianne saw, was *not* carved in Tatep's style or in Chornian's. This one was the work of an unfamiliar set of teeth.

Having shooed his child indoors, the Rejoicer squatted back on his haunches. In plain view of the street, he took up the bowl of nuts his child had left uncracked and began to crack them, one by one, with such deliberation that Marianne's jaw dropped.

She'd never seen an insolent Rejoicer but she would have bet money she was seeing one now. He even managed to make the crack of each nut resound like a gunshot. With the sound still ringing in her ears, Marianne quickened her steps toward Tatep's.

She found him at home, carving yet another nutcracker. He swallowed, then held out the nutcracker to her and said, "What do you think, Marianne? Do you approve of my portrayal?"

This one wasn't Halemtat, but his—for want of a better word—grand vizier, Corten. The grand vizier always looked to her as if he smirked. She knew the expression was due to a slightly malformed tooth but, to a human eye, the result was a smirk. Tatep's portrayal had the same smirk, only more so. Marianne couldn't help it . . . she giggled.

"Aha!" said Tatep, rattling up a rainstorm's worth of sound. "For once, you've shared the joke without the need of explanation!" He gave a long grave look at the nutcracker. "The grand vizier has earned his keep this once!"

Marianne laughed, and Tatep rattled. This time the sound of the quills sobered Marianne. "I think your work will get you clipped, Tatep," she said, and she told him about Pilli's child.

He made no response. Instead, he dropped to his feet and went to the chest in the corner, where he kept any number of carvings and other precious objects. From the chest, he drew out a box. Three-legged, he walked back to her. "Shake this! I'll bet you can guess what's inside."

Curious, she shook the box: it rattled. "A set of beads," she said.

"You see? I'm prepared. They rattle like a laugh, don't they?—a laugh at Halemtat. I asked Killim to make the beads red because that was the color you painted your scalp when you were clipped."

"I'm honored. . . ."

"But?"

"But I'm afraid for you. For *all* of you."

"Pilli's child wasn't afraid."

"No. No, Pilli's child wasn't afraid. Pilli said even Halemtat wouldn't dare *hashay* a child." Marianne took a deep breath and said, "But you're not a child." And I don't know what *hashay*ing does to a Rejoicer, she wanted to add.

"I've swallowed a talpseed," Tatep said, as if that said it all.

"I don't understand."

"Ah! I'll share, then. A talpseed can't grow unless it has been through the"—he patted himself—"stomach? digestive system? of a Rejoicer. Sometimes they don't grow even then. To swallow a talpseed means to take a step toward the growth of something important. I swallowed a talpseed called 'human rights.' "

There was nothing Marianne could say to that but: "I understand."

Slowly, thoughtfully, Marianne made her way back to the embassy. Yes, she understood Tatep—hadn't she been screaming at Clarence for just the same reason? But she was terrified for Tatep—for them all.

Without consciously meaning to, she bypassed the embassy for the little clutch of domes that housed the ethnologists. Esperanza—it was Esperanza she had to see.

She was in luck. Esperanza was at home writing up one of her reports. She looked up and said, "Oh, good. It's time for a break!"

"Not a break, I'm afraid. A question that, I think, is right up your alley. Do you know much about the physiology of the Rejoicers?"

"I'm the expert," Esperanza said, leaning back in her chair. "As far as there is one in the group."

"What happens if you cut a Rejoicer's spine"—she held up her fingers—"*this* close to the skin?"

"Like a cat's claw, sort of. If you cut the tip, nothing happens. If you cut too far down, you hit the blood supply—and maybe the nerve. The quill would bleed most certainly. Might never grow back properly. And it'd hurt like hell, I'm sure— like gouging the base of your thumbnail."

She sat forward suddenly. "Marianne, you're shaking. What is it?"

Marianne took a deep breath but couldn't stop shaking. "What would happen if somebody did that to all of Ta"—she found she couldn't get the name out—"all of a Rejoicer's quills?"

"He'd bleed to death, Marianne." Esperanza took her hand and gave it a firm squeeze. "Now, I'm going to get you a good stiff drink and you are going to tell me all about it."

Fighting nausea, Marianne nodded. "Yes," she said with enormous effort. "Yes."

"Who the *hell* told the Pincushions about 'human rights'?" Clarence roared. Furious, he glowered down at Marianne and waited for her response.

Esperanza drew herself up to her full height and stepped between the two of them. "Martin Luther King told the *Rejoicers* about human rights. You were there when he did it. Though you seem to have forgotten *your* dream, obviously the Rejoicers haven't forgotten theirs."

"There's a goddamned revolution going on out there!" Clarence waved a hand vaguely in the direction of the center of town.

"That is certainly what it looks like," Juliet said mildly. "So why are we here instead of out there observing?"

"You're here because I'm responsible for your safety."

"Bull," said Matsimoto. "Halemtat isn't interested in clipping *us*."

"Besides," said Esperanza. "The supply ship will be landing in about five minutes. Somebody's got to go pick up the supplies—and Nick. Otherwise, he's going to step right into the thick of it. The last mail went out two months ago. Nick's had no warning that the situation has"—she frowned slightly, then brightened as she found the proper phrase—"changed *radically*."

Clarence glared again at Marianne. "As a member of the embassy staff, you are assigned the job. You will pick up the supplies and Nick."

Marianne, who'd been about to volunteer to do just that, suppressed the urge to say, "Thank you!" and said instead, "Yes, sir."

Once out of Clarence's sight, Marianne let herself breathe a sigh of relief. The supply transport was built like a tank. While Marianne wasn't any more afraid of Halemtat's wrath than the ethnologists were, she was well aware that innocent

Dirt bystanders might easily find themselves stuck—all too literally—in a mob of Rejoicers. When the Rejoicers fought, as she understood it, they used teeth and quills. She had no desire to get too close to a lashing tailful. An unclipped quill was needle-sharp.

Belatedly, she caught the significance of the clipping Halemtat had instituted as punishment. Slapping a snout with a tail full of glass beads was not nearly as effective as slapping a snout with a morning-star made of spines.

She radioed the supply ship to tell them they'd all have to wait for transport before they came out. *Captain's gonna love that, I'm sure,* she thought, until she got a response from Captain Tertain. By reputation he'd never set foot on a world other than Dirt and certainly didn't intend to do so now. So she simply told Nick to stay put until she came for him.

Nick's cheery voice over the radio said only, "It's going to be a very special Christmas this year."

"Nick," she said, "you don't know the half of it."

She took a slight detour along the way, passing the narrow street that led to Tatep's house. She didn't dare to stop, but she could see from the awning that he wasn't home. In fact, nobody seemed to be home ... even the bazaar was deserted.

The supply truck rolled on, and Marianne took a second slight detour. What Esperanza had dubbed "the Grande Allez" led directly to Halemtat's imperial residence. The courtyard was filled with Rejoicers. Well-spaced Rejoicers, she saw, for they were—each and every one—bristled to their fullest extent. She wished she dared go for a closer look, but Clarence would be livid if she took much more time than normal reaching the supply ship. And he'd be checking—she knew his habits well enough to know that.

She floored the accelerator and made her way to the improvised landing field in record time. Nick waved to her from the port and stepped out. *Just like Nick,* she thought. *She'd told him to wait in the ship until she arrived; he'd obeyed to the letter.* It was all she could do to keep from hugging him as she hit the ground beside him. With a grateful sigh of relief, she said, "We've got to move fast on the transfer, Nick. I'll fill you in as we load."

By the time the two of them had transferred all the supplies from the ship, she'd done just that.

He climbed into the seat beside her, gave her a long thoughtful look, and said, "So Clarence has restricted all of the *other* ethnologists to the embassy grounds, has he?" He shook his head in mock sadness and clicked his tongue. "I see I haven't trained my team in the proper response to embassy edicts." He grinned at Marianne. "So the embassy advises that I stay off the streets, does it?"

"Yes," said Marianne. She hated being the one to tell him but he'd asked her. "The Super Plenipotentiary Etc. has issued a full and formal Advisory to all nongovernmental personnel. . . ."

"Okay," said Nick. "You've done your job: I've been Advised. Now I want to go have a look at this revolution-in-progress." He folded his arms across his chest and waited.

He was right. All Clarence could do was issue an Advisory; he had no power whatsoever to keep the ethnologists off the streets. And Marianne wanted to see the revolution as badly as Nick did.

"All right," she said. "I *am* responsible for your safety, though, so best we go in the transport. I don't want you stuck." She set the supply transport into motion and headed back toward the Grande Allez.

Nick pressed his nose to the window and watched the streets as they went. He was humming cheerfully under his breath.

"Uh, Nick—if Clarence calls us . . ."

"We'll worry about that when it happens," he said.

Worry is right, thought Marianne, but she smiled. He'd been humming Christmas carols, like some excited child. Inappropriate as all hell, but she liked him all the more for it.

She pulled the supply transport to a stop at the entrance to the palace courtyard and turned to ask Nick if he had a good enough view. He was already out the door and making his way carefully into the crowd of Rejoicers. "Hey!" she shouted—and she hit the ground running to catch up with him. "Nick!"

He paused long enough for her to catch his arm, then said, "I need to see this, Marianne. It's my *job*."

"It's *my* job to see you don't get hurt—"

He smiled. "Then you lead. I want to be over there where I can see and hear everything Halemtat and his advisors are up to."

Marianne harbored a brief fantasy about dragging him bodily back to the safety of the supply transport, but he was twice her weight and, from his expression, not about to cooperate. Best she lead, then. Her only consolation was that, when Clarence tried to radio them, there'd be nobody to pick up and receive his orders.

"Hey, Marianne!" said Chornian from the crowd. "Over here! Good view from here!"

And safer too. Grateful for the invitation, Marianne gingerly headed in that direction. Several quilled Rejoicers eased aside to let the two of them safely through. Better to be surrounded by beaded Rejoicers.

"Welcome back, Nick," said Chornian. He and Chaylam stepped apart to create a space of safety for the two humans. "You're just in time."

"So I see. What's going on?"

"Halemtat just had Pilli's Chippet clipped for playing with a Halemtat cracker. Halemtat doesn't *like* the Halemtat crackers."

Beside him, a fully quilled Rejoicer said, "Halemtat doesn't like much of anything. I think a proper prince ought to rattle his spines once or twice a year at least."

Marianne frowned up at Nick, who grinned and said, "Roughly translated: Hapter thinks a proper prince ought to have a sense of humor, however minimal."

"Rattle your spines, Halemtat!" shouted a voice from the crowd. "Let's see if you can do it."

"Yes." came another voice—and Marianne realized it was Chornian's—"Rattle your spines, Great Prince of the Nutcrackers!"

All around them, like rain on a tin roof, came the sound of rattling spines. Marianne looked around—the laughter swept through the crowd, setting every Rejoicer in vibrant motion.

Even the grand vizier rattled briefly, then caught himself, his ruff stiff with alarm.

Halemtat didn't rattle.

From his pouch, Chornian took a nutcracker and a nut. Placing the nut in the cracker's smirking mouth, Chornian made the bite cut through the rattling of the crowd like the sound of a shot. From somewhere to her right, a second crack resounded. Then a third. . . . Then the rattling took up a renewed life.

Marianne felt as if she were under water. All around her spines shifted and rattled. Chornian's beaded spines chattered as he cracked a second nut in the smirking face of the nutcracker.

Then one of Halemtat's guards ripped the nutcracker from Chornian's hands. The guard glared at Chornian, who rattled all the harder.

Looking over his shoulder to Halemtat, the guard called, "He's already clipped. What shall I do?"

"Bring me the nutcracker," said Halemtat. The guard glared again at Chornian, who had not stopped laughing, and loped back with the nutcracker in hand. Belatedly, Marianne recognized the smirk on the nutcracker's face.

The guard handed the nutcracker to the grand vizier— Marianne knew beyond a doubt that he recognized the smirk too.

"Whose teeth carved this?" demanded Halemtat.

An unclipped Rejoicer worked his way to the front of the crowd, sat proudly back on his haunches, and said, "Mine." To the grand vizier, he added, with a slight rasp of his quills that was a barely suppressed laugh, "What do you think of my work, Corten? Does it amuse you? You have a strong jaw."

Rattling swept the crowd again.

Halemtat sat up on his haunches. His bristles stood straight out. Marianne had never seen a Rejoicer bristle quite that way before. "Silence!" he bellowed.

Startled, either by the shout or by the electrified bristle of their ruler, the crowd spread itself thinner. The laughter had subsided only because each of the Rejoicers had gone as bris-

tly as Halemtat. Chornian shifted slightly to keep Marianne
and Nick near the protected cover of his beaded ruff.

"Marianne," said Nick softly, "that's Tatep."

"I know," she said. Without meaning to, she'd grabbed his
arm for reassurance.

Tatep. . . . He sat back on his haunches, as if fully at ease—
the only sleeked Rejoicer in the courtyard. He might have
been sitting in Marianne's office discussing different grades
of wood, for all the excitement he displayed.

Halemtat, rage quivering in every quill, turned to his
guards and said, "Clip Tatep. *Hashay.*"

"No!" shouted Marianne, starting forward. As she realized
she'd spoken Dirtside and opened her mouth to shout it again
in Rejoicer, Nick grabbed her and clapped a hand over her
mouth.

"No!" shouted Chornian, seeming to translate for her, but
speaking his own mind.

Marianne fought Nick's grip in vain. Furious, she bit the
hand he'd clapped over her mouth. When he yelped and removed it—still not letting her free—she said, "It'll kill him!
He'll bleed to death! Let me *go*." On the last word, she
kicked him hard, but he didn't let go.

A guard produced the ritual scissors and handed them to
the official in charge of clipping. She held the instrument
aloft and made the ritual display, clipping the air three times.
With each snap of the scissors, the crowd chanted, "No. No.
No."

Taken aback, the official paused. Halemtat clicked at her
and she abruptly remembered the rest of the ritual. She turned
to make the three ritual clips in the air before Halemtat.

This time the voice of the crowd was stronger. "No. No.
No," came the shout with each snap.

Marianne struggled harder as the official stepped toward
Tatep. . . .

Then the grand vizier scuttled to intercept. "No," he told
the official. Turning to Halemtat, he said, "The image is
mine. *I* can laugh at the caricature. Why is it, I wonder, that
you can't, Halemtat? Has some disease softened your spines
so that they no longer rattle?"

Marianne was so surprised she stopped struggling against Nick's hold—and felt the hold ease. He didn't let go, but held her against him in what was almost an embrace. Marianne held her breath, waiting for Halemtat's reply.

Halemtat snatched the ritual scissors from the official and threw them at Corten's feet. "You," he said. "You will *hashay* Tatep."

"No," said Corten. "I won't. *My* spines are still stiff enough to rattle."

Chornian chose that moment to shout once more, "Rattle your spines, Halemtat! Let us hear you rattle your spines!"

And without so much as a by-your-leave the entire crowd suddenly took up the chant: "Rattle your spines! Rattle your spines!"

Halemtat looked wildly around. He couldn't have rattled if he'd wanted to—his spines were too bristled to touch one to another. He turned his glare on the official, as if willing her to pick up the scissors and proceed.

Instead, she said, in perfect cadence with the crowd, "Rattle your spines!"

Halemtat made an imperious gesture to his guard—and the guard said, "Rattle your spines!"

Halemtat turned and galloped full tilt into his palace. Behind him the chant continued—"Rattle your spines! Rattle your spines!"

Then, quite without warning, Tatep rattled his spines. The next thing Marianne knew, the entire crowd was laughing and laughing and laughing at their vanished ruler.

Marianne went limp against Nick. He gave her a suggestion of a hug, then let her go. Against the rattle of the crowd, he said, "I thought you were going to get yourself killed, you little idiot."

"I couldn't—I couldn't stand by and do *nothing*; they might have killed Tatep."

"I thought doing nothing was a diplomat's job."

"You're right; some diplomat I make. Well, after this little episode, I probably don't have a job anyhow."

"My offer's still open."

"Tell the truth, Nick. If I'd been a member of your team fifteen minutes ago, would you have let me go?"

He threw back his head and laughed. "Of course not," he said. "But at least I understand why you bit the hell out of my hand."

"Oh, god, Nick! I'm so sorry! Did I hurt you?"

"Yes," he said. "But I accept your apology—and next time I won't give you that option."

" 'Next time,' huh?"

Nick, still grinning, nodded.

Well, there was that to be said for Nick: he was realistic.

"Hi, Nick," said Tatep. "Welcome back."

"Hi, Tatep. Some show you folks laid on. What happens next?"

Tatep rattled the length of his body. "Your guess is as good as mine," he said. "I've never done anything like this before. Corten's still rattling. In fact, he asked me to make him a grand vizier nutcracker. I think I'll make him a present of it— for Christmas."

He turned to Marianne. "Share?" he said. "I was too busy to watch at the time. Were you and Nick mating? If you do it again, may I watch?"

Marianne turned a vivid shade of red, and Nick laughed entirely too much. "You explain it to him," Marianne told Nick firmly. "Mating habits are not within my diplomatic jurisdiction. And I'm still in the diplomatic corps—at least, until we get back to the embassy."

Tatep sat back on his haunches, eagerly awaiting Nick's explanation. Marianne shivered with relief and said hastily, "No, it wasn't mating, Tatep. I was so scared for you I was going to charge in and—well, I don't know what I was going to do after that—but I couldn't just stand by and let Halemtat hurt you." She scowled at Nick and finished, "Nick was afraid I'd get hurt myself and wouldn't let me go."

Tatep's eyes widened in surprise. "Marianne, you would have fought for me?"

"Yes. You're my friend."

"Thank you," he said solemnly. Then to Nick, he said, "You were right to hold her back. Rattling is a better way than fighting." He turned again to Marianne. "You surprise me," he said. "You showed us how to rattle at Halemtat."

He shook from snout to tail-tip, with a sound like a hundred snare drums. "Halemtat turned tail and *ran* from our rattling!"

"And now?" Nick asked him.

"Now I'm going to go home. It's almost dinner time and I'm hungry enough to eat an entire tree all by myself." Still rattling, he added, "Too bad the hardwood I make the nutcrackers from is so bitter—though tonight I could almost make an exception and dine exclusively on bitter wood."

Tatep got down off his haunches and started for home. Most of the crowd had dispersed as well. It seemed oddly anticlimactic, until Marianne heard and saw the rattles of laughter ripple through the departing Rejoicers.

Beside the supply transport, Tatep paused. "Nick, at your convenience—I really *would* like you to share about human mating. For friendship's sake, I should know when Marianne is fighting and when she's mating. Then I'd know whether she needs help or—or what kind of help she needs. After all, some trees need help to mate. . . . "

Marianne had turned scarlet again. Nick said, "I'll tell you all about it as soon as I get settled in again."

"Thank you." Tatep headed for home, for all the world as if nothing unusual had happened. In fact, the entire crowd, laughing as it was, might have been a crowd of picnickers off for home as the sun began to set.

A squawk from the radio brought Marianne back to business. No use putting it off. Time to bite the bullet and check in with Clarence—if nothing else, the rest of the staff would be worried about both of them.

Marianne climbed into the cab. Without prompting, Nick climbed in beside her. For a long moment, they listened to the diatribe that came over the radio, but Marianne made no move to reply. Instead, she watched the Rejoicers laughing their way home from the palace courtyard.

"Nick," she said. "Can you really laugh a dictator into submission?"

He cocked a thumb at the radio. "Give it a try," he said.

"It's not worth cursing back at Clarence—you haven't his gift for bureaucratic invective."

Marianne also didn't have a job by the time she got back to the embassy. Clarence had tried to clap her onto the returning supply ship, but Nick stepped in to announce that Clarence had no business sending anybody from his ethnology staff home. In the end, Clarence's bureaucratic invective had failed him and the ethnologists simply disobeyed, as Nick had. All Clarence could do, after all, was issue a directive; if they chose to ignore it, the blame no longer fell on Clarence. Since that was all that worried Clarence, that was all right.

In the end, Marianne found that being an ethnologist was considerably more interesting than being a diplomat . . . especially during a revolution.

She and Nick, with Tatep, had taken time off from their mutual studies to choose this year's Christmas tree—from Halemtat's reserve. "Why," said Marianne, bemused at her own reaction, "do I fell like I'm cutting a Christmas tree with Thomas Jefferson?"

"Because you are," Nick said. "Even Thomas Jefferson did ordinary things once in a while. Chances are, he even hung out with his friends. . . ." He waved. "Hi, Tatep. How goes the revolution?"

For answer, Tatep rattled the length of his body.

"Good," said Nick.

"I may have good news to share with you at the Christmas party," added the Rejoicer.

"Then we look forward to the Christmas party even more than usual," said Marianne.

"And I brought a surprise for Marianne all the way from Dirt," Nick added. When Marianne lifted an eyebrow, he said, "No, no hints."

"Share?" said Tatep.

"Christmas Eve," Nick told him. "After you've shared your news, I think."

The tree-trimming party was in full swing. The newly formed Ad Hoc Christmas Chorus was singing Czech carols—a gift from Esperanza to everybody on both staffs. Clarence had gotten so mellow on the Christmas punch that he'd even offered Marianne her job back—if she was willing to be dropped a grade for insubordination. Marianne, equally mellow, said no but said it politely.

Nick had arrived at last, along with Tatep and Chornian and Chaylam and their kids. Surprisingly, Nick stepped in between verses to wave the Ad Hoc Christmas Chorus to silence. "Attention, please," he shouted over the hubbub. "Attention, *please*! Tatep has an announcement to make." When he'd finally gotten silence, Nick turned to Tatep and said, "You have the floor."

Tatep looked down, then looked up again at Nick.

"I mean," Nick said, "go ahead and speak. Marianne's not the only one who'll want to know your news, believe me."

But it was Marianne Tatep chose to address.

"We've all been to see Halemtat," he said. "And Halemtat has agreed: No one will be clipped again unless five people from the same village agree that the offense warrants that severe a punishment. *We* will choose the five, not Halemtat. Furthermore, from this day forward, anyone may say anything without fear of being clipped. Speaking one's mind is no longer to be punished."

The crowd broke into applause. Beside Tatep, Nick beamed.

Tatep took a piece of parchment from his pouch. "You see, Marianne? Halemtat signed it and put his bite to it."

"How did you get him to agree?"

"We laughed at him—and we cracked our nutcrackers in the palace courtyard for three days and three nights straight, until he agreed."

Chornian rattled. "He said he'd sign anything if we'd all just go away and let him sleep." He hefted the enormous package he'd brought with him and rattled again. "Look at all the shelled nuts we've brought for your Christmas party!"

Marianne almost found it in her heart to feel sorry for Halemtat. Grinning, she accepted the package and mounded the table with shelled nuts. "Those are almost too important to eat," she said, stepping back to admire their handiwork. "Are you sure they oughtn't to go into a museum?"

"The important thing," Tatep said, "is that I can say anything I want." He popped one of the nuts into his mouth and chewed it down. "Halemtat is a talemtat," he said, and rattled for the sheer joy of it.

"Corten looks like he's been eating too much briarwood," said Chornian—catching the spirit of the thing.

Not recognizing the expression, Marianne cast an eye at Nick, who said, "We'd say, 'Been eating a lemon.' "

One of Chornian's brood sat back on his/her haunches and said, "I'll show you Halemtat's guards—"

The child organized its siblings with much pomp and ceremony (except for the littlest, who couldn't stop rattling) and marched them back and forth. After the second repetition, Marianne caught the rough import of their chant: "We're Halemtat's guards/We send our regards/We wish you nothing but ill/Clip! we cut off your quill!"

After three passes, one child stepped on another's tail and the whole troop dissolved into squabbling among themselves and insulting each other. "You look like Corten!" said one, for full effect. The adults rattled away at them. The littlest one, delighted to find that insults could be funny, turned to Marianne and said, "Marianne! You're spineless!"

Marianne laughed even harder. When she'd caught her breath, she explained to the child what the phrase meant when it was translated literally into Standard. "If you want a good Dirt insult," she said, mischievously, "I give you 'birdbrain.' " All the sounds in that were easy for a Rejoicer mouth to utter—and when Marianne explained why it was an insult, the children all agreed that it was a very good insult indeed.

"Marianne is a birdbrain," said the littlest.

"No," said Tatep. "*Halemtat* is a birdbrain, not Marianne."

"Let the kid alone, Tatep," said Marianne. "The kid can say anything it wants!"

"True," said Tatep. "True!"

They shooed the children off to look for their presents

under the tree, and Tatep turned to Nick. "Share, Nick—your surprise for Marianne."

Nick reached under the table. After a moment's searching he brought out a large bulky parcel and hoisted it onto the table beside the heap of Halemtat nuts. Marianne caught a double-handful before they spilled onto the floor.

Nick laid a protective hand atop the parcel. "Wait," he said. "I'd better explain. Tatep, every family has a slightly different Christmas tradition—the way you folks do for Awakening. This is part of my family's Christmas tradition. It's *not* part of Marianne's Christmas tradition—but, just this once, I'm betting she'll go along with me." He took his hand from the parcel and held it out to Marianne. "Now you can open it," he said.

Dropping the Halemtat nuts back onto their pile, Marianne reached for the parcel and ripped it open with enough verve to satisfy anybody's Christmas unwrapping tradition. Inside was a box, and inside the box a jumble of gaudy cardboard tubes—glittering in stars and stripes and polka dots and even an entire school of metallic green fish. "Fireworks!" said Marianne. "Oh, Nick. . . ."

He put his finger to her lips. "Before you say another word—you chose today to celebrate Christmas because it was the right time of the Rejoicer year. You, furthermore, said that holidays on Dirt and the other human worlds don't converge—"

Marianne nodded.

Nick let that slow smile spread across his face. "But they *do*. This year, back on Dirt, today is the Fourth of July. The dates won't coincide again in our lifetimes but, just this once, they do. So, just this once—fireworks. You do traditionally celebrate Independence Day with fireworks, don't you?"

The pure impudence in his eyes made Marianne duck her head and look away but, in turning, she found herself looking right into Tatep's bright expectant gaze. In fact, all of the Rejoicers were waiting to see what Nick had chosen for her and if he'd chosen right.

"Yes," she said, speaking to Tatep but turning to smile at Nick. "After all, today's Independence Day right here on Rejoicing, too. Come on, let's go shoot off fireworks!"

And so, for the next twenty minutes, the night sky of Rejoicing was alive with Roman candles, shooting stars and all the brightness of all the Christmases and all the Independence Days in Marianne's memory. In the streets, humans ooohed and aaahed and Rejoicers rattled. The pops and bangs even woke Halemtat, but all he could do was come out on his balcony and watch.

A day later Tatep reported the rumor that one of the palace guards even claimed to have heard Halemtat rattle. "I don't believe it for a minute," Nick added when he passed the tale on to Marianne.

"Me neither," she said, "but it's a good enough story that I'd *like* to believe it."

"A perfect Christmas tale, then. What would you like to bet that the story of The First Time Halemtat Rattled gets told every Christmas from now on?"

"Sucker bet," said Marianne. Then the wonder struck her. "Nick? Do traditions start that easily—that quickly?"

He laughed. "What kind of fireworks would you like to have *next* year?"

"One of each," she said. "And about five of those with the gold fishlike things that swirl down and then go *bam!* at you when you least expect it."

For a moment, she thought he'd changed the subject, then she realized he'd answered her question. Wherever she went, for the rest of her life, her Christmas tradition would include fireworks—not just any fireworks, but Fourth of July fireworks. She smiled. "Next year, maybe we should play Tchaikovsky's *1812 Overture* as well as *The Nutcracker Suite.*"

He shook his head. "No," he said, "*The Nutcracker Suite* has plenty enough fireworks all by itself—at least *your* version of it certainly did!"

An explanation of Christmas for youngsters.

TRAINING TALK NO. 12
David R. Bunch

IT WAS DECEMBER now and snow was feather-sliding down toward our dirty windows, like billions of bleached seed floats sterile from some great ice tree in the sky, I sometimes thought—floating pieces of the world's great gloom-and-cold, I sometimes thought. But the air outside was full of the crisp jingle and tinkle of things, and the programs for weeks now, when I had tuned in for weather and world news, had been sneaking in a few words concerning the Terrible Thing. Little Sister at her doll beds and Little Brother at his soldiers and launch pads had turned and looked with a frightening kind of awe, and hope, at each small mention I allowed of the Terrible Thing—before I could flick the knob over. Little Sister, I had to think, looked something like a starving little squirrel, her slender face and funny blunty nose poked tautly toward the hedges of her uncombed yellow hair; and Little Brother must have looked like a starving heavyweight boxer in miniature, with his fine square build and sturdy legs and bull-like mien made incongruous by the thinness and scrawniness that started just below his neck around his collarbone and ex-

tended like a blueprint of poverty across his well-sprung ribs.
I fed them enough, hell knows. But sometimes I thought they
weren't happy and maybe discontent was the reason they
didn't progress in flesh. But we didn't come here to be happy.
NO! We came here to KNOW!

"Little Sister! Little Brother!" I yelled. "Leave off the dolls
and the launch sites and come here." They came and when
they were planted at attention, trembling slightly before me, I
said, "No, it isn't for portraits this time. It's for training talk.
And I had sought to avoid this one. Partly because it just isn't
worth a training talk and partly because it is so tied up with
the many other lectures that I, your one remaining staunch
parent, will be forced to give you, that somewhere it must all
seem redundant. I really think if we could hold off on this
thing until I could give you all of the other talks and you
could see the whole big picture of this life situation you'll be
forced to go into, this training talk about the Jollies would be
entirely beside the point. Unnecessary, I mean. But every time
you hear a certain word, this awful word, or some reference
to it, you both look at me. Little Sister looks at me like a
squirrel looking out of dirty yellowish fall hedges, and Little
Brother, you look at me as though you were remembering
something. Maybe you're both remembering something. At
any rate, you can see how you force my hand."

"Didn't intend it, Pop," Little Brother said. He was half
past five. "I'm sure we didn't intend to do it, Daddy," Little
Sister, who was somewhere after four, said.

"All right! I'll take your word for it. We won't argue it.
Now, let's get on. Every year, about this time, something happens. Perhaps you have both noticed it, ever since you have
been big enough to remember. And perhaps you—at least
you, Little Brother—remember a time when you mother—
But enough of that!" I got a firm stranglehold on an iron lump
just starting to feel like a big twisted nail in my throat, almost
before it even started. I hoped the kiddies hadn't noticed. Certainly I could have none of that. I coughed and blew my nose.
"Hell, if it's another cold—" I said. "All right! Where were
we? Oh, yes. Every year about this time something happens.
Even though we stay in the house and don't go out at all, and

I sit here at my easel and paint fiery pictures of summer with big droughts burning up hope, and we watch the weather and world news and have everything we need sent up to us, and you kiddies just play busily with your homemade toys all day, we'll still somehow know about this threat that's fast forming. They'll noise it in the streets, they'll cry it on the programs, and they'll even sky-halloo it from planes and drag it across us, hitched behind the lighter-than-air the big tire companies own. And in a place downtown, the biggest place downtown—I'll let you in on this, because I know from the years I used to go out—it's the same sound, and I know what's going on!—in this biggest place downtown they've got a rubber bag. It's colored all red, except for black patent and some white-fluffy tufts to make like real fur. And it's got the longest, whitest shimmer of wave-curled ersatz hairs—well, about as long as the chin crop on that old man reaping there." I pointed at the big picture of the gaunt man and the scythe I have featured on our walls. "But this thing in the place downtown is not a lean, fine harvester like that old man working there. It's silly fat, I say; it's soft. And you may not believe this, but it's true, take my word for it—this hollow fatty bag sits there in the front window of the biggest place downtown for a full month and a half, day and night, beats two black patent lumps together on a couple of sticks it has got sticking out from a little removed from a thinned place for a neck, and it laughs about things. It goes, 'Ho! ho! ho!' I know it! I've seen it. I've heard it. I know! And sometimes when the wind is right, in latter November and almost all of December, we can hear this ogre-shape even this far laughing at us, taunting at us about how we're caught and surrounded and soon to be gulped and eaten by the soft fat dangerous Jollies coming through the air, riding in on the wind, volplaning— from EVERYWHERE! Haven't you heard that laugh? Haven't you?" They both denied it. But just then a gale burst whipped smartly at our windows, and I'm almost sure I heard a very faint, very hollow ho-ho-ho rolling in on the wind, from toward that big place downtown.

"And what really happens when this awful thing gets going, when it firmly takes hold, in latter November and almost

all of December? Not the hollow rubber monster-bag that
shouts up all the Jollies and laughs at us when we're caught
and surrounded, I don't mean that. I mean the thing, the
threat, the event he's part of, the agitation for utter implausi-
bility of action, for dismissing the guards and surrender!" I
covered my face and my shoulders shook and knots began to
form in my stomach and there was a wintry feeling of great
hopelessness locked in my bowels. "God!" I said. "And I
don't mean God," I said. "Because that's part of another
training talk; so forget I said God," I said. "But God!" I said.
"What happens? WHAT REALLY HAPPENS to everything
in latter November and almost all of December?"

They could tell I was getting agitated, and I knew they
feared for me, and I was sorry for them; so I said, "It's all all
right, kiddies, I'll hold it down. What happens," I whispered,
raspy and sick and low out of a cracking throat, "in latter November and almost all of December?" Then, quite unexpect-
edly, I collapsed upon the floor; and when I came back to
consciousness, I was at full length looking into their scared
thin faces peering down at me like poultry; and all at once I
knew I would never be able to tell them enough of what I
knew about the horrors of this invasion. "We'll stay inside,"
I said. "We'll lock all our doors until it's over," I said. "I'll
paint night pictures of haystacks and the moon on fire in July.
I'll have red-black monster-bags, fur-trimmed, fleeing pitch-
fork clouds through whirling scuds like tornadoes. I'll demol-
ish the Jollies in a pair of black cyclones. We'll nail the
windows!"

"How about the chimney?" Little Sister asked, with a noise
that was a shimmering tremolo of hope, I knew, like sounds
out of a whole clothesline full of little golden bells might be,
shaking in a great black sleety wind. "Mightn't a Jolly
squeeze down through there? If it really tried? Even a big, big
one all thicky-wide with a sack?"

"We'll shove the bathtub under there," I shrieked, "and
keep it always full of boiling water. We'll heat flatirons and
big andirons. I'll set up another interior guard; we'll take
turns. And just to make sure this thing doesn't get into us,
doesn't take hold of us and soften us for the invasion, we'll

start wearing our earplugs again and take vows against looking out the windows. And to help out, I'll take one more trip outside for some things I'll need in my painting, and I'll try to bring back some small models of the hollow rubber ogrebag I was telling you about being all decked in the biggest place downtown. And we'll dip these things in sooty dirty water until they're all black all over, and then I'll sketch new faces on them just above the long, waved hairs to look like scared men screaming. After that we'll practice darts at these dirty little duds until the middle of next month next year— Would you like me to do that?"

"Darts, oh boy!" Little Brother said. But Little Sister, dazed and desperate, just nodded yes at me without meaning it, and with a moist, sentimental expression that somehow told me that Little Sister's heart, no matter how much I might try it, would always be on the soft, untenable side of the Jollies. She'd buy this big deal and she'd hope; she'd see fat sacks squeezed through even the smallest smoke flues and cold winds alive with gold bells of Xmas, in spite of all I could say.

The end of a Christmas tradition.

THE LAST BELSNICKEL
Chet Williamson

"DER BELSNICKEL KOMMT."

How long had it been since he had heard those words? How many years? Every Christmas Eve he listened, his old ears frozen from the wind and weather. At least he thought they were frozen. He had not felt the cold for centuries, not since the Christmas Eve he had been called upon to be a Belsnickel.

There had been many of them then, going from house to house on Christmas Eve with their bags full of treats and their switches. Oh yes, the switches were the most important things, far more important than the treats. The switches and the fear. He did not like to frighten the children, and he never really struck any of them with the switches he swung through the air, but it was necessary for them to know that this life was full of frightening things, things that could hurt them if they did not follow their parents' teachings. And if they were *truly* bad, the Belsnickel might even *take them away*.

How they shivered with fright when he burst in through the door of the cottage on Christmas Eve, dressed in his patched and tattered clothing, his fur cap pulled down so that the brim touched his thick eyebrows. Often they ran behind the skirts of their smiling *mutters* or the legs of their grinning *vaters*, but to no avail. They would be gently schussed out, and he would walk up to each one and glower and slap his switch against his leg. "Have you been *good*, child?" he asked them, and often as not they answered neither yes nor no, but simply stood before him in terror.

"Have you said your prayers at night, child?"

"Have you obeyed your parents, child?"

"Have you done your chores without being told, child?"

Little nods of little heads followed as his voice grew less harsh. Every now and then a child, most often a boy, proved surly, as though suspecting that the Belsnickel was in reality his uncle Otto. And then the Belsnickel would take his great black book from his sack, consult it, and say to the offender, "Two weeks ago you took a potato from your sister's plate when she wasn't looking. Shame on you, child!"

The boy blanched, and the required fear spread over his face as he realized that the theft of the potato, so small, insignificant, and secret a thing, could have been detected only by supernatural means.

"You had better hope, child," the Belsnickel went on, "that the Christkindel's gold book contains enough good deeds to outweigh those bad ones listed here." And now the child would quake, believing at last, and that was fine. For now the child would believe as well in what he *needed* to believe in— *der Christkindel*, the Christ Child, who would come later in the night, after everyone was asleep, and leave gifts for the family to remind them of the greater gift—His coming.

But first the Belsnickel would leave his own treats from his pack—a cookie, a piece of candy, some nuts or dried fruit, perhaps an orange to sweeten his visit, and then he would go on his way, his task completed. His gruffness had prepared the way for the Christ Child's kindness and gentleness. No one saw the Christkindel come, not even the Belsnickel. When the houses were dark, he would go on his way, a weary wanderer for another year, until Christmas should come again, and the parents would say the words—

"Hist! Hist! Der Belsnickel kommt!"

And he would come, knowing that he was wanted.

But he had not been wanted for many years. Times had changed. He had followed the families from their home countries to the new land, a land where the *alten* still wanted to preserve their memories, to keep the old ways alive. And so they did for many years. But times changed and customs changed as the years went by and the country grew and prospered and forgot about old ways, old values. A year could pass before he met another Belsnickel walking down some country path. Then it became years.

Now, this Christmas Eve, he had not seen another of his kind for a quarter century. Oh, there were those false Belsnickels, poor imitations who did in museums what used to be done in cottage and farmhouse. They would enter a room filled with children (for there was safety in numbers, and we can't have the children *frightened*, now, can we?), and roar for a moment, swing a thin little twig through the air, and then, without asking a single torturous question of his grinning and unafraid charges, would pass out the goodies— whole bars of candy, toys bought in stores, balloons, whistles, treasures that made his assortment of nuts and fruit and bite-sized sweetmeats seem poor fare indeed.

The last time he had been called was four Christmases ago, by an ancient *grossmutter* who, in her dotage, remembered the joys and terrors of the Christmas Eves of her youth, and murmured to her grandchildren, "Listen now, *der Belsnickel kommt. . . .*"

He came, as he had been directed, to find confused and annoyed parents and cautious and less than cordial children, while the grandmother who had beckoned him immediately forgot her incantation and began to call him Karl, mistaking him for someone long dead. The family, thinking him an old friend of Grandma's, suffered his presence for a time, the children answering his questions flippantly, and accepting his treats with less than good grace.

"An orange," the daughter said flatly, and sighed. "Thanks."

The Belsnickel received no more effusive show of thanks

from her younger brother for the nuts and dried fruit he was given, and was relieved to quit the house.

What thankless children, he thought. The time had been when a handful of nuts or an orange would have brought a look of unbearable joy to a child's face. In many cases, one orange a year was all that any child got, and the bright fruit was a thing of wonder.

But now all that was changed. Most children got whatever they asked for, and Christmas had become nothing but an orgy of buying presents, a *gorgerei* that would have been unheard of in days gone by. He began to think, as he had every year for he couldn't remember how long, that a Belsnickel had no place in today's tawdry version of Christmas. People did not want to be reminded of the frightening aspects of life so as to more greatly enjoy the advent of the Christkindel and the kingdom He brought. No, they ignored such dark visitors as the Belsnickel, for, no longer believing in the better world to come, they lied to themselves, trying to make Heaven out of their pitifully ill earth with electric lights and feasts and gifts bought with money, not with love. Their god now was Santa Claus, that jolly, red-suited amalgamation of Saint Nicholas, the Christkindel, a wealthy and generous uncle, and yes, the sack-toting Belsnickel, whom no one called anymore, not for four long years.

The Belsnickel sighed, looked from the top of a hill down into a town below where brightly colored lights heralded the advent of the glut of present exchanging that would come the following morning. No, he thought sadly, no place in this world for a Belsnickel.

"Der Belsnickel kommt. . . ."

Had he heard it? Or had he merely wanted to? He listened.

"Der Belsnickel kommt. . . ."

Yes, it was there, very faint and faraway, but there. The wonderful call, the call that acknowledged not only him, but Him whose path he had prepared every Christmas Eve for so many centuries.

"Der Belsnickel kommt. . . ."

There was no need to call again. He would come, and come quickly. He closed his eyes and obeyed the summons.

When he opened them again, he was standing in a small, dark room that smelled of urine and disinfectant. Through the soiled panes of the window, the light from a streetlamp dimly illuminated the only other person in the room, a very, very old man lying in a bed whose painted iron frame was chipped. There were no flowers in the room, and no Christmas cards. Only one small, framed picture sat on the enamel cabinet that served as a nightstand. It was that of a smiling woman in her twenties, and had faded from its original black and white to a dull yellow-brown.

"Belsnickel?" said the man on the bed in a voice as cracked as the plaster of the walls.

He raised his right arm to swing his switches through the air, then stopped. There were no children here, only the old man. Why had he called? What could he have been thinking? Was he addled too, like the old woman a few years before?

"Belsnickel?" the old man said again. "Is that you?"

The Belsnickel sighed, and lowered the arm with the switches. "Can you not tell?"

The old man smiled. "I'm blind. But now that I hear your voice, I know it's you. It's the same."

"I came to you before, then? As a child?"

The old man chuckled. It sounded like stones rattling down a well. "Don't you remember? I thought you had everything in that black book of yours."

"Where are the children?" the Belsnickel asked.

"I didn't call you for children. Or for my great-grandchildren, who I never see. . . ." His voice trailed off, then came back stronger than before. "I called you for me."

"For you?" The Belsnickel frowned even more deeply than usual. "Why? I bring only fear, and a smattering of things to eat. Your teeth are gone, so you cannot chew the nuts or the dried fruit. My candy is too hard for you. Why then do you call me? To be frightened?"

With great effort the man shook his head. "The things I've seen in my life, the people I've lost, the way I've ended up—life has nothing more to scare me with except the thought of drawing it out even longer. That's the one thing that terrifies me. And that's why I called you tonight. Because I remembered my *grossmutter* telling me that if I was bad, the Belsnickel might come and carry me away."

"Carry you away . . ."

"Oh, I was never really afraid of that. I knew that someone kind enough to give us treats, even if he did scare us first, would never take a little child, even a naughty one, somewhere he didn't want to go." Suddenly coughs shook the old man's frail body. When they were finished, he breathed deeply and went on.

"Then I started to wonder a few days ago, with Christmas coming—I started to remember you, and wondered if you did carry someone away, where you would carry him to. And I thought that it might really be someplace wonderful."

"No," the Belsnickel said, beginning to understand. "No, this is not right, this is not what I am here for."

"I know why you're here," said the old man. "I didn't know as a child, but I know now. You prepare the way for the Christkindel. You remind us that we have to go through all the pains and terrors of this world before we can enter the next." The old man's face turned toward the Belsnickel, and for a moment the Belsnickel thought that the milky eyes actually saw him. "I've been through this world. Been in it long enough. Now take me away. Carry me off. Please, Belsnickel."

For the first time in his existence, the Belsnickel was speechless.

"Please," the old man said again.

"I—I never have before," the Belsnickel said. "I don't know if I can."

"You can. I know you can. When I was little, what I wanted most in the world that Christmas Eve was an orange. And you came, and you gave it to me, and it was the sweetest thing I had ever tasted." He gave a long sigh. "Give me what I want now."

The Belsnickel looked at the switches in his right hand. Since he had taken up his duties, he had never laid them down. But now, as if guided by a stronger will, his fingers opened and the switches fell without a sound to the floor.

"All right, child," he said. "Here. Take my hand. We will

try and go together, try and leave this world. I promise nothing but to try."

The old man reached out in the darkness and put his hand in the Belsnickel's. His hand was cold, the Belsnickel thought, as cold as his own.

"Can you rise?" the Belsnickel asked.

"I can."

With the Belsnickel's help, the old man got to his feet. The Belsnickel put his arm around him, and together they shuffled to the window, where they stood for a moment.

"I don't know what to do," the Belsnickel began to say, but never finished, for at that moment the glare of the streetlamp was diminished by a far brighter light that began to bathe the room in a warm radiance, a light more intense than any the Belsnickel had seen in all his centuries of life, but a kindly light, a welcoming, transcendent light.

Then the Belsnickel saw a shape begin to come out of that light, a form, a face, and the old man heard him gasp, and asked, "What is it? I cannot see."

"You will, child," said the Belsnickel. "I promise you now you will."

"But what is it? What is there?"

"Der Christkindel," the Belsnickel said, and his mouth that had never worn a smile now smiled in wonder, and his eyes that had never shed tears now did so as they beheld the Glory.

"Der Christkindel kommt."

—For Laurie

You better watch out, you better not cry.

A CHILD'S CHRISTMAS
·IN FLORIDA
William Browning Spencer

THE WEEK BEFORE Christmas, Luke Haliday killed the traditional mud turtle, gutted it, and gave its shell to his oldest
son, Hark. Hark painted the shell with Day-Glo colors and
wore it on his head, where it would remain until two days before Christmas when the youngest of the children, Lou Belle,
would snatch it from his head, run giggling down to the
creek, and fill the gaudy shell with round, smooth stones.

"I miss Harrisburg," Janice Mosely said to her husband. "It
should be cold at Christmas. There should be snow." Her husband didn't say anything, but simply leaned over his newspaper as if he might dive into it. Well, Al could ignore her if he
pleased. She knew he missed Pennsylvania too and just didn't
care to talk about it. There was no getting around it: Christmas was for colder climes, everyone all bundled up and hustling from house to house with presents, red-faced children,
loud, wet people in the hall peeling off layers of clothing,
scarves, boots, gloves, shouting because they were full of hot
life that winter had failed to freeze and ready for any marvel-

ous thing. And snow, snow could make the world look like
the cellophane had just been shucked from it, was still crackling in the air.

"Barbara says is snowed eight inches last week," Janice
said. Barbara was their daughter. Al Mosely looked up from
his newspaper and regarded his wife with pale, sleepy blue
eyes. A wispy cloud of gray hair bloomed over his high forehead, giving his face a truculent, just-wakened cast. In fact,
he had been up since five (his unvarying routine) and regarded his wife's nine-o'clock appearance at the breakfast
table as something approaching decadence.

"She'll have to get that dodger"—Al always referred to
Barbara's live-in boyfriend as "that dodger," an allusion to the
young man's ability to avoid matrimony—"She'll have to get
that dodger to shovel her walk this year," Al said. "She was
the one who was so hot for us to retire to Florida, and we
done it and we'll just see if she gets that layabout to do anything more than wait for the spring thaw."

"Oh Al," Janice said, waving a hand at him and turning
away. She walked into the living room and stared out the window. Not only had they moved to Florida, they had moved to
rural Florida, land of cows and scrub pines and cattle egrets.
Her husband had said, "Okay, I'll go to Florida, but not to
some condominium on the ocean. I don't want a place full of
old folks playing bridge and shuffleboard. If I'm gonna retire,
I'm gonna retire right. A little place in the country—that's the
ticket."

Janice watched a yellow dog walk out into the road. Its image shimmered in the heat, like a bad television transmission.
Christmas. Christmas in Loomis, Florida. Dear God. Why,
none of her neighbors had even put up lights. And maybe
they had the right idea. Why bother? There was no way this
flat, sandy place could cobble up a Christmas to fool a half-
wit.

As Janice Mosely stared out the window, three boys, the
tallest of them wearing a funny, brightly colored beanie,
marched by. A tiny little girl ran in their wake. The boys were
carrying a Christmas tree. With an air of triumphant high spirits, they wrestled it down the road, shouting to each other,

country boys in tattered jeans and T-shirts and home-cropped haircuts, boys full of reckless enthusiasm and native rudeness. Janice smiled and scolded herself. "Well, it's a perfectly fine Christmas for some, Mrs. Janice 'Scrooge' Mosely," she said out loud. Still smiling, she turned away from the window and walked back into the kitchen. Her husband was listening to the radio, the news, all of it bleak: war, famine, murder, political graft.

"What's the world coming to?" Janice asked her husband.

"Let me think about it before I answer," Al said.

Hark was the oldest boy, but he wasn't right in the head, so Danny, who was three years younger, was in charge. "You don't do it that way," Danny said. "You will just bust your fingers doing it that way. Boy, you are a rattlebrain."

"Shut up," Hark said. "If you know what's good for you, shut up."

"What's the problem here?" their father asked, coming into the backyard. Luke Haliday was a tall, lanky man with a bristly black mustache. There wasn't any nonsense in him and his children knew it. He had been very strict since their mother left. Now he said, "Maybe you would rather fight than have a Christmas?"

"No, no!" shouted little Lou Belle, who was so infused with the spirit of Christmas that it made her eyes bulge. The boys, Hark, Danny, and Calder, all shouted: "No, no."

"I was just trying to explain to Hark that you got to tie these traps onto the tree first and then set 'em. You do it the other way, you just catch all your fingers," Danny said.

Luke laid a hand on Hark's shoulder. "Is this the first tree you ever decorated?" he asked his son.

"No sir," Hark said.

"Well then," Luke said.

"Tie 'em, then set 'em," Hark said, kicking dirt.

Luke stood back from his children and regarded the Christmas tree; the boys had dug a hole for the trunk and braced it with wires and stakes. The tree stood straight, tall and proud, the field rolling out behind it. "That's a damned fine tree,"

Luke said. "You children got an eye for a tree. You take this one out of Griper's field?"

"Yes sir," Danny said.

"It's a good one," their father said. He reached down, picked up one of the mousetraps, and tied it to a branch with a piece of brown string. Then he set the trap and stood back again. The tree already had a dozen traps tied to various branches. "If a tree like this can't bring us luck then we might as well give up. We might as well lie down and let them skin us and salt us if a tree like this don't bode a fine Christmas."

The children agreed.

Their father turned and walked back to the shack, and the children set to work tying the remaining traps to branches. Later they would paint colored dots on them. "I want blue," Lou Belle insisted. "I want mine blue." Her voice was shrill, prepared for an argument, but Danny just said, "Sure. Why not?"

"Hello," Janice shouted, when she saw the little girl again. "Hello, little girl." The child turned and stared at Janice for a long time before finally changing course and toddling toward the old woman.

"Lou Belle," the little girl said in answer to Janice's question. What a sweet child, Janice thought, with such full cheeks—they cried out to be pinched—and those glorious, big brown eyes. The girl wore corduroy overalls and a white T-shirt. Her feet were bare.

"What's Santa bringing you for Christmas?" Janice asked.

The girl shrugged her shoulders. "Santa don't come to our house," she said.

"Oh, I'm sure he does." Janice knelt down and placed her hands on the child's shoulders. Lou Belle was a frail little thing. "Santa wouldn't miss a sweet little girl like you."

"Yes'm," the girl said. "He don't come anymore. He left. He and my mommy. They went to live in sin."

"Goodness," Janice said. What an odd child.

Janice stood up. "Would you like to see my Christmas tree? I just finished decorating it, and I thought, There's no one around to see it except Al—that's my husband, and he couldn't care less about such things. And then I looked out the window and there you were, and I thought, I bet that little girl would like to see this tree."

"Yes'm," Lou Belle said, and she followed Janice Mosely into the house, and she studied the evergreen that Janice had harried her husband into buying and which she had then decorated carefully, all the while listening to Christmas music and ignoring her husband's grumblings and general humbuggery.

Lou Belle touched the glass ornaments. Lou Belle leaned close and blinked at the hand-sewn angels. She even rubbed the Styrofoam snowman against her cheek—it made a *skritch*, *skritch* sound—but finally she stepped back and said, "It won't catch nuthin'."

Lou Belle thought about it that night when she couldn't sleep. Silly old lady. What could you catch inside a house, anyway? Even with the best of traps?

Lou Belle couldn't sleep because tomorrow was Omen Day, the third day before Christmas. Last night they had baited the traps, and this morning they would get out of bed while it was still dark out; they would wake their father and he would make them eat breakfast first, while they craned their necks and peered out the back window, trying to squint through the darkness. Father would move slow, especially slow out of that meanness that adults have, and he would fix eggs and toast and talk about everything, as though it weren't Omen Day at all but any normal day and finally, finally, when they had all finished and were watching and fidgeting as their father mopped up the last of his eggs with a bread crust, he would say, "All right, let's see what we've got."

And it would still be dark, and he would grab up the big lantern flashlight and they would run down to the tree.

Who could possibly sleep the night before Omen Day?

And when it finally did come, when Lou Belle could stand it no longer and ran into her brother Hark's room and woke him and then the two of them fetched Danny and Calder and the long, long breakfast was endured, they pushed the screen door open and ran out into the darkness of the yard. Her heart thrummed like a telephone wire in a hurricane. The grass was wet under her feet.

She thought she would faint when her father, moving the flashlight over the tree, said, "There's a lizard. That's a red dot. Calder, that's you." She wanted to cry out, "No! Not Calder! I'm the Chosen!" But before she could scream, her father spoke again, in a low, awed whisper. "Well, would you look at that." And Lou Belle followed the flashlight's beam with her eyes, and there, flapping awkwardly, caught, like a wound-down toy, was a black, furry lump, and her breathing flipped backward and she said, in a hiccup of triumph, "Bat!" And she knew, before her father called out "Blue, that's Lou Belle," that it was hers.

And she didn't need her father to tell her that bat was best, that bat was the king of good luck. She clapped her hands and laughed.

"Light the tree, Lou Belle," they urged her, and she smelled the kerosene smell that was, more than anything, the smell of Christmas, and her father gave her the burning straw and she thrust it forward, and the whole tree stood up with flame, *whoosh*, and in the brightness she could see the bat, her bat, and she squealed with joy. Then her father started it off, with his fine, deep voice. "Silent night, holy night," he sang. They all joined in. "All is calm, all is bright."

"Listen," Janice said to her husband. "Do you hear that?"
"What?"
"Carolers," Janice said. "Isn't that nice?"

Because Lou Belle was the Chosen, she stole the mud turtle shell from Hark and filled it with smooth stones. And on Christmas Eve, just before twilight, Lou Belle distributed the stones among her brothers, and they each made their wishes on them and solemnly threw them into the lake, and then they all climbed into the back of their father's pickup truck and drove into town and on past the town and down to Clearwater and late, very late at night, with the salt air filling her lungs, Lou Belle fell asleep, her head resting on a dirty blanket smelling faintly of gasoline. When she woke it was dark, thick, muggy dark, and Hark was urging her out of the truck. She ran after them, instantly alert. A bouncing, silver ball on the grass was the orb of her father's flashlight.

They were in a suburb. She heard glass break and then Danny was beside her. "Come on, come on," he was whispering.

Oh. Her father had pushed open the sliding glass door to reveal, like a magician, a treasure of gifts, gaudily wrapped boxes, all strewn under a thick-bodied Christmas tree pin-pricked with yellow lights. Amid all the gift-wrapped boxes, a marvelous orange tricycle with yellow handlebars glowed.

"Oh," Lou Belle said. She pointed a stubby finger at the bike, and her father moved swiftly across the room, lifted the bike and returned to her.

"Shhhhhhhhhhh," her father said, raising a finger to his lips.

Hark and Danny and Calder were busy under the tree. Calder raised both hands, clutching a brand new air rifle, a smile scrawled across his face.

This is the best Christmas, the best, Lou Belle thought. Next year some of the magic would be gone. Other Christmases would bring disillusionment. She would learn, as her brothers already knew, that her father took great pains to discover a proper house, and that it was his vigilance and care in the choosing that was important, not the catch on Omen Day, not how fervently the wishes were placed on the turtle stones.

But for now it was all magic, and as they raced back across the lawn and piled into the truck, as the motor caught with a sound like thunder, as someone behind them shouted, Lou Belle sent a quick prayer to the baby Jesus, king of thieves.

Christmas in the future
with a special family.

LaZelle Family Christmas
Nina Kiriki Hoffman

Beryl's Tree

At my house, we talk our trees down for Christmas. The youngest who's gone through the transition sickness and has Earth skills does the tree talking, and this year, that was me. So, with Mama driving, I sat in the front seat of the van, where I hardly ever get to ride because my brothers, Flint and Jasper, and my sister Opal usually fight for it first (my sister Gypsum gave up scrambling for the front seat a while back). All alone, Mama and I drove up to the mountains above the Southern California town of Santa Tekla.

"I hate this," I said, clutching my pouch with my left hand and the door handle with my right, as Mama negotiated the twists and turns of the narrow mountain road.

"You say that every year, Beryl."

"Why do we need to kill a tree?" We were rising above the fog line. In winter, the fog drifts in off the sea in the mornings, usually burning away in the afternoons. For my tree day, Mama and I started early, driving through the gray. Now when I looked up past the tree branches tangling above the road, I saw blue sky with drifts of gray across it, cloud constellations and galaxies that shifted as I watched.

"It's tradition," said Mama above the purring labor of the engine. "It reminds us of important things."

"I don't understand," I said. I had looked at trees for thirteen years, watched them die under the weight of Christmas, and I had never understood. "Maybe I can find a tree that's already dead."

"Beryl!"

"Then it won't mind so much."

"When you find the right tree, it will come of its own accord, because you persuade it."

"How can I persuade it when I don't believe in what I'm doing? Why couldn't Flint do the tree? He liked doing it the last two years."

"It's a tradition for the youngest capable one to do it, and traditions don't exist without a reason," said Mama, in her "that's final" voice. I'm the youngest, and I'll stay the youngest for years. Even if my oldest sister Opal married and had babies, I'd have to wait until her kids went through transition, which usually happens at thirteen. I hugged my pouch and frowned at my future as a tree killer.

A few more kinks in the road, and Mama pulled over into a wide space and said, "Here is the place for you to start." She gestured toward a narrow gap between shoulders of dusty, tree-clutched cliffs. I opened the door and dropped to the ground, slinging my pouch over my shoulder.

The air was chill, and quiet except for the purring of a little creek between the mountain flanks. I smelled something sharp and sweet and spicy, my favorite plant odor, though I didn't know what made it. Sycamores had dropped leaf stars on the road, and beyond their dusty mosaic trunks I saw live oaks. I knelt and said the little star prayer that asks for guidance, then rose, picked my way down to the creek bed, and hopped rocks away from the road. I listened for tree talk. Great-Uncle Tobias had taught me how. For a little while I was deaf to anything but the brief murmur of leaf on leaf above and around me, and then I heard whispers: "Sun sun sun WATER bug sun sun sun carbon dioxide!" "Wind bring me bits of other to join with self, make seeds big and fat." "Water, water, sun."

"Seek," I whispered, "I seek I seek." I whispered and sang it as I walked, and after about half an hour, they realized there was something new in the conversational atmosphere.

"Seek what?"

"Seek one who desires to die."

When that penetrated, they got louder, and talked faster. "Axe murderers!" "Fire hands!" "Teeth faces!"

They were so loud I felt scared they would fall on me. Great-Uncle Tobias told me trees had a stretchy sense of time. Usually people walked past so quickly the trees didn't notice them, unless the people did something obnoxious. I wanted to run back to the car, slip out of the conversation and beneath their notice, forget all about the Christmas tree. But I remembered Mama saying that traditions existed for a reason. I waited, murmuring, "I seek one who desires to die, for tradition's sake."

Eventually they stopped speaking about things they'd suffered or heard of other trees suffering. I kept repeating myself. Tree voices dropped away, until I was standing, cold, in the forest, talking to myself.

I quieted. I waited. I wondered whether I should go back to the car and tell Mama there wasn't going to be a tree this Christmas. Then I noticed a small voice saying, "For tradition's sake?"

I walked toward it, and discovered the speaker was a small oak sapling.

"Speak to me," it said.

"If you come with me, I will cherish you. I will try to keep the life in you as long as it can be kept without soil. I and all my family will worship you, make offerings to you of things that look beautiful to us, and stare at you, each time reminding ourselves that you are a wonderful life-form and you and your seedmates share the Earth with us and we love you. And you will die. And we will love you even as you die and lose your chance to scatter seed." I murmured the words over and over, and somewhere deep inside I wondered what Flint had said to his trees the two years he did this, before I went through transition. The first year he brought home a pine, a small one with two tops. The second year, a eucalyptus sapling. I said, "We will celebrate your death with fire, the great transformer, and keep the image of you in our memories forever."

At last the little tree said, "I will come. I give up my seeds to you."

I felt stabbed to the heart. What did any of the things I said mean to a little tree? Why should it care if humans remembered it, or decorated it? What did that have to do with the perpetuation of its seedline? I opened my pouch, already murmuring the ritual thanks to the Lady and to the Lord, to the Elements and to the Spirits, to the falling of the fates. I took out my packet of tobacco and offered some to the tree and to the Earth that raised it. I got out my bottle of water and poured it at the base of the little tree, then dug with my hands and with my trowel to loosen the earth binding the roots. I was just going to add the unrooting powder that would let the roots become slippery and muscular enough so the tree could follow me back to the van when I stopped.

"Why?" I said. "Why do you say yes to me?"

"Trees have traditions. Every cold time, someone goes to live as humans, always the ones who are most curious. I grew knowing it might be me, thinking I might not mind choosing a death instead of waiting for an unknown one, realizing that at least my curiosity would be satisfied, and that this is a piece of the great Greenwork I can do."

"Thank you," I said, and loosed the unrooting powder, and the words to give the tree mobility. All the way back to the van, as I walked with one hand clasped to one of my tree's branches and the tree shuffled and rustled beside me, I pictured two peoples having traditional ceremonies that intersected at their heights, each achieving something mysterious, each not understanding what the other was accomplishing. Just before my tree and I climbed up to the road where the van waited, some other tree dropped an acorn on me. I put it in my pocket, and wondered: Was this too a part of the ritual of the trees? What part did I play?

"A beautiful tree, Beryl," Mama said, opening the back door of the van. I helped the tree up into the van and bound wet earth around its roots and sat beside it all the way home, one hand around a branch, the other cupping the acorn, wondering who answered whose prayers.

Flint's Lights

I always thought, when I hit eighteen, bam, out of the house, away from the family, GOOD-BYE.

It's much harder than that, though. I'm going to be eighteen two days after Christmas, and I'm having second thoughts. Now I understand why none of the others have left. Opal's the oldest, twenty-four already, and I never heard one movin'-on word come out of her mouth, before she turned eighteen or since. Jasper acts restless, but he doesn't leave, either; sometimes he goes off for a while, but he always comes back. And what could Gypsum do if she went out in the wide world, among the ungifted? Ungifted herself, but raised in the expectation of gifts. The world must look even scarier to her than it does to me, and my gifts are strong.

I always thought, gifts after transition. Stick around long enough to have Great-Uncle Tobias train me in them. Then go out and wreak havoc. Toe-to-toe with the wide world, and I planned to cheat, win, grin, and start over. But that's another broken dream. Used to be, when all my world was what could balance on a skateboard, my only dream was thrashing with the guys. I couldn't wait to gift so I could zoom up walls and across ceilings, maybe over water, maybe *under*water! Crash, tinkle. Gifts don't work like that. All mine did was make me scared of everything, because when I address my gifts, I never know what they'll give me.

Mama told me I was in charge of the lights this year, since Beryl's doing the tree now. "Strike some sparks, Flint," she said, which was her idea of a joke.

I went upstairs to try making lights, in case it was a skill that needed practice. I didn't want to ask Great-Uncle Tobias about it because he always tells me more than I want to know about things. Jasper wasn't home, and even if he had been, he might have been in a mean mood. He might withhold information just to spite me. Opal was concentrating on her own Christmas project, a special ornament, and she was sneery anyway. So I went to my room, turned on the goosenecked lamp by my bed, and sat on the rug between piles of dirty laundry, pieces of driftwood I'd been studying for the shapes inside, and pieces of driftwood I'd carved to let the shapes out. I stared at my hands in my lap.

Lights. We needed lights to put on the tree, and last year Jasper summoned up enough lights to festoon my tree, and dot the front of the house, making it look like a fairy palace after nightfall. He'd even placed lights on the ceiling of the living room. Was Mama expecting me to do all that? Jasper was always better at everything than I was, which was why I got interested in things I knew he wouldn't like, like wood carving.

How the hell did you make a light?

I thought about Jasper's gifts. He seemed so much more in control of his than I was of mine. If he wanted to turn Gypsum green or make it rain on me, he did it, no hesitations, no problems. He probably just said "Lights, appear," and his gifts obliged. No, he probably said something that rhymed. He was good at that stuff, what Great-Uncle Tobias called a power lubricant, something that made the interaction with gifts work better and easier.

I held my hands up. "Lights, appear before me here," I said, and felt the stirring under my skin that meant something gifted was happening. Then a small purple rip shimmered in the air in front of me. It widened into a floating curtain about a foot high and two feet wide, strings of purple and lavender beads made of light that shifted as if a wind were blowing them. It was beautiful and strange. The rustling in my hands went on, and tiredness stole over me. Great-Uncle Tobias said my main problem was learning when to stop supplying power and let what I had reached for exist by itself. I closed my hands into fists, cutting off the flow of power. The lights shivered and slipped away, a bead string at a time.

"This won't work," I said as the last strand of lightpearls winked out. Why wasn't the curtain there enough to stay,

when I had put so much power into it? Jasper hadn't played
battery for his lights last year. He just set them up and left
them.

I went down to the kitchen. It smelled like warmth and butter and fresh cookies. Gypsum was there, dropping spoonfuls
of batter on cookie sheets, looking wild and fuzzy and contented. She had dough in her hair, a streak of chocolate across
her nose, and a dusting of flour on her shirt. I grabbed a
cookie off a cooling rack and bit into it, then said, "How do
you make light?"

She shoved one tray in the oven and pulled another one
out. "It's an emission in the electromagnetic spectrum somewhere between heat and X rays," she said. "I can't remember
if everything makes it or if reflections count. I mean," she
held up her hand, staring at the outstretched fingers, "if the
light is coming from the fixture on the ceiling, and it hits me,
am I emitting photons or does the light bounce off—no, I'm
all mixed up. Anyway, you could try getting something hot
and heat it up into the visible spectrum, or you could do what
I do—turn on a light."

I finished my cookie (chocolate chip, still warm and
chewy) and held out my hands. "Tree lights, free lights," I
said, and suddenly there was a swarm of little green lights
above me. I closed my hands right away to stop the power
flow. These lights didn't disappear. They started out in a globular cluster, then peeled off, darting everywhere. Some flew
into the living room, some headed for the dining room, three
flew into Gyp's bowl of cookie dough, and one landed on her
forehead.

"Hey!" she yelped, reaching up to touch it.

"Is it hot?" I asked, going to her.

"No. Is it still there?"

"Yes." It looked like a glowing green penny, pressed into
her skin just above her nose.

"I can't even feel it."

"It looks funny."

"Thanks a lot! Free lights! What kind of powers do they
have?"

"I don't know," I said.

"How long are they going to last? How do I get it off?"

"It looks kind of neat, actually," I said.

She frowned at me and looked at the lights in the cookie dough. At first I thought they were just perching on the mountain of tan-and-chocolate-chip dough, but then I noticed—

"They're *eating* it," said Gypsum. The three lights in the dough were sinking into pits of their own creation. She lifted a wooden spoon. "Shoo!" she said, swatting at them. They giggled and tunneled deeper into the dough. "Damn!" she said. "This is no way to make light," she told me.

"But it worked. Better than the last thing I tried."

"Get specific," she said, leaning her elbows on the counter and staring at me. The light on her forehead looked like a third eye, greener than her other two, staring harder. "Map out exactly what you want, then put it into rhyme on paper, *then* try it out loud, okay?" Like the rest of us, she had sat through a lot of lessons with Great-Uncle Tobias. Nobody knew ahead of time who would gift and who wouldn't. She remembered her lessons better than I did.

"That's too worky," I said.

"A little work won't hurt you. It doesn't hurt me."

"Sure it does," I said, grabbing three more cookies and heading for the door. "You should see your face." Conjured cookies never tasted as good as ones somebody actually made from scratch.

In my room, three cookies later, I sat on the bed. I held up my hands. "Uh—lights on house, lights on tree, lights on ceiling, lights on—" I had been about to say me, but that would never do. Tomorrow was a school day, and effects I had conjured before sometimes lasted two weeks.

Despite my breaking off the rhyme before the end, I felt a prickling that started under the skin of my palms and spread up my arms, washing over my shoulders and down my chest and back. Oh, no. A major effect. At this point there was nothing I could do but wait and see what my gifts brought me, and try to pretend I had done it on purpose.

Heat flushed along my skin. I felt the power rising, flowing

out of me, felt it take the form of needles that rushed everywhere, poking holes in things, tiny punctures that let light
through from some other place. A moment, and my ceiling
was speckled with constellations; through my connection with
my power, I knew that all the ceilings in the house were, and
the front of the house was, and off on some road, needles
dived into the open window of the van and poked light holes
through the air around Beryl's tree.

I tensed my muscles to cut off the power flow, and waited
a moment, exhaustion pressing down on me like a lead blanket. Yes, I had managed to stop the flow. And yes. There were
still lights on the ceiling. After that, I fell asleep.

I woke up some time later, and there was no light on the
ceiling. Great-Uncle Tobias was sitting in a chair by my bed,
watching my face. His thick white hair looked more peaky
than usual, and his eyes looked tired, and they danced.

"What you did, Flint," he said.

"Yes?"

"It was fascinating. And very dangerous. It took your
mother and Hermetta and me to undo it."

I sighed. "What was wrong with it?"

"Well, the place the light was coming from is closer to a
source than we like to be. More than light was coming
through. Hard radiation, too. Not good for people and other
living things."

"I'm sorry, Uncle."

"Well," he said, and patted my knee. "You'll do it differently next time, won't you?"

"Yes."

He left.

I sat up, still tired in my bones, like I'd been skateboarding
down the biggest hill ever, tense the whole way because I
needed to pick a direction at the bottom, which was coming
faster and faster, and I couldn't see far enough ahead.

"Light," I said, staring at my hands. "Light."

I got up and went to my desk, opened the top right-hand
drawer, and fished my cash stash out from behind a stack of
graph paper, old math assignments, and some chewed pencils.
I sat on the floor and counted it. Twenty-four dollars, sixty-

three cents. It ought to be enough to buy some normal Christmas lights.

Maybe next year I'll get it right.

Gypsum's Cookies

Nobody can do anything without ingredients. That's what I tell myself, because in one sense it's true, and so it makes what I do as important as what the rest of my family does, even if what I do is less impressive. So what if one of their main ingredients is magic? So what if that's still a secret ingredient to me? So, I can still bake a good batch of cookies, and none of my siblings bothers to read recipes and learn methods, so that's beyond them. So there.

Before I came up with the Gypsum Theory of Ingredients, the kitchen in our house was just a big place I went several times a day in hopes that somebody had powered up some raw stuff into something edible, which they usually had. Everybody in the household was supposed to do some work, and I usually chose dishes, because I knew how to do dishes; my brothers and sisters and I had learned how in the years before they went through transition sickness. Grown-ups did all the cooking back then.

I woke up one morning when I was about twenty-one and thought about that. In the novels I'd been reading, I'd noticed that normal people cooked their own food instead of waiting for somebody with magic to do it for them, and it occurred to me that I wasn't just ungifted and incompetent and pitiful. I was *normal*. So why not try doing things like cooking? So it took longer, who cared? If it didn't work, that would be what everybody expected of me, and if it did work, I could surprise them all.

Now the kitchen is the heart of the house for me. I write things on the shopping list. I know what the more obscure tools are for. I've left my fingerprints here: I've scored the breadboard while chopping vegetables, and I melted a hole in the plastic spoondrip once when I left it too near the burner. A lot of what I've learned strikes my relatives as arcane and beyond them, so one of the secret things I cook up in the kitchen is my own smile.

This is the second year I tackled the Christmas cookies. This year I actually bought a book of cookie recipes, and I tried things that didn't even seem like they'd taste good. I didn't have to eat them. I just wanted to make mountains of cookies that would sit around the house testifying to my worthiness, and if I made cookies nobody wanted to eat, that meant my monuments would last longer.

Everybody wanted Tollhouse chocolate-chip cookies, though, so first I made millions of those. Then I started frenzying my way through a bunch of recipes with foreign names like *Berlinerkranzer, Krumkake, Pfeffernusse,* and *Sandkager.* It was weird how big a difference the way you treat butter, sugar, flour, and eggs made. I loved that.

It was like a spell, the ingredients the magic, the expression a result of how I shaped them.

I was rolling pieces of *Berlinerkranzer* dough to form wreaths when Jasper came in from outside, taking off his gold motorcycle helmet and running a hand through his light hair.

"You have something green on your forehead," he said.

"One of Flint's lights. He decorated me by mistake—I think."

Jasper picked up a piece of dough and bit it. "Yum," he said. Then he frowned. "Orange?"

"Orange rind. I think baking will make it taste better."

"It's pretty good now, just weird."

I watched him sample the dough again and thought, I wish we were children. Jasper and I were close before he went through transition. We got into so much trouble together Mama seriously considered sending one of us off to live with cousins, but Daddy talked her out of it. I worked the dough again, rolling it into pencil-thin lengths, then joining the ends. Jasper watched me load a baking sheet with cookies. I brushed their tops with meringue and added green and red candied fruit accents, then put the cookies in the oven, and he still stood there, a slight frown drawing a line between his brows, his hazel eyes shadowed.

"What?" I said as I went to the fridge for more dough.

"This stuff you're doing is so picky. You've already made the dough. I could spell it into those little rings in half a minute."

"Don't you dare," I said, then clapped a hand over my mouth. I hadn't said no to Jasper in a long time. It wasn't safe.

But he didn't look mad. "Why not?"

"Because, this is what I'm doing for our celebration," I said. "You do your part, and I'll do mine." It had been years since my heart was in the prayers we offered up on Christmas, because I thought the gods we honored had abandoned me; I was tired of petitioning them to take me back. I was normal, and I would make do with a normal lack of faith. Still, I said the prayers. And now, I discovered, I wanted to make my offering, too, whether there were gods to receive it or not. The people were here. They would receive. "This is a part of the job I like," I said.

"Cutting little leaves out of green fake fruit?"

"It's citron."

"Whatever it is, it's taking you longer to make these things than it will take us to eat them. They'll disappear, Gyp."

"That's the way cooking always works."

"I could snap them out, and you could have the rest of the afternoon off, do something more important or interesting."

"I want to be right here, doing this right now."

His frown deepened. I was afraid I had gone too far. Suppose he spelled me into living in the kitchen, baking endlessly until he was tired of the joke? Suppose he ignored me and snapped my cookies done anyway? Jasper could outspell everybody in the house except Mama, and she almost never interfered; "let them fight it out" was the LaZelle philosophy of child-rearing.

When Jasper didn't say anything, I leaned across the table and took one of my finished wreaths from the cooling rack. I held it out. He reached for it, his gaze still on my face.

"This is my spell," I said. I dropped the cookie in his hand, and the little wreath broke.

For an unbearable moment, we stared into each other's eyes. At last Jasper blinked, then turned away. "Thanks," he muttered. He stalked out of the kitchen, the broken cookie in one hand, his helmet in the other.

I pinched a ball off the chilled dough and tried to roll it into a snake. My fingers trembled too much. I got out the kitchen stool and sat down, staring at the floured surface of the butcher-block table, the leftover morsels of dough, the big ball, the little bit I had tried to work. Was I lying to myself? Was this work silly? Worthless? A waste of time?

"I smell something burning."

I turned. Helmetless, Jasper stood just inside the kitchen door, his face haunted. I jumped up and looked into the oven. "Damn," I said, and pulled out the sheet of burnt-bottomed cookies. I turned the sheet over the trash can and shook it till all the cookies fell into the trash.

"All that work," said Jasper.

"Yes, well," I said.

"Can I—"

I wiped the burnt bits off the nonstick cookie sheet with a paper towel. When Jasper didn't go on, I glanced at him.

"Can I try it?"

So many things to say jumped into my mind, but I let one after the other pass unsaid. I brought the cookie sheet to the table and reached for my abandoned dough, then glanced over my shoulder at Jasper. After a moment, he came to join me. I gave him a piece of dough. "You roll it out, like this," I said, and thought, Thanks.

Jasper's Carol

I find it hard to be thankful for something I'm still suspicious of. Thanks for the cake (are you sure it isn't poisoned?). Thanks for the toy (I think it's broken).

Thanks for my powers. (How come they work this way? How come Gyp's don't work at all?) They work really well. (When are you going to make me pay for them? If I use them wrong, will you take them away?) Merry Christmas.

Mama told me I was to write the carol this year, an expression of praise and thanksgiving for a whole year given us by the powers, Elements and Spirits, Lord and Lady, the Source, and of course, I should toss in a verse about hope and thanks for the year to come. I said I'd rather do any other Christmas chore than this.

She said everything else was too easy for me now.

But what if the carol wasn't good enough?

"It will be," she said, and smiled her "or else" smile.

I noodled on the piano and brooded about this year, wondering what had been good about it, and how I could express that in music. Art wasn't like magic; I couldn't just say, Okay, gifts, here's some notes, give me back a meaningful song that'll make everybody cry and feel good at the same time. I might be able to work backward, though; start with the feelings, and say, Please supply the notes to make these feelings happen. Of course, I'd need to be having the feelings first. Not very likely.

What did we have to be thankful for? Gyp got a job tutoring English at the community college. I had a new girlfriend. Flint managed to stay alive, in spite of everything. Beryl retained most of her innocence. Opal was prettier than ever. Mama and Dad still loved each other, and Great-Uncle Tobias hadn't moved out. Those were all things we could probably agree to be thankful about. So how come I felt mad instead?

I played the chords for anger, stomping doom chords, to get that out of my system. I thought about the Christmas carols I heard at the mall or on the radio, and tried making up something bright and gladdened, prancy and bouncy. That was easy, and incredibly unsatisfying. I started fitting words into the catchy melody I had come up with, and when I found myself rhyming "Presence" with "presents," I slammed the lid down over the keyboard and stomped out of the living room. I had figured out where the anger came from. Mama wanted me to feel something I didn't feel, thanks/glad/appreciate/love/return/blessing. Of all the sins I had committed, one I'd stayed away from was forcing anybody to feel something they weren't feeling. I'd avoided that one without realizing it, and now I was trying to violate my own somewhat elastic code of ethics.

I paced through the front hall, then through the dining room, the kitchen, the back hall, the study, and the living room again. I nearly tripped over the cord to Flint's lights as I stalked past the tree. The tree rustled at me, and I glanced at it, annoyed. It was a scruffy little oak tree, wearing Flint's white electric lights as if they were a pearl necklace. After a minute, I went over and collapsed on the couch, amid puffy squashed pillows that belched dust. I stared at the tree. "Look at me," it said, "look at me!"

"I'm looking," I said.

"I see you," it said, its voice faint but joyous, and I thought about my trees. I had collected seven before Flint figured out how to tree speak, and each year I'd been glad to go, because something happened in the course of finding a tree that made me feel like no matter what I was like, or who I was, I was doing something right. Trees didn't care that I'd hurt my sisters or terrorized my little brother. Trees didn't care that I was spiteful and mean at school. Trees just wanted to acknowledge that I was a human and they were trees and here we were, on the planet together, and it was nice to think about that at least once a year.

"You are beautiful," I told Beryl's tree.

"You are beautiful," it told me.

We stared at each other for a long time, and then I went to the piano and played what that felt like. It was a song with no words, and it wasn't really about gratitude or anything like that. It just said we're here together and I'm glad. I worked it over until it felt just right, then talked to the piano. It accepted the song. It liked it. It went on playing after I stood up, and I wandered out to the hall with my carol going on behind me. The house felt different. I ran upstairs and lay on my bed and fell asleep to the muffled sound of the carol seeping into the walls.

Opal's Ornament

I held them all when they were babies, even Jasper. I remember when he was an infant and I was two and a half, I sat on the big couch and Mama put Jasper into my lap. I hugged him so hard he squeaked. Mama taught me to be gentler with my love. I adored them all, before they could talk.

Something happens when babies start talking. I'm not sure what, but you just feel differently about them.

I was thinking about my ornament. I'm sure Mama just gave me this assignment because she couldn't think of something more useful for me to do. My gifts aren't up to anything major; she's already tested me on lights and Spirit invocation and fire, and I flunked them all. I'm not musical like Jasper, and even if it was all right for the eldest to tree talk, I never succeeded at that, either. So for the past six years I've made an ornament for the tree.

Last year, all I thought about was how to make my ornament more beautiful than the ones I'd made before; that's been my focus since I started. Beauty is something I understand. This year, though, I was thinking about babies instead of silver lace snowflakes inside iridescent bubbles, or mirror-bright stars with faint images of flowers etched into their surfaces.

Babies, and traditions. If the heart of the Christmas tradition was love and thanks for the family being together, maybe I should try to illustrate that somehow. I thought about loving my family, and somehow it got all tangled up with babies— nontalking babies. I took some woodchips I'd stolen from the woodpile, and cupped them in my hands, and thought, Gift me with the beloved image of Jasper, please, and there in my hands was a tiny baby with hazel eyes, wearing nothing but diapers.

The same thing happened when I asked for the beloved images of Gypsum, Flint, and Beryl.

I set the babies on the pink bedspread and studied them, and felt my heart melting. They looked wide-eyed, curious, wistful. Jasper reached up a chubby hand. Gypsum had her hands clasped over her belly. Flint was curled on his side, leaning on his fist. Beryl's hands lay open at her sides. I loved them all.

I took some more woodchips and asked for the beloved image of Opal, please. For a moment a tiny haze clouded my hands; when it cleared, I found the figure of a little blond girl with wide violet eyes. She was sitting back on her heels, her hands flat on her thighs, and looking down. She wore a flan-

nel nightgown with teddy bears patterned on it. She looked
about four. I felt like crying and didn't know why.

I set her among the others.

I took a stick and asked for the image of the beloved
Daddy. He looked just like he always does, shy, smiling, his
hair a little mussed. The image of the beloved Mama made
her look different: she wore a smile I couldn't ever remember
seeing on her face, so that she looked soft and pleased. The
image of the beloved Tobias came out just like him, tense and
relaxed at the same time, his smile broad.

I thanked my gifts for their help. I set everybody on the
bedspread and spent time arranging them, seeing who they'd
be next to, logically. Mama and Daddy together, of course,
standing to the rear, looking down at the children. After a hesitation, I put Gypsum and Jasper next to each other, because
when they were babies, they were inseparable, though since
transition it's another story. I put Beryl on Gypsum's other
side, and Flint on Jasper's other side. That left Great-Uncle
Tobias and me as loose pieces. We didn't fit together. I knew
Great-Uncle Tobias loved Jasper and Gypsum the best. I
asked my gifts to change him from a standing to a sitting position, and my gifts obliged. I set Tobias at Jasper and Gypsum's heads, just in front of Mama and Daddy.

And was left with me.

I held my image in my hand and cried.

After a while I rearranged everybody into a chronological
spiral, Great-Uncle Tobias at the outer edge, Beryl in the middle. It satisfied my desire for order, but it looked stupid. I put
everybody back the way they had been the first time, and then
put me, kneeling at the babies' feet, facing toward Great-
Uncle Tobias and my parents. That, at last, felt right. I was a
little outside, a little beyond, looking back at them. They were
absorbed in each other.

I gripped a stick of wood and asked my gift for a solid
cloud big enough to hold my little beloveds, and a cloud
formed in my hands, puffy and pearl-gray and strong enough
to support a whole family. I set everybody on it the way I had
planned. I hung it in the air and stared at it for a long time.
Maybe everybody would laugh at it. They had all said they

liked my earlier ornaments, but maybe that was the Christmas talking and not them. Maybe Jasper would hate being a baby. I listened to all these thoughts, and wondered if there was something better I could make, and decided there wasn't.

I took my ornament downstairs to the living room, where Beryl's tree stood, garlanded with Flint's lights. The music of Jasper's carol was playing, coming from everywhere, not from the stereo. A big plate of Gypsum's cookies sat on the piano. Daddy was alone in the room with all these things; he was sitting in his armchair, just looking. I walked over to him and held out my ornament. He accepted it. He studied it slowly, the way he looks at everything, turning it this way and that, looking at it from below and above, and at last he looked up at me with bright eyes and said, "Oh, Opal." He put my ornament on a side table and got up and then he hugged me so hard I almost squeaked. Then I knew everything would be all right, no matter what everybody else said.

A Christmas romance,
of passion and sorrow.

IXCHEL'S TEARS
José R. Nieto

❄

I

WALKING STEADILY OVER packed snow, frigid water seeping into his inadequate boots, Francisco found that he couldn't stop thinking about the argument. It had started over nothing; an errand forgotten by Elizabeth, his fiancée; a piece of mail undelivered. Annoyed by her calm disposition, he made the mistake of accusing her of not apologizing enough. Elizabeth in turn accused him of always accepting her apologies.

"What am I supposed to do?" Francisco said, incredulously.

"You're supposed to say that it's okay," Elizabeth responded, "that I shouldn't worry about it. You should say that you love me, no matter what I do. When you tell me 'I accept your apology' in that tone of yours—you know, that official voice you put on—it makes me feel awful, like I've done something beyond forgiveness. I mean, does a letter really matter that much to you?" While she spoke Elizabeth squinted her eyes, as if she had trouble focusing.

Francisco shook his head. "It's just cultural," he said to dismiss the issue. Often when they disagreed, when he was tired

or horny and did not feel like going at length, he was quick
to raise the spectre of ethnic difference. It saved the effort of
a good argument. Because of their disparate backgrounds—
he, the product of a large working-class San Juan family; she,
from a privileged Boston suburb—the subject carried the
weight and significance of a veiled threat. In normal circumstances the mere mention of culture would serve to stymie the
most heated debate, almost as if he had drawn a line on the
ground, a fragile border that Elizabeth did not dare cross.

This time, though, maybe because of the holidays, or possibly due to the impending nuptials (still six months away),
the two of them went on to rehash the rest of their disagree-
ments: city or country residence, casual wedding or formal re-
ception. Foolishly, Francisco revived an old fight about the
language and religion of their future children. That one kept
them at it until Elizabeth crossed her arms, glanced down at
her shoes and started to cry.

"I don't think we're ready for this," she said. It was those
words and that image—Elizabeth closed off, tears flowing in
thin rivulets, her face flushed to a pale red—that had sent
Francisco out carelessly into the brutal winter, thinly clad. His
shoes leaked, the overcoat had small rodent-type holes on the
back. Its lining had ripped weeks after he'd bought it at a
fancy secondhand store. He wished he'd forgone style and
bought sensible winter wear; as a graphic designer he made
enough to afford it. As it was, he usually wore the ragged
coat with a number of layers, or at least a sweater. Tonight he
had on only a T-shirt and cotton sweatpants.

His flight, Francisco now understood, had been propelled
by guilt and apprehension. For all their arguments he still
cared deeply for Elizabeth. They shared a history, a passage
through time. Their relationship (and he thought of it as an individual entity, a growing, living thing) had withstood passion
and indifference, conflict and resolution, even a year of separation while Francisco attended art school in Madrid. When
he'd first seen her, calmly sipping Grand Marnier from a
brandy snifter at a friend's dinner party, he had become convinced that they would end up together. That was three years
ago, but he could still picture her perfectly; wrist turned awk-

wardly, moist lips barely touching the contoured crystal as if
she were kissing a relic, bare legs crossed under the kitchen
chair, face and glass lit subtly by flickering candlelight. Right
then he had fallen in love with her.

The blustering wind sprinkled loose snowflakes on his
beard and hair, then swirled around his feet and crawled up
his legs to fill his clothes. Even inside the deep pockets his
fingers felt stiff and painfully dry. Across Cambridge Street
he noticed the colorful lights of a flower shop, gaudily decorated for the holidays. It was then that it hit him: a gift for
Elizabeth, that was precisely what he was after. The window
display looked like a magic screen, a tempting portal to a lush
tropical paradise. Improbable greens mingled with rich reds,
purples and yellows, tones made brighter by the dirgeful gray
of winter. Most of all, though, the plants promised soothing
temperatures. They reminded him of home. Francisco could
think of nothing better right now.

Christmas in Puerto Rico: *Noche Buena* up in the mountains, the family gathering as heavy raindrops played a quick
rhythm on the tin roof, heavy smell of roasted pork and
gandules hovering around Francisco like thick cigar smoke.
Loud, dissonant conversations over rum and watery beer . . .

The light changed and Francisco rushed across the street,
almost slipping into a pool of dirty slush. When he reached
the shop he opened the door so abruptly that the counter
person—a short brown man with shiny black hair and inset
eyes—jumped from his stool as if startled. The warmth and
green scent hit Francisco like a Caribbean wave; for a moment he stood at the entrance and let himself be enveloped.
He shook the snow from his face and clothes, then stomped
his feet.

"How can I help you?" said the man behind the counter.
His words came out with difficulty, twisted by a heavy accent.

"I'm so glad you're still open," Francisco said, "being like
it is Christmas Eve and all."

The man didn't respond. His leathery face showed a tenta-
tiveness that Francisco thought he recognized. He tried again,
this time in Spanish. The man smiled and perked up, as if a
weight had been removed from his back.

"Last minute we usually do good business," he said, "*plantas y flores*, people don't want to buy them too early. But I was going to close up soon."

"Well, I'm glad you didn't because I am in serious need of something nice for my *prometida*. It's kind of an emergency, really."

"Go ahead, look around. I can wait."

"*Gracias, hermano,*" Francisco said, turning toward a majestic display by the left wall. The plants were arranged in shelves, stacked all the way to the ceiling; giant succulent leaves shared space with delicate orchids and spindly lilies. On the floor, plastic buckets held cut flowers: carnations, violets, daffodils and many others Francisco had never seen before. A whole corner was crowded with red poinsettias—*Flor de Pascuas*, as they called them back home.

The possibilities baffled Francisco. He had no idea what would best serve as a peace offering, what would once again open the channels of communication.

"Is this all you have?" he said.

"No, no, no, we have a refrigerator in the back, you know, with the delicate ones, roses and things."

Roses, that sounded better to Francisco.

"Could I see them? That might be more appropriate."

"Sure, hold on a minute." The man got off the stool and walked to the front door. Immediately Francisco noticed a significant limp; he seemed to drag his right leg rather than step with it. He took a key chain from his stained orange apron and locked the door with some difficulty.

"I'm by myself here," he explained as he fumbled with the lock.

"No problem," Francisco said. The short man turned around and led him to the rear of the store. As they pushed through a little swinging gate behind the counter Francisco wondered if the limp was due to a war wound. The man's accent placed him someplace in Central America, where crippling violence seemed a likely possibility. Francisco considered asking, but thought better of the idea.

"So you're doing the Anglo thing," the man said, "giving Christmas presents, *Santa Clos* and such."

"Yes," Francisco said, then reconsidered. "Well, no, actually. See, I got into a big fight with my *prometida* tonight, that's what happened. Probably holiday stress, I think, combined with the wedding it's making us kind of edgy."

"That's what I've been telling people, why do they go crazy with the gift-giving thing on Christmas? I mean, isn't the baby Jesus gift enough for everybody? Take it easy, I tell them, wait until the sixth. . . ."

Francisco shrugged. "Well, I'm from Puerto Rico," he said, "and we give presents on both Christmas and Three Kings Day. We kind of play it both ways, I guess."

"Oh," the man said, as if disappointed, "I didn't know they did that in Puerto Rico."

For a moment Francisco expected to become enmeshed in an argument about the Americanization of Puerto Rican culture (Lord knew that he'd heard them before), but as the man limped down the hallway he did not say another word.

They walked past a cluttered supply room—black bags of potting soil, miniature hoes, fertilizer—then through a glass sliding door covered with mist. From inside, the refrigerated case reminded Francisco of a small *bodega* aisle, if slightly colder. Harsh fluorescent lights illuminated the space, somewhat diminishing the impact of the colorful arrangement. Still, the packed shelves were stunning. Each level displayed hundreds of flowers: roses, cut orchids, tulips. As an artist Francisco was quick to detect subtle permutations of hues and shapes, careful patterns that served to enhance the visual experience; round petals mingled with insectlike blossoms, wiry stigmas hung from bright red poppies and reached lovingly into the adjacent bellflowers.

"Did you do this?" Francisco asked.

"What do you mean?"

"I mean, did you put this room together?"

The man looked around and smiled. "Yes," he said, "that was me. My cousin Eriberto, he owns the store and he used to keep the place in such a mess, but I straightened it out."

"It's beautiful," Francisco said absently. The man smiled again and nodded, but did not speak.

"Why don't we do this," Francisco said, "why don't you

put together an arrangement for me. Put your nicest flowers together in a bouquet, I'll pay whatever it costs."

"We've got catalogues if you want to see them. . . ."

"No, that's fine, I trust you."

"Bueno," the man said, then with a quick wave of his arms sent Francisco out to the front of the store.

While he waited for the flowers Francisco paced back and forth, framed by walls of greenery, and in his mind he kept running Elizabeth's words—"I don't think we're ready for this . . ."—and with every repetition they became more definite, until, after a couple of turns, they had changed to "I know we're not ready for marriage . . ." and finally "We shouldn't get married." The weight of the imagined statement stopped him in midstep and made him shudder.

A few minutes later the man came forth with the finished bouquet. To his surprise Francisco found it rather disappointing. Not that the arrangement itself was ugly, far from it. The lavender orchids looked sublime nestled within a bunch of yellow chrysanthemums, and the single, central rose, red like a burning torch, conveyed a sense of longing and desire. But as he cradled the flowers in his arms Francisco wondered if such a gift was really suitable. Within weeks, he realized, the blooms would be nothing but wilted stems and dried petals— not exactly the message he'd wanted to deliver to his fiancée.

Francisco stared at the bouquet for a moment, then glanced quickly at the man. He was smiling, apparently satisfied with his work. Francisco couldn't blame him; he'd really done a good job.

"This is fine," he said as convincingly as possible, "they're beautiful. Now, how much do I owe you?"

The man dropped his smile just as Francisco finished the question. "Make it twenty," he said in a dry voice, "that'll be fine, twenty."

Francisco paid the man, thanked him, then headed for the door. Outside it started snowing again; thick clumps slid slowly down the tempered glass, leaving watery trails like tears. People walked hurriedly on the frozen sidewalk, wrapped tightly in bright ski jackets and woolen hats. Francisco paused just as he was about to push the door open,

right hand stuck to the cold glass. Suddenly he couldn't face
the prospect of going back to the apartment, of stepping na-
kedly into the sharp wind, carrying with him such a slight offering.

"What is it?" the man asked.

Francisco said the first thing that came to mind: "It's the
cold, I just can't stand this freezing weather."

After a moment the man said, "Why don't you come out
back to the office, I'll make some *café con leche* so we can
heat up your insides. It's not like I want to head out there either."

"My name's Agustín Irriñosa," the man began. He held the
coffee cup right under his nose and took a deep breath.

"Francisco Arriví."

"You said you're from Puerto Rico, is that right?"

"I live here in Cambridge now, but that's where I'm originally from. I left the island when I was eighteen. . . ."

"I've heard it's nice down there," Agustín said, smiling.

"Well you know," Francisco said, then paused to take a sip.
The liquid burned his tongue but felt good going down; he
could feel it drip all the way to his belly. "It's home so you
don't really think about it much until you're gone."

"Bet you think about it now," Agustín said, "with this
weather I mean."

"Yes I do," Francisco said plainly.

"I think about home too, Guatemala." Agustín stroked his
chin, then leaned back on the chair. Francisco rested his elbows on the crowded desk and sighed.

"Must've been rough," he said. "I've read horrible things
about the war."

"The war was one thing," Agustín said, his free hand fluttering, "but there was so much more to life than that. People
think it's hell, but we had our share of happiness, me and my
family, when the fighting stopped we made *milpe* grow with
our hands, we drank *balche* and watched the sun being smothered by the rubber trees. And when the stars came out we told
stories to each other, tales of *Cha-Chaac* and *Kukulcan*, but
most of all, no matter what the soldiers did to us, we were al-

ways warm, and the trees never died and in the river the water always flowed."

Francisco nodded hesitantly and drank from the steaming cup. At first he did not know how to respond; what Agustín described was so far from his staid urban experience. Instead he stared at a small framed picture of Jesus hanging on the opposite wall. Between his pierced hands he held a realistic-looking heart, like an Azteca sacrifice. *Sagrado Corazón*, Francisco thought.

"What about snow," he said after a moment, "what did you think of it when you first saw it."

Agustín turned away like he'd smelled something awful.

"Bah," he said, "it's just frozen water, that's all it is."

Francisco chuckled, splashing coffee onto the desk. "I was never too hot on it myself," he said as he reached for a napkin to clean the mess. Soon Agustín was laughing as well.

"You hate it here too, huh?" he asked.

While considering the question Francisco ran a hand through his hair and glanced blankly at the paneled ceiling. Originally he'd come to Boston only for school, fully intending to return to the island. But then his parents divorced and going to Puerto Rico lost some of its urgency. He got a lucrative job, he made good friends in the city, he met Elizabeth. He fell in love.

He remembered the walk to the flower shop, icy gusts running through his flimsy clothes like needles.

"I don't know," he said, "sometimes. I miss a lot of things about Puerto Rico; the language, old San Juan, my family. Adjuntas, up in the mountains where my grandparents lived. I miss the sea, I guess, water warm like from a bathtub. Not like here, *verdad*? Anyway, my fiancée and I talked once about moving down, but you know, Elizabeth has her career, she doesn't speak any Spanish, she's real close to her family—"

Agustín seemed taken aback for a moment. "Elizabeth?" he said like it was a mouthful. "You mean she's a *gringa*?"

"She's Anglo," Francisco said, annoyed by the man's reaction. He'd gotten the same words, the same expression from

a number of Latino acquaintances. In his mind Francisco
dusted off a long list of arguments to explain his decision.

"I'm sorry," Agustín said, quickly regaining his composure,
"I didn't mean to—"

"I understand," Francisco said, and was immediately
brought back to his argument with Elizabeth. The thought
made something twist uncomfortably in his chest. It was time
to go home, he'd been away long enough, almost an hour.
Though he wasn't looking forward to facing his fiancée,
Francisco realized that gift or not he had little choice. There
were, after all, matters left unresolved.

"Listen," he said as he pushed away from the desk, "I really should go back to my *prometida*. Thanks for your
hospitality—"

"*Espérese un momentito,*" Agustín said quickly, "are you
sure that's what you want to take to your fiancée?" He
pointed at the bouquet on Francisco's lap. "The way you
looked at it," he continued, "you know, when I handed it to
you, it was like you didn't care for it at all."

"Well it's beautiful," Francisco said, gently stroking the
rose petals, "but ... I don't know, maybe I should get her
something that's going to last. I thought of getting a plant, but
that just wouldn't have the same effect as the flowers. I mean,
I already got her a Christmas present, a really nice bracelet in
fact, but this, this has to be different. . . ."

Francisco paused, then looked down to the coffee cup. "We
really went at it tonight," he said. "Jesus, you should have
heard us! And, well, I have a feeling that when I get home tonight, I think there's a chance she's going to tell me that it's
over. So you see, what I want, it has to be something special. . . ."

Excited, almost laughing, Agustín stood up and walked to
Francisco's side. "I think I have exactly what you need," he
said.

With quick steps (considering the man's prominent limp)
Agustín led Francisco down a dusty stairwell, past heating
ducts and clanking water pipes, then through an iron gate and
into the tiny basement. Right across from the entrance, stand-

ing slightly askew against the cracked wall, stood a smaller version of the refrigerator upstairs; this one could have actually been a soda dispenser. On the middle shelf there was a delicate ceramic vase decorated with jaguar paws and proud quetzal birds. Within it lay a sole cut orchid, unlike any Francisco had ever seen. Huge silver-colored petals reflected the fluorescent glare like distorted mirrors.

"It's an Ixchel's tear, a moon orchid," Agustín explained, "it came from El Petén, near my home in Guatemala."

"I've never . . ." Francisco began, but let his voice trail off as he approached the refrigerator door.

"Most people haven't. Only a few of them grow in the entire Yucatán peninsula."

Francisco opened the door and knelt down in front of the flower. From up close the orchid's reddish center seemed to glow, as if it contained a dying ember. Had it not been for the way the petals quivered under his breath, he would have sworn they were made of steel.

"This is," he said, stumbling with the words, "this is unbelievable. Why, I mean, why would you keep it down here, hidden away?"

"Because it's not for sale," Agustín said, looking at the floor. "Eriberto, he doesn't know what to do with it, he doesn't even have a price for it yet."

"If you're not selling it then why are you showing it to me?"

Agustín paused and stroked his cheek and walked closer to Francisco. He put a heavy hand on his shoulder. "Because I'm giving it to you, that's what I'm doing."

"I don't understand," Francisco said.

"It's Christmas," Agustín said with a forced grin, "and that's what you do for Christmas, right?"

"But won't your boss—"

"What is he going to do, fire me? I'm his cousin and I work for nothing, just room and board. Besides, that orchid didn't cost him a cent. It was me who got it, you see, I brought it with me when I came from Guatemala." For a moment Agustín seemed angry, but at what Francisco could not tell.

The thought of receiving such a gift seemed unreal to Francisco. It was as if a stranger had offered to buy him a house or a car; it just didn't happen. He stepped away from the flower and pursed his lips, then slowly shook his head.

"Take it," Agustín said with some urgency, "I'm telling you, that's what you want."

"How long will it last?" Francisco asked sheepishly.

"That's the thing," Agustín said, "my Quiché *mama*, she used to tell me tales of the moon orchid, and what she said to me was that the blossoms, even if they're torn from the plant, they last forever. They never die. This one my mother got years ago, I carried it with me in an ammunition box. I waded across wide rivers and pushed through thick forests, I ran with it across two borders, and now look at it, it's still as beautiful as when she found it."

Perhaps because Agustín seemed to him like a kindred spirit—as much of an artist with flowers as he was with brushes and pens—Francisco found it natural to believe his story about the undying orchid. Aesthetically it made sense; blossoms had always been used to represent feelings of love and affection. Why should they, then, perish?

Reverently, Francisco reached into the refrigerator and took the vase in his hands. To his surprise there was no water inside. He rested it against his chest and felt a strange warmth exuding from the blossom—almost like a living thing—and he thought, Agustín's right: this is exactly what I need. When Elizabeth sees the orchid she will be overwhelmed by its beauty, by the utter perfection of its form, and she will see, actually see, what I truly feel for her. In her slim hands she will hold the full extent of my devotion.

Before, he had told Agustín that he wasn't looking for a Christmas present. He'd been wrong. The moon orchid was the perfect Christmas gift, not just for Elizabeth, but for their relationship; a symbol concretized, like the baby Jesus, an embodiment of the permanence of love.

"Thank you," he said, "thank you. You don't know how much you've helped us. I think with this you've given us a future."

Agustín opened his mouth but did not say a word. Instead

he took Francisco's left hand and shook it vigorously. With visible effort he lifted his fused leg and limped to the cement stairs. Still in awe, Francisco followed.

Once upstairs the man spent a few seconds playing with the lock, then pushed the door open. Immediately, the arctic wind rushed in, tussling the poinsettia leaves and stinging Francisco's face and bare hands.

"Feliz Navidad," he said and stepped into the cold. Through the glass window he saw Agustín mouth the same words.

After tucking the orchid under his coat, he walked to the curb and hailed a cab.

II

From the street the second-floor apartment appeared empty; there were no lights on in the windows and at eight-thirty Francisco thought it too early for Elizabeth to have gone to bed. Could she had moved out of the house so quickly? He shook his head to dispel the painful thought; his *prometida* would have never acted so rashly.

As soon as he'd stepped inside Francisco flicked the light switch and yelled "Elizabeth!" but there was no response. Out of habit, he reached behind the couch and plugged in the Christmas tree. The bulbs lit up immediately, but took a few minutes to start alternating. This year, because of all the wedding preparations, the smallish fir had ended up sparsely decorated. A single long strand of colored lights clung awkwardly to the abundant needles. Under the tree they kept a wooden manger scene complete with mother, father, baby and animals. The Three Kings—small stubs with golden crowns—stood impassively on the other side of the room. Every night before going to bed Francisco would move them closer to their destination.

He walked with a quick gait to the kitchen and carefully placed the moon orchid on the counter, right by the maplewood cutting board. Taped to the pantry, Francisco found a hurriedly scrawled note from Elizabeth. In it she explained that she had not felt like being alone tonight, so she'd gone to her sister's, who lived only a few minutes away. At the bottom of the torn sheet she wrote down the phone number (as if he could forget that number) and next to it she inscribed in tall letters CALL ME.

Immediately Francisco reached for the wall-mounted phone and picked up the receiver. He'd already pressed the first digit when he thought, No, no, there you go again, acting, talking without thinking. That's what got you in trouble in the first place, *idiota*!

What was he going to say? He'd placed all his hopes in the orchid, in the meaningful act of gift giving. How could he have known that he would first have to talk to Elizabeth? Once again he felt the familiar sting of muted panic. It was as if he were standing in front of an empty canvas, pencil tip pressed lightly against the smooth surface, images turning fast inside his head, too fluid to capture in a single frame. The words were all there, but not quite in the right combination.

He sat on the kitchen stool, cracked his knuckles, then shook his arms to loosen up. Obviously he needed a clear mind, and patience. Much patience.

All of a sudden a thought crossed Francisco's mind that he tried hard to ignore; in Spanish he would know exactly what to say to Elizabeth. For all his years in Boston, he still found it easier to communicate emotions in his native language. Even the word *amor* seemed to hold more significance than its English equivalent. In Spanish, after all, he would never say "I love pizza," or "I loved that movie," uses that served to cheapen the expression, making it less meaningful. The phrase *te amo* implied a certain level of passion, a careless ardor that could never be conveyed in English; to Francisco it was almost magical. He'd only used it frivolously once—in an ill-fated attempt to bed a stunning classmate—and he had immediately regretted it.

He closed his eyes for a moment. Rubbing his forehead, he said out loud, "Maybe I should wait for her to call me." Yes, that was the rational thing to do, make sure she has had a chance to cool off. Taking the initiative could only make things worse.

Francisco took a cookie from a porcelain jar in the pantry

and began to bite methodically around the sprinkled center. Soon he was staring at the moon orchid. The glittering petals reminded Francisco of his conversation with Agustín, of how easy it'd been to talk to him about his life in the island. When he blurted in Spanish that he missed Puerto Rico the man simply nodded and accepted the statement. If he'd been talking to Elizabeth he would have had to explain so much that in the end he would have given up and said nothing. Sitting as he was on that wobbly stool, staring deep into the fiery heart of Ixchel's tear, Francisco could not deny the attractiveness of cultural symmetry; one person talking in precise, descriptive terms, another listening intently, comprehending fully. How he wished it were that easy with Elizabeth.

He remained still on the stool more than an hour, absorbed by the blossom's delicate curvature. Inside the folds he could see twisted reflections of himself and the kitchen—light particles dancing in swirling, concentric patterns, like water down an open drain. Yes, that was the image; a tiny but powerful maelstrom, its flow drawing the fear and discomfort from him, leaving behind a strange but satisfying emptiness.

He was roused by the persistent ringing of the buzzerlike doorbell. Annoyed by the interruption, he stood up slowly and headed for the downstairs foyer. As he walked through the living room, Francisco discovered that the strand of colored lights had slipped from the Christmas fir. It now lay coiled around the tree's base, blinking arrhythmically.

"Jesus," he said. Before he could take a closer look the doorbell rang again.

He climbed down the stairs as quietly as possible since he didn't want to disturb the Portuguese family on the first floor. The two little girls had to be asleep already. After only eight months in the states they had come to take Santa Claus very seriously.

In the tiny viewer Francisco saw the man from the flower shop. Agustín stood on the porch shivering, even though he was wrapped in a large padded coat that looked like a comforter. Without hesitation, Francisco opened the door.

"Well, this is a surprise," he said. Agustín paid no heed to the pleasantry and pushed past him, then limped fast up the

wooden staircase. Hanging from his left hand there was a
rusted-green ammunition box. Francisco turned to look at the
curious sight but did not move from the foyer.

"Where's the flower, the moon blossom?" the man yelled
from upstairs. Francisco reacted like he'd just been shaken
from a fond reminiscence. He rushed up the stairs after
Agustín. By the time he made it to the kitchen the man had
already taken Ixchel's tear from the ceramic vase and was
placing it tenderly inside the box.

"Tell me," he said, closing the metal lid, "are you still in
love with your fiancée?"

"Of course," Francisco said. As if to convince himself he
repeated, "Of course I love her."

Shaking his head, Agustín ran stubby hands over his face
and drew closer to him.

"Where's Elizabeth, Francisco?" he said.

"At her sister's, she went to her sister's after our fight this
afternoon. Anyway, what does that have to do with my orchid?"

Agustín pulled on a small metal handle to close the latch
on the ammunition box. He took off his coat and laid it out
on the kitchen stool, then with one smooth motion lifted himself and sat on top of it.

"In the jungle we believe in circles," he began, "for many
years my *mama* tried to explain that to me. Strange that it's
in the States where I finally understood."

"Circles?" Francisco asked.

"We Quiché believe that Ixchel's tears are a gift from *la
luna*, the sun's consort. So sad is she when she's alone in the
sky that she cries, and her tears, when they hit the ground
they turn to beautiful things, moon blossoms. So you see,
from sadness comes something of beauty.

"But the thing is, it doesn't stop there, because the moon
orchids live by sucking the life out of plants around them,
they pull *la esencia*, that's why the flowers can live forever.
When you find them they're almost always in the middle of
an open clearing, surrounded by rotten trees. The Mayas, they
used the tears to open up the forest for the *milpe* fields. Better

than burning, I'm sure. So you see, death leads to food, to life."

Francisco was reminded of the scene in the living room. "That's what happened to my Christmas tree," he said, "that's why you kept the flower all by itself in that tiny basement. Well, if that's all, we'll just keep it someplace—"

"Do you realize that Elizabeth is still waiting for you?" Agustín interrupted. The harsh tone made it sound less like a question than an accusation.

Francisco felt like he'd just slipped underwater. All of a sudden he became aware of the stupidity of his thoughts and behavior since he'd arrived at home with the flower. How could he have waited so long to go after his fiancée? Pointing tentatively at the box he said, "Was that, I mean could that have been . . . ?"

Agustín nodded. His eyes were covered with red lines, like cracked marbles.

"But how?" Francisco said.

"After the empire fell apart, *curanderas* like my *mama* found out that Ixchel's tears could also drain strong feelings from people; hate, anger, jealousy. They can soothe someone who's in pain, or end a fight between brothers." He paused for a second, then said, "They can suck the love from even the most passionate couple. . . ."

Francisco took a step back and glared intently at Agustín. The man lowered his head and began to speak in a low, pleading voice. Throughout his hands remained on his lap, still.

"It was the cold, that's what it was. You walked into the shop and your face was the color of snow and your hands were shaking and you told me how much you hated the cold, how much you wished you were back home, and the thing is, you *can* go home, you can take a plane tomorrow and you'll be there. Me, I'm stuck here. You see, about a year ago I struck a soldier who'd been trying to burn our fields, and since then my life's been worthless in Guatemala. That's why I ran away, that's why I had to come to this frozen hell to work for my cousin.

"I long for my home as much as you do, but I can't go anywhere, you understand, I don't have a green card, no permits or anything, and if I'm caught they'll send me back to die. But you, all that keeps you here's a woman, a *gringa*. . . ."

"You had no right," Francisco began in anger, but stopped when he realized that Agustín was quietly weeping.

"I know, I know," he said, "but the thing is, I thought I was helping you, I thought I was giving you the warm beaches and the green mountains, I thought I was giving you back to your family. I mean, what better gift is there than something you wish you could give to yourself?"

Francisco leaned against the counter and put his hands in his pockets. He took a couple of deep breaths, then said calmly, "Why are you here then?"

Agustín looked up. His face glistened with tears.

"Before you left, you said something that stuck in my mind, even after I locked up the store and headed home I just couldn't stop thinking about it. You said that I had given you your future, and I kept thinking about what my Quiché *mama* said to me when she handed me the Ixchel's tear, right before I left. She handed me that ammunition box, and she told me, if you want to feel better, if you miss us too much, open the box and let it clean your mind. I never did though, even when I was starving in refugee camps, even when I broke my knee and spent months in a leper's hospital. You see, she gave me a choice—"

"Which you are now giving me," Francisco interjected. Agustín closed his eyes and nodded quickly.

"The moon orchid can help you," he said, almost whispering. "It can drain the things that make you fight with your *prometida*. But the thing is, it would also let you think, and maybe then you'll decide that it's better to go back home, that you belong in your *islita*. The question is, do you want to take that chance?"

For an instant—perhaps because of his tears and the blue glimmer of the fluorescent lights—Agustín's eyes looked blank, as if he were blind. Francisco was momentarily taken aback by the illusion. Then a curious thought crossed his mind: Agustín's mother, she must have been a wise, wise woman. Right then and there he knew he had the answer.

"Take it away. Please take the flower with you."

Agustín nodded and jumped down from the stool. He slipped on his coat, took the ammunition box and put it under his arm and walked out of the kitchen. The limp made his body bounce awkwardly, like a needle on a scratched record. A minute later Francisco heard the muffled bang of the outside door being shut and knew that Agustín and Ixchel's tear were gone.

Back to square one, he thought. Guess the man was right about circles.

Elizabeth's note was still where he'd found it, taped to the pantry. The last line—CALL ME—seemed larger than before, as if in the ensuing hours it'd grown in importance. Instinctively Francisco looked at his watch. Five minutes past midnight; maybe it was too late to call.

He picked up the phone anyway. As he dialed his heart beat as if his chest were empty; every palpitation seemed to echo against his ribs and slowly fade away.

"Hello?" The voice took him by surprise; there had barely been a ring. Elizabeth must have been sitting right by the phone.

"It's me," he said.

"Where have you been?" she said angrily. "I've been waiting here for hours! How could you walk away like—"

Francisco blurted out, *"Te amo, Elizabeth."*

Elizabeth was quiet for a minute. "Francisco," she finally said, and the way she said it—the tenderness in her voice, the music in her inflection—made it clear that she understood.

Christmas among the immortals.

A Midnight Clear
Wil McCarthy and Gregory R. Hyde

"Something temperature something something," said the old man to Solov. The man's face looked like a pile of spilled linen, white and dry and wrinkled. From within the pile, two gray orbs looked down at him, their too-shiny surfaces flashing and flickering in the light of the iron-caged fires. The mouth hung partway open, and within writhed a tongue that was wet and dark.

"Get me back," Solov tried to say. His skin crawled with the sensation of wind, with the eerie, open feeling of the night sky over his head. "I can't stay here, I can't live here." His voice was a stuttering croak, and he imagined his own face softening and wrinkling.

A portion of folds separated beneath the gray eyes, the mouth working and changing shape. "Something effects of the fever something something," it said. The man leaned over Solov, brought a hot and leathery hand against his forehead. His breath smelled of decay, of living things consumed.

Solov was very cold despite the rags draped and piled upon him, and the breeze seemed to pass, unwarmed, between the fires. But a fever? No, that was not possible. Perhaps the word had been *fear*, or *flavor*, muddled by quick and breathy tones. Such a strange voice.

Not human, Solov reminded himself. The man was shant, mammalian, burning and withering with the free-radical fires of an oxidation metabolism. Someday he would . . . Breath would cease and blood would congeal and the fires within him would cool and he would . . .

"It's cold here," Solov said as heavy darkness reached up to pull him down again, into unquiet sleep.

With a start, he sat upright, opening his eyes, rubbing out the cobwebby filaments of sleep. On three sides of him rose walls of dark wood, with rectangular openings spilling light in across the floor. The fourth wall was open, swung wide like the door of a cabinet. Outside were other structures, great wooden boxes with jointed doors and window shutters all folded out, like puzzle boxes half as high as the leafless trees. A lattice of shadows dusted the hard-packed ground and the flattened grass.

The day was bright with sunlight, but Solov's eyes adjusted slowly, until he could see that the walls around him were covered with shelves and drawers and narrow slots. In a few, he saw children sleeping. A ladder with rollers reached to the top shelf, where Solov saw jugs, and crates, and bales of what seemed to be gigantic leaves.

Another jug lay beside him, its neck stoppered with a wooden peg. Carefully, he picked it up and sniffed it. Grimaced. This was strong solvent, pungent even through the primitive seal. He remembered having some of it poured on his tongue, scouring his dry mouth, burning and freezing the insides of his head.

The boxes outside seemed to be stationary a few millimeters off the ground. Underneath, Solov saw, almost invisible in the daylight, the faint blue tint of a float field.

"So you are something something live," said a voice behind him. Solov turned and saw the man with the wrinkled face standing in an opening in the far wall. Behind him, a small heard of oxen grazed in a savanna.

Solov clutched the coarse blankets to his chest.

Shanty, my God I'm in a shanty. He swallowed back an urge to panic. The shantytowns never stayed put for long. The structures, hovering on their float fields, were endlessly pulled around by oxen teams. Journey without end, without destination. Solov had never actually seen a shanty, but he'd seen their trails from the sky during his infrequent trips between Unders; four burn marks on the ground, a swath of bare, trampled earth. He glanced at the ground and decided they hadn't been camped here much more than a few days.

How long had he been asleep?

The shant was eyeing him calmly, showing no desire to speak further or move from where he was standing. He regarded Solov with interest, as if watching him weaken and dry out in the untreated air.

How had Solov come to this terrible place? He remembered his ill-fated decision, casually made, to visit Under-Evans. He wanted to see the delicate crystal sculptures they made there, to compare them to the crystal sculptures in UnderPike and in UnderGreen, his home. Solov had a high regard for fine crystal. But the lorry's float coils had burned out, and it had heeled over and slipped down through the air, and the Austin Bluffs loomed large as he jammed and jammed on the useless brake pedal. He remembered the feeling of dread, remembered the impulse to scream, nothing else.

Had the Rangers looked for him? Surely he had been reported missing. Would they think to look in a shanty?

"Something cold-blooded something something," said the man. He stepped forward, picked up the jug next to Solov's bedroll, and tipped it back, taking a long drink. "Daily nutrition is a something something of the way we something in the winter," he said, drawing his sleeve over his mouth. "We don't turn away, like people something something under the mountain." He handed the jug to Solov.

Solov took it, not knowing what else to do. He set it down again where it had been.

The man walked slowly to a shelf, pulled a bowl out of a wooden rack, filled it with an assortment of things from barrels on the wall. Pieces of plants, and, Solov thought, of animals as well. From an urn, he added water to the bowl, and then he sat down on a low stool and began to stir the bowl's contents with his fingers.

The mixture looked sticky as he scooped it into his mouth.

Solov felt a tingling sensation up and down his back, up and down his scalp. He had known this, he had known that wild things did this, but to actually *see* it was . . .

For one life to continue, other lives must . . . The lives of plants and animals and even people must . . .

Solov must have made a face, because the man laughed at him. "Something something out here you need something to sustain. You take something, you have something and something something. You die from having nothing."

The man laughed again, folds and eyes transforming. Solov looked down at the ground, saw a trampled flower, wrinkled and dried. Old, he thought.

Old.

The man's laugh sounded like failing float coils, like the eroded bearings of the gate down to UnderGreen. Worn out. Up for replacement. Solov looked at the man, his wet and wrinkled mouth, his withered and spotted skin.

And Solov looked at his own outstretched arm, and saw that brown spots had begun to form there as well. The flesh seemed to hang more loosely than it should.

"Something something," the man, the old man, was mumbling.

"Do the boots fit something comfortable something?" The old man asked, slowly, in a voice that seemed genuinely interested in his satisfaction.

"It's very cold," Solov said. The day was fading again, and in the growing chill Solov could see mist rising from the man's mouth as he spoke. The air was sharp.

They were walking on the edge of the savanna, on the edge of the forest. Solov and the old man and a dozen or so shants, men and women in various states of decay, and perfect little children. They wore clothes the color of soil and autumn leaves, smoked pipes, and occasionally laughed. Snow crunched under Solov's feet. On the horizon, above the forest, the mountains were gray and brown and white.

Across the expanse, at the distant horizon, the setting sun ignited a spectrum of colors he was sure he had never seen before, not even in crystals. He had seen mountains and sky before, from the windows of float lorries. But the trip between Unders was quick, an inconvenience rather than a process in itself, and he had taken little interest in the view. Now, standing out in it, feeling it against his face, in his lungs, thumping in his heart, he marveled that he had ever confused the tiny window view with the world that now surrounded him.

He would remember this, he told himself. He would produce a crystal that would convey the Earth, air, and water, the burning blue skies and whispering leaves.

He bent down to pick up a small rock. Examining it, he noticed his hand, noticed the veins that had risen to the surface, bulging out against sagging skin. Noticed the fingers that had grown thin and were starting to curl and twist.

Suddenly weary, he glanced up at the sky and drew in a long breath. He felt that if he inhaled deeply enough he could fill his lungs with stars. The thought brought a burning to his chest.

"Something something to see all them stars," said the old man.

"Yes," said Solov, hearing the word fade in his ears.

The old man tugged at his sleeve. "Beautiful, yes, but not these stars, something something I speak. Come."

Solov allowed the man to pull him back to the shanty. How many shanties floated across the savanna? Solov wondered. Why didn't they settle together, stop moving? On the way back he tried to get a count on how many shants were in this group. In the fading light he counted several dozen, guessed at least twice that many more were currently inside the shanties. And this was but one group of many.

A thought nagged at Solov: Nearly everyone had gone down, gone Under, for the Process made delicate the bodies that it healed. There had been some who refused the Process, and others whose bodies had rejected it. But *few*, damn it, and so very long ago. Where had all these people come from?

"These stars, *these* stars!"

They returned to the shanty. Those inside watched them as the man led Solov to a cupboard in the far wall. The man knelt on one knee, reached out and pulled open the doors.

The light from the caged fire behind them filled the cupboard with liquid color: blues, greens, reds, and purples spilled out onto the floor, danced up and down along the walls.

"My God," Solov whispered.

"Yes!" the man agreed. "Yes, correct!"

Solov thought of the fine crystal things he had made back at his home. Nothing compared to the multicolored stars twinkling from the cupboard.

"If only we could share," said the man. "Something something, it is like those who have." He touched Solov's cheek, his hand hot and rough. "And then again those who haven't." He touched his own cheek, staring absentmindedly at the crystals. Solov was about to ask where they had found these crystals when the man touched him again. "Those who shall, and those who shant," he said softly, putting an arm around Solov. Solov looked down and saw two children standing next to him. The crystal reflected off their eyes, vibrant. He wondered who had and who hadn't.

He looked at the man's withered face. He found it hard to believe that the man would someday ... It didn't seem fair. Surely, someone with his understanding, his compassion and wisdom deserved to live forever. This man had heat. Caring heat. Free-radical heat. The first made him unique, the second made him ... impermanent.

"No," Solov whispered.

"Warm blood or cold makes no difference for purposes of something something. We all of us are made of something something."

Solov looked around him. The shanty was suddenly crowded. They moved around, putting up decorations, lighting candles. A pine tree had been erected in the middle of the

shanty and Solov thought of an antiquated custom he had
once heard about.

"Do you something know what something night it is?"
asked a child, tugging on his sleeve. The little girl's eyes sparkled, her face fresh and expectant.

"No," Solov said, looking helplessly at the man.

The man put his hand on Solov's shoulder and squeezed a
little, fingers barely strong enough to be noticed through the
bulk of the coat. "You will stay always in this world."

"And you?" Solov asked, though he knew the answer.

The old man nodded his head toward the opening. The
shants had parted. On the savanna, he saw a multitude of
shants, hundreds and hundreds of them, settling into a large
circle. A bright white light glowed from the middle of the circle. Solov stepped outside, watched oxen pulling wooden
boxes, blue light touching the ground beneath them.

"Tonight something something very special. Most special
night of the year," the man said. "Come."

Solov followed them. Dust scratched at his throat, at his
lungs, but he didn't care. He noticed the newly arrived shants
watching him as he walked past the perimeter. It seemed to
take forever to approach the light. He heard others walking,
felt their presence in the darkness behind and around him.

The light grew brighter.

When they arrived, Solov saw the small rock formation,
something in the center of it incandescent. A shanty floated
up next to them, and a handful of men opened one of the
sides. Its shelves were filled with decorations and colorful
packages. People started bringing things out, setting them up
around the rock.

When they had finished, the children joined hands around
the rock and began singing. Their words were slurred and almost impossible to understand, but the melody was vaguely
familiar, an echo of something he once had known. Had he
heard songs like this before? Had he sung them himself? He
wished he could remember.

"Every year we come here, yes," said the man. "We give
something, something to each other and the crystal something
give us light."

Sparks shot from the rock formation, disappearing into the night, falling back to the earth like dust, faintly glowing.

"How do you do this?" Solov asked, gesturing at the huge, glowing crystal.

"Why, we just something come and it awakens for us. And all the other days we find others, bring them something here. Something something, the more brotherhood, the brighter."

A bright, blue-yellow light moved over them. At first Solov thought it was a spark from the crystal, but then he saw its shape and the way it reflected the light from below, the way its underside glowed like the floats of a lorry.

The Rangers had found him.

The light slowed and descended, settling down a short distance from the shants. The singing quieted, all faces turned toward the intruding vehicle. A sliver of brightness became a yellow doorway framing two human silhouettes. The two Rangers disembarked and walked toward them. It had grown so quiet, Solov could hear their boots squeaking against the snow.

"Solov 367," said one of the uniformed men when they were close enough.

"Solov 367, we almost gave up on you," said the other.

Solov blinked, stared. The Rangers were holding dark objects in their fists, brandishing them, waving them around. Solov felt the warmth inside him shrink back. He pointed at the objects. "I recognize those. I know what those are for."

"You've been injured," said the first Ranger. "We will take you back Under."

"I might not want to come with you," Solov said. His voice was weak, rattling. "I might want to stay here."

"Solov 367, that is not possible and you know it. Come with us now. We'll have you back to UnderGreen in time to be rebaselined."

Solov looked back toward the large crystal. He was startled when he realized pictures were shaping in his head.

"Do not look," said one of the Rangers. "The intense light will harm your eyes."

Solov pulled his eyes away from the light. "You see it, don't you?" he said, glancing back at the Rangers.

"We see nothing, Solov 367. Come with us now."

"What am I not supposed to see?"

The old man touched Solov on the shoulder. "See something something what you want to see," he said. "Let the crystals shine in your heart, see something something what you see. No one can tell you what that something something is."

"Do not speak with the shant," one of the Rangers said sternly, taking a step forward, raising his weapon. "You must maintain the balance."

"You mean I must maintain obedience," Solov said. Just then, the other Ranger shoved his way forward, stopped just in front of the old man, weapon pointed at his head.

"Stop!" yelled Solov. "I'll come with you. Leave him alone."

Solov turned to look one final time at the scene taking shape in the crystal. Smoke, the color of the crystals, filled his head. Within the smoke, he saw—

"Now!" shouted the Ranger, redirecting his aim at the crystal.

"Something something," said the old man. The words, *carry rest-mass*, or perhaps *many crystals*, struck a familiar chord deep in Solov's heart.

"Yes," he said. "Many Crystals."

Water was leaking from the old man's eyes, so that reflected colors sparkled his cheeks. Solov remembered the word, *weeping*, and in the reflection off the tears, he saw the image he'd seen in the crystal light.

He saw happy faces, old faces, a newborn baby and a bright star. And as he saw them, they were all sheathed in clear and unclouded crystal.

Solov thought, again, that he really could stay here. Let the flesh darken and wither off his bones, let the earth open up to embrace what remained of him, to share with him the peace that the crystal had shown.

But he knew the Rangers would not let that happen.

"I'm coming," he said, his voice a hoarse whisper.

Silently, they boarded the scout ship and lifted. Through his window, Solov looked down at the shanties, at the great ringed city they formed around the crystals. In each of them, a different bright color filled the spaces within the walls.

"Do not look out the window," one of the Rangers said to Solov.

"You will need to be counseled," said the other. "This incident may have confused you."

"Yes," Solov said, though he knew it was a lie.

Beneath, the lights joined together in lines, in angles and patterns. Half a thousand shanties were down there now, spreading across the plain like ocean of light, and out of their seeming randomness an image arose. Solov felt a flicker of memory, a momentary touch of something familiar as he gazed down upon the delicate tracing of a huge, hundred-pointed star. He knew this image! It meant . . . It had to do with . . .

He grasped at the memory, as one might grasp at smoke. Joy and sadness, and the hope of . . . eternal life? No, that made no sense. And yet, though they sped away from it, the star burned on, filling the lorry cabin with its warmth and light, and even when it vanished, Solov fancied he could still hear, in the distance, faint voices raised in song.

"A Christmas Carol" transformed.

HOUSEHOLD WORDS

OR THE POWERS-THAT-BE

Howard Waldrop

His theory of life was entirely wrong. He thought men ought to be buttered up, and the world made soft and accommodating for them, and all sorts of fellow have turkey for their Christmas dinner. . . .

—Thomas Carlyle

He was the first to find out the immense spiritual power of the Christmas turkey.

—Mrs. Oliphant

UNDER A DEEP cerulean November sky, the train stopped on a turn near the road one half-mile outside the town of Barchester.

Two closed carriages waited on the road. Passengers leaned out the train windows and watched as a small man in a suit as brown as a Norfolk biffin stepped down from the doorway at the end of the third railcar.

Men waved their hats, women their scarves. "Hurray, Charlie!" they yelled. "Hoorah, Mr. Dickens! Hooray for Boz!"

The small man, accompanied by two others, limped across the cinders to a group of men who waited, hats in hand, near the carriages. He turned, doffed his stovepipe hat to the train, and waved to the cheering people.

Footmen loaded his traveling case and the trunk of props from the train into the last carriage.

The train, with barely a lurch, moved smoothly on down the tracks toward the cathedral tower of the town, hidden from view by trees. There a large crowd, estimated at more than three thousand, would be waiting for the author, to cheer him and watch him alight.

The welcoming committee had met him here to obviate that indignity, and to take him by a side street to his hotel, avoiding the crowds.

When the men were all in, the drivers at the fronts of the carriages released their brakes, and the carriages made their way quickly down the road toward town.

Promptly at 8 P.M. the lights in the Workingman's Hall came up to full brilliance.

Onstage were three deep magenta folding screens, the center one parallel to the audience, the two wings curved in slightly toward them. The stage curtains had been drawn in to touch the wings of the screen. Directly in front of the center panel stood a waist-high, four-legged small table. At the audience's right side of the desk was a raised wooden block; at its left, on a small lower projection, stood a glass and a sweating carafe of ice water; next to the water were an ivory letter opener and a white linen handkerchief. The top of the table was covered with a fringed magenta cloth that hung below the tabletop only an inch or so.

Without preamble, Charles Dickens walked with a slight limp in from the side of the stage and took his place behind the desk, carrying in his hand a small octavo volume. When he stood behind the thin-legged table his whole body, except for the few inches across his waist, was fully visible to the audience.

There came a thunderous roar of applause, wave after wave; then as one the audience rose to its feet, joyed for the very sight of the man who had brought so much warmth and wonder to their heater-sides and hearths.

He stood unmoving behind the desk, looking over them with his bright brown eyes above the now-familiar (due to the frontispiece by Mr. Frith in his latest published book, *Pip's Expectations*) visage with its high balding forehead, the shock of brownish hair combed to the left, the large pointed beard and connected thick mustache. He wore a brown formal evening suit, the jacket with black velvet lapels worn open showing his vest and watch chain. His shirt was white, with an old-fashioned neck stock in place of the new button-on collars, and he wore an even more old-fashioned bow tie, with two inches of end hanging down from the bows.

After two full minutes of applause, he nodded to the audience and they slowed, then stopped, sitting down with much clatter of canes and rustle of clothing and scraping of chairs, a scattering of coughs. From far back in the hall came a set of nervous hiccups, quickly shushed.

"My dear readers," said Dickens, "you do me more honor than I can stand. Since it is nearing the holiday season, I have chosen my reading especially as suits that most Christian of seasons." Murmurs went around the hall. "As I look around me at this fine Barchester crowd, I see many of you in the proud blue and red uniforms of Her Majesty's Power Service, and I must remind you that I was writing in a time, more than two decades gone, when things in our country were neither as Christian as we should have liked, nor as fast and modern as we thought. To mention nothing of a type of weather only the most elderly—and I count myself among them—remember with absolutely no regrets whatsoever." Laughter. "As I read, should you my auditors be moved to express yourselves— in matters of appreciation and applause, tears, or indeed hostility"—more laughter—"please be assured you may do so without distracting or discomfiting me in any adverse way."

He poured a small amount of water from carafe to glass and drank. "Tonight, I shall read to you *The Christmas Garland*."

There were oohs and more applause, the ones who guessed

before nodding in satisfaction to themselves and their neighbors.

The houselights dimmed until only Dickens, the desk, and the central magenta panel were illuminated.

He opened the book in his hand, and without looking at it said, "*The Christmas Garland.* Holly Sprig the First. 'No doubt about it, Marley was dead as a doorknob . . . ' "

Dickens barely glanced at the prompt book in his hand as he read. It was the regular edition of *The Christmas Garland*, the pages cut out and pasted in the center of larger bound octavo leaves. There were deletions and underlinings in red, blue, and yellow inks—notes to himself, directions for changes of voice, alternate wordings for lines. The whole had been shortened by more than a third, to fit into an hour and a half for these paid readings. When he had begun his charity readings more than ten years ago, the edition as printed had gone on more than two hours and a half. Through deletions and transpositions, he reduced it to its present length without losing effect or sense.

He moved continually as he read, now using the letter opener as Eben Mizer's quill, then the block of wood—three heavy blows with his left hand—as a door knocker. He moved his fingers together, the book between them, to simulate Cratchitt's attempts to warm himself at a single glowing coal. His voice was slow, cold and drawn as Eben Mizer; solemnly cheerful as the gentleman from the charity; merry and bright as Mizer's nephew. The audience laughed or drew inward on itself as he read the opening scenes.

"For I am that Spirit of Christmases Past," said the visitant. "I am to show you things that Were. Take my hand."

Eben Mizer did so, and they were out the window casing and over the night city in a slow movement. They flew slowly into the darkness to the north.

And then they were outside a house and shop, looking through the window at a large man in old-fashioned waistcoat and knee-breeks, with his spectacles pushed back on his forehead.

"Why, old Mr. Fezziwigg, to whom I was 'prenticed!" said Eben Mizer.

"Ho!" said Fezziwigg. "Seven o'clock! Away with your quills! Roll back the carpets! Move those desks against the walls! It's Christmas Eve and no one works! . . ."

As Dickens acted out preparations for the party, his eyes going to the prompt book only twice, he remembered the writing of this, his most famous story. It had been late October of the year 1843. He was halfway through the writing of *Martin Sweezlebugg*, had just, in fact, sent the young hero to America—the place he himself had returned from late in 1842, the place that had become the source of one long squeal of protest when he had published *Notes on the Americans* early in the year. He had gone from triumph to disdain in less than six months. For the first time in his life, the monthly numbers had been a chore for him—he was having troubles with *Sweezlebugg*, and the sales were disappointing. As they had been for *Gabriel Vardon: The Locksmith of London* of two years before. (The Americans who were outraged with his travel book were the same who had named a species of Far Western trout after Gabriel Vardon's daughter.) Between finishing the November number of *Sweezlebugg* on October 18, and having to start the next on November 3, he had taken one of the steam trains to the opening of the Manchester Institute of that city. Sitting on the platform, waiting his turn to speak, the idea for *The Christmas Garland* had come to him unbidden. He could hardly contain himself, waiting until after the speeches and the banquet to return to the quiet of his hotel to think it through.

And since he had a larger and larger family each year to support, more indigent brothers and sisters, in-laws and his importunate mother and father, he conceived the story as a separate book, to be sold at Christmas as were many of the holiday annuals, keepsakes, and books of remembrance. Illustrated, of course, with cuts by John Leech. The whole plan was a fire in his mind that night and all the way back to London the next day. He went straight to Chapman and Hall and presented the notion to them. They agreed with alacrity, and began ordering up stock and writing advertisements.

He had had no wild success since the two books that had made his reputation, *Tales of the Nimrod Club* and *Oliver Twist*, parts of them written simultaneously, in overlapping monthly numbers, six years before. He had envisioned for *The Christmas Garland* sales that would earn him £3,000 or more.

"Show me no more, no more!" said Eben Mizer. "These are things long past; the alternate miseries and joys of my youth. Those times are all gone. We can no more change them than stop the tides!"

"These are things as they were," said the Spirit of Christmases Past. "These things *are* unchangeable. They *have* happened."

"I had forgotten both pleasure and heartache," said Mizer. "I had forgotten the firewood, the smoke, the horses."

"In another night, as Marley said, you shall be visited by another, who will show you things as they are now. Prepare," said the Spirit. As with the final guttering of a candle, it was gone. Eben Mizer was back in his bed, in his cold bedchamber, in the dark. He dropped his head to the horsehair pillow, and slept.

Twenty-two years had gone by since Dickens wrote the words he read. He remembered his disappointment with the sales of *The Christmas Garland*—"Disappointment?! Disappointment!" yelled his friend Macready, the actor, when he had complained. "Disappointment at selling twenty thousand copies in six days! Disappointment, Charlie?" It was not that it had not sold phenomenally, but that it was such a well-made book—red cover, gilt-edged pages, four hand-tinted cuts, the best type and paper, and because of Dickens's insistence that everyone have one, priced far too low—that his half-copyright earnings through January 1844 only came to £347 6s 2p when he had counted on thousands. *That* had been the disappointment.

Dickens spoke on. This was the ninety-fourth public reading of *The Christmas Garland*, his most popular, next to the trial

scene from *The Nimrod Club*, and the death of little Dombey.
At home these days he worked on an abridgement of the
scenes, including that of the great sea storm, from *The Copper-
field Record of the World As It Rolled*, which he thought would
make a capital dramatic reading, perhaps to be followed by a
short comic scene, such as his reading of Mrs. Gamp, the hit
of the otherwise disappointing *Martin Sweezlebugg*.

What a winter that had been . . . the hostile American press,
doing the monthly numbers of *Sweezlebugg*, writing and seeing to the publication of *The Christmas Garland* in less than
six weeks, preparing his growing family—his wife, an ever-
increasing number of children, his sister-in-law Georgina Ho-
garth, the servants and dogs—for the coming sojourn to Italy,
severing his ties with *Bentley's Miscellany*, thinking of starting a daily newspaper of a liberal slant, walking each night
through London streets five, ten, fifteen miles because his
brain was hot with plans and he could not sleep or rest. He
was never to know such energies again.

There was his foot now, for instance. He believed its present pain was a nervous condition brought on by walking
twelve miles one night years ago through the snow. The two
doctors who had diagnosed it as gout were dismissed; a third
was brought in who diagnosed it as a nervous condition
brought on by walking through the snow. Before each of his
readings, his servant John had to put upon the bare foot a fo-
mentation of the poppy, which allowed him to put on a sock
and shoe, and make it the two hours standing up.

He still had a wife, though he had not seen her in six years;
they had separated after twenty-three years of marriage and
nine children. Some of the living children and Georgina had
remained with Dickens, taking his side against the mother and
sister. One boy was in the navy, another in Australia, two others in school. Only one child, Mamie—"young Tinderbox," as
Dickens called her—visited freely between the two house-
holds, taking neither side.

The separation had of course caused scandal, and Dickens's
break with Anthony Trollope. They belonged to the same clubs.
Trollope had walked into one; several scandalized members

were saying that Dickens had taken his sister-in-law as mistress. "No such thing," said Trollope. "It's a young actress."

So it was; Trollope said he was averting a larger outrageous lie with the truth; Dickens had not seen it that way.

Her name was Ellen Ternan. She and Dickens had performed in charity theatricals together, *The Frozen Deep* and Jonson's *Every Man in His Humour*. She was of a stage family—her mother and two sisters were actresses. Her sister Fanny had married Anthony Trollope's brother Tom in Florence, Italy, where she had gone to be his children's tutor after the death of Tom's wife Theodosia.

The world had been a much more settled place when the young fire-eating Boz had published his first works, and had remained so for some time afterward. But look at it now.

The Americans had just finished blowing the heads off first themselves, and then their President; had thrown the world in turmoil—which side should we take?—for four years, destroying a large part of their manpower and manufacturing capabilities. What irked Dickens was not their violent war—they had it coming—but that he would not be able to arrange a reading tour there for at least another year. An American had shown up two weeks ago at his publisher's office with an offer of £10,000, cash on the barrelhead, if Dickens would agree to a three-month tour of seventy-five readings. Both his friend Forster and the old actor Macready advised him against it for reasons of his health. Besides his foot, there had been some tightening in his chest for the last year or so, and his bowels had been in straitened circumstances long before that.

Ah, but what a trouper. He found even with his mind wandering he had not lost his place, or missed a change of voice or character; not given the slightest hint that his whole being was not in the reading being communicated to his forward-leaning, intent auditors.

Eben Mizer opened his eyes. How long had he slept? Was the Spirit of Christmases Past that bit of undigested potato, that dollop of mustard? he thought.

There came to his bedchamber a slight crackling sound; the air was suffused with a faint blue glow. Mizer reached into the watch catch above his bed and took down his timepiece. It was 12:00, he saw by the glow, which slowly brightened about his bed. Twelve! Surely not noon! And not the midnight before, when the Spirit of Christmases Past had come. Had he slept the clock round, all through the sham-bug Christmas Day? He grasped the bedclothes to haul himself out onto the cold bare floor. The overall bright glow coalesced in the corner nearest the chair.

The popping became louder, like faraway fireworks over the Thames on Coronation Day, or the ice slowly breaking on a March day. There was a smell of hot metal in the air; the sharp odor before a thunderstorm, but without heat or dampness. And then it was there, in the room behind the chair!

It was a looming figure, far above normal height, shrouded in a gown of copper and mica, and above its head, at its top, glowing green and jagged with purple, was one of Faraday's Needles. . . .

The listeners jerked back, as always. There was a rustle of crinoline and starch as they hunkered back down. Most knew the story as they knew their own hearts, but the effect on them was always the same.

Dickens knew why; for when he had written those words more than two decades before, his own hair had stood on end as if he were in the very presence of the Motility Factor itself.

It was from that moment on in the writing of *The Christmas Garland* that he had never wavered, never slowed down; it was that moment when, overcome by tiredness at his desk, he had flung himself and his hat and cane out into the (in those days) dark London night, and had walked till dawn, out to Holborn, up Duckett Lane, across to Seven Sisters, and back up and down Vauxhall Bridge Road, to come in again just as the household was rising, and throw himself fully clothed across his bed, to sleep for an hour, and then, rising, go back to his ink bottle and quills.

The crackling sound grew louder as the Spirit shook his raiments, and a spark danced between the Needle and the ceiling, leaving a bright blue spot there to slowly fade as Eben Mizer watched, fascinated as a bird before a snake.

"Know that I am the Spirit of Christmases Current, Eben Mizer. Know that I am in the form that the men who hire your accountancy worship, as you worship the money that flows, like the Motive Force itself, from them to you."

"What do you wish of me?" asked Eben.

The Spirit laughed, and a large gust of blue washed over the room, as if day had come and gone in an instant.

"Wish? Nothing. I am only to show you what takes place this Christmas."

"You mean this past day?"

"Past? Oh, very well, as you will!" The Spirit laughed again. "Take my hand."

"I will be volcanized in an instant!" said Mizer.

"No, you shall not." It held out an empty sleeve. Mizer felt invisible fingers take his. "Come," said the Spirit. "Hold on to me."

There was a feeling of lightness in Mizer's head; he became a point of light, as the flash of a meteor across the heavens, or the dot of a lightning-bug against an American night, and they were outside his nephew's house in the daylight.

"As before, you are neither seen nor heard," said the Spirit of Christmases Current. "Walk through this wall with me." They did, but Mizer had the sensation that instead of walking directly through they had, in a twinkling, gone up the windowpane, across the roof tiles, down the heated air of the chimney, across the ceiling, and into the room just inside the window, too fast to apprehend. The effect was the same, from outside to inside, but Eben Mizer had the memory of doing it the long way. . . .

Dickens's voice became high, thin, and merry as he took on the younger tones of Mizer's nephew, his nephew's wife, their in-laws and guests at the party where they were settling in for a game of charades before the Christmas meal.

Actors on the stage of the time said that Dickens was the greatest actor of his age; others thought it beneath his dignity to do the readings—authors should be paid to publish books,

not read them for money. Some of his readings he had
dropped after they did not have the desired effect—comic or
pathetic or terrific—on the audience. Others he had prepared
but never given, because they had proved unsatisfying to him.
By the time any reading had joined his repertoire, he had re-
hearsed it twenty-five times before its debut.

He knew that he was a good actor—if he had not gone into
journalism, covering the courts and the Parliament when a
youth, he would have gone on the stage—but he knew he was
not great. He knew it was the words *and* the acting that had
made his readings such a success. No matter how many times
they had read and heard them, audiences still responded to them
as if they had come newly dry from his pen that very morning.

Dickens paused for another drink from the glass, mopped
his brow with the handkerchief that a moment before had
been Mizer's nightcap. The audience waited patiently, the
slight hum of the fans in the ceiling purring to let the accumulated warmth of 1,500 bodies escape into the cold night. The
glow from the selenium lights against the magenta screen
added nothing to the heat.

He put the glass down, eyes twinkling, and went back to
his reading.

"If only my uncle were here," said his nephew.

"Oh, why bother?" asked his pretty young wife. "He's
probably at his office counting out more profits from the
Greater Cumberland and Smythe-Jones Motility Factory, or
the United Batchford Motive-Force Delivery Service. And no
doubt got poor Bob Cratchitt there with him, chained to his
stool. . . ."

"Hush, please," asked the nephew.

"Well, it's true. A man like Eben Mizer. He does sums for
seventeen different power brokers, yet his office is still lit
with candles! He lets poor Cratchitt freeze in the outer office.
And poor Bob with the troubles he has at home. Your uncle
should be ashamed of what he pays him, of how he himself
lives. . . ."

"But, after all," said her father the greengrocer, "it is a free
market, and he pays what the trade will bear."

"That's wrong too," said the young wife, hands on hips. "How the workingmen are to better themselves if their wages are so low they have to put their children working at such early ages is beyond me. How are they to make ends meet? How are they to advance themselves if there are no better wages in the future, perhaps even lower ones, and they can't live decently now?"

"The Tories won't be happy if women such as yourself get the suffrage," said her father with a laugh. "Neither would anyone on the board of directors of a motive-power company!"

"If I did not love you as a father," said the young wife, "I should be very cross with you."

"Come, come," said her husband the nephew. "It's Christmas Day. Where's your charity?"

"Where's your uncle's?"

"He does as the world wills," said the nephew.

"Only more so," said another guest, and they all laughed, the young wife included.

"Well, I invited him," said Mizer's nephew. "It's up to him to come or no. I should welcome him with all the gladness of the season."

"As would I," said his wife. "Only you might as well wish for Christian charity to be carried on every day, in every way, throughout the year, in every nation on Earth!"

"Why show me this?" asked Eben Mizer of the Spirit. "No love is lost betwixt my nephew's wife and myself. My nephew means very well, but he does not grasp the full principles of business to his bosom. He has done well enough; he *could* do much better."

"Come," said the Spirit of Christmases Current, grabbing Mizer's hand in its unseen own. There was another crackle of blue lightning, and they were away, up a nail, across the roof, down the gutter pipe, and off into the day.

After this reading, Dickens had two more in the provinces, then back to St. James Hall in London for the holiday series. He would read not only *The Christmas Garland* there, but also both *The Chimes* and *The Haunted Man*, his last Christmas book from back in 1848.

In London he would also oversee the Christmas supplement of *Household Words*, his weekly magazine. This year, on a theme superintended by Dickens, and including one short story by him, was the conceit of Christmas at Mugby Junction, a station where five railway lines converged. Leaning over the junction would be the bright blue towers of the H.M.P.S., from which the trains drew their force. Indeed, Wilkie Collins's contribution was the story of a boy, back in London, who proudly wore the crisp blue and red uniform, imagining, as he sat on duty with his headset strapped on, Mugby Junction and the great rail lines that he powered, on one of which was coming to London, and to whom he would be introduced on his fortnight off duty, his brother-in-law's cousin, a girl. Dickens had, of course, made Collins rewrite all the precious parts, and bring Father Christmas in for a scratch behind the ears—"else it might as well take place during August Bank Holiday!" said Dickens in a terse note to Collins when the manuscript had caught up with him at his hotel in Aberdeen yesterday.

Just now, the letter opener in his hand had become the cane of old Mr. Jayhew as he walked toward the Cratchitts' door.

Such a smell, like a bakery and a laundry and a pub all rolled together! The very air was thick with Christmas, so much so that Eben Mizer wondered how he detected the smells, unseen and unheard as he was, as the sputtering blue and purple Spirit stood beside him.

"Where's your father?" asked Mrs. Cratchitt.

"He's just gone to fetch Giant Timmy," said the youngest daughter.

"Your brother's name is Tim," said Mrs. Cratchitt. "It's just the neighbors call him that," she added with a smile.

The door came open without a knock, and there stood Katy, their eldest, laden with baskets and a case, come all the way from Cambridge, where she worked as a nanny.

"Mother!" she said. "Oh, the changes on the trains! I thought I should never reach here!"

"Well," said Mrs. Cratchitt, hugging her, "you're here, that's what matters. Now it will be a very merry Christmas!"

"I must have waited in ten stations," said Katy, taking off her shawl, then hugging her sisters and giving them small presents. "Every line its own train, every one with its own motive-car. Absolutely nothing works right on Christmas Eve!" She looked around. "Where's Father? Where's Tim?"

"Your father's off fetching him . . . and his pay," said Mrs. Cratchitt.

"When can *I* go to work, mumsy?" asked Bobby, pulling at his pinafore.

"Not for a long time yet," said Mrs. Cratchitt. "Perhaps you'll be the first one in the family goes to University."

"Don't tease him so," said Katy.

"Well, it's possible," said his mother.

"Not with what Mr. Mizer pays Father, and what I can send when I can, nor even with Tim's pay," said Katy. "And unless I am mistaken, his rates have gone down."

"All of them are down," said Mrs. Cratchitt, "what with the Irish and the potato blight. The streets here are full of red hair and beards, all looking for work."

There was a sound outside in the street, and the door came open, Mr. Cratchitt's back appearing as he turned. "This way. No, no, this way." He tugged twice, and then was followed.

Behind Mr. Cratchitt came Tim. He weighed fifteen stone though he was but twelve years old. He wore a white shapeless smock, with the name *Wilborn Mot. Ser.* written in smudged ink across the left chest, and white pants. His skin was translucent, as if made of waxed parchment, and his head had taken on a slight pearlike appearance, not helped by the short bowl shape into which his hair had been cut. There were two round notches in the bowl cut, just above the temples, and small bruised and slightly burnt circles covered the exposed skin there.

But it was the eyes Mizer noticed most—the eyes, once blue-green like his father's, had faded to whitish gray; they seemed both staring from their sockets in amazement, and to be taking in absolutely nothing, as if they were white china doorknobs stuck below his brows.

"Tim!" yelled Katy. She ran to him and hugged him as best she could. He slowly lifted one of his arms to wrap around her shoulders.

"Oh! You're hurting!" she said, and pulled away.

"Here, sit here, Tim," said Bob Cratchitt, making motions toward the largest chair. It groaned as the boy sat down.

"There is a small bonus for Christmas," said Mr. Cratchitt. "Not much." He patted the corner of the pay envelope in his pocket. "Not enough to equal even the old pay rates, but something. They've been working especially hard. The pay-master at Wilborn's was telling me they've been hired as mo-tive power for six new factories in the last month alone."

"Oh, Tim," said Katy. "It's so good to see you and have you home for Christmas, even for just the day."

He looked at her for a long time, then went back to watch-ing the fireplace.

Then there was the steaming sound of a goose coming out of the oven, hissing in its own gravy, and of a pudding going in, and Mr. Cratchitt leapt up and started the gin-and-apple punch, with its pieces of pineapple, and oranges, and a full stick of cinnamon bark.

Halfway through the meal, when healths were going round, and Mr. Mizer's name mentioned, and the Queen's, Giant Timmy sat forward suddenly in the big chair that had been pulled up to the table, and said, "God Bless . . . us all each . . . every . . ." Then he went quiet again, staring at his glass.

"That's right, that's exactly right, Tim," said Bob Cratchitt. "God Bless Us All, Each and Every One!"

Then the Spirit and Eben Mizer were outside in the snow, looking in at the window.

"I have nothing to do with this," said Eben. "I pay Cratchitt as good as he could get, and I have *nothing* to do, whatsoever, with the policies of the companies for whom I do the accounts." He looked at the Spirit of Christmases Current, who said nothing, and in a trice, he was back in his bedcham-ber, and the blue-purple glow was fading from the air. Ex-hausted as if he had swum ten miles off Blackpool, he dropped to unconsciousness against his stiff pillow.

Dickens grew rapidly tired as he read, but he dared not now let down either himself or his audience.

In many ways that younger self who had written the story

had been a dreamer, but he had been also a very practical man in business and social matters. That night in Manchester as he waited for Mr. Disraeli to wind down, and as the idea for *The Christmas Garland* ran through his head, he thought he had seen a glimpse of a simple social need, and with all the assurance and arrogance of youth, what needed to be done. If he could strike the hammer blow with a Christmas tale, so much the better.

So he had.

The Spirit of Christmases Yet to Come was a small implike person, jumping here and there. It wore no mica or copper, only a tight garment and a small cloth skullcap from which stood up only a single wire, slightly glowing at the tip. First the Spirit was behind the chair, then in front, then above the bureau, then at one corner of the bed.

Despite its somewhat comic manner, the Spirit frightened Eben Mizer as the others had not. He drew back, afraid, for the face below the cap was an upturned grin, whether from mirth or in a rictus of pain he did not know. The imp said nothing but held out a gutta-percha covered wand for Mizer to grasp, as if it knew the very touch of its nervous hand would cause instant death, of the kind Mizer had feared from the Spirit before. Mizer took the end of the wand; instantly they were on the ceiling, then out in the hall, back near the chair, then inside something dark, then out into the night.

"I know you are to show me the Christmas Yet to Come, as Marley said. But is it Christmas as it *Will Be*, or only Christmas Yet to Come if I *keep on* this way?"

The imp was silent. They were in the air near the Serpentine, then somewhere off Margate, then back at the confluence of the Thames and Isis, then somewhere over the river near the docks. As Eben Mizer looked down, a slow barge transformed into a sleek boat going an unimaginable speed across the water. As he watched, it went in a long fast circle and crashed into a wharf, spewing bodies like toy soldiers from a bumped table.

He looked out toward the city. London towered up and up and up, till the highest buildings were level with his place in the middle of the air. And above the highest buildings stood giant towers of every kind and shape, humming and glowing blue in the air. Between the tall stone and iron buildings ran aerial railways, level after crossing level of them, and on every one some kind of train; some sleek, some boxlike, moving along their spans. The city was a blaze of light; every corner on every street glowed, all the buildings were lit. Far to the horizon the lights stretched, past all comprehension; lights in a million houses, more lights than all the candles and lamps and new motility lights in Eben Mizer's world could make if all lit at once. There was no end to the glow—the whole river valley was one blue sheen that hurt his eyes.

Here and there, though, the blue flickered. As he watched, some trains gathered speed on their rails three hundred feet above the ground, and on others higher or lower they stopped completely. Then he and the imp were closer to one of the trains that had come to a halt. The passengers were pressed to the windows of one of the carriages, which had no engines or motive-cars attached, and then in a flash around a building came a spotted snake of light that was another train, and there was a great grinding roar as the two became one. The trains were a wilted salad of metal and wheels, and people flew by like hornet larvae from a nest hit by a shotgun blast. They tumbled without sound down the crevasses between the buildings, and cracked windows and masonry followed them as rails snapped like stretched string.

Something was wrong with the sky, for the blue light flickered on and off, as did the lights of the city, and the top of one of the towers began to glow faint red, as if it were a mulling poker.

Then he and the imp were on the ground, near a churchyard, and as they watched, with a grinding clang that died instantly, a train car from above went through the belfry of the church. Bodies, whose screams grew higher and louder, thudded into the sacred ground, snapping off tombstones, giving statues a clothing of true human skin.

The imp of Christmases Yet to Come drew nearer a wooden cross in the pauper's section, pointing. Eben Mizer stood transfixed, watching the towers of buildings, stone attached to iron, and the twisting cords of the railways above come loose and dangle before breaking off and falling.

With a deafening roar a ground-level railway train came ploughing through the churchyard wall, tearing a great gouge in the earth and, shedding passengers like an otter shakes water, burst through the opposite wall, ending its career farther out of sight. It left a huge furrow through the cemetery, and at the cemetery's exact center a quiet, intact railway car in which nothing moved. Here and there in the torn earth a coffin stood on end, or lay cut in two, exactly half an anatomy lesson.

Eben Mizer saw that one of the great towers nearby had its side punched open, as neat a cut as with a knife through a hoop of cheese. From this opening shambled an army, if ever army such as this could be. . . .

They were huge, and their heads too were huge, and the sides of their heads smoked; the hair of some was smouldering, which they did not notice, until some quite burst afire, and then those slowly sank back to the ground. Others walked in place, only thinking their thin legs were moving them forward. A higher part of the tower fell on twenty or thirty of them with no effect on the others who were walking before or behind them.

Great fires were bursting out in the buildings overhead. A jagged bolt lanced into the Thames, turning it to steam; a return bolt blew the top from a tower, which fell away from the river, taking two giant buildings with it.

A train shot out of the city a thousand feet up. As it left, the entire valley winked out into a darkness lit only by dim blazes from fires. Mizer heard the train hit in Southwark in the pitch blackness before his night vision came back.

All around there was moaning; the small moaning of people, larger ones of twisted cooling metal, great ones of buildings before they snapped and fell.

He began to make out shapes in the churchyard slowly, here and there. There were fires on bodies of people, on the wooden seats of train benches. A burning chesterfield fell onto the railway car, showering sparks.

The staggering figures came closer; they were dressed in

loose clothing. By the light of fires he saw their bulbous shapes. One drew near, and turned toward him.

Its eyes, all their eyes, were like pale doorknobs. They moved toward him. The closest, its lips trying to say words, lifted its arms. Others joined it, and they came on slowly, their shoulders moving ineffectually back and forth; they shuffled from one foot to the other, getting closer and closer. They lifted their white soft grub-worm fingers toward him—

WHAP!!! Dickens brought his palm down hard on the wooden block. The whole audience jumped. Men and women both yelped. Then nervous laughter ran through the hall.

Eben Mizer opened the shutter. The boy in the street had another snowball ready to throw when he noticed the man at the window. He turned to run.

"Wait, boy!" Eben Mizer called. "Wait! What day is this?"

"What? Why, sir, it's Christmas Day."

"Bless me," said Eben Mizer. "Of course. The Spirits have done it all in one night. Of course they have. There's still time. Boy! You know that turkey in the shop down the street? . . ."

His foot was paining him mightily. He shifted his weight to the other leg, his arms drawing the giant shape of the man-sized turkey in the air. He was Eben Mizer, and he was the boy, and he was also the poulterer, running back with the turkey.

And from that day on, he was a man with a mission, a most Christian one, and he took to his bosom his nephew's family, and that of all mankind, but most especially that of Bob Cratchitt, and that most special case of Giant Timmy—who did not die—and took to his heart those great words, "God Bless . . . us all each . . . every . . . "

Charles Dickens closed his book and stood bathed in the selenium glow, and waited for the battering love that was applause.

REQUEST YOUR FREE BOOKS!

2 FREE NOVELS
PLUS 2 FREE GIFTS!

KIMANI™ ROMANCE

Love's ultimate destination!